FORGED

FORGED

THE JOE MACK ADVENTURES - VOLUME ONE

GAIL Z. MARTIN

LARRY N. MARTIN

Charlotte, NC

FALSTAFF
BOOKS

WWW.FALSTAFFBOOKS.COM

PART I

CAULDRON

1

July 1892– Homestead, Pennsylvania

I'd never been to war before.

Bullets whizzed past my head, and I ducked, trying to stay out of the firefight. All I had was a rock, and my aim had never been that good. I didn't want to die tonight here on the riverbank, but I wasn't a coward. I stood shoulder to shoulder with my fellow workers, determined not to let the Pinkertons reach the steel mill behind us.

Two men already lay dead: one of ours, and one of theirs. I knew the Pinkertons fired first, but later, they'd claim we did, if any of us survived. The agents kept up a barrage from their boat, firing blindly into the crowd. I heard men cry out in pain and fear. Women prayed, calling on God in Polish, Russian, Hungarian—all the languages of the mill. Boys too young to shave clamored for a spot on the front line, thinking it all great sport.

I knew better. This riverbank would be soaked in blood before dawn.

Someone spilled oil into the river and lit leftover fireworks from the parade along with a few sticks of dynamite, tossing them toward the Pinkerton boats, trying to make them go away.

My heart froze in my chest. Fighting the king's men back in Hungary, or the hired guns of Carnegie and Frick, it was all the same. One side could afford an army of soldiers, and the other side offered up their own blood and sinew, all that they had, daring to demand pay enough to buy bread.

"Hey, Magarac. You think we're gonna win this?" Piotr Kowalczyk, my best friend from the mill, stood next to me with his own pile of rocks.

"I hope so," I replied, figuring a lie was better than the truth. Piotr crossed himself. I didn't, and Piotr either didn't see or didn't mention it.

The Pinkertons kept firing. Higher up the hill, our side fired back. The whole town was out here—men, women, and children. I'd heard that the owner of the hardware store donated all his ammunition to the cause. Shots rang out around us. I saw the bullet strike Jakob Nowak in the chest, sending up a spray of blood. His arms flew out from his body, and his head snapped back, then he fell and didn't move.

We screamed in fury. Those closest to the shore threw whatever they could get their hands on, pelting the Pinkerton boats. Flames rose in the night. Some of the workers lit a barge on fire and sent it toward the boat with the hired muscle. More dynamite went off, sending up a wall of water and nearly swamping the agents' boats. Still, they fired on us. And I knew that come dawn, there'd be more of them.

All I'd wanted was a job. I'd come to America, to this little town outside of Pittsburgh, from my native Hungary with my wife and baby son to make a new start. We didn't have enough to eat in the Old World. Work was scarce, and the police in my village were dishonest. My uncle Stanislaw left first, making his way across the ocean, and sent back for me. I brought my wife, Agata, and our baby son, Patryk, with me because I believed we would have a better life here.

Within a year, they were dead of a fever, and I was alone. I stopped praying to the Holy Mother the night I'd buried my family. If I prayed at all, which wasn't often, I called on the Old Gods, the ones I'd heard my great-grandmother whisper about in the dark of night. Carnegie and Frick claimed Jesus and the Apostles. But the Old Gods weren't beholden to the men who owned the mills and thought they owned our bodies and our lives. They were ancient and powerful, and they did as they pleased. Whether or not they cared about the likes of us, I wasn't sure.

"Magarac! Look—the Pinkertons are leaving!" Piotr crowed, elbowing me. I looked down toward the dark waters of the Monongahela River. Sure enough, the barge was withdrawing. A cheer went up from our side, and voices shouted taunts in a dozen languages.

"We won!" Piotr cried out, lifting his arms in the air in victory. "We drove the sons of bitches back!"

4

I could not share his glee, or join in the celebration going on all around me. Good men were dead, and our "win" wouldn't comfort their kin. I knew that men like the robber barons didn't give up so easily, not to the likes of us. We stayed encamped around the mill, holding it prisoner, while the men who led our union went to Pittsburgh in good faith to negotiate terms. The camp had a holiday air about it, giddy with having driven back the hired guns. Women brought us food from town, and young boys ran through the strike camp, chasing each other with sticks for rifles and pinecones for rocks, acting out the victory. I forced a smile and stayed with my friends, but in my heart, I knew it wasn't over.

Vengeance came swiftly. There had to have been thousands of armed soldiers.

We didn't stand a chance.

Bullets flew, and bayonets flashed. Piotr died with a look of shock on his face, cut down when a slug took off part of his head. His blood and brains splattered my face and soaked my shirt. He'd raised his hands in surrender, and they didn't care. "Fucking Polocks," the soldier shouted, right before he fired.

I didn't have a gun, but I screamed a curse in Hungarian and hurled a rock at the man who killed my friend, and clipped his shoulder. All around me, men fell as shots rang out.

The soldier didn't bother to reload. He turned the rifle in his hands and slammed the stock into my head. I stumbled, and two of his buddies were on me, beating me with fists, kicking my ribs and groin with heavy boots, stomping down on my chest and face. I couldn't see with blood running into my eyes. They kept beating me, kicking and punching, and my breath came with a wet rattle as I brought up blood. All the while, they cursed me, vile words against my homeland and my people, mocking my accent and telling me to go back where I came from.

I knew the only place I would go from here was the churchyard at St. Michal's.

When the soldiers had their sport, they left me for dead among the corpses and rounded up the survivors, marching them back to town, perhaps to jail. From where I lay, I could see Piotr, his face pale, eyes staring.

Rage filled me, for Piotr and all the others, for the men dying around me amid the gun smoke and the fire. I drew a painful breath and called on the only being I trusted to hear my cry.

Krukis, god of blacksmiths.

I had seen his image in an icon my grandmother hid behind a likeness of St. Peter. I'd always been drawn more toward Krukis, with his bare chest and strong arms, striking iron on an anvil with a powerful hammer and a raging fire, than I had been by the serene man in white robes with a halo. My world had dirt and ash and flame, and Krukis wasn't afraid to get dirty.

Through the smoke, I saw him, striding toward me like an ancient predator. Perhaps it was a vision brought on from being at death's door. Krukis stood at least seven feet tall, broad-shouldered and thick-muscled from the forge. His black hair hung long around his stern, handsome face. Slate gray eyes surveyed the carnage, afraid of no one.

"Jozef Magarac. Why have you summoned me?"

The deep voice rang in my head. Maybe I was already dead, come to judgment day. No, not dead yet. The air still stank of blood and piss, and my mouth tasted of ash. I again wondered if this was delusion caused by the pain, but I decided it didn't matter. If there was any chance, any chance at all...

"Give me justice, for the men killed today," I begged. I wasn't afraid to die. Life was a constant struggle. Death meant rest or peaceful oblivion. But I would not die like an animal, unavenged. *"Make me the instrument of your vengeance."*

Krukis's laugh rumbled through the air like thunder. *"Think yourself up to the task?"*

"If not me, then who?" Clearly, being almost dead made me insanely brave to challenge a god.

Krukis stopped laughing. He regarded me with a gaze that seemed to see down to my bones, assessing my paltry courage and many failures. It took everything I had not to shrink beneath that scrutiny, but fury made me bold. I stared back, unflinching.

"Very well, Jozef Magarac. I will grant your prayer. To you, I give the strength of a mule team and the speed of a racehorse. You possess the heart of a warrior, but to that courage, I add magic, when you call on my name. Your bones will be steel, and magic can make your skin metal for a short time. You will not age and cannot die but by the hottest of fires. You will be my servant, meting out my justice, and I will be your god."

"Agreed. By my blood and bone, make it thus."

Lightning struck me, coursing through my veins, setting bone and skin and sinew on fire. I screamed, never having felt such agony before. Then, abruptly, the pain stopped. I drew in a breath, and nothing hurt.

My blond hair was still matted with blood, but the gash on my forehead, the swollen eye, the split lip—all were healed.

I opened my eyes and found Krukis giving me an appraising look. *"I will be watching, as will my companions. Expect to hear from us, now and again. I shall be quite interested to see what comes of this vengeance of yours. Do not forget the fires that forged you."*

With that, Krukis vanished, leaving me alone with the dead.

2

1928–Cleveland, Ohio

B en Lavecchia ran the best blind tiger in Cleveland.

The Hathaway Theater hosted the top vaudeville show in the city, with a mix of traveling performers and an impressive cast of local talent that many people said put New York and Chicago to shame.

I'm pretty sure that the people who said that had never actually been to New York or Chicago, but it was a nice fiction that made Ben happy. Considering the guy was both a powerful *strega* and the youngest son of Vincent Lavecchia, Cleveland's biggest crime boss, telling Ben what he wanted to hear was smart.

I'm smart, but I'm also an asshole. Ben puts up with me anyhow.

"You got any Caribbean tigers in there?" I asked when I bellied up to the huge mahogany bar. This being Prohibition and all, there were no bottles of distilled spirits on the backbar, although there were several oddly shaped containers of medicinal potions and elixirs, famed for their "curative" powers.

"Never sure what kind of tigers we have around," Ben said with a shrug. He took my money, rapped on a wooden panel, and dropped the coins into a hidden drawer. A moment later, the drawer opened again, holding a glass filled with an amber liquid that looked a lot like rum.

"Might be your lucky day, Joe," Ben said, handing me the glass. "Caribbean tigers are hard to come by." I knocked back the shot and held out a couple more coins.

"I can't say I got a good look at that tiger," I said with a grin. "I'd like to try again. I'll look real hard, this time."

Ben rolled his eyes, repeated the trick with the hidden drawer, and handed off my rum. "Leave some for the other patrons tonight, will ya?" he added, but I knew he wasn't pissed because he hadn't racked his shotgun.

"I'm your best customer, Ben." It was true. And thanks to my deal with an ancient Slavic god, I also couldn't get more than mildly buzzed, no matter how much I drank.

"I try to keep everyone happy," Ben replied, glancing around the smoky room. His gaze never missed anything, a habit that went with living on a knife-edge. Rumor had it that once upon a time, Ben and his big brother Tony never missed a party. Then Tony went to war and didn't come back, and Ben's party days were over.

Ben's "blind tiger" speakeasy operated out of a private room in the basement of the theater, which conveniently had several exits, hidden and not. It was a sanctuary that catered to a strange mix of people, myself included. Theater folks came down after their performances, often still in costume, and mixed with the bankers, socialites, well-off wastrel sons, card sharps, and Mob gentry. Hank, the piano player, was as blind as the fictitious tiger, with a perfect memory and a keen ear for voices. There wasn't anything worth knowing in this town that Hank hadn't overheard.

"You ever get anyone who actually thinks you've got a real tiger?" I asked, sipping my second rum.

"Now and again," Ben replied. "Vito, one of my boys, brought one of the new guys in last week. Big fellow, but young and green as grass. You'd have thought someone kicked his puppy when he found out there weren't no tigers."

I don't know who came up with the idea of charging patrons for a "special exhibit" of seeing an exotic blind tiger, then giving them "free" alcohol with their ticket in order to get around the law, but the name stuck. Then again, no cop with two brains to rub together would try to close down Benny Lavecchia's place. That is, if he didn't want to find himself fired and dead, not necessarily in that order. Not that Ben himself would have anything to do with it. Ben had gone as straight as his circumstances would allow. Didn't stop his overprotective papa and big brothers from making sure no harm came to their youngest.

Not to mention that Ben was a powerful *strega*. Even Capone knew not to mess with a witch.

"Hey, Mack." A beautiful dark-skinned woman with bobbed, wavy hair and a sultry voice leaned against the bar next to me. Her beaded dress clung to her curves like liquid silver.

Most people said that when they were speaking to a stranger, but I knew Millie meant me. I'd gone by "Joe Mack" for close to sixteen years now, ever since I'd been in Cleveland. The thing about immortality is, after a while, people notice you don't age. I'd probably look thirty-one forever. In a few years, I'd need a new name and a new city, but for now, I liked where I was.

"How'd your show go?" I asked, as Millie slipped coins to Ben and he passed her a tiger that smelled a lot like gin.

"Almost a full house. Tried out a couple of new songs. They went over real good." Millie had a voice like a fallen angel, and when she sang a torch song, she smoldered. I could read in her eyes that she'd lived the blues she sang about. The Deep South drawl made it clear she wasn't from around here.

"You could sing my grocery list and get a standing ovation." I wasn't flirting; it was the truth.

"You, sir, are a silver-tongued devil," Millie said, wagging a finger at me with a grin. "But keep talking. I like what you're selling."

"Just telling it like I see it," I replied. I liked the fact that Millie and I knew where we stood with each other. There hadn't been anyone for me since Agata died all those years ago, and there wouldn't be, ever again. Wouldn't be fair to them, what with me not aging. And I couldn't stand watching someone I loved age and die. As for Millie, she sang enough "done me wrong" songs that I believed her when she said she had sworn off on men. I believed her even more when she slipped an arm around Nicolette, the show's French contortionist.

"Sure is jumpin' down here tonight," Millie drawled.

"You'd think Lucky Lindy had dropped by," I replied, glancing around to make sure Lindbergh hadn't actually done just that. You never knew who might show up at Ben's. He knew everyone and the dirt on them, as insurance.

Millie gave an unladylike snort. "I wouldn't be here talking to the likes of you if Charles Lindbergh was here. Be over asking for an autograph."

"You don't need a man to fly," Nicolette murmured, quietly enough I wouldn't have heard her if I'd still been mortal.

I rolled my eyes and returned my attention to the crowd. I liked Ben's speakeasy because people mixed here when they couldn't other places. Everybody played nice, or they got bounced with a warning to forget what they'd seen, *or else*. Millie was royalty here, and so were some of the show's more unusual performers. Samson, the "mighty midget" strongman, mingled with the crowd, receiving compliments on tonight's performance. Tom and Tad, identical twin tap dancers, still wore their tuxes. Mirabella, the fan dancer, wore a lacy dress that stopped just short of illegal. She carried a small version of the big feather fans she used onstage, in case people didn't recognize her with her clothes on.

Grace McAllen Harringworth caught my eye and winked, one of my frequent partners in crime. She looked like she had just stepped out of a bandbox, gussied up in a dress that probably came from New York, or maybe Paris. I wasn't surprised to see her on the arm of Frank Shilling, Cleveland's golden boy. Shilling had flown in the Great War, gone up against the Red Baron and lived to tell about it. He had an impressive number of kills to his record, though the fame and his good looks—not to mention family money—seemed to have gone to his head. I wondered if Grace was really sleeping with the bloke, or just pumping him for information. Maybe both.

Over in the back corner near the piano, Georgina, the bearded lady, was their fabulous self, holding court with admirers, dressed in a gown that was a peacock splendor of blue and green silk. Miroslav, Georgina's besotted lover, watched from a distance, content to let Georgina have the limelight.

My gaze lingered on Miro a tad longer than usual. He seemed worried, but I doubted jealousy had anything to do with his mood. Rumor had it that Georgina had killed to protect him, long ago in another city. I knew he'd come mighty close to killing a theater-goer who spoke ill of Georgina. They were blood bound. No, it had to be something else. Miro looked up, noticing me and realizing I'd been staring. He headed my direction.

"Mack."

"Hello, Miro. Something on your mind?"

Miro was Russian, one of the many who'd found their way to the factories and steel mills of the Northeast after the War and the Revolution. I'd picked up some Russian over the years in the mill, but I wasn't fluent. Unfortunately, Miro's English was still dodgy, though he and

Georgina seemed to communicate just fine. He worked at the green-grocer and always reeked of onion and garlic.

"Mr. Ben told me I should speak to you," Miro said in a hushed voice. I drew him away from the crowd.

"What's going on?"

"People in my neighborhood, they've been...going gone."

I frowned. "Leaving?"

He shook his head. "They just suddenly go."

"Disappearing?"

"Yes. That. Going gone, suddenly. No reason. I think something bad is happening."

Ben's Aunt Frederica ran a rooming house near the theater that mostly catered to the performers, like Millie, Sampson, and Georgina, who would have had difficulty finding safe lodging elsewhere, but she didn't have room for everyone on Ben's payroll. That meant Miro probably lived in one of the neighborhoods filled with other new arrivals from Eastern Europe.

I had an idea of what Miro's neighborhood was like, having lived in Homestead's crowded tenements. Each group—Poles, Italians, Hungarians, Russians, and more—had their own few blocks, complete with bars, churches, and stores that catered to them. God help the poor bastard who wandered into the wrong territory.

"Did they owe money? You think the cops took them?"

"No. Not these. Good people. I think, maybe something in the dark."

"They're being kidnapped?"

"No, Mack. I think they're being eaten." He looked around, worried someone might have overheard.

Oh. *That* kind of "something" in the dark. "You got any proof?"

"*Nyet.* But coming home late at night, I see things," Miro confided. "Red eyes in the shadows. Shapes that move too fast to be a person. I think something is hunting."

"How have you stayed safe?" I asked.

Miro dug beneath his shirt and pulled out a silver medallion. "Saint Boris protects me." He kissed the medallion and slipped it back next to his skin. "But maybe I am lucky too. I do not wish to find out, how you say, the hard way."

"Okay," I said. "I'll check into it." Miro gave me directions to his rooming house, and I resolved to have a look later that night. He thanked me with embarrassing gratitude and drifted off to join Georgina. I headed back to the bar, in search of another island tiger.

Heavy footsteps sounded overhead, in the now-closed theater. The room quieted. New patrons paled, expecting a raid.

"That's just Gertrude," Ben announced, naming the theater's resident ghost-diva. "She wants her song. Play it, Hank."

Hank swung seamlessly into "Let Me Call You Sweetheart," and the ghostly tantrum immediately stopped. Satisfied, Gertrude apparently went off to wherever ghosts go when they're not making things go bump in the night.

Grace sidled up beside me. "Hello, Joe. Fancy meeting you here." Her cultured voice held a promise of classy naughtiness.

"Hello, Grace. How come your swell date is making you get your own drinks?"

Grace chuckled. "Frank? He's busy telling stories. Hasn't even noticed I've moved," she replied. A glance told me she was correct. "And he's just a friend. Arm candy. His heart belongs to Freddy."

"That photographer who's always hanging around?" I hadn't seen that coming.

"Can you think of a better cover?" Grace was right. I'd been fooled, because what I saw fit what I expected. It reminded me that the Hathaway's speakeasy provided a sanctuary, but the word outside wasn't nearly so welcoming. So far, immortality hadn't redeemed my faith in human nature.

"What can I do you for?" I asked, resisting the urge to knock back my drink.

"I need a date."

I nearly snorted rum through my nose. "Excuse me?"

"Not a real date, silly," Grace replied in fond frustration, batting at my arm. "More like a hunky 'Hunky' bodyguard for an event I need to attend."

"I'm Hungarian," I said with an exaggerated sigh. "And 'Hunky' isn't any more polite than 'Polack.'" I knew Grace didn't mean anything by it, but my time in the mills had exposed me to plenty of people who did.

"Then I need a handsome Hungarian with muscles," she said imperiously.

"And Flying Frankie can't escort you?"

Grace rolled her eyes. "It could get dangerous. He can go zoom-zoom when bullets fly. I need a man who can go pow-pow."

Several ungentlemanly comments occurred to me, and I resisted them all. I saw the sparkle in Grace's eyes that said she knew exactly what she'd said. "That aside," I replied, clearing my throat, "why me?"

Grace slipped an arm through mine and led me away from the bar, closer to where Hank's piano music would make eavesdropping difficult. "I've been asked to go to a luncheon by Countess Antonina Demidov. Sounds very impressive," she said with a dismissive hand wave, "but I'm certain she means to ask for money for a pet cause."

Grace leaned closer. "The Countess is an Imperialist," she confided.

"Not going to do much good, after the Bolsheviks shot the royal family."

"Some live forever in hope. Oh, it's likely a con of some kind. They've found a missing princess. Or the *tsarevich* was secretly spirited away. But I promised my dear friend, Jack West, I'd keep an eye on her."

This time, I did snort a bit of rum. "You're asking me to do Jack West an indirect favor?" West was an arrogant prick, and a Supernatural Secret Service agent as well. Too close to a Pinkerton in my book.

"It's really doing *me* a favor," Grace replied, turning the wide, pleading eyes on me that we both knew had absolutely no effect. Almost.

"Why can't Jackie-boy escort you?"

"He might be recognized."

"More like he wants us to pull his chestnuts out of the fire," I grumbled. West and I had crossed paths a few times. I'd grudgingly admit that he was probably one of the good guys, but doing so left a bad taste in my mouth.

"I can count on you, right, Joe?" Grace pressed.

I sighed like a martyr, but she knew she had me from the time she walked up to the bar. "Sure. Where and when?"

"You're the bee's knees, Joe," Grace said with a saucy wink.

"Pretty sure I'd be an awfully big bee."

"I had your monkey suit pressed," Grace told me. I escorted her to enough fancy-pants parties that she'd had a tuxedo custom-made for me. I felt like an organ grinder's pet in it, but Grace assured me I looked swell.

"Yeah, yeah. I'll do it."

Grace stood on tiptoe to give me a peck on the cheek. The feather in her headband tickled my nose, and the beaded fringe on her flapper dress tinkled like a glass chandelier to my enhanced hearing.

"Better get back to Frankie before he gets jealous," I said, with an affectionate shooing motion. "Then Freddie will have to bash me with his camera."

"See you around," Grace said with a look over her shoulder. "Don't be late."

For some reason, watching Grace walk away made me suddenly melancholy. The crowd's gaiety struck me as a bit desperate. Then again, the horrors of the influenza and the Great War weren't far behind us, reminding mortals that their time was brief. Mine, on the other hand, was long. On nights like this, I felt the weight of the bargain I'd made. I didn't exactly regret it, but it weighed on me, nonetheless.

I took my empty glass back to the bar. Ben gave me a look. "You get roped into another job, Joe?"

"Just doing a favor for a friend."

Ben's eyes narrowed. "Sure you are. Just don't let that metal head get you into trouble." Ben was one of the very few who knew my secret. His witchcraft saw right through me.

I rapped my knuckles lightly against my forehead. "No different than any other day," I said with a grin and walked out into the night.

MIRO'S NEIGHBORHOOD lived down to expectations. Locals referred to it as "Moscow Heights." It reminded me of the squalid tenements back in Homestead, though the air here smelled more of borscht, less of cabbage. Clotheslines crisscrossed over my head, though the washing would be gray from coal smoke minutes after hanging it on the line.

Teenage boys and older men sat out on the stoops, smoking cheap cigarettes. Even with the windows closed, voices carried. I spoke enough Russian to get by, but I didn't need to speak the language to understand the gist of most of the conversations. Mothers screamed at children. Husbands growled at wives. Dogs barked, and babies screeched. I remembered the whole glorious mess from my mortal days.

I had changed clothes after the speakeasy. What I wore now didn't look much different from how the men on the stoops were dressed, but they knew I didn't belong here. I considered stopping to ask about the missing people but suspected everyone would suddenly "forget" how to speak English. I'd played that game a time or two myself, before.

But as I walked, I picked up an uneasiness that didn't come from being poor. I knew that discomfort well enough. Taking a second glance, I saw that the men didn't sprawl on the steps, they huddled, as if no one wanted to be at the edges in the dark. First-floor windows were shuttered, odd on a night without a storm. Few other walkers passed me, and as I walked farther, toward the mills on the other side, I saw no one at all. The street lamps were few and dim, making the shadows long.

The steel mill hulked like a behemoth along the river, huge and dark. In silhouette, the many pipes and conduits looked like the ribs of a great beast, and the burn-off chimney cast hellish shadows. A shiver went down my spine.

I'd never been a very imaginative man before my almost-death, so I wasn't given to flights of fancy. My sudden jitters told me something was truly wrong.

"Open," I murmured, igniting Krukis's borrowed magic. I blinked, and the world changed around me. Colors, sights, and sounds grew sharper, but what mattered most were the faint, blood-red wisps I could see in the air, the tell-tale sign of dark magic, like the lingering scent of a cigar.

Something unnatural and magical had come this way and gone toward the steel mill. Even with all my advantages, there was no way in hell I wanted to chase a monster into the chaos of rail yards and storage buildings. Not when I had no idea what I might be facing, or how many there were.

But I went, anyhow.

I followed the red traces only I could see. They wafted like smoke, and I needed to hurry before the wind took them away. It took strong magic to leave a resonance like that, which worried me. A neighborhood witch shouldn't have that kind of power. Usually, someone like that used their abilities to protect the group. If not, everyone knew who was behind the hexes and curses and drove the witch out.

Milo hadn't said anything about a local magic user, which made me think the traces of power came from an outsider. I strained to suss out more from what had been left behind. The magic was definitely tainted. I could feel the malice, as well as an overwhelming hunger. Not the normal need to eat; no, whatever left behind the echo of its essence needed to destroy and consume, to rip its prey out of existence.

I followed the trail of a monster, not a predator.

Closer to the steel mill, hundreds of workers came and went, working round-the-clock shifts. Out here, in the rail yard, I saw no one. Empty train cars awaited bars or rolls of new steel to carry across the country. Heaps of coal and stacks of raw materials littered the gravel lot, each of them a potential hiding place. Sheds that housed equipment hulked in the darkness, too many to search, and all of them perfect places for a killer to go to ground. I knew from my own time in the mills that no one went into every storage building every day. Some weren't visited for weeks or months, depending on what was needed.

They would be ideal for lying in wait—close to vulnerable prey and yet difficult for someone to notice. The cops wouldn't listen to a guy like Milo. Even if they did, they'd be sitting ducks against dark magic. I edged closer, still trying to figure out what would have left a trail like the blood red traces of power that grew fainter with every breeze.

Sorcerer. That alone made my blood freeze. I'd never really tested my borrowed magic. Maybe Krukis would give me what I needed, when I needed it. That made me understandably nervous. I didn't want to bring a knife to a gunfight hoping it would become a rifle, only to be left with a pig sticker. I didn't even know if Ben Lavecchia could hold his own against a true sorcerer. I hoped we didn't have to find out.

But my gut said more than blood magic left the traces. Whatever had been here wasn't human.

The traces led me to one of the sheds. A lock on the door didn't keep me out; I snapped it with a jerk of my wrist. As soon as I opened the door, the smell of rot and old blood assaulted my nose. The nearly empty shed clearly hadn't been used for anything except a monster's lair in quite a while. My vision, enhanced in the dark thanks to Krukis, could make out lumps that I felt certain were the remains of the missing people from Milo's neighborhood, and probably from elsewhere as well.

The red wisps and the stink of their dark magic lingered stronger here, but I could tell that the source of the power was gone. I moved slowly, expecting an ambush, staying close to the wall. In the far corner, I found a pile of filthy blankets and bloodstained, ragged clothing. Something had made its nest here, feeding to gain strength. When it was ready, it moved on, leaving behind what it no longer needed.

Shit. The creature had been dangerous enough in its weakened state. Now, I wasn't sure what it would take to stop it. I had gained my abilities from Krukis, but he wasn't the only god who might want a champion, and some of the other options were the stuff of nightmares.

Nothing I found gave me a clue about the nature of the monster, and I didn't want to be found with a bunch of corpses. I slipped out of the door, leaving it ajar behind me so that someone might find the missing people and give their worried relatives the news. As I headed back across the no man's land toward Milo's neighborhood, I heard the attacker closing on me right before he struck.

The werewolf lunged, hitting me in the chest with its full weight. A normal-sized wolf with a man's bulk would have been bad enough, but the huge creature looked more like a direwolf, bigger in every way. If he'd hit me before I'd powered up with magic, he'd have taken us both to the ground, and I'd be hurting. As it was, he chomped on metal skin, clanging as his teeth hit unyielding steel.

I seized that moment of surprise to flip us, pinning him with my weight. Thanks to the steel bones, I'm always heavier than I look, and when the skin turns to metal, that adds to the heft. The huge wolf let out an *oof* as I knocked him breathless. He clawed and snapped, but I had him, and finally, he bared his neck in surrender, waiting to die.

"I don't want to kill you. I just want answers. Now shift. And if you try to get away, I might change my mind on the whole killing you piece."

The bones beneath me began to shudder and realign, and the body expanded and contracted. Fur sloughed off, changing to skin, and in minutes, I found myself pinning a very large, very naked man to the ground.

Not the most awkward moment of my life.

"Why are you here?" I growled.

"Why are you? What are you? Did you kill them?"

"Kill who?"

"Don't bullshit me! I can smell them. Your clothing stinks of death."

A wolf's sensitive nose would be able to find the rotting corpses in the shed despite the heavy coal smoke of the mill.

"Did you?"

My prisoner had a raw-boned, Eastern European look, not unlike Milo or the men I'd known from Romania, Bulgaria, or the Ukraine. I wondered if he was from the neighborhood, or had come as a favor to someone who lived there. He looked at me in shock.

"Me? I'm here to find them. My cousin Mikhail disappeared." He regained some of his bluster. "You're not from the neighborhood, and you're sure as hell not human."

"I came because a friend asked me to see if I could find them. Maybe we're on the same side."

I could tell from the look in his eyes that he didn't trust me, but he was freaked out by not being the biggest dog in the fight. "Do you know what killed them?"

"Not one of us." By that, I took him to mean a shifter. "I would have smelled it."

Probably true. "What then?" I had my suspicions, but I needed to know what he considered likely.

"One of the fey? A hound of the gods? Perchta, come to winnow the herd?" He shook his head and gave up any pretense of a fight. "All I know is that it killed my cousin and many others. It must be stopped."

"I came here to hunt it. Do you have any idea where it might have gone?"

He shook his head. I believed what he said, given the grief I saw in his eyes. Deciding to take a chance, I eased up, moving off him. The man drew his legs up in a belated attempt at modesty, or maybe he was just cold. "No. Perhaps it got what it wanted and left."

Or maybe it just changed forms, like a butterfly leaving a cocoon. That thought did nothing to lift my mood. Neither did the suspicion burning in my gut. If the monster wasn't a shifter gone wrong, the most likely culprit was a vampire—who also practiced the dark arts.

"Maybe," I agreed, more because I needed to wrap up this little heart-to-heart before the mill security goons caught us. "Get out of here. Whatever hunted the neighborhood isn't likely to come back. You found your cousin. Now, leave the revenge to the professionals."

He gave me a disdainful look. "I am Romanian. We do not walk away from vengeance."

"I'm Hungarian. And we know better than to take on a fight we can't win." Not true in my case, but he didn't need to know that. "I promise you, in the name of Svarog and Krukis, your cousin will be avenged."

His eyes widened. Apparently, I wasn't the only one who still remembered the Old Gods. The shifter scrambled to his feet, not bothering to cover his bits. "Thank you." He made a shallow bow. "*Mulțumesc.*"

"Go home. And...put some clothes on."

He loped toward the darker shadows at the edge of the lot and shifted back to his wolf form before vanishing into the night. I didn't have all the answers, but I'd accomplished something.

Miro wasn't imagining the disappearances, and whatever was snatching people wasn't just a sick human being. It stank of foul magic, and it wasn't human or a shifter. That narrowed down the possibilities, at least a little. I smiled. I had a job to do.

By the time I got back to the rooming house where I lived, dinner was over. Mrs. Branson, the landlady, included a hot supper in the cost of the room, which I appreciated and rarely missed. She had put a plate in the icebox for me, and the meatloaf wasn't completely cold yet.

I sat down at the table and tucked a napkin under my chin. Just as I started to eat, Officer Colin Kennedy, a beat cop with the Cleveland police, trudged in and grabbed the remaining plate from the icebox.

"Long day?" I asked, although I already knew the answer.

"My feet are killing me." Colin ate like the food might disappear. So did I. I'd gone hungry too many times growing up to ever waste a good meal, and Mrs. Branson's cooking was surprisingly good.

"There you are." Aislin, Colin's wife, swept into the kitchen with a big smile for both of us. "You're both late tonight."

"Can't be helped." Colin sighed.

"Goes with the job," I said with a shrug.

Our rooming house wasn't near the theater, but Mrs. Branson was also one of Ben Lavecchia's people. She took in odd ducks, like me, and didn't ask nosy questions. I suspected that Oscar, the other tenant, was a shifter of some sort. So long as no one got eaten when the moon was full, it really wasn't any of my business.

"You know anything about people going missing over in the Russian neighborhoods?" I asked through a mouth full of meatloaf.

Colin frowned. "Heard something like that. Not much. Those folks stick pretty much to themselves. Why? You got a lead?"

"Maybe." I told him about my stroll. "I don't think whatever's taking people is human." Colin and Aislin were among the few who knew my secret. Colin and I had helped each other out a time or two, hunting down the bad guys.

"Interesting," Colin said, wiping his mouth. "We've been on alert for anarchists. Some dotty Brit is spouting off about the end of the world, and that's got dodgers here thinking that if the world's going to end, there's no need for government."

I was just about to respond when an insistent knock sounded at the door. Colin drew his service weapon, and Aislin, never one to be left out of the action, grabbed an iron frying pan from the stove. I went to the door and found a flunky from the speakeasy nervously twisting his cap.

"You Mr. Mack?" he asked, avoiding eye contact. The skinny kid barely came up to the middle of my chest and looked like a stiff wind would blow him over. "Mr. Lavecchia sent me to fetch you. Says it's important."

My eyes narrowed. *"Which* Mr. Lavecchia?" Ben was a friend but damned if I'd dance to his father's tune.

"Mr. Ben. Please, he said to bring you right back."

"Is everything okay?" Colin called from behind me.

I didn't know what business Ben needed help with, but I didn't want to drag Colin into it. "Yeah, I'm good. I need to go deal with some trouble over at the theater." With that, I grabbed my coat and followed the messenger outside.

I wondered what had gone wrong enough for Ben to send for me. He couldn't exactly call for the cops if he had a problem at the speakeasy— another reason I didn't want to involve Colin—but the Lavecchias had their own muscle to deal with troublemakers.

The messenger brought me in one of the back entrances to the club, and my intuition told me something was very wrong. For a few seconds, I wondered if it was a set-up, but Ben had no reason to be angry with me, and since he knew what I was, I didn't figure him for stupid. That meant that whatever had gone wrong had spooked Ben, and a guy who was that mobbed-up didn't scare easily.

Ben was waiting in the back hall, near the secret tunnel they used to bring in shipments of illegal liquor. He stopped pacing and waved me over. I looked down and found a dead man on the floor.

"We've got trouble," Ben said, gently turning the man's head with the toe of his wingtip. "See those marks? This isn't a Mob hit, or a stick-up. We've got a vamp on the loose."

3

Mack. Why am I not surprised to see you here?" Special Agent Jack West, Supernatural Secret Service, took one look at me and pinched the bridge of his nose as if to hold off a migraine. I had that effect on some people.

"Probably because you're reasonably smart, and you know I belong here, same as you."

West and I had history. He knew about me, and we'd tangled several times over the years. Sometimes we were on the same side, other times, not so much. With his slicked back hair, sharp suit, and fedora, West looked more like a hotshot gambler or Chicago hitman than a Fed. The SSS dealt with supernatural problems—something I had no issue with—and kept an eye on people with special abilities—something I most definitely had a beef about. On the other hand, West had pull, so he could be handy to have on my side—when he wasn't being an asshole.

"You seen any vamps around?" West asked me, raising an eyebrow.

"Not as such, no. But people have been going missing over in Moscow Heights. I went to take a look—favor to a friend. Something with dark magic has been there. I didn't see who or what it was, but there was no mistaking the traces they left behind."

I was doubly bound to get to the bottom of the problem, first because of my vow to Krukis, and second, because I'd been invited— more like conscripted—into the Shadow Council, a loose alliance of people with extraordinary abilities who tried to keep the world safe from supernatural threats. West knew about Krukis, but not about the Council.

"You get anything from the stiff?" West asked, jerking his head toward the dead guy.

Ben cleared the room, leaving just him, West, me, and the corpse. I closed my eyes and called my magic. When I opened my eyes, I saw what usually stayed hidden. Ben's aura glowed a deep blue—not surprising for a witch of his power. West had a slightly silver glow, something I'd confronted him on in the past. He always blew me off or made a joke of it. I suspected his "intuition" might be a bit more psychic than he wanted to admit.

When I peered at the dead man, I saw faint traces of the blood-red wisps I'd seen in Moscow Heights. Could there be two creatures snatching people? Sure. Was it likely? No.

I looked back at Ben. "Can you see it?"

Ben nodded. "You?"

"Yeah. Same red glow I saw in Miro's neighborhood. Which means we don't just have a vamp gone feral, but a witch-vamp." It wasn't illegal to be a vampire in Cleveland, so long as you didn't snack on unwilling people or kill anyone. Like the shifters, vamps tended to do their best to avoid coming to the notice of guys like West—or me. We got called when one went rogue.

"Where'd you find him?" West asked. He knelt beside the body, tipping up his hat to let him see better, but he didn't touch anything, just gave the dead guy a very intense once-over.

"Out back, with the garbage," Ben said. "One of the kitchen boys found him when they took out the trash."

"You turn any of their kind away from the club lately?" West always cut right to the chase.

"No. They're welcome like anyone else, long as they pay their tab and don't make trouble."

The dead man was poorly dressed, probably a vagrant, and smelled like he hadn't bathed in a long time. Most vamps who weren't absolutely desperate for blood were more discriminating, and not just because of an excellent sense of smell. They usually had no difficulty finding willing donors who enjoyed the danger. The only vamps I'd ever known to start chomping on hobos were outcasts. But that didn't square with the traces of power I'd seen.

"Any reason for someone from the family business to decide to leave you a warning?" I asked.

"None that I've heard about," Ben replied. "I do my best to stay out of what they do. But fucking around with the vamps isn't like them."

"You brought us down here," I said.

"I brought *you* here. *He* showed up on his own," Ben said with a pointed glare at West. "What was I gonna do? Call the cops?"

Figured. "Fair enough. But you didn't have your boys take care of it. Why?"

Ben looked like he was deciding how much to say. "I've been hearing things, about the vamps. Not the ones who've lived here for a while—they know their place and how to get along. But there've been whispers about some new vamps who don't play by the rules. *Russian* vamps."

West and I exchanged glances. I'd been in Cleveland for more than a decade without any trouble from the Russians. Now I had Ruskies coming out my ears—Miro's missing neighbors, Ben's dead vamp, Grace's Countess-in-exile, and Colin's anarchists.

"Is there a turf war no one's told us about?" West asked, standing and brushing non-existent lint from his suit. "Maybe the Russian Mob making a move on your old man's territory?"

Ben snorted. "Seriously? No. First—if I thought it was related to business, you two would be the *last* people I'd call. And second?" He shook his head. "No. The Russians are thugs. Muscle. Not *businessmen.*"

Once upon a time, back when I was mortal, I might have had objections to being allied with someone like Ben Lavecchia, a man with criminal ties and unholy powers. Then I saw the pain and death that "legitimate" businessmen like Carnegie and Frick caused, and my moral compass tilted a little. Ben—and West, in his own way—had honor. I could work with honorable men.

"I have some contacts among the vamps," I said. "I'll see if anyone is willing to talk."

"We have people in Moscow Heights," West said.

Of course he did. I reined in my anger, reminding myself that the SSS wasn't the Pinkertons. West wasn't above throwing his weight—and his badge—around, but he'd told me flat out when we first met that, in his unofficial opinion, the Pinkertons had fucked up big-time in Homestead. "I'll ask around."

Ben nodded. "Yeah, I already put out the word. But I don't expect to hear anything from the Family. This wasn't a hit, and it wasn't a shakedown gone wrong. This guy was dinner, and whoever drank him tossed out the leftovers with the trash."

West and I left the speakeasy together. "Where's your shiny Buick?" I asked. As usual, I'd walked, but then again, I didn't have West's stylish reputation to uphold.

"I parked it a couple of blocks away. Didn't want to make Lavecchia's pop nervous."

"And you just happened to be in town when a vamp goes feral?" I didn't try to hide my skepticism.

"How about we go get a cup of coffee and talk?" West lifted his collar against the cold wind.

If I were going to trust a Fed—which I wouldn't, at least not completely—I'd probably trust West. And maybe I should get over the fact that a goddamn Pinkerton beat me to death, but I'm pissy like that and hold grudges. Still, what happened before wasn't West's fault, and he'd been decent to me while still being a pain in the ass. So I figured that I might as well go along with it, because my gut told me that whatever was actually going on was big.

The all-night diner smelled like bacon grease and burnt coffee. West hailed a waitress to bring us two cups of java and slices of their best pie. Betty, the waitress, gave him a bright smile, and when she brought our food, she slipped him a note that I figured said when she got off work. West had that effect on people. A real charmer—when he wasn't being a son of a bitch. Guess which side of him I got to see?

"So, talk." I stirred more sugar than usual into my black coffee and drank it fast, letting the heat and sweetness cover up the bottom-of-the-pot taste.

"I think the dead guy was a warning." West got us a table in the corner so we could both sit with our backs to the wall and have a view of the door while being far away from the big glass windows. The diner's neon sign cast the sidewalk in a crimson glow.

"I'll buy that he was a message. But who was supposed to get the hint? Ben? His pops?" I'd ended up with a piece of the banana cream pie and intended to enjoy it.

West shrugged. "Dunno. But I think we're being played for chumps here, and I don't like it."

"Well, at least we agree on something." I finished my coffee and hoped that when the waitress refilled it, she'd have a fresh pot. "What do you know about anarchists?"

West's eyebrows rose. "They're bad news. Why?"

"C'mon. You want info from me, you're gonna have to share, too."

West's expression soured, but it could have been the coffee. "We've had reports that there are troublemakers in town. Eastern European—maybe Russian."

"Bolsheviks?" We'd all heard about the bloody revolution and the deaths of the Tsar and his family. I didn't figure the guy had been a saint, but at least his kids and his dog deserved better.

"White Russians," West replied. "Anti-Bolsheviks. I appreciate that they're against the Reds, but most of them are nutty as a fruitcake. There's always a lost prince or princess showing up to lay a 'true claim' to the throne. They don't just want to toss out the Leninists—they want a new monarchy."

"Do you think that any real heir survived?" From what I'd seen in the paper, the wily monk Rasputin, the Tsar, and the entire royal family—along with their loyal servants—got massacred in cold blood.

"Doubtful," West said through a mouthful of pie. "I mean, if you go out far enough, there's probably a second cousin who might technically be next in line since everyone else is dead, but that's not the kind of claim that's going to hold water."

I was thinking about the fancy luncheon Grace had asked me to attend. That crowd was the upper crust end of the same sad pipe dream. "I know what it's like to have to leave my homeland," I said quietly. "Many people dream of things getting better so they can go back again."

West stared at me like he was seeing me for the first time. Maybe he was just remembering that I'm a lot older than I look. "I can buy that," he said finally and finished the rest of his coffee without wincing. Betty swooped in to refill both our cups. This batch didn't smell any better. Maybe the regulars liked it burned.

"The thing about anarchists is, they just like to burn things down and have riots," West continued. "And if they organize—"

"Organized anarchists?" I mocked. "Isn't that—"

"An oxymoron?" West replied with a twitch of a smile. "Maybe. But stay with me. If they *loosely* organize, they might decide to pick another target. An *American* target. And once the rioting starts, the Pinkertons get called in, and no one is too precise about who's who when the brass knuckles come out."

He had me, and he knew it. Hell, I'd kinda figured that much out on my own. "I hear there's a Countess in town who's got the caviar crowd all a-twitter," I replied, figuring I owed him something.

West's smile broadened. "Ah, Grace Harringworth's at it again, isn't she? Cleveland's debutante spy. Whatever she drags you into, be sure to take notes, and try not to get anyone killed."

I gave him a look that was as bitter as my coffee. "Do you think the Countess has any connection to the anarchists?"

West took his time to answer, like he was thinking it over. "Maybe indirectly. If so, the money is calling all the shots, and the anarchists are the muscle. There's probably someone in the middle, playing both ends. Whoever that is could be the connection to the rogue vamps. But we're missing pieces. I can't figure out the big picture."

"I speak a little Russian," I said before I could stop myself. "Understand it better than I can talk it, but I can follow a conversation. Lots of guys in the mills spoke it."

I could see West sizing me up, figuring out what I was offering without me even having to put it into words. "You think you could infiltrate a meeting?"

"Maybe. I can certainly look the part."

He nodded. "It could work. If you went to one of their rallies, you might be able to tell whether they're just blowing smoke, or if there's actually a plan."

"Or I could be the unlucky SOB who's in the wrong place at the wrong time when a riot breaks out."

"Maybe," West agreed. "I can get you sprung if you get arrested. Not much even Ben can do if you get dead. Again."

"Funny. So if I'm carrying tales from what Grace hears and being your shill in the anarchist meeting, what are you doing besides sitting on your thumbs?"

West smirked. "Doing what I do best. Intimidating the cops and charming the ladies."

"Better than the other way around, I guess."

West muttered a phrase not usually said in polite company, but then again, the crowd in the diner didn't look like they'd care. "I'll work my channels, you work yours. I've got the feeling that there's mutual benefit here, much as it pains me to say it."

I grinned. "Admit it, Jackie. You missed working with me."

"Like a bad case of the clap," he replied. "I'm just pragmatic."

"I always said you were a prick."

He glowered. "That's not the same."

For as much fun as it was to rile West up, I didn't need him as an enemy. All things considered, he wasn't a bad guy—as Feds went. "Geez-Louise, West. Can't you take a joke? Somebody put too much starch in your shorts?"

West rolled his eyes. "You're incorrigible."

"Maybe. Takes one to know one."

He opened his mouth, then shut it again, and I took that as a victory.

"Anarchists and countesses aside, we still need to figure out the vamp angle and who's snatching people in Moscow Heights," I reminded him. "I've got no idea how that ties in. But I'm going to find out—and I need you to back me on it."

He gave a bored wave of his hand. "Yeah, yeah. Just try not to get the whole Cleveland PD on your tail. Even I can only pull so many strings."

I NEVER DID promise anything about not ending up crosswise with the CPD. I know better than to guarantee something I don't control. Still, West came through with an address and a time for the next anarchist meeting, and I dug out some dungarees and an old shirt that had seen a lot of wear to look the part, down to my hard-worn boots and faded kerchief.

My room at the lodging house isn't fancy—just a bed, a lamp, a chair, and a desk, plus a beat up armchair I pulled out of the trash. The bathroom is down the hall, but at least we've got electric lights and running water—a big improvement over what I had back in Homestead. Still, seeing myself in clothes like I wore in the mill made me melancholy. I didn't dress like that anymore, unless I was going out on the sly, like tonight.

The face that stared back at me didn't look changed at all by the last thirty-six years. I should be gray-haired, a grandfather at sixty-seven. But my blond hair was the same as ever, my face still unlined, and even the scars I'd earned in bar fights or at the steel mill were gone, courtesy of Krukis. Everything stayed the same, except for the eyes. I thought my blue eyes looked every bit my true age, and then some.

I figured I'd best get going before I went all maudlin. The past was past, and as much as my dreams still remembered flames and blood, nothing could bring those people back, or my beloved Agata and Patryk.

But maybe, if I could get my ass in gear, I could stop a riot or worse from destroying someone else's life.

The anarchists met in an old dance hall that rented out to meetings on weeknights. It didn't look like it got much business on the weekend, either, judging from the worn, sagging wooden floor and the faded paint on the walls. I imagine it had been quite the place for a hot date years ago, but time had passed it by, and now it just got by the best it could. I knew the feeling.

"Ain't seen you before," a man said in Russian when I drifted toward the middle of the crowd. People milled about in front of the stage where other nights, a band might play.

"First time," I replied, in the same language. "Wanted to see what all the fuss was about."

"Keep your ears open," he said. "There's plenty to hear."

Inwardly, I sighed with relief at having passed the first test for fitting in. The man who'd spoken to me moved away, chatting with others, but I didn't get the feeling he was ratting me out. I avoided eye contact, not wanting to test the limits of my remembered Russian, working my way toward a point where I'd still be hidden in the crowd but could see or hear whatever happened on stage.

Meanwhile, I listened to the conversations around me. It was hard to follow a single voice in the babble, especially when I had to work to translate the words in my head. I quickly gathered that people weren't happy with their wages at the mill, the beef at the butcher shop was tough this week and the grocer's potatoes had bugs, and that beets here didn't cook up as well as they did back in Russia. I heard comments about the pilot, Amelia Earhart, comparing her with Charles Lindbergh. One of the men said he'd seen a motion picture with a whistling mouse and a steamboat and thought America was very strange.

I'd almost decided this was just a group of gossipy old roosters when I caught a word that made me snap to attention. "Tsar." I tried not to swivel my head, looking for the speaker. In the noise of the crowd, I couldn't pick out who had spoken. Maybe someone was just nostalgic for the old days. Or perhaps, there really was a link to darker purposes.

Just as the bells in the clock tower struck nine, a man bounded out onto the stage, greeted by a smattering of applause. He didn't look like an actor and didn't move like a politician. His thinning light brown hair gave him a prominent forehead, and he had a spare, gaunt look to him that I associated with priests and professors. The man wore a suit and tie, but even I could tell that they weren't of good quality, though he looked better than most of his audience. The ill-fitting suit made me wonder whether it was second hand, and how an anarchist earned his bread.

"Good evening, loyal Russians!" he greeted the crowd, which answered with less enthusiasm than I anticipated for a bunch of rabble-rousers. I'd expected a pack of young wolves, eager for a fight. There were a few groups of men in their twenties and thirties, but more of them were in their middle years, looking worn and disillusioned. If this group intended to riot, they'd best do it before supper and early bedtime, or they'd lose half their protesters.

"I bring you news from England, and a prediction from Spencer Percival, Junior!"

That was a name I didn't recognize, but it sounded hoity-toity, and I wondered if this Spencer guy wrote things to rile people up.

"He has published an article just this month, sent to me from friends across the waves. In it, Percival confirms that we are soon to see the end of the world. Make no mistake—things are grinding to a halt. This wisdom is reserved for the few brave enough to hear it, brave like you!"

The crowd perked up at that, with more applause. The young men hooted and hollered, which didn't seem to bother the man on the stage. Out of a crowd of perhaps thirty people—all men—about half looked to be young enough to cause a problem. I tried to get a good look at them, without drawing notice.

Now that I paid attention, I realized that the crowd had divisions aside from age. The older men looked like tradesmen I'd expect at the union hall, or down at the pub drinking at the bar. Perhaps they came for something to do, or because talking politics was more exciting than going home to their wives. They didn't seem angry enough to be anarchists, just tired and maybe bitter from a bad run of luck.

The younger men, on the other hand, seemed to be looking for a fight. They talked loudly, reacted to the speaker with whistles and stomps, egging each other on. When the speaker paused, they filled the silence with cries of "burn it down!" and "throw out the trash!" The man on the stage didn't address them directly, but he looked pleased with their outbursts, while those around me appeared uncomfortable and dismayed.

"We have been given this knowledge for a reason!" the man on the stage declared. "Now that we know that the world is corrupt and broken, on its last legs, we can rise up and reveal the rot for all to see! Cast out the vipers and break down the walls they've used to keep you from claiming your fair share of all that you've labored to build."

"Percival says the end of the world is coming—and he's right," the man on the stage shouted. "But he doesn't understand what he's said. It's not our world that's coming to an end—it's his! It's the world of privilege, the robber barons, the gilded thieves—their world is ending. Our world is just beginning—a world of equality! Where men are paid fair wages for hard work! Where the hired thugs and the Pinkerton goons get what's coming to them, where they're the ones thrown in jail, not us!"

The huckster on stage painted a pretty picture. Men around me called out in support, clapping and cat-calling. Salted throughout the crowd were other men I was certain were shills; they shouted and yelled, trying to get the others to follow their lead. The speaker spun an appealing fantasy, but I'd been around long enough to doubt his promises. I could see some of the audience hesitate, trying to make up their minds, enticed by a yarn they desperately wanted to believe.

As the speaker continued, saying very little new or concrete but repeating the same ideas in different words, I sensed the crowd shift. He didn't need magic to win them over; he held out their wildest dream, dangled it in front of them, and described it in loving detail until the attraction overwhelmed them and pulled the crowd to him. I saw the hope in their eyes and realized that it was as powerful as any drug. That made me angry because I knew in my bones that the huckster on the stage intended to use these men, in his own way, just like Carnegie and Frick and their ilk had done, and leave their bones behind.

I caught a glimpse of the vamp out of the corner of my eye, but I knew what I'd seen. When I first scanned the crowd, I'd been on alert for non-humans. I knew there were shifters around, as well as vamps, and Ben Lavecchia wasn't the only witch in Cleveland. Even though I hadn't quite figured out the huckster's angle and what was in it for him, I knew why the mortals were gathered here. But a vamp? He didn't care about the likes of Carnegie, Frick, and their gilded friends. A vamp would outlive them all. He wouldn't be forced to take a shitty, dangerous job in the mills or mines to put food on the table and keep a roof over his family's heads. Vamps, like other predators, could fend for themselves. So why would one of them come to a rally like this?

I didn't know, but I intended to find out.

As the huckster wound up the crowd with another pitch, I shouldered my way toward where I'd glimpsed the vamp in the crowd. The last thing

I needed was to have him spook an already emotional crowd into a stampede or a fight. That would bring the cops down on the gathering for sure, and no matter how much I distrusted the man on stage, I didn't want to see a bloodbath. The police wouldn't believe reports of a vamp, but they'd go hard on the anarchists—dangerous or not.

But maybe I could draw off the vampire, pull him away from the crowd, or scare him off. I caught sight of him again, a short, slightly-built fellow with yellow hair like a haystack and an unnaturally pale complexion. We were both caught by the crowd, trying to make our way to the exit without attracting the wrong kind of attention.

I jostled a man who didn't like being distracted. He glared at me, and he might have looked menacing if he hadn't stood half a head shorter and been about forty pounds lighter than I was—not to mention my other unfair advantages. My height helped me keep track of the elusive vampire, since I could see over the heads and shoulders of the crowd around me, while he had to fight his way blind toward the wall.

If he made it out the door ahead of me, he'd vanish in the seconds it took for me to follow. He was holding back on his immortal speed here in the crowd, not wanting to be noticed, but he'd take off like a shot into the dark, and as fast as I was, I wasn't sure I could overtake him. That meant I had to catch him before he got outside.

Muttered curses followed me as I hurried toward the door, bumping shoulders in the crowded hall. I reached the door a heartbeat before the vamp and brought my steel grip down on his shoulder.

"I'd like a word," I said in a quiet rumble that left no room for debate. The vamp squeaked as my fingers dug into his bicep. His eyes widened as he tried to figure out what I was, because vampires aren't used to being manhandled.

I steered him outside. As soon as the door clicked shut behind me, he tried to pull out of my grip, and when that didn't work, he showed me his fangs and went for my throat.

I stiff-armed the son of a bitch and held him six inches off the ground, out of reach of his kicking feet and his nasty teeth. Just for good measure, I gave him a shake.

"What the fuck is your problem?" the vamp spat.

"I want to know why a vampire showed up at a labor rally," I replied, keeping him dangling. "Were you scouting for dinner or spying for someone else?"

He didn't answer right away, so I shook him like a dog with a rabbit, back and forth quick enough to blur, with enough strength to have snapped his neck if he hadn't already been undead. When his brain was suitably rattled, I stopped. "Are you going to tell me what's going on, or you want another shake-up? I can do this all night."

"No!" The vamp must have figured out that whatever I was, I could hold my own. He probably hadn't run into anyone who could take him since he'd been turned, and wasn't sure what to make of it.

"Start talking. What's your name?"

"Thaddeus. Tad for short."

"All right, Tad-for-short. Spill it." Just for good measure, and because I could, I gave him a little shake.

"Okay!" Tad glared at me. "Stan, my maker, sent me. Told me to size up the crowd, see what the guy on stage was selling, and report back."

"Were you going to eat anyone?"

Tad's gaze slid away. "Of course not." I shook him back and forth a few times. "All right! Maybe. I hadn't made up my mind yet. Did you smell those guys? Phew! Besides, their blood's probably half moonshine."

"What did your maker want with a bunch of loser factory stiffs?"

"I don't know." When my grip tensed for another shake, he cringed. "Honest! He doesn't explain himself; he just gives orders."

"Why do you think he was interested?" I tightened my fingers. He'd have bruises for sure. Tad was smart enough to realize that I could just as easily break his arm, or rip it clean off. Vampires can heal from a lot of damage, but I'd never known one to grow a limb back. I gambled he'd want to stay in one piece.

Tad looked from side to side and licked his lips, a nervous gesture left over from his mortal days. "He'll kill me if he finds out I talked to you."

"I'll kill you if you don't," I replied with a shrug. "So you can take your chances that he won't find out, or piss me off and get a sure thing."

Tad slumped in defeat. I didn't ease my grip, not trusting him half as far as I could throw him. "It's the Russian vamps," he said. "Nothing's been right since they got here. I think they've got something on Stan, or they've threatened him. He's had us keeping tabs on the anarchist guys, and on the shifters, and a couple of Mob bosses. Not doing anything, just watching and reporting back."

"Is he interested in any particular kind of information?" My hand was starting to cramp, and I hoped that I could finish the evening without getting blood all over my clothes.

"He wants to know what they say, who they see, how many show up to meetings, that sort of thing," Tad replied. "Useless stuff. I think he tells the Ruskies, but I don't know why they'd care." He dropped his voice. "And I think Stan's scared. When we're not being his spies, he keeps us real close, like he's afraid to let us out of his sight. That ain't like Stan. He's not usually afraid of anybody."

I believed him. Stan wasn't likely to tell his flunkies what was really going on, especially if it made him look weak. And getting ordered around by out-of-town vampires definitely wouldn't do good things for Stan's ego—or his authority.

"Now, we can do this hard or easy," I told Tad. "I could just set you down. Unless you're going to try to go for my throat, in which case I'll knock you into next week. Or, I can throw you down the street, no guarantee on how you land. Your choice."

"Just put me down. You've made your point." Tad sounded like a sore loser.

"Get out of here," I said. "Find dinner somewhere else. I'm sure we'll cross paths again. When we do, I'll want an update. You want to help Stan?"

Tad nodded. I figured that Stan might not be the best leader, but Tad realized there were worse options.

"Then when I see you again, you're going to tell me everything you can about those Russian vamps. The more you tell me, the more I might be able to do to get them out of your hair for good."

Tad looked skeptical. "You're going to help me?"

I raised an eyebrow, and he winced and rubbed his sore upper arms where I'd gripped him. "I've got my reasons. You want rid of the Ruskies? I'm your best bet."

Tad hesitated, then nodded. "Yeah. Okay. I'll see what I can find out. But Stan can't know. Doesn't matter if it would help him—he'll be sore if he knows I talked about our business to an outsider."

"So you'll just have to be sneaky," I replied. "Just make sure you keep your eyes and ears open. I'll find you. Now, get gone."

I blinked, and Tad was gone. A glance in each direction told me that no other vampires or creatures lurked around the outside of the meeting hall. No human criminals, either. Since I got what I came for, I ambled off, trying to figure out what the hell was going on, and why Cleveland was Little Russia, and what that meant. Whatever it was, it couldn't be good.

4

S tand still. Your bow tie isn't straight." Grace Harringworth stretched up on tip-toe to adjust my tie. I grumbled but stopped fidgeting.

"I look ridiculous." A tux was wasted on the likes of me. The suit probably cost more than my wages for a year, back when I worked in the mills. Grace had it custom-made for me, since I was her go-to partner in crime and needed to look presentable. Still, the jacket felt constricting across my shoulders, the fancy shoes pinched, and I would have felt better with my Colt 1911 holstered instead of jammed into the waistband of my trousers.

"You clean up well," Grace said and patted my cheek.

"How did you get invited to this shindig again?" I asked, resisting the urge to tug at my tie.

"Money, darling. I have it, and they want it. Occupational hazard," she added with a smirk.

Grace McAllen Harringworth was the embodiment of something I never thought I'd see—wealth with a conscience. She was the only child of James "Baron" McAllen, a Pittsburgh steel magnate and Carnegie rival. Her husband, Henry—heir to the Harringworth coal fortune—ended up shot by the angry boyfriend of one of his many mistresses. His death left Grace obscenely wealthy and completely independent, free to pursue her real passion—vengeance.

"So how does this whole social register invitation thing work?" I asked, snarky as ever. "Is there a secret handshake?"

Grace rolled her eyes. "No. It's all in the pedigree. Florence Abingdon, tonight's hostess, went to boarding school with my mother. Her father's sister was married to my father's second cousin. I dated her nephew when I was young and foolish." She leaned closer as if to impart a secret, though it was only the two of us and her butler. "And Mrs. Abingdon's parents were part of The Club."

I knew what that meant. Grace's shift from socialite to socially conscious was the result of being indirectly part of a great American tragedy. Like many of the Pittsburgh and Cleveland elite, her parents had been part of the South Fork Rod and Gun Club, a sporting organization with its own private campground and artificial lake. Back when Grace was a child, the dam that formed the lake gave way after a torrential rain, causing the Johnstown Flood, wiping a city off the map and killing almost two thousand people. Eavesdropping on the conversations of her elders, Grace realized that the club owners had been warned that the dam would break, and didn't care. When the disaster finally happened, they packed up, moved out, and never paid a dime in reparations. When Grace came into her own, she decided to use her connections, money, and inside information against the worst of the oligarchy—under the table, of course. Our paths crossed, and the rest is history.

"All you have to do tonight is look suitably menacing," Grace said, fussing over my sleeves and collar. "The strong and silent type. Watch the crowd, listen to the conversations. I'll have my lockpicks in my purse if we need them. I honestly don't know what to expect, but I've got a feeling it'll be interesting."

With Grace Harringworth around, I knew the evening wouldn't be dull.

We arrived at the downtown brownstone precisely at eight. Steven, her regular driver, pulled the Rolls Royce up at the curb and went around to open the rear door for her. He looked natty in his chauffeur's uniform. I got myself out of the passenger seat and took my place a few steps behind Grace as Steven went to park the car and wait in the vehicle.

I was glad for the weight of my gun, even though I didn't think I'd have cause to shoot up the place. Still, even as just a bodyguard, I could protect Grace better from thugs and purse snatchers if I were armed. That went double for Russian troublemakers.

The brownstone glittered with crystal chandeliers, candles in faceted sconces, and newfangled electric lights. Gilt-framed mirrors reflected the glow. Antique tables covered with expensive figurines and oil paintings furthered the show of wealth, as did fancy imported carpets and lots of silver bric-a-brac. At the same time, while all the furnishings were expensive, they also looked a bit worn. Like maybe the Countess hung on to her old stuff not because it was valuable or for sentimental reasons, but because she couldn't afford to buy new. That would make sense if she'd fled the Revolution. I imagined that keeping up appearances might be all she had left.

Grace should have been an actress because as soon as we entered, she was suddenly on stage. Everything about her was "more" than usual—her smile, her laugh, the way she casually flirted or dropped compliments and names. Everyone else in the room seemed equally animated, and either they had all drunk way too much coffee, or they were trying to out-impress each other.

I hung back, watching not just Grace but all the attendees. It reminded me of a fancy version of church picnics I attended back when I was mortal. Everyone was on their best behavior and knew each other at least to say hello, but old rivalries were barely concealed behind a little lipstick and rouge. Back then, jealousies ranged from who had the best covered dish casserole to who was wearing a new dress or a fancy hat. I suspected the stakes were higher here, but not altogether different in their pettiness.

Tux-clad waiters carried silver trays with shrimp and puff pastries, along with flutes of champagne. I watched them as carefully as I did the guests, heeding the jumpiness I felt as a sign to be on guard. Two of the men looked familiar, although I couldn't place them. That made me even more uncomfortable, and I shifted my position to stay within a few strides of Grace at all times.

"Gather round, everyone. Gather round." The old woman's voice had a tremor beneath the thick Russian accent, and she tapped her crystal goblet with a silver spoon to call the group to order. "We'll be going into the drawing room in a minute to meet my special guest," the Countess said. "I want you all to know how thrilled I am to have you here with me on such a momentous occasion."

Countess Antonina Demidov looked to be on the far side of seventy, with white hair, carefully styled, and a matronly dress that still probably cost as much as a car. I don't know much about jewelry, but I'd bet money the diamonds and gems were real and worth a fortune. She didn't look like anyone's grandmother, and I caught a glint in her eyes that told me she was a survivor.

"You all know the tragedy that brought me here to America," Countess Demidov continued. "And that so many of my people fled with just the clothes on their backs ahead of those awful, barbaric Bolsheviks." She spat the last word like a curse. I didn't doubt that the emotion in her voice was real, but I thought she was also every bit as good an actress as Grace. All I was missing was the popcorn.

"My guest is here to share his vision for freeing my homeland from the clutches of those savages," the Countess said. "My friends, you know how dear this cause is to my heart. I ask that you hear him out, and if you're moved to help my people take back their country and put the rightful heir on the throne, please consider making a modest contribution to the cause."

I swallowed wrong and had to stifle my cough. Where I came from, a "modest contribution" was a few bucks, enough to cover a beer or a sandwich. These folks could drop a wad that could buy and sell men like me many times over and never even notice the money was gone.

Grace let some of the others go into the drawing room ahead of her, hanging back, so I wasn't far out of reach. Maybe she had a bad feeling about tonight, too. The drawing room's dark wallpaper and floor-to-ceiling bookshelves gave it a warm, close feel, as did the fire in the fireplace. Countess Demidov made her way to a large wing-backed chair at one end of the room.

A tall, raw-boned man in the brown cassock of a priest stood next to the chair beside her. He had a long, hollow-cheeked face, deep-set eyes, shoulder-length dark hair, and a straggly beard. I caught my breath, recognizing two things right off the bat. First, he was a dead-ringer for Rasputin, the Russian monk who had been an adviser to the Tsar. And second—he was a vamp.

"My friends, I present Father Rasputin, returned to us by a miracle to set my people free!" Countess Demidov clapped enthusiastically as her stunned audience stared, then managed a smattering of applause in response.

"Good people," Rasputin began, speaking with an even heavier accent than the Countess. "Thank you for coming. We have much work to do, after the tragedy that befell my beloved royal family."

"We have contacts inside Russia who remain loyal to the Tsar," the Countess said. "Father Rasputin has laid the groundwork for us to put a

Romanov on the throne of Russia and rid our homeland of the Stalinists. I will let him tell you more." She sat down and folded her hands on her lap, looking to Rasputin like he was a saint.

Later, I couldn't have told you exactly what Rasputin said. I'm not sure it made sense, but maybe the words didn't matter. The man had a way about him that made people want to believe, the kind of personality that drew them like flies to honey. Maybe it was his vampire glamour, although, from the little I'd read in the newspapers, I had the sense Rasputin was a good con man even before his death.

How he ended up as a vamp, I couldn't imagine, but now all the Russian vampire info made a lot more sense.

To my relief, Grace's eyes remained as flinty and skeptical as ever, though her expression matched the besotted looks of those around her. Everyone else looked ready to swoon.

"My dear, dear friends," Countess Demidov said when Rasputin finally stopped speaking. "Thank you for listening. Of course, I don't expect you to make a contribution tonight, although I welcome your pledges if you feel so moved. Next week, for those of you whose hearts yearn for a free Russia, we will meet again, and this time, with a *very* special guest. I am certain that once you meet our guest, any reservations you have will be swept away, and you will welcome a chance to change history!"

The applause came quicker this time and felt more genuine. Rasputin sat back with a look on his face as if he was above being excited over such things, but I didn't miss the satisfied glint in his eyes. Some of the other guests moved forward to talk with the Countess and the monk. I navigated closer to Grace.

"We need to leave," I murmured. Grace nodded, and with a bow to our hostess, who was deep in conversation, we made our way to the door. None of the servants from before were in the outer room, and a single maid in the foyer returned our coats and bid us good night. Steven must have parked where he had a good view of the door because he pulled up minutes later.

"I can't shake the feeling that something's wrong," I said once we were inside the car.

"Did you see him? Could that really be Rasputin?" Grace asked, a little breathless with excitement.

My attention was focused out the back window. We drove away from the swanky neighborhood where the Countess lived, onto a darkened stretch of roadway. Shadows kept pace with the car, and once we moved away from a busy area, they grew larger and closer.

Everything happened at once. I remembered where I'd seen those waiters. I recognized the shadows for what they were. And I pushed Grace down with a shouted warning, as a huge wolf sprang at the window.

"Stay down!" I yelled at Grace. "Get us out of here!" I ordered Steven.

The werewolves were bigger, heavier, and stronger than normal wolves. I heard one rake across the metal roof with its claws, as fangs snapped outside the window. I pulled my gun, and when I looked at Grace, she held a Derringer. Considering her evening wear, I didn't want to know where she'd hidden it.

Steven hit the gas, but the wolves kept up. I rolled down the window.

"What are you doing? Are you insane?" Grace yelled.

"I'm shooting, and probably so," I replied. I got off three shots, winging one of the wolves and missing two more. A loud thump on the roof told me that another wolf had landed, and I heard it tearing at the metal like a can opener.

I shot again, hitting a wolf in the face when it tried to launch itself at the window as an easy target. That definitely hurt, but despite the bloody injury, the werewolf didn't stop. *Shit, I should have brought silver,* I thought, but it was too late now.

Grace moved to roll down her window, but I put a hand on her arm to stop her. "That pea shooter isn't going to do anything at a distance," I warned. "Save it, and hope you don't need to shoot close range."

Another wolf lunged at my window. I hung onto the inside handle and slammed the door open, knocking him loose. The wolf tumbled into the street and rolled. Unfortunately, I didn't seem to do real damage.

"Hold on," Steven warned. I slammed my door shut and braced. He swung the car around at high speed, and suddenly we were heading back the way we came. Steven rammed one wolf, sending it flying, as the others scrambled away, but they quickly came after us again.

We shot past a dark Buick, and seconds later, I realized that I'd recognized the driver.

"I've got an idea—take the next ramp." The wolves were after us, and we couldn't lead them into more populated areas. But the ramp led away from houses toward a commercial area, where we'd have more maneuvering room.

Steven zoomed up the ramp, with the wolves close behind us. That's when I saw the Buick was behind them—and the driver was halfway out his window, steering with one hand and shooting at the wolves with the other.

"West never misses the chance to make an entrance," I grumbled, though I was secretly glad for the help. What's more, the wolves West shot didn't get back up again, letting me know that the son of a bitch had come ready with silver bullets.

I kept shooting, figuring that even though my shots wouldn't kill the wolves, it had to slow them down, which gave West better odds.

There had been a dozen wolves after us at one point; now, I only saw five. Just then, a wolf appeared right in my face, clinging to the doorframe and perched on the running board. I swung a punch, cold-cocking it in the nose. Before it could recover, I cranked up the window, trapping its snout. That left it desperately trying to hold on as Steven maneuvered, with me hoping we'd have at least one of the werewolves alive to interrogate. West's steady shots made me doubt there'd be a lot of survivors.

By the time I looked back again, the rest of the wolves were dead, injured, or they'd run away. Steven brought the car to a halt, and West pulled up next to us. I jammed the barrel of my gun into the end of the werewolf's muzzle.

"Stay right where you are. We've got some questions for you," I growled, as West came up behind the beast with a sawed-off shotgun.

"He's going to roll down his window, and you're going to step down off that running board *very* slowly," West ordered. "Then we're all going into that warehouse to have a little chat."

Steven reached under his seat for a gun of his own. Grace slipped her Derringer into her beaded clutch and got out.

"I'll get the door," she said, striding toward the warehouse.

Steven, West, and I had our guns trained on the wounded werewolf. "Shift," I ordered. "We don't speak wolf."

The creature's yellow eyes fixed me with a glare. Seconds later, its body began to ripple, tearing itself apart and reforming. Fur sloughed off, leaving bare skin. A gasping man on his hands and knees replaced the fearsome beast. A very naked man.

"Wrap this around yourself," I said, handing off my tux jacket. The werewolf took the jacket and tied it as best he could to cover himself, then limped ahead of us toward the warehouse. By that time, Grace had the door open and waited for us with her gun drawn, just in case the werewolf got any ideas.

West sent Steven back for the Rolls, and he brought it up to the door so that the headlights lit up the inside of the warehouse. I found a chair and motioned with my gun for the werewolf to sit down. That let me get a good look at him. He wasn't one of the men I'd recognized from the anarchist rally who posed as waiters. This guy looked a few years older, a little rougher. Even if he'd bothered to shave, he'd have never looked polished enough to get into the Countess's brownstone, not even as a servant.

"What's your name?" West asked. The man remained silent until West chambered another round in the shotgun.

"Flint."

"Who sent you?"

Flint stayed silent, giving me a baleful look with brown eyes flecked with yellow. West brought his shotgun up to nudge the prisoner's temple. "My bullets are silver. I can shoot you once, and it'll be all over. Or...my friend here can shoot you lots of times, and you still won't die. What's it gonna be?"

I saw Flint's gaze flicker briefly between West and me, and he swallowed hard. "Look, all I did was follow orders," he said, licking his lips nervously. "We were supposed to chase the Rolls, scare you off. That's all."

I raised an eyebrow skeptically. "It sure didn't *look* like that was all you wanted. You were trying to tear my door off."

"We just thought we'd chase you," the man said. "We didn't expect you to shoot at us."

"You don't like it when your prey fights back?" West needled.

"They weren't prey until they attacked us."

"Pretty sure you attacked us first," I pointed out. "So...whose orders did you follow?"

He looked like he was going to balk, so West poked him again with the shotgun.

"All right! Clyde, our pack Alpha, said he wanted to scare you off."

"Just us, or the other guests, too?"

"All of you," Flint replied. "Shake you up, make sure you didn't go see the old Russian biddy again."

"What about the Countess?" Grace asked. "What's she got to do with it?"

"And why were some of your pack members at the anarchist rally last night?" I added. "Since when are werewolves interested in politics?"

"Since the vamps started throwing their weight around. Clyde said there'd be a vampire at the party tonight, trying to get the swells to give money to some cause. Said that if they did, we'd never be rid of the vamps and they'd try to take over. So we had to scare you off, so you wouldn't pay up."

West and I exchanged a look. The werewolf's story mangled some of the details, but it rang true for how the situation might look from Clyde's point of view.

"And the anarchists?" I probed.

"A lot of our pack works in the mills or the factories. We get our hands dirty, not like the vamps," Flint added with a sneer. "Gotta actually earn a living for our families. So what's good for the workers is good for the pack. Last thing we need is some fancy Russian vampires coming in and thinking they're in charge."

It made sense, in a fucked up sort of way. "What else do you know about the Russians?" I asked, keeping my gun in hand but no longer pointing it at Flint.

"They've been a thorn in the paw since they got here," he replied, voice thick with contempt. "They swagger in, acting like they're the only ones who aren't human, like they're better than everyone. The Russians are the worst. Like they think they're princes or some shit like that." He glanced at Grace and blushed. "Pardon my French."

Grace murmured something in French that I didn't understand, but I was pretty sure was far more creatively obscene than Flint's mild curse. "Were you supposed to kill the people from the party?"

Flint shook his head. "No. Just scare them. But, when the prey fights back, and we're in wolf form, it's hard to think straight."

"Don't you dare make it our fault that you almost ate us!" Grace snapped. She leveled her Derringer at Flint's groin. Her small caliber gun wouldn't do much damage elsewhere, but a strategic shot like that would hurt like a son of a bitch.

"Geez, lady, watch where you point that thing!" Flint yelped, closing his knees on reflex. "We weren't gonna eat anyone. I swear. Things just got a little out of hand."

That might be an understatement, considering that there were bodies of dead wolves—or naked men—strewn along a main street for the police to find. In the distance, I heard sirens and realized that the cops were probably swarming already.

"Here's what you're going to do, Flint." I folded my arms over my chest. The werewolf was solidly built, but I had him by several inches of height and a good thirty pounds. Hell, I even out-muscled West, which I knew he hated. But sometimes, the best way to avoid an all-out fight was to leverage a little intimidation.

"You go back to Clyde and tell him he needs to leave the Countess and her guests alone. My friend and I are on it. Now, if you want to help, we might be able to use some muscle down the road—and any information you can get on the Russians. But this is our show, not Clyde's. The wolves that got shot tonight—that didn't have to happen. Clyde needs to understand that we're handling it our way, and if he tries a stunt like this again, more wolves will die—and we'll be pissed off enough to come after him."

The glimmer in Flint's eyes told me he was thinking, *You can try*, but then he took another look at me, and I let a little of my magic slip, just enough for another supernatural creature to pick up on. Flint's eyes widened.

"What are you?"

I smiled. "Nobody you want to cross. Neither's he," I added with a nod toward West. Grace cleared her throat loudly. "Or her. Got it?"

Flint hesitated, then nodded. I exchanged a look with West. I'd had my fill of killing, and would just as soon not if I had a choice. And we did have a choice with Flint. In fact, sending him back to Clyde with our message might ultimately save a lot of trouble.

"You're going to leave here and go right to Clyde," I said, adding a little magic to my order, although I wasn't entirely sure it would work on a shifter. "Give him our message. We see you or your pack again anywhere near the Countess, and that's it. Understand?"

Flint nodded again, managing to look like a beat dog even in his human form.

We stood back to give him a clear path to the door, not taking any chances. "Go," I said. "And you'd better be out of sight by the time we get outside."

Flint glanced again between West and me, maybe wondering whether we'd shoot him in the back. I guess he figured he had nothing to lose because he took off faster than a mortal could run and disappeared into the night.

"Sirens sound close, Mrs. Harringworth. It might be good to leave," Steven said as we headed back to the car.

I looked at the ruined Rolls and sighed. "I don't think those scratches are going to buff out." Deep gouges marred the doors and the roof, trailing down the back.

"I'll have Richards handle it in the morning," Grace replied, referring to her long-suffering butler. Steven held the door for her, and she got back into the Rolls as if it were nothing more than a minor dent.

"Go with them, in case Wolfie and his friends come back," West said. "I'll follow you, and once we see Mrs. Harringworth safely home, how about you and I get some coffee? We've got a lot to talk about."

5

I thought diner coffee was supposed to be good." I glared at the sludge in the heavy ceramic cup.

"Probably got the bottom of the pot again," West replied with a shrug, and finished his, setting aside his cup for a refill.

"I miss having these meetings in bars," I grumbled. There was a lot that changed since Prohibition went into effect, but sometimes I missed the bars themselves more than the alcohol.

"Didn't think Ben's was the place for this discussion." West managed a distracted "thank you" to the waitress who refilled his cup, rather than his usual charm. "So...tell me what happened at the Countess's big party."

West listened with unusual patience as I told him about the event. He didn't interrupt once, which for West must have been a personal best. "So you're sure the guy claiming he was Rasputin was a vamp. But was he really Rasputin?"

I'd been asking myself that question all night. "Maybe. It's possible. If not, they picked a perfect actor." I frowned, remembering the way the man could sway a crowd. "But my gut says it's really him. You should have seen how he had everyone eating out of his hand. I don't know whether it was magic, or vamp glamour, or—"

"Charisma," West said. "Rasputin had it in spades. Every account says that he was an ugly man, looked like a vagrant, and didn't smell good. But as soon as he started to talk, it was like everyone was mesmerized, like he'd cast a spell on them."

"Yeah. Only I'd know if he'd done magic, and he didn't. At least, not any kind of magic I'm familiar with."

"Rasputin's enemies said he'd made a pact with the devil," West said off-handedly, stirring sugar into his coffee. "Could he be a demon?"

"I'm usually pretty good at picking up on sulfur," I replied. "And I didn't notice any. Let's not make this more complicated than it is already. Rasputin is back as a vampire, with some squirrelly conspiracy that requires raising a lot of money from moonstruck swells. And while the local vamps don't like the Russians, they're cooperating, probably because they figure they'll get a piece of the action. So we've got Imperialist vampires—"

"And Leninist werewolves," West said in a tone that let me know he was wishing his coffee had a slug of whiskey. "I guess that makes sense, in a weird sort of way. The vamps and the shifters almost always end up on opposite sides—lucky for us."

"I still think there's a piece we're missing." I toyed with the handle of my cup, unsure my stomach would survive much more of the bitter drink. "Something big. If Clyde's wolves didn't scare off the Countess and Rasputin, she hinted about another event and a big surprise."

"If it really is Rasputin, wolves won't scare him. Rumor has it he controlled werewolves with his dark arts back in Russia."

"He was a witch?" That added a whole new angle.

"Hard to say. He had plenty of enemies because of how connected he was to the Tsar and Tsarina. They weren't above making shit up to discredit him. Then again, he spouted a lot of mystical bullshit, and for all his talk of being a priest, he often came across more like a fortune teller. He never said he was, but he didn't outright say he wasn't."

"So being a vamp isn't bad enough?" I swore under my breath. "Wonderful."

"I'm more worried about his talk of putting a Romanov back on the throne," West said, leaning back against the diner seat. "Conditions aren't good in Russia, but at least they're stable. If Rasputin returns from the dead with a pretender to the throne, it'll cause a bloodbath. Stalin and his supporters won't go easily. And to be honest, Nicholas II wasn't too great of a king, though I imagine he still has his loyalists. The question is—what would it do to the rest of Europe?"

I felt a sick twist in my gut. The Great War had been over for ten years, but the damage would last for a generation, maybe longer. The last time, one assassin's bullet had triggered a cataclysm. What would happen if Russia tore itself apart with a civil war?

"So if Russia goes up in flames, do we get another Great War?" I asked, bile rising.

"Maybe. In fact, probably," West replied, meeting my gaze. "Think about it. All the monarchs of Europe were related through Queen Victoria. There are still pacts and alliances between all the powers, which is what created the whole damn mess the last time. If other countries thought they could take some of Russia's territory, we could be back to trench warfare in no time."

"Shit. How do we stop it?"

West drummed his fingers against the coffee cup. "I don't know," he said, and I saw a muscle twitch in his jaw, an indication of how much he hated admitting that. "I asked for backup. But the SSS isn't a big department—"

"Did you mention the possibility of a second Great War?"

West looked weary. "I strongly hinted at it. The exact reply was 'you and everyone else.' Bottom line—everyone's busy putting out fires that might or might not lead to the end of the world. Government bureaucracy being what it is, there is no backup coming."

I swore under my breath. We'd been left to twist in the wind.

"Look—maybe it's not all bad. If I bring my bosses in on this, frankly, they'll make a hash of it. They'll sweep in here with Black Mariahs and Tommy-guns, and it'll be a bloodbath."

He was right; that's exactly what would happen. The Feds didn't do anything half-way, and sometimes that worked well. I didn't have a reputation as a subtle guy myself, and West only had one setting—full throttle. But even I realized that rolling in like Elliott Ness and going gangbusters on the vamps and werewolves would be a very bad idea. I didn't have a problem with the body count if it came to that. But the fight needed to happen out of sight, not splashed across the papers in big, bold headlines.

"So it's you and me, saving the world? Not sure about those odds."

"If it comes down to it, we've got Ben on our side," West said. "I dare say Grace could come up with enough money for a private little war, so we won't run out of ammo. And...desperate times make strange bedfellows. Vincent Lavecchia might have a stake in this as well."

My eyebrows rose. Had West just suggested an alliance with the Mob? "How do you figure?"

He fell silent as the waitress refilled our cups. This time, the java actually tasted like coffee instead of acid. "The Mob here is tied in tightly with the Old Country. What affects Italy affects New York and Chicago—and Cleveland. And another world war would definitely have an impact on Italy. Plus this wouldn't be like the last time, with the U.S. coming in to save the day in the final year. If American money put a Romanov back on the throne and it all explodes, we'd be pulled in early. That's bad for business—legit and Mob-run."

I nodded. "What about the werewolves?"

West pinched the bridge of his nose like he was staving off a headache. "I heard that there was a dust-up between the Mob and the wolves last night—unofficially."

"Of course," I replied with a smirk. "What happened?"

"Ben was bitching to me before I headed over to stake out your fancy dress party," West said. "The wolves picketed the wrong mill. Turns out Lavecchia had a finger or two in that pie, and he didn't much like seeing operations shut down. It didn't go quite as badly as Homestead, because the Mob used its own bullyboys, but there was quite a fight. In the end, the wolves backed down. For now. I wouldn't consider the matter to be settled."

"So the wolves are a wild card," I summed up. "They hate the vamps and the Tsar, but they're also not buddy-buddy with the Mob." I frowned. "But if war came, wouldn't they benefit, working in a steel mill?"

"Getting conscripted would make for a lot of complications. A werewolf can't explain why he can't go, but he'd also stick out more for not going. And don't forget, the Mob has its own werewolves—Italian ones. The anarchist wolves are from Poland, Hungary, Romania. So you've got the Old World bullshit on top of the vamp-were stuff."

"The local vampires aren't happy with the Russians," I pointed out.

"Maybe not right now. But vampires are opportunists," West said. "If they had one of their own on the throne of a major country? That could upset the balance between vampires and wolves across Europe, and here, too."

"So is there a way to have the Mob *and* the wolves on our side? Because if this Rasputin is as wily as the stories make him out to be, he's not going to stop at anything until he gets what he wants."

West shrugged. "Once we know what the Russians are planning, maybe we'll have a better idea of how to pull together a defense. Stick close to Grace, and let me know what you find out at that next meeting."

FORTUNATELY, I didn't need my tux for the reception at the Russian tea room, because my jacket had gone home wrapped around Flint's privates and Grace's tailor hadn't finished the replacement. Grace handed me an expensive black suit to wear in the meantime. Of course, her outfit looked like it had come from Paris or at least New York, which it probably had.

Cleveland's tea room wasn't as famous as the fancy one in Manhattan, but it was swanky by this city's standards. The salon looked like an expensive parlor with large mirrors on the walls, comfortable uphol-stered chairs, and shelves filled with photographs and knick-knacks from Russia. In the middle of a large table that dominated the center of the room sat a silver samovar, the ultimate in tea-making. China plates around the table's edge were filled with delicate white *pryaniki* cookies, *zefir* meringue, and *pastila* confections. I didn't need to eat them here to remember their taste from my mortal days when the men at the mill would bring in trays of cookies their wives had baked for special occasions.

The restaurant was closed to anyone except the hand-picked group chosen by Countess Demidov. Once again, uniformed waiters carried trays of hors d'oeurves and glasses of wine for the ladies. I suspected that the men's drinks were vodka. I hung back, observing the room, keeping a protective eye on Grace as she worked the crowd. None of these waiters looked familiar, so if they were werewolves, they were ones I hadn't met. Rasputin hadn't made an appearance, and I wondered what his big surprise was.

If anyone else from the prior event had been menaced by wolves, they weren't talking about it and looked none the worse for wear. Though now that I thought about it, some of the women appeared to be drinking a bit more than usual, and the men stood in tight clusters, casting glances over their shoulders or peering out the windows at the darkened street.

Grace drifted back my way, with a new "friend" in tow. The woman looked to be a decade or so older than Grace, finely boned and delicate. Everything from her hair to her shoes reeked of old money. She was also, clearly, tipsy. Grace and I exchanged a glance. She'd obviously brought her "catch" to where I could overhear the conversation. That meant paying close attention while making it look like I wasn't.

"It's not just the travel," the woman gushed in response to Grace's careful questions. "Though it's beastly expensive to get to America from

Russia, so of course, it would be the same going the other way." She giggled at her own wording, and Grace snagged the woman another flute of champagne to replace her empty one. "We'll have to raise at least a little army, won't we? I mean, Stalin won't just throw his hands in the air and surrender!"

The socialite tittered again, and from Grace's frozen smile, I knew she was doing her best to be patient and not smack the woman. "Just think—a real Romanov!" Her hand went to her heart as if she might swoon. Then she leaned in confidentially. "But it's not just getting to Russia that's expensive," she whispered. "It's ransoming the Chalice of St. Theodore the Black so the ritual can be done right."

The tipsy woman's fingers went to cover her lips, and her eyes went wide. "Oopsie! I wasn't supposed to say anything about that." She laid a hand on Grace's arm, going a little off balance and sloshing some of her champagne. "You won't tell, will you? We girls have to stick together."

I missed the next bit of chit-chat, as my mind spun. What the hell was the Chalice of St. Theodore the Black, and what *ritual* required it? I certainly wasn't an expert on Russian royalty, but the tingle that went down my spine told me that the ritual was likely to be much darker than a simple coronation.

The chatty socialite meandered off, teetering on her heels, greeting everyone like a long-lost friend. Grace, of course, said nothing, but I knew from the way her eyes narrowed that she had caught the slip and was puzzling it out.

The crowd mingled for another half hour. Under the pretense of sticking close to Grace—no one seemed to question the need for a body-guard after what happened at the last meeting, and several other guests had brought their own security—I moved among the guests. Many spoke to each other in Russian, but I could pick up the gist of their conversations. They were abuzz about the possibility of restoring the Romanovs, punishing the usurpers, and most of all, returning home. Many—men and women—teared up at the possibility of going back, rebuilding, and picking up the pieces of their shattered lives.

I felt anger flare. If this was, indeed, a con, it was particularly cruel. My circumstances differed, but I knew an immigrant's longing for home, and while I'd been in America for longer than a mortal lifespan, my heart would always be Hungarian. Building up these people's hope to take advantage of them was unforgivable.

I felt fidgety, and I knew Grace well enough to guess that she did, too, just from her posture and the way her perfectly manicured nails tapped against her wine glass. Just when I thought nothing more would come of the gathering, the Countess tapped her crystal flute with a spoon to call us all to attention. The older woman seemed to be vibrating with excitement.

"My dear friends. Please gather in the next room—we have a truly unforgettable secret to share with you!"

The group buzzed with conversation as we entered the private dining room. As before, Rasputin was already there, standing next to a small dais with a curtain across the back, likely used for musicians. The holy man's serene expression couldn't entirely hide the smug satisfaction I saw in his eyes.

"At this point, I must tell you that we can only share this with those who are committed to our cause," the Countess said. "The stakes are too high for us to have this secret shared with those who are not ready to do all within their power to free Mother Russia from the grip of its looters and restore it to its rightful rulers."

I'd known Rasputin was a con man, but I started to have second thoughts about the Countess, too. At the first meeting, I thought she might have been a well-intentioned shill so besotted with the idea of going home that she bought what Rasputin was selling. Now as I watched her work her so-called "friends," I decided she was as much of a flim-flam artist as he was.

"Forgive my forwardness, but in order to stay for the remainder of the event, I must ask for a surety in the form of a check for three thousand dollars." In other words, twice as much as I'd made in a full year of back-breaking work in a steel mill.

A murmur spread through the crowd, but to my surprise, no one became indignant. Then again, despite the fact that these were former nobles without a home, there were enough gems and expensive furs to suggest they'd managed to escape with at least part of their wealth, which was still substantial. Maybe to these folks, three grand was like paying for a round of drinks at the pub. Didn't change how I felt about them getting conned.

The swells formed a line, either writing checks on the spot or signing notes promising to have their accountant do so right away. I noticed Grace took her place in line, and I sighed. The excitement on her face wasn't fake, although I knew she didn't believe in Rasputin. Grace Harringworth loved the thrill of the chase, betting on long odds, taking wild risks and coming out unscathed. Perhaps for her, it was no more cash than she might lose at one of those swanky underground casinos I'd heard about.

In the end, only four couples left without paying. No one chided them openly, but even I sensed the disapproval.

"Don't let the disbelievers weaken your resolve!" the Countess urged. "Restoring Russia to her former glory will require men and women with strong spines and much courage. We're better off without doubters. Let them go, and may they find peace with their choice." Her fake generosity dripped with disapproval. I'd seen the same kind of tactics from tent revival ministers fleecing their flock. If I hadn't been committed to seeing Countess Demidov and Rasputin fail before, this just firmed that resolve.

Once the doors closed behind the non-believers, the Countess went to stand beside Rasputin. "Now you will see what we mean when we tell you that Russia will rise again," she said, her eyes shining with fervor. "You will see why no one will doubt our cause is righteous."

Rasputin looked out over the anxious gathering like a predatory clergyman assessing his followers for the most likely patsies. "Everything they told you about what happened that awful night is a lie," he said in a deep, thickly accented voice. "They wanted to break your spirit, to make you believe that the damage could not be undone. But they lied!" His voice rose. "Here is our proof!"

The curtain twitched. Rasputin spoke a command in Russian which I knew meant "come forth." The velvet drapes parted, and the crowd caught its collective breath. Two of the women fainted. Men cursed or crossed themselves, dumbstruck.

I found myself staring at the zombie of Tsar Nicholas II.

6

Grace, West, and I sat at a table in the back of Ben's speakeasy with tumblers of whiskey in front of each of us. West's eyes had damn near bugged out when Grace and I told him about the undead Tsar.

"You're sure he's a zombie?" West asked. I'd never seen him look shaken before. Grace was also usually completely unflappable, but this had given her a jolt. Me, I didn't know what to think. I'd seen a lot of strange things in my time—including zombies. Just never one quite so famous, or with so much at stake.

"Yeah, I'm sure," I replied. Maybe no one else caught the whiff of embalming fluid, but to my senses, it was potent. "What I don't know is what method Rasputin used to raise him."

Grace blanched. "There's more than one?"

"Dark magic's been around for a long time," I said. "Everybody does it a little differently."

"Guessing that Rasputin's probably not big on Voodoo." West swirled the booze in his glass as if he'd find the meaning of life in its depths. I knew from experience it wasn't there.

"Probably not. There are Norse traditions that would be more likely. And Slavic magic, which is something we don't see a lot of here." I made up my mind to go for a long walk after this to see if Krukis had any great ideas. Sometimes he answered; sometimes he didn't. I figured it couldn't hurt to ask, since I was cleaning up someone else's mess and a lot was riding on the outcome.

West took another swig of his whiskey. "I made a few calls. That chalice your tipsy friend mentioned is a priceless Russian relic. It went missing during their Revolution, and everyone figured the Bolsheviks melted it down for the gold and gems. Apparently, it had quite a history. The gems are older than the Russian monarchy, and legend has it they were given to the first Romanov by some guy named Veles."

I swore potently in Hungarian. West raised an eyebrow, and Grace gave me a curious look. "That makes everything worse."

"Why?" Grace asked. "I mean, we're already staring down the barrel of another Great War. What could be worse than that?"

"Dark Slavic gods," I replied, tossing back my drink and wishing it actually had an effect on me. "Veles is the horned god."

"Satan?" West asked, looking curious despite himself.

"Not exactly, although the Church probably borrowed from the drawings." I felt the burn in my throat but absolutely nothing in my blood, so I poured myself another, even though I knew it was useless. "Veles is chaos and destruction. Svarog, the Light God, holds him in check. They're always battling each other, down through the ages, using people to do their bidding."

"Like puppets?" Grace looked more angry than surprised.

"More like bribery. Find out someone's weakness, deepest desire, and then offer to grant it—for a price."

"I stopped going to Sunday School a long time ago," West said, setting his glass aside. "I don't believe in fairy tales."

I shrugged. "Some of those stories are real, whether you believe in them or not. Krukis made me what I am. He serves Svarog. That makes me a sworn enemy of Veles."

"Like we didn't have enough players," Grace said, reaching for the bottle. "Tsars. Vamps. Werewolves. The Mob. And now...gods and monsters. Anyone have an idea about how we're going to win this?"

I grinned. "Actually, I do. We find the chalice of St. Theodore the Black and steal it before Rasputin can 'ransom' it."

WEST WENT to call in his connections—legal and otherwise—to find the chalice. I'd always figured him to be one of those guys whose idea of walking the "straight and narrow" was really balancing on the line between light and dark. I'd sold my soul for vengeance, so I really wasn't one to talk. Whatever works.

Grace had Steven drive her back to her brownstone in one of her other cars, since the Rolls was totaled. I imagine once the hangover wore off, she'd put the touch out to her contacts—friends in high and low places—to see what she could turn up.

I intended to find god.

Krukis didn't answer my prayers—no surprise there—so I figured I'd try Plan B. Which explained why I was walking through a forest looking for a woodcutter.

Steven gave me the keys to Grace's Packard. I promised to bring it back without a scratch and hoped I could keep that vow because being the champion of a dark god didn't pay nearly enough to replace a car like that. I drove into the countryside, looking for a farm that sold firewood. A boy directed me into the woods, where his grandfather was cutting down trees.

Boruta. I hope you're listening, because your buddy, Krukis, isn't answering. I shared West's skepticism about prayer in general, although the response to my dying wish ruled out atheism. Most of the time, Krukis was like that annoying person who was home but refused to come to the door when you knocked. I knew he could hear me; he just didn't feel like responding.

Fortunately, some of his friends were easier to reach.

The rhythm of an axe against wood led me to a gray-haired man chopping logs. He looked up with a frown when he saw me, wary and surprised. Then I saw the instant when the old farmer was pushed aside, and Boruta, god of the woodlands, took over.

"Joe Magarac. It is always good to see you."

I don't know what the farmer's real voice sounded like, but I was willing to bet he didn't have a thick Hungarian accent. I made a shallow bow, since it's always good to be reasonably polite to gods. "Boruta. Thank you for hearing my prayer."

He chuckled, a deep, rich sound. "I'm a bit more hands-on than my brother. What troubles you?"

I didn't ask the gods for much. I already owed my soul, and even when I was alive, I didn't like being in debt. Most of the time, the gifts Krukis had bestowed when he raised me from the dead took care of my needs. He'd also set me up with a billfold that magically replenished and couldn't get lost, always enough to cover my necessary expenses, with a little extra thrown in randomly from time to time. I no longer got sick, and my injuries healed rapidly. It was as fair a deal as could be expected. But sometimes, like now, I wanted advice. I'd averted plenty of catastrophes in my time, as well as righting less important wrongs. But now, the weight of the world settled on my shoulders, and I really didn't think I was the right guy for the job.

"Rasputin is a vampire. He's done something—necromancy, probably —to bring back the Tsar. If I can't stop him, he'll probably cause another Great War. And I...don't know how." I felt no shame admitting my lack. After all, I was just a mill hunk from Pittsburgh.

"So you have graduated, I see." The man's large hand came down on my shoulder as if he were congratulating me.

"I don't understand."

Again, a laugh like rolling thunder, and a glint of light in the old man's eyes that was otherworldly. I doubted the farmer would remember any of this when Boruta left him.

"You've served Krukis as a faithful champion-in-training," Boruta replied. "Stopping monsters. Righting wrongs. Serving justice that would not otherwise be done. You acted and learned. This is your first true test."

"Stopping another world war?" My voice rose an octave. "I'm not ready."

Boruta's smile was sad, wise, and impossibly old. "You will never be ready, so you do what you can, and it will have to be enough."

"I need your help," I begged. "Is Veles involved? Because that changes the stakes completely."

"Does it? All things, large and small, test the balance between chaos and creation. All that changes is the scale."

Fucking gods. Why did they always talk in riddles? "Please. This chalice—is it more than it appears? Are the legends true?"

Boruta leaned on his axe. "The chalice was forged in offering to Svarog by a warlord five hundred years ago. A rival stole it and sought to use it for his own ends. That was the beginning of the first of the chalice's wars."

"So it's cursed?" Just what we needed.

"Perhaps. Or maybe it has just been witness to many terrible events throughout history."

"Does it have magic of its own?"

"Legend says that the chalice was enchanted by a powerful shaman and that possessing it makes the bearer lucky in war."

"If you can get the chalice and keep it," I supplied.

Boruta inclined his head in agreement. "Precisely. The kind of men who start wars are usually willing to do anything to win."

"How do I destroy it, once and for all?" One Great War was more than enough. The world didn't need more bloodshed, certainly not on that scale.

"There is a ritual for objects such as the chalice. The rite hasn't been done in a very long time, never—obviously—for the chalice. But there has never been one like you," Boruta said, giving me an appraising look. "Perhaps the time has finally come."

"What do I need to do?"

"I will show you." He took a step forward and touched a finger to my forehead. I felt warmth, then the knowledge blossomed in my mind—ingredients, symbols, and the words to say. I knew what had to be done, and why I had to do it—even if it destroyed me.

"Thank you," I said as Boruta stepped back. He inclined his head in acknowledgment.

"Blessings on you, my son. We will be watching." With that, a tremor came over the old man's body. His eyes went glassy for a moment, and his mouth hung open. I feared he might be having a stroke. Then he collected his wits and looked at me, clear-eyed but confused.

"Are you lost?" he asked me. "Can I help you find your way?"

I smiled and shook my head. "I'm fine. Just came to ask about buying a cord of wood."

He rolled his eyes and named a price. "My grandson should have been up at the barn. He could have told you and saved you a trip."

"I didn't think to check," I lied, not wanting to get the young man in trouble. "Thank you. I'll be back with my truck."

"Wear decent shoes when you come back," the old man said with a pointed glance at my footwear, which wasn't made for hiking. "Those aren't farm shoes."

"No, sir," I agreed. "Thank you for your time. You've been more helpful than you know." That probably left him scratching his head as I retreated, but it was the god's honest truth.

"No one told us there were three damn chalices!" Grace paced in the kitchen of her brownstone, where she, West, and I met the next day.

"How can we tell which one is the real one?" West asked.

"More importantly, how can we make sure we steal the real one?" I believed in getting right to the point.

"The one at the Vatican would be quite the challenge," West replied.

"I can't imagine Rasputin being able to dicker with the Holy Father for one of their relics," I said. "Do we know where that chalice came from?"

West leaned back in his chair and stretched. The large kitchen smelled of coffee and gingerbread. One of Grace's many servants brought us a hot pot of fresh java, cream, and a tray of warm pastries. "Supposedly, the Vatican chalice has been in their collection since the turn of the last century," he said, reaching out to snag a crisp ginger cookie and shoving it in his mouth. "Before that, the chalice made its way across Europe, from cathedral to cathedral, until it was finally bought by the Vatican."

"Is it on public display?" Grace asked.

West shook his head. "No. Then again, they have a lot of treasures in their vaults that aren't."

"Any idea why it moved around so much?" I grabbed a cookie myself, dipping mine into my coffee before taking a bite.

"That's not unusual for relics," Grace answered. "Sometimes they 'tour,' and in other cases, cathedrals will swap a finger bone for a piece of the 'True Cross' if the Bishop feels a stronger connection to one item or another."

"Is it supposed to be good luck? Or bad? Any miracles to its credit?" I pressed. There had to be a way to narrow down the hunt without someone taking an ocean liner to Italy. My gut told me that if the real chalice was actually in Europe, Rasputin would be, too.

"It all depends on which Theodore we're really talking about," Grace replied. "There are more of them than there are chalices, and some of the lore gets muddy going back that far. From what I could find out, the Theodore whose chalice is in Rome is famous for defying the pagans—and then getting killed anyhow."

"Not exactly linked to giving one side or another a leg up winning a war," I muttered. "What about the other two? Is anything here in the United States?"

"One of them is owned by Jonathan Sprite, a very wealthy collector," Grace said. "He's a recluse, and everyone in the art world hates him because when he purchases something, it's permanently removed from view because he never lends his collection and never displays it to the public. It just disappears."

"So, we really can't validate whether or not he actually does own it because no one's seen it," West pointed out.

"There's a record of the chalice going to Sprite at auction, and my contacts confirmed that he took possession of a box that was supposed to contain the right object. But beyond that? No," Grace replied.

"I put a call in to a contact I have in Charleston," West said. "Someone who has a very good grasp of the occult. He dismissed the Sprite chalice as a replica at best and an outright fake at worst. Of course, I didn't tell him why I wanted to know, but I asked his opinion on that chalice's historic importance, and he clearly didn't think it had any."

"Where's this Sprite fellow located?" I asked.

"Chicago."

Still far from where Rasputin himself was, though arguably closer than Rome. "What about the third one?"

"You're in luck," West replied. "The third chalice is right here in Cleveland, at the new Museum of Art, in a touring exhibit that came from Washington, D.C. Interestingly enough, it's been on loan to the Smithsonian since it was donated by a mysterious benefactor," he added with a raised eyebrow. "It caused quite a stir."

"Bingo," I said with a grin. "I don't think Rasputin picked Cleveland by accident. After all, there's a large Russian community in Chicago for him to fleece if he needed to get the chalice away from Sprite. And the museum here has to be easier to break into than the Smithsonian." I shook my head. "Rasputin knows the real deal. If there's a chalice here in town, then my money is on it being the right one."

West nodded. "I agree."

I started to pace. Coffee didn't have quite the same effect on me as it used to when I was mortal. Then, it woke me up. Now, it just makes me twitchy. "So, why now? The revolution was ten years ago."

West tipped his chair back, balancing. Grace glared at him, and he dropped back down. "I asked my Charleston contact those same questions. I don't know where he gets his information, but it's never wrong. He said that the Bolsheviks stole it from the Romanovs before the October Revolution. That's when the Imperialists' luck really shifted. The chalice remained with Stalin, and while it did, he prospered. But then he had a falling-out with some of his co-conspirators, and my contact believes that Trotsky loyalists stole the chalice last year and smuggled it to America, passing it to the Smithsonian for safekeeping."

I nodded. "That makes sense. We don't know where Rasputin's been this whole time, but getting turned takes a while to adjust to. It probably took him a while to control his vamp urges and get out of Europe."

"Why come here?" Grace asked, pouring herself another cup of coffee. "He'd have been closer to the chalice in Europe."

"And closer to danger," West supplied. "In Europe, people are skeptical about the Romanovs *and* the Bolsheviks. They think they're both trouble. Here in America, among the Russian ex-pats, Rasputin and Nicholas would practically be gods."

"Maybe Rasputin's been tracking the chalice all along, waiting for the right time to grab it," I suggested. "Who made the decision to put the chalice on tour—to Cleveland? Even if the people who stole the chalice weren't supporters of the Tsar, Rasputin might have had sympathizers at the Smithsonian—and maybe at the museum here in Cleveland."

"It's probably not a coincidence that all the Russian trouble popped up just as the collection was about to arrive here in town," Grace said. "But what's he going to do with the chalice once he gets it? Europe's not going to support him leading an army against Stalin."

"He wouldn't have to," West mused, tapping his fingers on the table as he thought. "Rasputin gets the chalice, and its magic gives him the advantage. Then he reveals Tsar Nicholas II, apparently alive and well. And that rocks the U.S. government and Europe. Europe is afraid of Bolshevism. Some of the governments are going to favor the Tsar over usurpers. Once the Russian people see that the Tsar wasn't killed, they might turn on his murderers. Stalin loses power. Russia is thrown into chaos."

"Which brings us back to starting another Great War," I said with a sigh. "Because not everyone in Europe will be thrilled to see the Romanovs return. And others will want to benefit from the lack of leadership for their own purposes." I could imagine it playing out, another deadly domino cascade, picking up where the last bloody fight left off.

"Unless we steal the chalice and destroy it," West said. "Because our own government isn't above wanting an ace in the hole, either."

"That's why the SSS isn't coming," I said, as the last piece of the puzzle fell into place in my mind. "You never asked them to come. If they're here, they'd have to take possession, cart the chalice back to Washington."

West gave me a shark-like smile. "Whereas, one lone agent and some civilian helpers? The 'truth' is whatever story we choose to give them." He looked from me to Grace. "Are you in?"

I nodded, and Grace gave a long-suffering sigh.

"Yes. And I know we have to steal the chalice, and soon," Grace said. "The exhibit opens tomorrow, and it's only in town for a week. I just wish I weren't on the museum's board of directors."

I SPENT the next day gathering the elements Boruta had told me would be needed for the ritual to destroy the chalice. However he had transferred the information into my brain, I was in no danger of forgetting. It felt as if the words had been branded into my memory. Some were easy—a raven feather, bark from an aspen tree, and wormwood. Holy oil took a little maneuvering, but I got a priest to bless a vial after I invented a story about my sick granny. I figured that since we were going to destroy a holy relic, a couple more fibs wouldn't blacken my soul significantly.

A few other ingredients were harder to find until I happened upon a *bodega* that had a surprising amount of witchy stuff in its back room. The owner happily sold me all the candles and other items I needed when I paid in cash and promised not to tell anyone where I found my supplies.

That left one more item on the list, and Boruta's comment about my involvement suddenly made more sense. "Blood of the god-touched," I muttered. *Well, that's me. Can't imagine there are a whole lot of other candidates walking around.*

I collected everything into a satchel that would be easy to carry with me. As I packed, I debated the next step. Krukis had promised me magic if I called on his name. Then again, he didn't usually answer when I prayed to him, so I really didn't want to discover that we couldn't finish that part of the ritual because he'd decided to ignore me. Boruta's support didn't necessarily mean Krukis was paying attention. If I played this wrong, not only could we blow the chance to stop a huge war, but it might get me and my friends killed.

The other option meant making a deal with the Mob.

I guess if it'd been easy, the job would have been done a long time ago.

I slung the satchel over my shoulder and headed down to the theater. If I was lucky, I'd catch Ben in his office, where I could mostly explain why I needed his help. There were other witches in Cleveland—I'd even met a few of them. Some were decent folk, and others weren't, same as

Forged

non-witches. But Ben was the only one I knew enough to sort-of trust, and given the stakes, I couldn't afford to mess this up.

So I headed over to see a *strega* about a heist. Grace had gone to pay a visit to the museum, doing a casual stroll-through to case the joint, while West went off to make preparations. With luck and a little magic, we'd have the chalice in our possession tonight and destroyed by morning.

That worried me because I never would have said my luck was all that good.

LATER THAT NIGHT, we gathered in a darkened alley behind the Cleveland Museum of Art.

"Who are they?" West demanded when Ben Lavecchia showed up with six big guys who could only be described as "henchmen." Personally, I thought the answer was obvious unless we needed a football team.

"Backup," Ben said with a shrug.

West and I both looked the part of second-story men, dressed completely in black. Grace was also in an all-black top and trousers, but somehow, she just looked like she was going to the theater. Steven waited a few blocks away in a black Duesenberg Model J, a perfect—and stylish—getaway car.

Ben left his goons outside, and we headed to the back door, a staff entrance. The alley had no traffic this time of night, and thanks to the key Grace managed to procure, we didn't need to linger.

I'd been to the museum. West and even Grace might not figure me for the type, but it wasn't really the art that called me. It was the window on time that the paintings gave me. As immortality went, I was a youngster. Still, I'd outlived a lot of men my age, and those who hadn't died yet were old. I already realized that I'd feel more and more adrift as the decades passed, carrying me further from the time in which I belonged. Art let me look at a moment from my era, frozen forever, connecting me with the memories.

Tonight, thankfully, we were headed to different galleries than the ones I visited. Grace led the way. West and I had our guns, and I suspected Ben did, too. The museum's security lighting kept the huge building from being completely dark, though shadows pooled between the dimly glowing bulbs. In the darkness, the museum seemed less welcoming, maybe even dangerous. Every now and then, as I passed an entrance to another gallery, I caught a glimpse of a statue or a painting and jolted with a momentary fear that we'd been caught.

I thought we might find the chalice in a display of religious items. Instead, we followed Grace to a darkened gallery filled with mannequins dressed in elaborate ceremonial costumes and gilt-covered icons. My heart thumped harder. Dear gods, we were in a Slavic art exhibition.

I forced myself to focus. It made sense that the chalice would be part of a touring exhibit. That was the reason it was here in Cleveland, instead of safe back at the Smithsonian. Many collections were a traveling show of sorts, moving from museum to museum for curious crowds. I remembered what Grace had said about relics doing something of the same, hopping cathedrals instead of museums. Memory and nostalgia hit me hard as I looked at the items on display; I remembered some of the items from the church I attended in Homestead, and other, smaller pieces, from the household altars of my devout grandparents. And at the end of the row stood an entire glass case of chalices.

"Which one?" West hissed. Grace kept lookout, though she'd assured us that the night guard was known for sleeping through his watch in his office. Ben had his eyes closed, and his lips moved silently. I sensed his magic, and in my mind, I saw the light of his aura glow that much brighter. I figured he was placing a distraction spell, or perhaps assuring the guard slumbered deeply.

Time to open up my own magic. I sent up a prayer to Krukis—one of many tonight—and took a deep breath, centering myself and letting my senses roam. I didn't expect the rush of sensation that greeted me. Many of the objects here had a touch of something—if not magic, then perhaps, the divine—about them. I stretched out my borrowed power, touching some and shying away from others whose energy felt tainted.

Boruta had given me the liturgy, but only a glimpse of the chalice itself. A couple of the display pieces were close. I started at the top and moved from one to another, but none of them were right. Finally, when my magic touched a chalice near the bottom, I felt like the stars lit up, and I *knew*.

"There. That's the one," I said, pointing.

The Chalice of Thaddeus the Black didn't look like anything special. Lots of items in this museum were made out of gold or silver, and crusted with gems. For something that had the power to start wars and change the fate of empires, it seemed underwhelming. Then again, I'd heard someone say that if the Holy Grail was ever found, it would probably just be a wooden cup, what a carpenter would use. So maybe it made sense that a monk's goblet looked like he'd stolen a chalice from the abbey and marked it with esoteric symbols.

A tangle of emotions swirled through me. Elation that we'd beat Rasputin to the chalice. Disappointment that such an important piece was so ordinary. And fear, knowing what had to come next.

"Ben?" I pointed to the lock on the case. Ben nodded and closed his eyes again. Seconds later, the case door swung open. Grace reached in with a gloved hand and pulled out the chalice, carefully dropping it into the black cloth bag West held.

Uneasiness rippled through me, strong enough to make my gut clench. Ben's head came up at the same moment.

"We've got to get out of here," I whispered, trusting the magic.

"They're coming," Ben said. "Something unnatural—and something undead—are close by."

West took point this time, with Ben bringing up the rear, and Grace and me in between. We hurried as much as we dared, trying to keep our movement silent. Just as we reached the back door, I heard a man's scream of rage.

"Run!" I hissed.

Ben burst out of the doorway and held his hands up, gesturing to his goons not to shoot. They closed ranks around us as we ran toward where the cars were parked.

"A skinny man and three other guys went in through another door a couple of minutes ago," one of Ben's guards reported. "We didn't have a way to flag you, but we scoped out what we could. They've got a car around the other side."

Anything else he might have said was lost in the gunfire that kicked up the asphalt at our heels. Ben and his people peeled off toward their cars, while West, Grace, and I threw ourselves into the Duesenberg. Steven peeled out before the doors were shut.

"They know where to meet us," I gasped. "But we need to lose Rasputin and his gang first."

Steven chuckled. "Leave that to me."

Steven drove like a madman, making me wonder how often Grace had reason to outrun the cops. West and I hung on for dear life, while Grace merely braced herself, sitting forward with her eyes alight, as if this were the best adventure. I'd faced gods, vamps, and monsters, but sometimes that woman scared the shit out of me.

We took corners nearly on two wheels, screeched through round-abouts and tore through alleys so narrow I closed my eyes and found myself holding my breath. West turned in his seat, watching out the back, while I scanned from side to side for cops or Russians. I thought I glimpsed motion in the shadows, but whenever I checked, I couldn't see anything.

"Do you think Rasputin followed us?" West asked as the Duesenberg jolted over a pothole.

"No. Ben would have realized it, or I would have picked up on it," I replied. "The exhibit was going to leave in two days. Rasputin needed to make his move quickly. We're just lucky we didn't run into each other."

We parked in the shadows not far from a massive steel mill. This plant ran all day and all night, but I remembered from my own days as a mill worker that the night shift was still quieter than any other time. I'd worn clothing that would let me fit in, and with luck, I could join the stream of men reporting for work, maneuver my way near one of the massive cauldrons full of molten steel, and drop the chalice in to melt, after working Boruta's spell to make sure it stayed gone.

Steven kept the car running, but cut the headlights. Ben's cars parked next to us, and he came around to the side of the car sheltered from sight to help with the ritual, while Steven, West, and Grace stood guard, guns drawn. Ben's men spread out to check the perimeter. I had the feeling that we hadn't completely escaped Rasputin—just managed to give him the slip, for now.

I drew a circle in the gravel large enough to accommodate the chalice and me. Ben stayed outside the warding, using his magic to distract and deflect attention. We didn't know how much magic Rasputin had, but any working required energy, and someone attuned to that kind of power might be able to sense what where we were doing and where we were. That left actually doing the spell to me.

Did I believe that the Slavic god of the woodland gave me good information? Yes. Did that mean I felt confident that I was the right person for the job? Absolutely not. But since I seemed to be the only one dumb enough to accept the assignment, I guessed it fell to me to do the dirty work. I lit four candles, one at each of the quarter marks of the circle, then walked counter-clockwise as I spoke the first words of the spell.

"Svarog, god of light and order, I call on your power and protection." The words were in an archaic version of Hungarian, but I could still make out the meaning.

"Krukis, you'd better be listening and on duty," I muttered under my breath.

I added the holy oil, swirling it in the chalice as I said the next line of the spell Boruta had burned into my memory. "Oil of the Archangels, to purify with fire." Next, I added the raven's feather.

"Wings of the Watchers, to speed your way to the gods." Maybe it was my imagination, but the mixture seemed to take on a faint glow as I added the wormwood, absinthe, and aspen bark. "Strengthen my magic, gods above, and deliver us from the Dark One." The next elements were mistletoe and powdered asphodel. "Protect us, and grant us victory."

Time for the final piece: my blood. I pulled out my knife and made a quick cut on my finger, watching as it dripped into the cup. This time, I knew it wasn't my imagination when the elixir in the chalice took on a greenish glow. I swirled the mixture to coat the inside of the chalice, then sealed the magic by using the liquid to extinguish the candles, walking clockwise this time. My senses buzzed when I touched the chalice, and to my sight, it now had a shadow image, as if I could see the object and its "soul."

"Let's get this done," I muttered to Ben as I broke the warded circle.

We drove the rest of the way to the mill and parked in the shadows. The massive plant's silhouette hulked against the darker night sky. Burn-off flames rose from high chimneys, and electric lights on posts lit the parts of the lot closest to the building. The air smelled of coal smoke with the tang of metal, a scent I knew well.

I felt a tingle down my spine. Ben turned suddenly and stared into the darkness. "Wolves," he called out quietly to his enforcers. Steven stayed with the Duesenberg for a quick getaway, but Grace refused to be coddled and stood shoulder-to-shoulder with West and the goons.

"Go!" West snapped. "We'll hold them."

I walked quickly toward the line of men in worn shirts, overalls, and work boots who were making their way in to work the graveyard shift. Ben didn't look the part quite as much as I did, but he kept his hat low over his eyes and managed to make himself unremarkable—a bit of magic I figured only I would notice.

Once inside, we split off from the workers as soon as possible, which didn't attract notice since the men would go to many different areas of the mill. Ben and I suited up in the leather coats, long aprons, and gloves up to our elbows that provided scant protection against hellish conditions. At least the tinted glass of the welders' masks helped to hide our faces.

"This way," I said under my breath. I might never have been in this particular plant, but I knew my way around a steel mill. After all, thanks to Krukis, steel made up my bones and if needed, covered my skin. I hoped those changes weren't going to prove necessary. Then I thought back to Boruta saying this was my first real test. I prayed it wouldn't be my last.

"What is this? Hell?" Ben asked. No matter what the temperature outside, it was always sweltering inside the mill, and as we grew closer to the cauldrons, the whole area took on a reddish glow like the Pit itself.

"Next best thing," I replied. I felt the chalice's weight inside my jacket as if it realized it was nearing its destruction. With the shift change, the area had fewer people than usual. I'd learned long ago that if I walked as if I belonged somewhere, most people would believe that I did.

We climbed the metal stairs to the catwalk above the cauldrons where the molten steel glowed like lava. Huge cranes could maneuver the cauldrons and their contents to molds for everything from railroad engines to automobiles. The heat seared my lungs and made my skin feel sunburnt. My eyes stung, and my lips were dry as if I'd been in the desert.

Outside, Mob henchmen, a Secret Service agent, and a socialite squared off against werewolves. I had no idea whether the wolves had followed us, and if so, why. Perhaps they were headed to the mill to protest or cause mayhem, and we were unlucky enough to choose the same night to avert a war. I couldn't worry about it now; I had to trust West and the others to hold the line while we did what needed to be done.

"Almost there," I muttered. I'd grown used to Ben's magic, and I felt it covering us like an invisible blanket, deflecting notice and encouraging the few people who were around to busy themselves elsewhere. We just needed to get to the middle of the large cauldron, when I could say the last of the incantation and cast the chalice into the fires.

Of course, it couldn't be that simple.

Between one blink and another, Rasputin appeared, standing on the catwalk to block me from the cauldron.

"What are you?" He fixed me with a glare that might have glamoured a regular mortal, but I knew that neither Ben nor I could be captured by his vampire abilities.

"The servant of Svarog, and the champion of Krukis."

For an instant, I saw surprise in Rasputin's features before his lips twisted into a sneer. "Svarog has no power here! The flames belong to Veles."

For yet another time tonight, I prayed to Krukis and felt a shimmer over my skin. His magic didn't turn me into a tin man. My skin remained as supple as ever, with only a faint metallic sheen, but it became my armor and made me much harder to kill. With one exception.

Fire.

"Give me the chalice, and you and your friend can leave here alive," Rasputin said, holding out his hand for his treasure.

"Go to hell."

"I've been, and I won't go back." He lunged at me with vampire speed and strength. As solid as I was when I was mortal, that would have been enough to knock me over the railing and into the cauldron without my new strength. As it was, Rasputin only managed to push me a foot back down the catwalk. I shoved him in return, a push that should have sent an ordinary man tumbling, and felt as if I'd hit a stone wall.

I sincerely hoped Ben got the fuck out of the way because it was going to get brutal.

"Give me the chalice!" Rasputin repeated, and this time he tore at my jacket, where the tell-tale bulge revealed my prize. "I did not come this far to lose!"

I swung at him, but his reflexes were faster, and he dodged out of the way, still managing to ram me with his shoulder, and I stumbled. I grabbed for him and held on. We fell to the catwalk, and it shuddered with the impact. When I went full metal, I wasn't exactly light. Rasputin was as scrawny as he'd been before being turned, but now he was all vamp power, regardless of his skinny build.

We rolled on the narrow catwalk, high above nine-thousand-degree steel. I tried to pin the vampire, and he tried to use his speed to twist out of my grip. The chalice dug into my skin as we tussled, and would have broken my ribs without my metal "armor." Rasputin abruptly changed his tactics and went for my throat, fangs bared. I chuckled when he found himself with a mouthful of metal, and I used his surprise to flip him again.

"I'm not leaving without the chalice!" His breath smelled of old blood and rot. Fire and madness glinted in his eyes. He might not have been entirely sane as a mortal, but turning vamp hadn't helped.

This time, when he tore at my clothing with his sharp nails and clawed hands, he managed to rip at the fabric beneath the leather as he scrabbled for the chalice. I figured Ben was somewhere working his magic to keep us from being disturbed, but even he could only do so much and sooner or later, someone would notice the fight to the death up on the catwalk. I needed to finish this fast before bystanders got hurt—or worse, were used as hostages.

If the legends were true, the one who possessed the chalice held the upper hand in battle. I wasn't about to turn over that advantage to a damn vamp. I brought my knee up, hard, gambling that vampire nuts were just as sensitive as ever, and put my whole weight into it. From the way his eyes bugged out, I'd guessed right.

The chalice began to slip from where I'd secured it, and I needed to cast it into the cauldron, not lose it to the shop floor below. I pulled it from inside my coat, gripping it with all my strength, hard enough that I felt the metal give a bit beneath my fingers.

Rasputin surged beneath me, knocking me to one side, and his bony fingers tried to tear the chalice from my hand. I head-butted him, and he scored scratches in my metal skin with his vampire-strong fingers. We might tear each other apart before either of us emerged victorious.

I couldn't let him get the chalice. The world's future depended on me —me—to prevent another Great War and millions of deaths. Rasputin wanted the goblet for glory and power. His victory required him to leave here with his prize. Mine, technically, did not.

Maybe that was Krukis's test, to see whether I'd throw myself into the cauldron with the chalice, into one of the only forces that could destroy me. If so, passing his challenge meant he'd need to find a new champion, but it wouldn't be my problem anymore. I thought about all the friends who'd passed on before me, and the people like Ben and Grace, Colin and Aislin, and even West, who I'd leave behind. I didn't want to leave, but if it meant sparing the world another Great War, my loss would be a cheap price to pay.

Rasputin's grasp faltered, just for a second, just enough. I tore loose and sprang for the railing with the chalice in hand, a prayer to Krukis on my lips. I recited the last of the spell, staring at the fiery liquid where I would meet my end. As I reached the rail, Rasputin threw himself at me, grabbing for the chalice. He gripped the relic with all his vampire strength, and we began to tumble over the railing.

Just as my feet left the steel catwalk, I felt a force around me and heard Ben's voice above the din of the mill.

"Let go!"

Trusting fate—and Ben—I released the chalice. Rasputin clutched it against his chest in the second before gravity took over. Before he could grab for the rail, I punched him with all my might, sending him flying, and as he fell backward, I glimpsed realization in his eyes.

I hung, suspended in mid-air when I should have fallen to my death. Ben's magic dropped me back on the catwalk, hard enough to jolt the breath from my lungs, but so much better than the alternative.

I forced myself not to look away as Rasputin and the chalice plunged into the molten steel. Vampire or not, that heat would destroy him. Long ago, I'd seen a man fall into a cauldron, and he'd been burned to nothing almost before the metal finished closing over his body. They'd found no trace of him in the steel, not even bone or teeth. Superstition demanded setting aside the castings made from such a tainted pour, but cold greed overruled, and somewhere, a building held the last traces of that unfortunate worker.

Just like someday soon, the only remainders of the great Rasputin and the Chalice of St. Theodore the Black would be locked for eternity into the rails beneath a locomotive, or the I-beams in a skyscraper.

"Come on!" Ben urged, rousing me from where I stood, rooted in shock. We ran down the catwalk, slowing only when we got to the stairs. I didn't know how much longer Ben's magic could shield us; he'd been using a lot of energy, and I knew he couldn't keep it up forever. I guessed some of his ability to deflect attention was slipping when we drew notice hurrying toward the door.

"Hey! Where do you think you're going?" a floor supervisor yelled after us. We bulled our way past the few men who tried to stop us and burst from the door. Ben's magic locked it behind us, stopping our pursuers.

And trapping us with nowhere to go, in the middle of a war between vampires, mobsters, and werewolves.

"What the ever loving fuck is going on?" I took in the battle that raged across the parking lot, amazed that the local cops hadn't also gotten involved as well. Hell, call in the Army. The vamps and wolves went at it hand-to-hand, while the Mob guards, West, and Grace fired round after round to protect where they were pinned down behind the cars.

"I guess we need to break this party up," I said. With my metal skin, no regular bullets could hurt me, and Ben's magic, done right, would protect him. Two of us against more than twenty vamps and wolves wasn't the odds I preferred, but someone had to do something.

Just before we strode into the middle of the fight, four black Cadillacs pulled up, surrounding the battle. Someone reached out of the first car's passenger window and fired a Tommy gun into the air.

That got everyone's attention. To my surprise, when the rear door of the lead car opened, Vincent Lavecchia stepped out. He looked every inch the Mob boss—or powerful businessman—in a black mohair coat over his custom suit.

"Do I have your attention?" he called out in a raspy voice that suggested cigars and hard liquor. "Because I can have them shoot a little more if you're not listening." The silence that greeted him answered the question.

"This fighting, it's going to stop. Right now, it stops. I'm declaring a truce—between my people, the wolves, and the vampires. And you're going to accept the truce, because if you don't, I'm declaring war. If that happens, my boys will go hunting—loaded with silver."

I looked around, and at least a dozen burly men had gotten out of the cars, holding machine guns at their sides. I looked back and forth between the two sides, holding my breath. If the vamps and wolves didn't take the truce, this was going to be a bloodbath. They were fast, but a machine gun was faster.

I spotted Flint among the vampires. Two of their group conferred with a third, a tall, skinny man I guessed must be the leader, Stan. On the weres' side, I was glad not to see anyone else I recognized, but I had no problem picking out the Alpha, a tall, strongly built man talking with his advisors.

"Take your time," Vincent Lavecchia called out sarcastically. "We've got plenty before the cops arrive."

Stan stepped forward, glowering at the Alpha wolf, who also moved away from his followers. They stared at each other for a tense moment, then nodded, almost in unison.

"All right," Stan, the vampire, said. "We accept the truce—as long as *they* keep the bargain," he added, stabbing a finger toward the Alpha.

"And we accept, as long as the vamps play by the rules," the Alpha snarled.

"Neither of you is in a position to bargain," Lavecchia pointed out. "Remember that. Now get out of here, and understand—I'll be watching. Nothing happens in this city that I don't know about. Nothing."

The werewolves slunk away toward the shadows on the right, and the vamps vanished in a heartbeat, leaving Ben and me out in the open, West and Grace rising from behind Ben's car, and the Lavecchia boss and his goons in a quiet, darkened parking lot.

Before Vincent could say anything, another car pulled up, moving slowly as if to signal that it meant no harm. The black Maybach Zeppelin was long and sleek and on a normal night would have looked totally out of place in a steel mill parking lot. But tonight, between Vincent Lavecchia's Cadillacs, Ben's black LaSalle coupe, and Steven in the Duesenberg, we had a snazzy car rally going.

The Mob goons turned toward the newcomer. They didn't raise their guns, but no one could miss the weapons in the glare of the headlights.

The driver leaned out of his open window. "Don't shoot! It's the Countess—and her guest."

Vincent Lavecchia didn't look won over, and his goons didn't move, but they didn't start shooting, either—which I took as a good sign.

"He's coming out—unarmed," the driver shouted. "He wants to talk with the witch."

West cut a look at Ben, who shrugged. I stayed beside Ben and kept my metal skin since I had no idea what was going on, or who was in that car.

"It's Countess Demidov's Maybach," Grace said from where she stood next to West. "It's the only one in Cleveland."

Even the Mob goons gasped when Tsar Nicholas II climbed out of the back of the Maybach. He wore a uniform I recognized from the newspaper pictures, and he stood ramrod straight, carrying himself like a military man—and an emperor.

When he stopped in the glow of a streetlight, I caught my breath. Whatever magic Rasputin had worked to bring the Tsar back from the dead was failing. Nicholas's face was mottled with dark spots, his eyes had the sunken look of a corpse, and even at a distance, the smell of rot was unmistakable.

"Please," he called out in a voice like a death rattle. "I need the Italian witch. I followed the magic here. I beg of you—set me free."

A man like Nicholas didn't beg. But even across the distance, I glimpsed raw pain in his eyes. Ben exchanged a glance with his father, who gave a curt nod. Ben started forward, and I kept pace right beside him, not bothering to glance at the older Lavecchia for permission. If this went sour, I could get between Ben and bullets faster than anyone else.

We stopped a few paces from Nicholas. Close up, I could see where decomposition had set in, bloating his slender body, turning his skin a sickly green.

"I never asked to be brought back," Nicholas said, and I wondered if the scratchy voice was normal, or a side effect of rotting vocal cords. "He forced me to return," the Tsar added, contempt clear in his expression. "Like a trick pony. *Pozhaluysta*. Please. Let me return where I belong, to rest in peace with my family."

"I'm not a necromancer," Ben said. He closed his eyes and held up one hand, and I felt Ben's magic probe tentatively at the dead Tsar. In my mind's eye, I saw Nicholas's aura like an oily residue, and I could feel the taint of the dark god Veles's touch behind what remained of Rasputin's power. That's when I knew I'd be asking Krukis for another favor, but after the fight on the catwalk, I figured the god owed me.

"If we work together, I think we can break what's left of the magic that bound him," I said quietly. Ben nodded. I placed a hand on Ben's shoulder, and while he and I hadn't worked together quite like this before, I knew instinctively to "think" my power toward him, directing it to twine with his.

I didn't know what to ask Krukis for exactly, so I just sent, *Help me*. He was a god. He could figure it out.

Ben murmured something that sounded like Latin. Nicholas's whole body began to tremble. His skin drew up tight on his bones like a mummy, and his mouth opened in a silent scream. In the next instant, the Tsar crumpled to the ground as his body and uniform turned to dust. I moved my hand from Ben's shoulder and felt the connection with his magic sever like a shock that ran the length of my arm.

Before I could debate what to do with the ashes of the dead Tsar, a brisk, all-too-convenient wind scattered them into the night.

Which left us staring back at a small army of mobsters.

I knew the relationship between Ben and his father wasn't warm and fuzzy. After all, Vincent Lavecchia was a Mob boss, and Ben had defied his wishes to leave the family business. Now, completely outgunned in a dark parking lot, I hoped that this wasn't going to go horribly wrong.

Ben left my side with a glance that warned me not to follow. I stayed where I was as Ben approached his father. A few paces away, he inclined his head and made a shallow bow, like a prince before a king. Vincent placed his hand on Ben's head, and the large gems in the gold settings of his rings gleamed in the streetlight's glow.

"Thank you," Ben said. I could see what it cost him in the tight lines of his body and the stiff way his hands fought clenching into fists. Then again, Vincent Lavecchia had saved our asses. Maybe Ben and I could have taken the vamps and weres, but then again, maybe not. I'm glad we didn't have to find out the hard way.

"You're my son," Vincent replied as if tonight was unremarkable. "Bad business with the Tsar."

"You knew?" Ben asked, with a stunned expression.

Vincent shrugged. "I know many things." He looked beyond Ben to where West and Grace had come to stand next to me. "Not exactly the friends I'd choose," he said, fixing his gaze on West in particular. "Still, you got the job done." He clapped Ben on the shoulder, and then turned, walking with great dignity back to the Cadillac, where his driver hurried to hold the door for him. Ben remained where he was, looking after the Mob fleet until only the tail lights were visible.

Sirens sounded, growing closer. I suspected that Ben had done something to keep the factory guards from noticing us, but after all we'd done tonight, I doubted he could hold off the entire Cleveland police department, and from the number of wailing klaxons, that's exactly what it sounded like was closing in on us.

"Go," West said, taking charge. "I'll deal with the flatfoots. They can't touch me. We'll talk tomorrow."

Ben nodded, then walked to where his goons waited, got into his car, and drove off.

Exhaustion had begun to set in as the adrenaline from the fight crashed. I let my metal skin disappear and felt even more tired without its magic boost. When I stumbled, Grace rushed to get under my shoulder, slipping her arm around my waist.

"Come on," she said, patting me on the back. "Steven will drive you home. I don't know what happened in there, but I think you two just saved the world—with a little help," she added, grinning.

I'm not ashamed to say I fell asleep on the drive back.

EPILOGUE

W ell, that could have gone worse." Jack West sat back in his seat at the blind tiger, in the corner booth I'd started to think of as belonging to the three of us.

Grace Harringworth sat beside him, glamorous as ever in a beaded flapper dress. She took a drag from her long jade cigarette holder, with a grin that said she thought the whole thing had been a grand adventure.

"The museum got big headlines over the mysterious disappearance of the chalice. I've heard it was international art thieves," she added in a conspiratorial whisper, eyes alight. "They announced they were bumping up security—and donors are flocking in to help." She took another inhale and let out the smoke in a long stream. "I'm quite sure they'll come out ahead."

I watched Ben Lavecchia at the bar. He had greeted us as if nothing out of the ordinary had happened, though I caught his glances in our direction. We'd saved the world from another Great War two nights ago, and no one knew except the four of us. I've done a lot of things in my life that I'm not proud of, but this I could feel good about—even if nobody else would ever know.

"You never said what happened with the cops," I asked West. Given my own experiences, I tended to keep a close eye on such things.

West shrugged. "I told them I'd busted up a fight between off-duty mill hunks and a gang of anarchists, from an anonymous tip. Spun out the story that it was part of a larger, hush-hush investigation and that Washington would be very grateful for their cooperation," he added with a grin. "Fortunately, the chief bought it."

I'd asked Colin back at the rooming house if there'd been any excitement lately. He told me there'd been a problem over at the mill, with a look that said he strongly suspected I'd been involved, but he let it go.

"Do you think the truce will hold?" Grace asked. "It's going to be bloody around here if it doesn't."

I glanced at Ben, who was busy introducing a customer to his blind tiger. "It won't make the wolves and vamps best friends, but they're not stupid," West said. "I think it will hold, well enough, anyhow. Getting rid of the Russian vampires should help a lot."

The Countess had rolled on her accomplices pretty quickly, once she found out Rasputin and the chalice were gone. She'd promised to give back all the donations—Grace intended to make sure that happened. Countess Demidov had also proved helpful to West in steering him toward Rasputin's hench-vamps. West, Ben, and I had taken it from there. They were either destroyed or on a cargo ship headed back to Russia.

"Now what?" Grace asked, taking a sip of whiskey. "What are we going to do next?"

West opened his mouth to tell her that there was no "we," but I stepped on his foot—hard—and he shut his trap without saying anything. Frankly, I thought the four of us made a damn good team, and I felt sure that Colin and maybe even Oscar might be helpful future additions.

"I've got to go back to Washington," West said, finishing off his booze. He eyed the bar as if he were debating having another. Ben took the matter out of his hands, dispatching a waiter with a fresh drink. "But I have a feeling I'll be back soon."

He gave me a look. "There're whispers about warlocks near Reading, Pennsylvania, and a group that call themselves the Vril, stirring up problems with their hocus-pocus. Possibly tied in with the dicey things we're hearing out of Germany these days. I'm likely to need your help, Joe."

"Sounds right up my alley," I replied, draining my own glass. I couldn't help grinning at the thought of another case. "You wouldn't want me to get bored, would you?"

PART II

BLACK SUN

1

I couldn't help a smug smile when the werewolf's teeth clanged on metal as he bit down on my shoulder. Tough to know what was more entertaining—the shocked look on his face when he realized he'd broken a fang on my steel skin or the fear that came right after, recognizing that he wasn't the biggest badass on the block.

I grabbed him by the scruff of the neck faster than he could react, lifted him off the ground with one hand, and gave him a shake. Since he probably stood about six feet tall and weighed around one-ninety, I doubt anyone had done that to him since he was a pup.

Certainly not the mark he'd figured for an easy dinner.

"Bad wolf," I scolded, giving him another shake that might have made his vision blur. He kicked and struggled, snapped and snarled, but I held him far enough away from my body that he couldn't make his fists or feet connect. Not that it would have hurt me, but he might have broken a hand or a toe on my metal skin.

"There've been four deaths close to here—werewolf kills. Hearts ripped out, deep claw marks on the bodies. The only good thing I can say is that you didn't turn them. Probably went down so quick and easy there wasn't time," I said. "You know I can't let you go."

Sometimes, there's enough humanity left that the monster begs for a second chance, promises to be good, swears to turn over a new leaf. It almost never changes the outcome. Occasionally they try to bribe me and seem astonished when I turn them down. I have everything I need, and the things I want and can't get, even the gods can't give me. Once in a while though, I take a chance. It almost never works out, and we end up right back where we started, but it reminds me that I'm not one of the monsters.

At least, not yet.

The werewolf sealed his fate when he twisted, raking his claws down my chest in a move that would have ripped out my guts if I hadn't been, well, *me*. Instead, he made an awful screech of nails on metal, howled when he broke a claw, and tried to bite me—again.

Not the brightest pup of the litter.

I snapped his neck with a flick of my wrist. Then I put a silver bullet through his heart. Someone would find him shifted back, a naked man dead in an alley. Another nameless tragedy of the big city. They'd never know he'd been the big bad wolf, with a string of murders to his name.

I protect the ones who can't protect themselves. That's the vengeance I sold my soul for when I made a bargain with an ancient Slavic god as I lay dying.

Most days, I'm good with that. I make a difference. Because of what Krukis, the god of blacksmiths, made me into, the victims have a fighting chance. I keep people from dying because I kill the monsters first.

But on other days, the old memories of who I was and what I've lost crowd closer, and it's impossible to forget.

Immortality isn't all it's cracked up to be.

I thanked Krukis and felt his magic leave me. On my own, I'm a big guy, tall and brawny with muscles earned from hard work. Still not someone bad guys want to meet in a dark alley. But without Krukis's magic, I'm not strong as an ox, fast as a racehorse, almost impossible to kill, and I don't have metal skin or steel bones.

Without Krukis, I'm just Joe Mack.

I sighed, realizing that the werewolf had destroyed another good shirt. I thought about going back to my apartment for the night, but even with a successful hunt, my mood tonight was bleak, and it would be better if I weren't alone. But I'd need to change clothing so that I didn't scare the mortals.

The bouncer at the door of the speakeasy looked me up and down, probably figuring that I could easily move him out of the way. Then again, he knew I was one of Mr. Ben's friends, so he just waved me in without comment.

Ben Lavecchia ran the best "blind tiger" in Cleveland. Prohibition declared it illegal to sell alcohol, but charging admission to see a rare blind tiger was completely legal. So here in the relative secrecy of the basement under the Hathaway Theater, Ben offered people the chance to "see" a rare blind tiger for the very affordable price of a few coins.

Of course, if those same clients wished to enjoy a complimentary drink on the house while waiting to see those tigers, that was within the law. And if the tigers couldn't be persuaded to show themselves for viewing, well, that was understandable—since there weren't any tigers. Ben had to explain that reality once in a while to the very, very dense.

And because Ben's father ran the Italian Mob in Cleveland—and with it, the police department—the cops left his speakeasy alone. It didn't hurt that Ben was also a *strega*. Even Capone didn't mess with witches.

"Got any new tigers back there, Ben?" I asked. "Maybe some I haven't seen before?"

Ben gave me a look. "You've seen a lot of tigers lately, Joe. Keep it up, and you'll be the blind one, not the tigers."

I shrugged. "I can't get drunk. Part of the bargain. And it's that time of the year."

Ben's expression softened, and he handed me a shot of rum. "Take it easy," he said. "I might run out of tigers."

I nodded my thanks and sat back down at the bar. Ben was one of the few who knew my story. The "bargain" was why I was over eighty years old and still looked like I was in my mid-thirties—and why I always would. Immortality has its benefits. But since memory didn't fade with time, and my dreams were as vivid as ever, especially lately, I'd have to settle for vengeance instead of knowing that at some point, I'd find peace in death.

I'd come over to this country from my native Hungary looking for honest work and a safe place for my wife and me to raise our son, back when I was still Joe Magarac. We'd settled in Pittsburgh, and I'd gone to work in the steel mills. The hard, dirty work held plenty of danger, but it also put a roof over our heads and food in our bellies. Agata and our son died of fever, leaving me alone. Then came the Homestead Strike. I'd stood with my friends striking for fair pay. The Pinkerton agents hired by the mill owner shot us, clubbed us, beat us with fists, and left us to die.

I'd called out with my last breath to old Slavic gods, the ones my grandmother believed in, whose altars she hid behind pictures of the Christian saints. Krukis, god of blacksmiths, heard my prayer and made me his champion, with a charge to protect the weak and punish the oppressors. He gave me immortality, and when I call on his power, I'm nearly impossible to kill, except by the heat of the forge. I took a new name, Joe Mack, because when you're immortal, you have to reinvent yourself from time to time, or people wonder why you don't get any older.

Not a bad deal, all things considered. Except I kept the fuckin' memories, and this time of year, they haunted me. The sweet pain of remembering Agata's voice and my son's blue eyes. The smell of gunpowder and blood the day I died. I couldn't forget, and I couldn't get drunk. Instead I stayed busy, and when I wasn't busy, I stayed numb.

"Thought I might find you here."

I didn't look up at the sound of the familiar voice, as the newcomer slid onto the barstool next to mine. I knew what I'd see. Jack West, Supernatural Secret Service, in a natty suit and fedora hat. He looked like he'd stepped off a movie screen, too handsome to be a real tough guy. But I'd fought beside West more than once, and anyone who let his good looks fool them into thinking he was soft learned the hard way.

We didn't always see eye to eye, but Jack was also in the very small circle of those who knew the truth about me. Most of it, anyhow. I didn't completely trust him. But I didn't completely trust anyone.

On weeknights, the theater crowd filled the speakeasy and finding a seat took speed and patience. On a Tuesday like tonight, there were plenty of empty chairs. I knew West didn't come for a drink—he had a job for me.

"Does your boss know you drink here?" I felt like talking shit. West's a good guy, for a fed. He made it clear right up front he thought the Pinkertons were scum. So we had that in common.

"Yeah. My boss drinks here on even-numbered days, and I get the days that end in the letter 'y.'"

I knocked back the rest of my "Caribbean" tiger that tasted a lot like rum and set the glass down with a thud. "What's up?"

"Maybe I just felt like hanging out. Thought we could go see a baseball game." Now he was definitely poking the bear.

"You hate baseball. So do I."

West gave me his slick grin, the one that made most people want to smack it off his face. Me, I grudgingly respected brass balls.

"We've got a situation, and I think you'd be the perfect inside man."

Ben gave me a new shot, without me even having to ask. I plunked down my money. It probably costs a lot to feed those tigers.

"Explain." West and I didn't waste words. I wasn't in a mood to be chatty.

"Something weird is going on in Reading, over on the eastern side of Pennsylvania. Our witch informant got murdered. There've been *wehrwolf* attacks."

I raised an eyebrow. The way West pronounced the word sounded closer to German than English. "I thought that was some cheap novel. And the book wasn't even really about real werewolves."

"And I meant what I said," Jack replied. "*Der Wehrwolf* is a hack novel that is all the rage with the *Völkisch* groups, and with the folks back in Germany who sided with the Kaiser and like some of the young hotheads who are screaming in the streets over there."

I'd heard of the unrest and hoped it didn't come here to America. Such things did not end well.

"So, who's worried about these things? The government? The industrialists?" I asked. "And what's their fear? That people will rise up and ask for their due? Or that there's someone using dark powers?"

"We don't entirely know what's going on, or who's behind it. All the signs are there that whatever it is won't turn out to be a good thing," West replied, and I appreciated his honesty. "There's reason to think dark magic is part of it, and money. Right now, the activity is deep in the Pennsylvania German community. I'd like to send you because someone else might not take the time to tell the difference between good immigrants and bad immigrants, if you know what I mean."

I did, and dammit, West was right. "What do you want me to do— assuming I agree?"

I saw the quirk of his lips, an almost-smile that said he knew he had me. In my current mood, I couldn't bring myself to be annoyed. Maybe West was doing me a favor, although he didn't know it. Going out on a case might be just what I needed, to pull my head out of my ass and escape my dark dreams.

I slid him a sidelong look. "Same arrangement as usual?"

"Of course."

I might be the champion of an ancient dark god, but I didn't work for free —not for the feds. Gave the wrong impression. Part of my deal with Krukis involved a wallet that always refilled with enough money to cover my food, clothing, and rent, sometimes with a bit extra for a job well done. I didn't need much. But people value what they pay for, so my arrangement with West meant the Supernatural Secret Service handled my transportation and expenses, with a stipend on top. Usually I gave most of that stipend to the soup kitchen. Too many people were hungry, and I knew how that felt.

"All right," I said. "How sure are you this isn't a bunch of superstitious bullshit dreamed up by people who are still sore at the Germans over the Great War?"

West shrugged. "I'm not. That's why you're the one I trust to go in and sniff around. But you won't be on your own—Sarah and I are going to wow the swells and see what the beautiful people are up to."

I knew West could fight like a back-alley cutpurse. But he was best in an expensive suit cozying up to movers and shakers at some invitation-only ritzy party where schemes were hatched.

"How'd Sarah get involved in this?"

"We think that whatever's going on has something to do with the higher ups at the Reading Railroad," West replied. "And Reading Railroad also owns Reading Coal and Iron. Ring any bells?"

Oh, that rang plenty. Alarm bells. The Homestead Strike where I died was in 1892. But fifteen years before that, in 1877, there'd been the Reading Railroad Massacre, where the head of the railroad called in private security troops and the "official" toll was sixteen dead, fifty injured. I felt certain the true numbers were much larger. I had no love for the Reading Railroad.

"So she's working her Harringworth Coal connections?" I asked.

Sarah McAllen grew up among the Pittsburgh elite as the daughter of a steel magnate. She married the heir to the Harringworth Coal fortune, but dear old Harry ended up shot dead by one of his many mistresses. That left Sarah completely independent and obscenely wealthy.

Unlike most of her social group, Sarah had a conscience. She'd always felt guilt over her family being members at the South Fork Rod and Gun Club, whose badly managed earthen dam caused the Johnstown Flood and killed fifteen hundred people, even though she was just a child at the time. So she meddled, becoming a patron of mine and a supporter of West's sometimes off-the-books endeavors. It's how she gets her kicks, and to be honest, the lady is good with lock picks and a gun.

"Yeah. There's a swanky dinner up on Mount Penn this weekend and another reception at a big mansion. We'll work that angle, and you see what you can find out from the regular Joes." West paused. "You do speak German, don't you?"

Hungarian was my native tongue. But working in the mills, I picked up a lot from the men around me, all the languages of Europe. Mostly curse words. But whether it was Krukis's doing or something I had a knack for, learning languages came easily for me. I spoke enough German to get along, although I wasn't sure anyone would mistake me for a native.

"Well enough to get by," I answered. I knocked back the shot. "You know anything about these *Völkisch* groups?"

West nursed his second shot. He knew better than to try to drink me under the table. Hell, even when I was mortal, I could hold my liquor better than most men. Of course, my size helped. I had a couple of inches height on West, and probably forty pounds of muscle. He was fit, but I'd forged this body in the hard work of the steel mills. People tended to get out of my way.

"Mostly that they're trouble," West replied. "They sound nice and cultural, on the surface. Make you think they're going to do folk dances and tell stories. But dig down, and it's just some ugly shit about how being German is better than being anything else—and they have a short, very specific list of who they are especially better than," he added, loathing clear in his voice.

It didn't take much imagination to guess who was on that list. The usual suspects, the ones who got beat down every time some tinpot dandy wanted to make himself feel like a big man by pushing other people around. I had no patience for that sort. As far as I was concerned, that type of human garbage fell into my charge from Krukis to clean up the place and leave it a little better than I found it.

Knocking heads together for a good cause was a sure way to cheer me up.

West and I get on each other's nerves. We annoy the fuck out of each other sometimes. But he treats women with respect, and he isn't a dick to people because they talk with an accent or have a name he can't spell or aren't lily-white. He's a good man. I just don't say that to his face, because his head is swelled enough already.

I looked up at Ben, who was fiddling behind the bar, trying to look like he wasn't eavesdropping. "You know anything about this?"

Ben might have gone as straight as the family business would permit, but he was still Anthony Lavecchia's youngest son, and Ben's father and older brothers kept tabs on him. Which meant he heard stuff through Mob channels even if he didn't want a piece of the action. And being a *strega*, he heard the witchy gossip, too.

"Maybe." Ben finished drying glasses behind the bar and came over. I looked up at him, he rolled his eyes, and fetched me another shot; this time it was vodka.

"We have a new Russian tiger," he said and pocketed my money. "Be careful. He bites."

"So...the grapevine?" West asked.

"A lot of people who live here now lost family in the Great War, back in the Old Country," Ben said. He's always careful about what he shares, not a surprise given the circles he runs in. "They pay attention to what goes on over there. Germany remains a worry. The Germans lost, but they're very angry, and this *Völkisch* movement you mention, it says the loss was everyone's fault but the Germans'. People are nervous. They're trying to bring family over before something else bad happens."

That squared with what I read in the newspaper and heard at the pubs. It must have sounded right to West because he nodded. "Yeah, that's what my sources are telling me, too."

"You think people in Reading are disloyal?" I asked and sipped the vodka.

West grimaced. "The majority? No. They answered the call, and they served in the war with honor. But some...especially if they came over with high expectations and got the shitty end of the stick, I think they can start thinking the grass is greener on the other side of the ocean, if you know what I mean."

I don't know when West's people came over, but I figured it was long enough ago and from places that made him feel settled, like he belonged here. I knew what it was like to leave a home and a homeland behind. I missed things about Hungary—odd things, like cookies that were hard to find here, certain flowers I hadn't seen since I'd come over, the smell of the Turkish coffee my mother loved.

But none of that would move me to act against this country that took me in, although arguably, I too had gotten the "shitty end of the stick." I'd lost my family, my job, and my life. Still, I remembered the bad times in Hungary, the reason we risked everything to come here. I had no desire, even now, to return. I appreciated that West understood that most immigrants were loyal to their adopted country. Many didn't believe that, no matter the proof. Now I knew I had no real choice about helping settle the Reading problem.

"All right," I said, finishing my shot and, to Ben's great relief, finally turning my glass upside-down. I was still a long way from drunk, not even really numb. But oddly enough, now that I had a job to do, the darkness receded, at least for now. "Tell me the plan."

2

I couldn't shake the feeling that I was being watched. The train left Cleveland without incident, and I had a comfortable seat that wasn't in the fanciest section but wasn't in the worst, either. It was going to be a long ride, with stops all along the way.

West had arranged for my ticket and for my lodging once I got to Reading. Since it was going to take most of the day, I settled into my seat by the window and got as comfortable as a man of my size could.

Being on a case and going on a trip lifted my mood, but it did nothing for the nagging sense that something was wrong. I tried to interest myself with a newspaper or with the book I had brought and finally settled for watching the landscape slide by, noting the similarities and differences to my native Hungary.

Once or twice, I got up, under the pretext of using the lavatory or getting a cup of coffee from the commissary car. I paid close attention to my fellow passengers, trying to pin down the source of my uneasiness.

As I headed back to my seat, I angled past a wiry little man in the connector area between cars. I'd noticed him sitting on the opposite side of the row, a few seats behind me, but hadn't paid him much attention.

He bumped into me on purpose. "What are you?" he hissed, staring at me as if he wished he could see down to my bones.

"I don't know what you mean." I sniffed the air, wondering if he was drunk, but I feared a darker reason.

"Did you do this to me?" he demanded, voice rising, shrill with panic. I did not want to attract attention, but the stranger seemed beyond caring about social niceties.

"I've never seen you before." I didn't dare call Krukis's magic to me, but I wished for the "knowing" that it often conveyed.

The man was pale and sweating, with a twitchiness I'd sometimes seen in those who took too much patent medicine. With his dilated pupils and the way he licked his lips, I thought perhaps he'd gotten a bad batch of bathtub gin.

"You put a spell on me!" the wild-eyed man screeched. There was no helping it; people turned to look.

"You're mad," I said, my voice low and deep, hoping I could intimidate him into being quiet and taking his seat.

He shook his head so hard his glasses nearly flew off. "No, no I'm not. You're one of them! *Hexerei!*" he shouted, and now I could see the conductor striding toward us.

"Here now, what's going on?"

"I have no idea," I replied, doing my best to look sane and sober. "I was coming back from the lavatory, and he just started shouting at me."

The conductor turned to the stranger. The man's glasses sat tilted on his nose, and his hair looked as if he had been running his hands through it. "He hexed me!" the man accused, pointing at me, and I heard a buzz of conversation through the train car.

"That's enough of that nonsense," the conductor snapped. "Get back to your seat and stop bothering people, or I'll have you put off at the next station."

"I'm telling the truth! I've been hexed. And there's something not right about him," the stranger repeated, pointing to me once more. "So maybe he's the one—"

Whatever the man might have said next got cut off. He gasped as if he'd swallowed his tongue, then stiffened, going even paler, and his entire body began to tremble. Sweat poured from him, and he wheezed to draw air.

The stranger fell to the floor, half in and half out of the vestibule, and the shaking grew worse. Foam flecked his mouth, and he soiled himself. The other passengers gasped and drew back from the corridor but could not help staring in horror.

With one final groan, the man arched, then dropped back, dead.

The conductor collected his wits admirably. "I need a blanket and a stretcher," he told a porter who happened by. "Now!" The porter went running.

"I swear, I've never seen him before," I repeated, staring at the dead man.

"You never know what they've been drinking," the conductor said with a shrug. "There's bad stuff out there." He looked at me and let out a long breath. "Go back to your seat. If the police at the station have any questions, we'll find you."

I walked back to my seat with my now-cool cup of coffee still clutched in my hand. The other passengers stared at me, then averted their eyes. A whisper passed through the car, and I heard the same word repeated.

Verhext. Cursed.

I took my seat, set my coffee down on the tray, and unfolded the newspaper to create a screen between myself and the prying eyes of my fellow travelers. My mind raced, trying to figure out what I'd seen. I'd heard of illness that could cause a person to have a fit, but I'd never seen it. Doctors thought such things were a problem in the brain. Only the ignorant blamed witches and demons for sickness.

Except that I knew for a fact that witches, gods, demons, and magic were real.

Perhaps once I reached Reading, West could find out more about the unlucky passenger. Maybe he had nothing to do with our mission. But the unsettled feeling hadn't left me, and I found my jaw clenched and my shoulders tense.

After I'd read the paper twice and tired of pretending to study it further, I finally lowered my "shield" to find that the other passengers had gone back to their own diversions. Porters had removed the corpse, and I wrinkled my nose at the strong disinfectant they'd used to cover the smell.

We pulled into the Harrisburg station, and I watched out my window as the body was taken off on a litter, covered by a blanket. The conductor spoke with a policeman, but the cop either didn't consider the stranger's odd death to be his problem, or didn't want to bother. I couldn't shake the worry I felt, but at least it didn't look like I'd be delayed being questioned by the police.

Several people got off at Harrisburg, a few moving with panicky haste as if they suddenly decided to change their plans en route. My fellow passengers weren't staring at me; now, they made an effort to avert their eyes. Either they felt embarrassed by their earlier reaction, or they weren't taking any chances that I might put the evil eye on them.

New travelers got on, filling the vacated seats. A blond man in a well-worn tweed jacket settled into the aisle seat a few rows in front and to the side. He moved with purpose, and although he wasn't a large man, something about him commanded attention. The man had an intensity that drew the eye, even when he appeared to be at rest. I wondered if he were a politician, or perhaps a union organizer.

I'd dismissed the other new arrivals as uninteresting, until the last man ran for the train as it started to pull out of the station, catching hold and swinging up onto the step. I couldn't hear what he said to the conductor, but he was permitted through and made his way down the aisle to the nearest empty seat as the train swayed, picking up speed.

My eyes narrowed, as my gut warned me to watch out for the newcomer. The man wore an expensive suit, carried a leather valise, and his shoes had a fresh shine. Black hair and large, equally dark eyes gave him a face not easily forgotten. He looked like a showman, perhaps an actor or a con artist. But the prickle I felt at the back of my mind wasn't intuition. It was a warning from my patron god. Krukis had noticed the well-dressed stranger, and that couldn't be a good thing.

I hadn't planned on napping, not with everything that had happened, but the sun was warm through the window, and the clack of the wheels, coupled with the rocking of the car, put me under.

Or rather, Krukis wished to deliver a message.

In the dream, I stood in a cave, a dark, dank place that smelled of wet rock. The flickering light of a torch or lantern did little to drive away the shadows. I felt Krukis's presence before I saw him. Only fools or madmen would want to stand in the presence of a god. Even at a distance, the sheer power of his presence overwhelmed me. I respected him, gave him his due, but stubborn bastard that I am, I refused to kneel. That Krukis did not demand it made me regard him more highly.

"What is bound cannot be allowed to be set free." His deep voice made my bones tremble, like thunder close by.

Are there witches? Dream-me had a bit of moxie, to demand answers from a god.

"Veles seeks to interfere. The dark-haired man has some power, and the blond is a shill used without true understanding. Watch them closely, and be on guard."

Can I just kill them when we get off the train, and be done with it? I preferred a direct approach, clean and efficient. I would prefer not to kill, but monsters, like rabid dogs, gave me no choice.

"Patience. Events must play out if the worst is to be prevented, or Veles will just try again."

How can I stop a god?

"I will handle Veles. I rely on your stubbornness and talent for doing the unexpected to prevail against the mortals he controls. Do not forget: you are my champion."

I startled awake, just as the train's whistle sounded. Krukis's deep voice rang in my mind. I wasn't sure, but I thought he'd told me that my ability to be a pain in the ass was what would win the day. At least I could promise to live up to that expectation.

When I looked around, the blond man appeared to be sleeping. But the dark-eyed man had turned in his seat so that he could see me out of the corner of his eye. If he did, indeed, have some true magic, then perhaps he sensed a ripple because gods never walk softly. I tensed, expecting a confrontation, but after a while, he turned and picked up his book.

Several hours later, we reached the station in Reading. The blond man had left his seat before we came to the platform and did not return. I had hoped to at least get an idea of his destination. The dark-eyed man already had his valise down from the luggage rack, held between his feet. As soon as the doors opened, he sprang from his seat, pushing past those around him, to be one of the first out of the car. I had only a suitcase, so it didn't take me long to get off the train, but the man was gone by the time I reached the street.

I swore under my breath in frustration, and then stopped to get my bearings.

"Why is there a Chinese pagoda on top of that mountain?" I asked a man standing on the station steps.

I came to this heavily German city expecting knitting mills and hosiery factories, but the Japanese building had me stumped.

The guy looked at me like that was a weird question. He shrugged. "I heard some rich guy wants to build a ritzy hotel. Guess he wanted it to look different."

If that was the case, he'd succeeded. Mount Penn and its companion, Neversink Mountain, weren't anything like the Appalachians closer to Pittsburgh or the Mátra range back in Hungary. By comparison, these "mountains" were just really big hills. With a pagoda. Odd.

I knew I was still a number of blocks from my destination, but a trolley would get me where I needed to go. I hopped a streetcar, which took me up to Spring and Ninth. Still getting my bearings, I looked around, trying to get a feel for this new place. An odd, medicinal scent hung in the air, and I wondered if the Luden's factory a few blocks to the east had something to do with it. Up ahead in the foothills of Mouth Penn was the new Reading Senior High School, the huge, brick and stone building I'd heard someone refer to as the "castle on the hill." It had just opened a few years ago and looked solid enough to last for centuries. The area around me was an odd mix of row houses, factories, corner stores, and pubs. I'd passed a Catholic orphanage several blocks to the south, and an elementary school sat at the corner of Spring and Moss. Other churches, Catholic and Protestant, poked spires above the skyline.

The air smelled of coal smoke and horses. The milkmen and the ice trucks lumbered along with their horse-drawn wagons, seemingly unconcerned by the modern trolley that zipped past them. From what I gathered, the department stores were down on Penn, along with the other fancy stores. West's sources had all agreed that North Ninth Street was the place to go looking for information, a working man's neighborhood of mostly German immigrants.

I paused, listening. I heard the *ding* of the streetcar, the *clip-clop* of hooves, and voices coming from the open windows of the narrow houses, speaking the version of Low German people in these parts called "Pennsylvania Dutch." These folks were "Deutsch," not "Dutch," but they had long ago stopped correcting outsiders.

A boy who might have been about seven years old—still in short pants —followed the milkman's cart, carrying a bucket and pail. I figured he must live around here.

"Hey, you!" I called out. He stopped and looked at me.

"Mister?"

"I'm new in town. You know where Kemmner's Rooming House is?"

He scratched his head, then pointed. "Down that way, just before you get to the cough drop factory."

I couldn't help my curiosity. "What's the bucket for?"

"My mum pays me a nickel for horse shit to put on her garden," he replied proudly. I watched him run off after the receding wagon and had to chuckle at his enthusiasm.

Kemmner's Rooming House was a row home at the end of the block. Like the rest of the houses, it was one room wide and stretched from one street to the alley behind it, and rose four floors into the air. The homes looked fairly new, although the soot from the coal smoke made every-thing dingy. I walked in the front door, carrying my suitcase, and removed my hat.

"May I help you?" A matronly woman past her middle years looked up from a rocking chair in the front room and paused her knitting.

"I'm looking for a room."

The woman I assumed was Mrs. Kemmner looked me over from top to bottom. "How long?"

"That depends on whether I can find a job," I replied, nervously fingering my cap to give the right impression. West and I agreed to my cover story as a mill hand who was looking for work anywhere I could find it, preferably in one of the underground breweries. Reading never held much with Prohibition and apparently made only the barest effort at hiding its alcohol.

"If you can pay a week in advance, I've got a room," the woman said. "It's small, but you'd be by yourself. Everyone shares the bathroom unless you want to use the old outhouse by the back door. Rent includes a simple breakfast, a bag lunch, and a hot supper, family-style. No drunks, and no visitors. Do you smoke?" She peered over her glasses at me.

"No, ma'am."

"Good," she replied with a curt nod. "Because you'd have to do it outside in the alley. I don't hold with that." She named a price, and I paid it.

"Top of the stairs, second door on your right. If you want your washing done, that's on Tuesdays, and it costs extra."

I lugged my suitcase up the stairs and found my room. The narrow space held a single bed, a dresser, chair, and footstool. A window and a gas lamp in a wall sconce provided good light. Nothing in my bag was likely to give me away as being more than I claimed, although I figured Mrs. Kemmner might look askance at the Colt 1911 tucked into my waistband, the silver dagger in a wrist sheath, or the packets of salt and bottle of holy water in my jacket pocket.

I explored the hallway, enough to find the bathroom and a back stairway that curved down in a tight spiral to the dining room. The kitchen and small yard were to my left, and a dining room, sitting room, and front room were lined up end to end, bringing me back to where Mrs. Kemmner remained rocking and knitting.

"I see you found your way," she said. "You said something about looking for a job. Are you one of those Temperance people?"

"No ma'am," I replied. "I like a beer as much as the next man, although I don't overdo." Even when I was mortal, I'd never been a drunkard. Now, I could drink a barrel-full and feel none the worse for it.

"Can you keep your mouth shut?"

I nodded.

"Then if you don't mind hard work, Abe Minker's looking for men to move barrels. Deliveries come at night, and you'll have to avoid the cops. Don't know about the pay. You'll have to ask. Thought I'd mention it." She gave me instructions on where to go and what to do. Obviously, the work was as illegal as the speakeasy it provisioned.

"Thank you," I replied.

"You got a shiv?" Mrs. Kemmner asked.

I froze, wondering if she'd somehow noted the weapons beneath my jacket.

"If not, get one. The Seventh Street Gang causes trouble, and you might want protection, what with working nights." Then she gave me another once-over. "Although you're big enough, they might leave you alone. You look like you can handle yourself."

More than she could imagine. Still, I ducked my head and thanked her for the advice, filing it away. I didn't doubt that I could probably take on the whole gang and survive, but it would raise awkward questions best avoided.

A block from the Luden's factory, a small grocer's shop sat tucked between row houses on Eighth Street. The name over the door said *"Izzy's Market,"* and the display in the window showed canned foods, sacks of flour, sugar, and sewing notions, as well as a jar of hard candy.

I watched through the window as a stream of men went to the counter and turned in a receipt. Some were handed cash; others walked out empty-handed. I didn't have an inclination toward gambling myself, but I knew a numbers game when I saw it. Obviously the Minkers were running more than just bathtub gin.

I went around to the back, needing to turn sideways to navigate the small pass-through between buildings, and knocked at the door.

"Zhazhda," I said when a man opened the door. I spoke passable Russian and recognized the word for "thirst," the password Mrs. Kemmner had shared with me for the speakeasy.

"You're new," the man said.

"I heard you had a job open. I can load and unload wagons." That was no lie, and as the man looked me over, the truth of it was apparent.

"All right. Come in. There's work tonight. You do good, maybe there's more."

I followed him inside through a storeroom to a door that led to a basement. The underground room was wider than the row house, and I figured someone had knocked through to connect the cellars of two adjacent houses.

Back in Cleveland, Ben Lavecchia ran a classy speakeasy. Theater folks hobnobbed with socialites, but working folk weren't turned away if they were on good behavior. By comparison, Minker's speakeasy drew a rough sort, from the factories, the railroad, the trades. I knew how to fit in with this crowd. I'd been them, in my mortal days.

Since I had work, I stuck with one beer and nursed it, not that I'd feel the effects one way or the other. Belly up to the bar, it felt a little like Pittsburgh in the old days. That just made the ache of my memories sharper.

"Ain't seen you here before." The guy on my left barely looked at me, but I figured he'd already sized me up.

"Haven't been here before," I replied, with more accent to my words than usual.

"Reading's not a bad place," he replied. "Just gotta keep your nose out of things that don't involve you."

I wasn't sure whether I had somehow earned a warning, or whether the stranger merely dispensed advice to anyone who would listen. Since I'd only been in the hidden bar for a few minutes, I figured the latter was more likely.

"I already heard tell of the gangs," I said and took a sip of my beer. Not bad, for contraband. Ben's stuff was better. I wondered if Abe Minker was mobbed up, too. Minker was a Russian name, like the password. That worried me, since I'd had a run-in with some Russian vampires back in Cleveland who had gotten a bit too nostalgic for the Motherland.

The stranger shrugged. "*Ach*, there are ruffians everywhere. They mostly fight among themselves. I don't worry much about the gangs. The *hexerei*, on the other hand—"

I'd heard the word before. The same word the unlucky man had used on the train. It meant dark witch.

"Leave the witches alone, and they leave you alone," the man on the other side of the stranger said.

The stranger gave the other man a dirty look. "Like that *braucher* in York, in Rehmeyer's Hollow? Didn't work so well for him, did it?"

That was the contact of West's who ended up murdered. I listened closely without looking like the tale caught my interest.

"He wasn't a regular person," the second man insisted. "He was already a witch-healer. Who knows what goes on among witches?"

They agreed that witches couldn't be understood by the likes of us, and the conversation went back to complaints about rising prices, a debate over how long it would take to build the new theater, and squabbling over politics.

I let newcomers squeeze in between me and the stranger, figuring I'd learned all I could from him. The basement had an intimate feel, and the light from the kerosene lanterns didn't reach the corners, where shadows remained. Most patrons stood at the bar since all the stools were taken. The few tables were already claimed by men engrossed in card games with betting as illegal as their whiskey. Over to one side, two fellows played darts while their friends joked and jeered.

The cellar smelled of rotgut liquor, sweat, and the tang of coal oil. The man behind the makeshift bar didn't get the drinks from a drawer shoved through from a secret room. I suspected the cabinets behind the bar swiveled, presenting their blank wooden backs if anyone bothered to raid the place. The crowd didn't seem worried about that possibility.

"That's where the Free Society tried to make a difference," I heard a man say but didn't dare turn. Two men were walking behind me, heading back to their seats after refilling their drinks at the bar.

"The Society's gone. Just like the Thule," his companion replied.

"Damn shame. They had the right idea. That's what someone needs to do—pick up the work and carry it forward," the first man said.

The bar was busy enough; it took some pushing for the men to get through the crowd, which meant I had the chance to overhear at least that much of their conversation. I filed the words away for my next discussion with West. Much as I lamented my memories of some things, another effect of Krukis's blessing was near-perfect recall.

I mulled over what I'd heard. A strange word, "Thule." I knew I had heard it before, and that it was not a good thing. As for the "Free Society" —perhaps it was one of the *Völkisch* groups West sent me to learn more about. But I knew asking questions was the wrong way to go. I'd have to bide my time and keep my ears open.

The slap of a palm against the rough counter made me look toward the end of the bar. "You've had enough, Karl," the bartender said.

Karl shook his head. He looked a bit like a possum, with a pointy nose, pale skin, and a nearsighted squint despite his wire-rimmed glasses. "It's my going-away party," he announced. "Keep 'em coming." His accent wasn't German. Karl had the high cheekbones and the wary look I associated with Eastern Europe, farther east than Hungary. Romania, maybe, or Ukraine. I couldn't quite place his accent.

The bartender just nodded. "Is that so, Karl? Where are you going?" He clearly didn't take the man seriously, but he didn't sound unkind. Amused, perhaps. Karl didn't look like the type who caused trouble.

"To hell, I imagine," Karl replied, and that drew the attention of those around him, whose chatter came to an abrupt end. Karl looked a bit bleary, but he wasn't three sheets to the wind by any measure. I felt a prickle in the back of my mind, a warning.

"Hell, huh?" the bartender replied, and relented, pouring Karl another glass and taking his money. "What'd you do? Pay for the trolley with a slug? Make a little whoopie with somebody's wife?"

That last suggestion raised guffaws as if the others doubted Karl's virility.

"I was cursed by a witch."

Everyone eyed Karl as if he'd come down with the plague. Several of the men muttered prayers and crossed themselves. Others stepped back, making sure to remain a safe distance from Karl.

Karl seemed to enjoy being the center of attention. I guessed it was a rarity. He took the drink and knocked it back, sputtering. "I didn't know he was a witch when I bumped into him on the street. I tried to apologize. Then he called me a name, said he'd send me somewhere I belonged. He muttered something at me and waved his hands and told me I was a dead man walking."

He slapped the bar with more money, and I wondered if he meant to drink himself broke. "Gimme another round, Frederick," he told the bartender. "One for the road." He had a manic gleam in his eyes, and the cheer in his voice sounded forced.

I realized Karl believed the curse, and it terrified him. He'd come here, to the speakeasy, so that even if he wasn't really among true friends, he didn't have to die alone.

Frederick must have gotten the same hunch because he took the money and filled two large shots. If that didn't put Karl out of his misery, it would certainly send him on his way feeling no pain.

Karl raised the drinks, one in each hand. "*Ein Prosit!*" he shouted.

Every man raised his drink. "*Zicke, zacke, zicke, zacke, hoi, hoi, hoi!*" the crowd answered. We all took a slug of our drinks, and Karl knocked his back one after the other.

I stole a glance at Frederick, who was now watching Karl with concern rather than indulgent amusement. A flush came over Karl's pale skin, and sweat beaded his forehead. He took a step away from the bar, wobbly but still functioning. His gaze fixed on the plain wooden boards of the ceiling, which held a horror only he could see.

"I'm not gonna run. Come and get me, you bastard!" Karl raised a fist to the ceiling, more a cornered badger than a fainting possum.

Both his hands went to his throat, and his eyes bulged as his face reddened. The speakeasy's patrons scattered, cursing under their breath in German. I had no trouble making out what they said.

"*Die hexe!*" The witch.

Karl sank to his knees, fingers clawing at his neck, tearing at an invisible noose. I'd seen a man hanged once. I knew what was coming, the bloodshot eyes, swollen tongue, beet-red face. Karl's tortured wheezes filled the basement, which had gone quiet in horrified silence.

Then, as quickly as it began, Karl fell forward. Dead.

Men made the sign of the cross or dug saints' medallions from beneath their shirts with shaking hands and kissed the silver as they murmured half-remembered prayers.

One word repeated, whispered through the room. *Verhext.* Cursed.

"Lemme through! What's everybody staring at? Oh, Christ—is he dead?" A thin, dark-haired man with a face like a weasel plowed through the crowd. He wore a striped shirt with dark pants and suspenders, and his glasses were perched on top of his head as if Karl's death had interrupted doing ledgers.

This, I gathered, was Abe Minker, the speakeasy's owner.

Minker turned to me. "You. You're the new guy?"

I nodded.

Minker waved vaguely in Karl's direction. "Get him out of here. I don't care where—just not near here, get it?"

I nodded and scooped Karl's skinny body up knowing that whatever curse the witch had laid on him was no match for the protection of an Old God. The crowd parted around me as I carried the dead man up the stairs.

I had only been in town a few hours, and now I needed to dump a body—preferably without getting caught by the cops. I thought about it for a minute and came up with a plan.

It didn't escape my notice that Karl wasn't German. Neither was Abe Minker. Or me. The witch's curse sounded like it was grounded more in *Völkisch* nationalism than in any flub of Karl's since the comment about "sending him where he belonged" was ominous.

Minker might be mobbed up enough to get a pass. Or maybe he collaborated with the right people. I'd seen that in my homeland, at the worst of times, when a few people sold out those like them to save their own necks. Maybe someone was willing to protect Minker because of the racket he ran—or the protection money he paid.

But little guys like Karl died.

That feeling that I was being watched swept over me again. I glanced over my shoulder but didn't see anyone following. My instincts were good even when I wasn't drawing on Krukis's magic, and I had learned to trust my gut. For a moment, I debated calling on Krukis's power for protection. But I didn't want to tip my hand, and once I summoned the magic of an ancient god, I might as well shoot up a flare to any witches in the area.

I didn't dare travel far, but the alley behind the speakeasy was dark, and I figured Minker probably had the beat cop on the payroll. I slung Karl over my shoulder and went up a block, then over, and picked a house at random, then slipped through the wooden gate into the small back yard.

Mrs. Kemmner had told me the rooming house had an old outhouse at the back. I wagered other row homes did, too. Sure enough, a wooden privy sat next to the corner of the house. I opened the door, wincing as the hinge squeaked.

"Sorry, Karl," I muttered since he deserved more dignity than I'd be able to give him. I yanked his pants down, averting my eyes, sat the corpse up on the wooden seat, then shut the door.

When someone found Karl, they'd think he snuck in to take a dump and died from a bad heart. Such things happened. My family in Hungary still talked about a great uncle who died relieving himself. Not as much as they talked about the uncle whose heart gave out while he was fucking a barmaid, but still, he was almost famous, as family legends went.

I muttered in Hungarian. *My deepest condolences* didn't seem like quite the right thing, but what do you say to a dead man with his pants around his ankles? I had no idea what faith, if any, Karl had. But I learned long ago that customs serve the living, not the dead. I had abandoned my Catholic upbringing the night I died on the riverbank in Homestead when the Christian god turned a deaf ear, and the Slavic god of black-smiths heard my plea.

I turned away from the outhouse and felt a foul chill slither over me, like cooled blood running down my spine. For a second, my heart stuttered, and I stumbled, straining for breath. It felt like I was dying all over again. My hand went to my chest as if I could claw through my ribs to get more air. I thought of West and Sarah, afraid I would let them down. I fell to one knee, and my head felt as if it would explode.

Then unbidden, my patron's power swept in to sustain me, like a wave rushing from the ocean. It sluiced away the dark magic, which receded as if it were powerless to do otherwise. I felt the malicious magic withdraw and wondered if Krukis followed up his protection with a warning—or worse. Gods can be territorial about their pet humans.

I climbed to my feet as the headache receded and breathing came more easily. Fear still sent my heart jackrabbiting, a natural reaction, but no longer manipulated by someone with ill intent.

"Thank you," I said, turning my face up to the sky. Then I glanced around to make sure no one had seen me make the drop-off and slunk back to the speakeasy, keeping to the shadows.

"You came back." Frederick looked up when I tromped down the steps. Minker was nowhere to be seen. The crowd had thinned, not unusual since most people had work tomorrow. No one sat at the bar, although several card games were still going, and the dartboard remained popular.

I shrugged. "Of course I came back. I need a job. You said you had barrels to move." I decided not to mention the dark magic attack, since explaining how I survived would be awkward. The witch would probably try again, and I hoped that I'd be prepared to fight back.

A slow grin spread across Frederick's face like I had passed a test. "You're alright," he said.

"I hope there's extra for getting rid of a body? It should be more."

Frederick laughed. "You've got brass balls, don't you? Tell you what— I'll run you a tab, on the house."

I did not enlighten him, but my balls—like the rest of me—were steel, not brass.

"Does that sort of thing happen often?" I asked as Frederick slid a glass of beer to me. This time, I did not sip. I downed it in one go, and thumped my chest, as expected.

"Not from a hex," Frederick replied. "Sometimes a bad heart, now and again a knife fight if someone doesn't pay what's owed." He sounded like this was commonplace. "But the *hexerei* have grown bold. Best to avoid them."

"So...yes?"

Frederick refilled my glass, figuring I'd earned my tab. He didn't know the half of it. "More and more often," he replied, glancing around. He dropped his voice so low that I probably couldn't have caught his words without my god-enhanced hearing.

"Started out one here and one there, but in the last couple of months, more like one a week. Lately, even more often. Like the witches are building up to something," Frederick said. "And none of them German. Poles, Italians, Greeks, Jews, even a Romani guy. It worries me. Such things happened in the Old World. Here, we should do better."

Could the witch tell I was Hungarian? I had assumed the attack was connected to my mission with West and Sarah. Maybe I'd overestimated my attacker, and it was plain old hate-the-foreigner shit. Like we weren't *all* foreigners here.

Did that mean West and Sarah were in danger for not being German? Perhaps. I had no idea of their background, and it never occurred to me to ask. Since both of them enjoyed money and privilege, I had just assumed them to be German-English, as most of those at the top seemed to be. Still, I'd warn them, because they were my friends, and I had few enough of those.

Krukis, please protect them. I think you'd like both of them, even West. They've got...attitude.

I nodded like Frederick had shared great wisdom. "The barrels?" I asked again.

Frederick wiped his hands on a towel and gestured for me to follow him. We went back up the steps and through the tiny, fenced backyard, a postage stamp of grass and concrete, with a shed at one end, large enough for a car or a wagon. I followed him into the shed, and he opened a trap door in the floor. His lantern revealed a ramp that extended into darkness.

"There are tunnels under some of the homes, from a brewery that was here a long time ago. Not many people remember. Good place to store the beer," he said, slapping me on the back. "There's a door from the second room that connects, so we can take it in as we need it."

He left the lantern, and I followed him out to the alley where a man with a wagon waited. The horse nickered and snuffled, impatient. Frederick and the wagon driver and I made short work of the cargo, six barrels of beer and eight jugs of corn whiskey.

When we'd emptied the wagon, Frederick paid the driver and me in cash. Not bad for a night's work, even if it did involve stashing a body.

I thanked Frederick, and the bartender told me to come back tomorrow if I didn't mind being muscle to break up fights. I said I'd be there. The speakeasy seemed like a good place for information. I needed to find out more about the Free Society, as well as the Thule and the witches.

West's instincts were right. Something deadly was going on, and I wanted to find out what.

To my surprise, Mrs. Kemmner was still rocking and knitting when I came in close to midnight. She wore a chintz apron tied over her house-dress, with thick, wrinkled stockings and sensible black shoes. Her dark hair, shot through with gray, was rolled into a tight bun under a hair net. Her needles flew, and the light from the gas lamp glinted off her gold-rimmed glasses.

"Did you get the job?" she asked, without looking up.

"Yes. Thank you." I hesitated. "My shoulder is sore. Is there a healer nearby?" I asked for a healer instead of a doctor because I was hoping for a referral to a *braucher*, a good witch. Like most folk-healers, I figured they depended on word of mouth since the authorities took a dim view.

"There's one up the street at 949," Mrs. Kemmner said. "Thomas Zeigler. Tell him I sent you. He does good work."

"I can pay," I said, in case she doubted.

"That's good. Sometimes, he'll take a chicken or fresh-baked bread, if money is tight."

"I'll go see him after breakfast. I hope he can help." Mostly, I wanted to see what I could learn from him about witches since my deal with Krukis made my body self-healing. But I figured I could fake a few pulled muscles for a good cause.

I bid her goodnight, wondering as I climbed the steps how late she stayed up, and what she did with the things she knitted. I didn't ponder much, because I'd had a busy day. I undressed and then fell across my bed and let sleep take me.

3

The smell of sausage woke me. The rooming house where I stayed in Cleveland also included meals, and our landlady was a good cook. There was a seasoning in this sausage that smelled different, and I realized it was bratwurst, almost certainly locally made. That boded well, and I dressed quickly and washed my face, combing my dark hair to be presentable. Alcohol offered me no real respite, and I hadn't desired a companion since my Agata died, but good food was the balm of immortality.

"I didn't know if you'd be up this early," Mrs. Kemmner greeted me when I came to the table. The clock told me that it was after seven, and since no one else was at the table, I assumed that my fellow boarders had already left for work.

"I'm not a heavy sleeper," I said, settling myself at the table. A blue and white metal coffee pot sat on a trivet, next to a bowl of scrambled eggs, a plate of sausage links, and a loaf of homemade bread with butter. The strong, dark coffee had little effect on me now that I was immortal, but like alcohol, I drank it for the taste and the memory of who I used to be. I made a plate for myself, eating with gusto. Mrs. Kemmner looked on with approval.

"This is real good," I said with my mouth full. Her normally stern expression softened, and I wondered if she had sons my age—well, the age I appeared.

"Eat up. It won't keep. I already had all I want," she told me, and then left me to finish as she went to the kitchen to do the dishes.

I ate my fill and carried my plate out to the sink, as my mother trained me.

"You're a good boy," she said, patting my arm with a hand laced with blue veins and liver spots. I wondered if I'd been right about her having grown sons and where they were. I hadn't seen evidence of a Mr. Kemmner, and boarding houses tended to be widow's work. I thanked her for the food, and she reminded me to pick up my bag lunch when I came back from the healer.

On the way out, I paused in the living room. I hadn't looked around yesterday. A photograph of a young man in a military uniform from the Great War sat on top of the black upright piano, and beside it, an older wedding picture that was probably Mrs. Kemmner's. I suspected that both the husband and the son were dead.

Outside, Reading bustled with people who were in a hurry to get to their destinations. The milkman's wagon rolled by with a *clink* of bottles, and school children raced by, likely headed for class. The smell of bread meant either a bakery or *hausfraus* getting an early start on their chores. Underneath it all hung the smell of coal smoke and horse shit, and the cough drops from the factory.

Making my way down the sidewalk reminded me of what a hermit I'd become when I didn't have a case. I took my meals at the boarding house, where I had friends among the others who stayed there, and I drank at Ben's speakeasy, but otherwise, I kept to myself with my books and my radio. A solitary widower's life. Comfortable enough, I supposed, but quiet.

Sometimes, too quiet.

I pushed those thoughts from my mind, figuring that the anniversary of Agata's passing accounted for my gloomy thoughts. I had a case to solve and a city's secrets to uncover. That should certainly be enough to keep me from brooding, at least for a while.

A brisk walk brought me to 949 North Ninth Street, a red-brick row home with a stained-glass transom window above the door. I rang the bell and waited on the steps. As I stood there, I felt the same prickle between my shoulder blades that I had felt before when the dark witch attacked me. Had I brought danger to the healer just by showing up?

"Can I help you?" A man I guessed to be Dr. Zeigler opened the door. He wore a tweed jacket instead of a doctor's coat, with a pince-nez perched on a hawk-like nose. The man was all sharp angles, gaunt with a prominent brow, high cheekbones, and a strong jaw. His clothing hung from his tall, square frame like a scarecrow. Zeigler had a melancholy look to him, and he smelled like Macassar oil and peppermint lozenges.

"Mrs. Kemmner sent me," I replied. "Sore shoulder."

"Come in."

I followed him into a home set up identically to the rooming house, only with an office instead of a front sitting room. It looked comfortable enough. Ziegler motioned for me to sit in a wooden chair and crossed his arms over his chest as he looked me up and down.

"What seems to be the problem?"

I made a show of raising my left arm as if the shoulder hurt. "I've done something to my shoulder. I was hoping you could fix it."

"You know that I'm a healer, not a doctor. I use traditional methods."

"Yes, she told me."

Ziegler walked over and laid his hand on my shoulder. He closed his eyes, concentrating, and then recoiled, snatching his hand back.

"Who are you?" he asked, eyes wide and fearful. "You are *gott beruhren.*" God-touched.

"I'm a friend," I replied. "I came to Reading to protect the good witches. I came to you because you are a *braucher.* I'll help you if you will help me."

"Help you, how?" He didn't trust me. I didn't blame him.

"I saw a man die *verhext* last night. A friend of a friend was murdered for being a witch. I've been in town one day, and have already been warned about the *hexerei.* What I don't have is the information to connect those dots. I believe you *can* help me. But will you?"

Ziegler stared at me for a long time, and I wondered if he was using his abilities to decide whether not to believe me. Finally, he sighed and turned the sign on his door to "closed."

"Come into the kitchen. I will fix coffee, and then we talk."

I followed him through the next two rooms to the kitchen. Ziegler's home was tidy and modest, and he didn't make a show of his witchy abilities. Still, I knew what to look for—the bunches of dried plants, the protective "hex" signs, the smell of sage.

In the kitchen, he took a pot off the warming grate of the old coal stove and poured two cups of coffee. I knew before I smelled it that the brew would be dark, sharp, and bitter, even with sugar. I drank it anyhow, to show trust.

"I'm afraid I've put you in danger by coming here," I said.

He looked up, surprised. "How so?"

"I was attacked by a dark power last night. That god-touch you felt saved me."

Ziegler raised his eyebrow. "Do you know who attacked you? Or why?"

I shook my head. "Maybe he knew why I came here. Or maybe he realized I'm not really German. Like the others who died."

The healer ran a hand back through his hair. "I've heard." I thought he looked guilty—or maybe, ashamed.

"I've heard talk, around the neighborhood. Ugly things, like back over there, before the War." He looked haunted, and I wondered what had made him choose to come here. We all had our stories, none of them happy. "I don't wish to see those things happen here."

Ziegler's shaken appearance made me think he had lost something precious to that hatred. "How much do you know about the *hexeglaawe?*" he asked after a moment when he had collected himself.

I recognized the word. It roughly translated as "witch beliefs." "Some. Obviously not enough."

"The *hexerei* have grown stronger lately," Ziegler said. "They may be organizing. I've heard stories about a secret society of *armanenschaft*, occult priests who translate sacred mysteries, and cipher manuscripts."

"Secret societies like the Free Society?"

Ziegler looked as if he were debating with himself on how much to say. "And the Order of the Golden Dawn. Those groups date back into the end of the last century. Always they have been about denying that some people were German enough to belong, or that they were even human."

He licked his lips nervously. "Some groups drew the working people, but others attracted the most powerful and wealthy, who liked excluding those they considered to be inferior. Be careful, my friend."

I knew that, better than most. "That's why I look out for the ones who need help."

Ziegler gave me another long appraisal, and I wondered what he saw. I wondered, but I wasn't sure I really wanted to know. I had my own darkness, and plenty of blood stained my hands. I told myself I fought for the people who couldn't, the champion of a god who watched out for the regular folks, but in the hour of the wolf I knew that some of those deeds had cast a shadow on my soul.

"Did you know the healer of Rehmeyer's Hollow?"

"We crossed paths. When he died, powerful relics were taken from his house. Some of those relics enhance magic. Others bind dark powers."

"If you had to guess who killed him—"

"Look to the *Völkisch* groups. Some of them wish to see the dark gods rise again."

I felt a prickle on the back of my neck. "Any particular dark gods?"

Ziegler's worry showed in his eyes. "Veles, god of the underworld."

Holy shit. It would be an understatement to say that Veles did not get along well with my patron, Krukis.

"I have had dreams," Ziegler went on. "Of a black spot on the mountain. Then the sun turns black, and there are monsters in the deep places."

"Does any of that mean anything to you? It sounds bad, but it's also not very specific."

He shook his head. "No. My dreams are true sendings, but they are often riddles or filled with symbols. I saw a skull with crossed bones and a strange drawing of the sun."

"Can you show me what you saw?"

Ziegler reached for a pad and pencil, and drew me a wheel within a wheel, with crooked spokes like lightning bolts. I had never seen anything like it.

"Is it familiar to you?" I asked.

"No. But deep in my belly, I fear it." He paused. "I have something to show you—and a gift that may help."

He left me in the kitchen and walked into one of the other rooms, then returned carrying a piece of parchment and a fountain pen. Ziegler slid the parchment toward me and made a mark at the bottom with the fountain pen.

"This is a *himmelsbrief*," he told me.

I spoke German better than I read it, and the old-fashioned *fraktur* lettering on the document made it all the harder. Heavy strokes of ink and florid embellishments gave the yellowed parchment a medieval appearance. "A 'heaven letter'?"

"It holds divine protection," Ziegler told me. "It will protect you from evil and misfortune, and enable you to speak with the dead."

I had been about to object since I already had divine protection of another sort, but I shut my mouth because my deal with Krukis didn't do squat to help me talk to ghosts. That sounded like it might come in handy.

"What's the catch?" Magical items always came with a price. Best to know that up front.

"You must defend those who cannot defend themselves," he replied. I did my best to live up to that, and it was what Krukis required of me for our deal.

"I accept."

He folded the letter and handed it to me with a solemn expression. I felt like one of the knights of old, receiving a writ from the king.

"Be careful," Ziegler said. "I believe that most of our neighbors are good people. But the darkness is spreading, and sometimes even good people can be led astray."

"What about you? If they went after one healer, what's to keep them from coming after you?" I asked.

"I have wardings. Protections. I trust in magic—but I also carry a gun."

"Smart man. Thank you. If you need me, I'm down at Kemmner's boarding house."

He saw me out, and I found the sunny day did not lift my spirits. The speakeasy didn't need me until evening, and I had no reason to hurry back to the boarding house except to pick up my bag lunch, so I took a walk down to Penn's Commons, admiring the fountain and the statue of a large stag, and doing my best to appreciate the green open space as I ate my sandwich and apple, giving the City Jail a wide berth.

I didn't see anyone following me, and at the moment, I didn't feel a dark presence. But I still sensed that I had drawn the attention of something, or someone, not mortal. Intuition told me to seek it out, and I found myself drawn toward the far end of the park, toward Hill Road.

As I drew closer, I felt the weight of the *himmelsbrief* in my pocket as if it grew heavier with each step. When I reached the corner, the parchment felt leaden. The air around me grew cold, and a shudder went through me. An unassuming plaque, hidden off to the side, confirmed my suspicions. This was the potter's field, the burying place for the poor, condemned, and unlucky.

Their justice was long-overdue, but those who wronged the dead had passed beyond the reach of mortal vengeance.

Unless...the forces that I had come to Reading to contain also had a hand in the misfortune of the unnamed dead?

Dr. Ziegler had said that the *Völkisch* groups like The Order and the Free Society attracted people from every class—including those in powerful positions. In Reading, that had to include the men who ran the railroad—and owned the coal and iron mines.

That gave me an idea. I intended to come back here to the pauper's cemetery, once I had my questions ready for the dead. But I needed to go somewhere else first. Seventh and Elm, the site of the Reading Railroad Massacre.

It took me a bit to find the spot. Roads had been moved and renamed in the fifty years since the tragedy, and I wondered if that was, in part, to keep the place where the men died from becoming a shrine, to erase the memory of those who were killed. My feet seemed to know the way, and when I followed my instinct, the odd document in my pocket felt lighter.

The railroad's treatment of its striking workers had been so bad that not only did civilians join in fray on the side of the strikers, but one regiment of the state militia threw down their weapons and refused to act against the workers. That was when the railroad company brought in its private security goons, and things went from bad to worse.

Gooseflesh raised on my arms, and a cold wind rose from nowhere, mussing my hair and tugging at my clothing. There wasn't much left now except for a narrow cut between two high stone walls that allowed the tracks to run beneath the cross street.

I could smell the gunpowder and blood, and see the smoke rise in the air. Men shouted and cried out, jeered and cursed. Different voices, different accents, but not so far removed from those memories of my last breaths fifteen years later, on a different slope.

That's when I realized I wasn't just imagining the view of the massacre, or reliving my final moments in Homestead. The magic of the *himmelsbrief* showed me the tragedy as it unfolded, or perhaps made it possible for me to see through the eyes of the dead.

I heard voices all around me.

"—*monsters in the mines.*"

"—*couldn't command us, so they brought hell spawn from the depths.*"

"—*summon the power of hell, and call forth the Vril-ya.*"

I staggered, putting my hands to my ears. The voices went silent, and I stumbled to the side of the embankment, well away from the tracks, to catch my breath and still my pounding heart. Despite Krukis's gift, I knew that I had—would always have—what the soldiers from the Great War called "shell shock" or "soldier's heart" from the horror of my death. Those memories haunted my dreams, made me flinch, and sent my heart pounding from loud noises, or doused me in cold sweats.

What I had just experienced was not the wrestling of my damaged mind to come to grips with my violent death. I knew what I had heard was real, the ghosts of the massacre trying to stop a new and perhaps even worse calamity from befalling their hardworking brethren.

My hands shook, my shoulders heaved as I struggled to regain control, and I knew if a policeman were to find me at this moment, he would be certain I was drunk. After a bit, I steadied, though inside, I felt shaken to my core.

"Thank you," I murmured. "*Danke.*" I gathered my wits and headed back toward the rooming house, wondering if I would encounter other spirits along the way.

Fortunately, no more messengers from the restless dead accosted me. I closed the door of the boarding house behind me and breathed a sigh of relief.

"Mr. Mack? Is that you?" Mrs. Kemmner had left her rocker, although her knitting project remained on the seat, awaiting her return. She bustled in from the kitchen.

"Did Dr. Ziegler help?" she asked, peering at me over her spectacles.

"He was very helpful. Thank you," I said, which was the truth so long as I didn't mention my shoulder.

"There's a note for you." She pointed to a sealed envelope lying on top of the piano. "A man dropped it by earlier."

I thanked her, and she headed back to the kitchen. The handwriting on the envelope was West's, and I wondered for a second if Mrs. Kemmner was the sort to steam open the seal in search of juicy gossip, but I saw no signs of tampering.

Joe. New developments on the job. Meet me by the fountain in the park at six tonight. Watch your back. —W

I checked the clock on the mantle. My meandering had used up a good bit of the afternoon, but I still had a couple of hours to clean up and eat dinner before I went to meet West and then headed back to the speakeasy. Mrs. Kemmner had the radio playing. First a spirited march, then a lively polka. Despite everything, the music made me smile. No matter how the world changed, I knew that polka would never die.

I debated taking a rest and decided against it. Thanks to the Gift, I don't require much sleep and can go without it longer than if I were mortal. I've never tried seeing just how long I could do without, and I hope I never have to find out the hard way.

When I came back downstairs, Mrs. Kemmner had placed a large pot of ham, beans, and potatoes in the middle of the table, along with a loaf of homemade bread, plenty of butter, and bowls, so the lodgers could serve themselves.

Two other men, my fellow lodgers, were already at the table, ladling out ample portions. I found a seat and saw that Mrs. Kemmner was busy in the kitchen. Given the gusto with which my companions attacked the food, I feared she might not get some if she waited.

"Can I make a bowl for you?" I called to her. She turned, startled, and then beamed at me.

"That's very kind. I would appreciate that. Thank you."

The other men gave me a look, and I shrugged. I wasn't trying to win favor. My mother raised me to be polite; God rest her soul.

I filled a bowl for Mrs. Kemmner and grabbed a couple of pieces of bread as well, which I set next to her place, then did the same for myself. It was a good thing that I served her first because the ladle scraped the bottom of the pot by the time I was finished.

"You're the new guy," the man across the table and to my left said. He had reddish-blond hair and a square jaw. Broad shoulders and calloused hands told me he had done plenty of hard labor in his life.

"Yeah, that's me," I replied, digging in to my food before it cooled.

"Where're you from?" The man across and to my right spoke through the mouthful of bread that puffed out his cheek like a squirrel. He had short black hair and a dark five o'clock shadow.

"Here and there," I said off-handedly. "Pittsburgh, Cleveland. Thought I'd come east and see how I liked it."

"Ain't never been out west," the dark-haired man said as if Cleveland was a land of cowboys and tumbleweeds. "Is it different?"

"The buildings are newer," I replied with a shrug. "People are people wherever they are."

As the blond ate, the sleeve of his shirt rode up, and I saw a mark like two lightning bolts on the inside of his forearm. The only men I'd met who had tattoos were sailors or criminals. I wondered which he was and decided to keep a close eye on my belongings.

"So where are you really from?" the blond asked. "You know, before America."

"A little village on the German side of the border with Austria," I replied. That was part of the cover story West and I had created.

"You don't sound German."

I shrugged. "I moved a lot." I managed a smile that I hoped made me look friendly but a bit dim-witted. "So, how about you?"

"I came from Düsseldorf," the blond said. He jerked his head toward his companion. "He's from Berlin."

"Big cities," I said. "Must have been interesting."

"Polluted," the blond replied. "Full of people who shouldn't have been there."

"The same," the dark-haired man added. "Vagrants and wastrels."

"That's too bad." I tried not to sound interested. These two might be the connection I needed to the groups I'd need to investigate.

"Have you read *Der Wehrwolf?*" Blondie asked. I remembered West mentioning the book that had caused trouble in Germany.

"What's that? A potboiler?" I asked, wanting to see what they'd say.

"A cautionary tale," the dark-haired man said. "A warning about protecting what's ours from thieves and bandits. In the book, a man builds an army to protect his fortress." He glanced at his companion. "That's what we mean to create. An army to protect our folk. The Alliance of the *Wehrwolf.*"

I understood enough German to realize from the way he said the word that he didn't mean creatures that changed in the full moon, monsters I knew to be real. He meant war-wolf, defender-wolf. He was a goddamn tree-pisser, marking his territory.

I plastered on a smile that I hope covered my thoughts. These two were dangerously crazy.

"You look like a man who believes in hard work," Blondie said.

"I do what needs to be done," I replied.

"If you're interested in finding people who feel the same way, there's a meeting tomorrow night at the old Highland House hotel, up on Neversink Mountain," the blond man added. "I'm Jakob. Just tell the man at the door I invited you. Not everyone is welcome."

"And I'm Hans," the dark-haired man said.

"Joe," I answered. We were busy with food, so we did not shake hands. That was fine with me, because if they were the sort I suspected them to be—the sort I had come to Reading to find—I did not want to be their friend.

"Thanks for the invitation," I said. "What time?"

"Nine o'clock," Jakob replied. "You'll find out what the Free Society is all about, and how you can make a difference. There are a lot of us. You'll fit right in."

I smiled, pretending that I didn't answer because my mouth was full. Mrs. Kemmner had finished her meal and gone to the kitchen. I wondered if she was trying to get the dishes done so she could go back to her knitting, or if perhaps she didn't like her other two boarders.

Jakob and Hans finished eating and said good night, leaving their dishes on the table. I sopped up bits on my plate with a piece of bread and finished with one of the sugar cookies from a platter in the center of the table. Then I gathered up all of the plates and silverware and carried them out to the kitchen.

"*Ach*, Joe. You are a good boy."

It bothered me that she seemed so surprised at such a simple kindness. I wondered how long she had been widowed and whether she was alone in the world. I helped to clear the table when Agata cooked for us, and I made sure our son Patryk helped as well. My mother had always told me that being poor did not excuse a dirty face or bad manners.

"It's nothing," I replied. She looked careworn, and I knew that running this house must be hard on her.

"It *is* something," She turned and looked at me like a worried mother. "Be careful around those men, Joe. Don't let them lead you astray."

My first inclination was to joke about it, but her concern silenced me. "You're more worried about their folk club than the moonshiners or the gangs?" I asked, genuinely interested in her answer.

She didn't look at me as she spoke, just kept doing the dishes. "I can't speak for all the gangs, but the Eighth Streeters aren't bad boys. They keep the riff-raff out of the neighborhood, and they look out for each other. Not enough jobs for young men these days. As for the moonshiners, there have always been whiskey-makers in these parts, law or no law. It's an honest profession, even if the government doesn't agree."

"But…"

She shrugged as if she didn't care, but her movements in the dishpan had grown jerky and quick, a sign that something had upset her. "This is a big country. Room enough for everyone. As it should be. My Johan and I, we came here because in Germany, our neighbors said we should not marry. He went to one church; I went to another. Same God, so who cares about the building? He was Polish. I am German. They said, 'stick to your own kind.' I asked them, 'What kind is that? Human?' But they would not leave us be. So we came here. Where we can all live together. I don't want that to change."

I'd already decided that Hans and Jakob were going to have to go. I didn't want them showing disrespect to Mrs. Kemmner. Now, I suspected that they made her feel unsafe or brought back troubling memories. So they would have to go even sooner, and I would not be gentle.

"I'll be careful," I promised. I didn't dare tell her more without the possibility of being overheard. It both bothered me and warmed me that she worried. No one had been concerned like that for me in a long time. West and Sarah had my back, and we were friends. But my mother was many long years in her grave. Despite everything, I had never outgrown liking a bit of mothering, now and then.

"Don't you have work?" she asked, changing the subject. I took that as my cue to leave.

"Soon. Thank you again for such a good dinner." Providing a meal was part of my rent. Making it a good meal worth eating was a benefit, not a requirement.

I needed to meet up with West before I went to the speakeasy. Since I'd already changed clothing, I just went back to my room for my gun and knife, and my jacket with a few "extras" in the pockets.

I had plenty to tell West and lots of questions. I only hoped that he and Sarah had discovered some answers because I couldn't shake the feeling that things were likely to get ugly real soon.

4

West sat on a park bench near the fountain in Penn's Commons. Instead of his usual suit and hat, West wore a canvas jacket over wool pants and a cabbie hat. I suppose that was so he didn't look out of place talking to the likes of me. I sat down on the other end of the bench, close enough to hear him but with enough distance that people would not think we were together.

"How are things?" West asked. "You get settled in okay?"

"The rooming house is good. I like the landlady." I gave him a quick rundown of my conversation with Dr. Ziegler and the unexpected invitation from Jakob and Hans. I left out ditching poor, dead Karl in the outhouse, but I did fill West in on the hexing and what had gone on at the speakeasy.

"Damn, you move fast. Good work," West replied.

I appreciated the praise, although part of me wanted to remind West that I didn't work for him. "How about you?"

"Learned a bit more about some of the dangerous *Völkisch* groups," West said, staring out at the fountain as if we were discussing the weather. "The Order of the Golden Dawn started at the end of the last century, dedicated to occult practices. Some of its members overlapped with the Thule, another *Völkisch* occult society, with some troubling political ties."

"And the Free Society?"

"That would be the Free Society of Teutonia. Started as a drinking club," West said.

"Really? And they are dangerous, why?"

He shrugged. "I guess they started talking politics with their beer and got taken over by some of the hotheads who don't like the treaty from the last war, hate the Bolsheviks, and aren't keen on a lot of other people, either."

"Sounds like the kind of group that would attract guys like Hans and Jakob," I said. "But not the sort to win over the swells."

"No, that's The Order and for the inner circle, the Thule," West agreed. "I'm nearly certain that the president of Reading Railroad during the massacre was an Order member. Same with the next railroad president, who cut wages and caused the Great Railroad Strike of 1922."

"What about the current president?"

"Odds are good he's also a member. Maybe we'll find out when we go to the event. If the dark magic we're looking for goes all the way to the top, then there's something in it for them, or they wouldn't bother," West said. "So if the workingmen think they're going to throw off the shackles of their oppressors, what are the oppressors expecting?"

"That's a good question. Maybe someone is playing both ends against the middle," I mused.

"Almost certainly," West agreed. "And while you're cozying up to those two rough chaps, keep your eyes open. There are some symbols to look for. The *wolfsangel* looks like two lightning bolts or two of the letter 'S' drawn with sharp angles."

"Ah," I replied. "Hans had that tattooed on his forearm." Well, that decided my earlier question. Definitely criminal, if he held with the likes of the Free Society.

"There's also the *totenkopf*—a skull and crossbones. And the *sonnenrad*, a wheel within a wheel with *wolfsangels* as the spokes."

"The *braucher* I went to see had a vision with the skull symbol and the wheel," I told him. "He didn't know what they meant, but he was frightened of them."

"Interesting. Keep your eyes open when you go to that gathering they invited you to—and for god's sake, Joe, watch your back."

"What are you and Sarah doing?" I asked.

"Hobnobbing with people we have reason to think are part of The Order. A mesmerist by the name of Erik Jan Hanussen has been taking Washington D.C. and Harrisburg by storm with his performances, and he came to Reading for a special event. We managed to finagle an invitation. Hanussen is hip-deep in dark magic, and he's got dodgy friends back in Germany. I'm nearly certain he's *hexerei*."

"So what do you need from me?" I asked. A glance at my watch told me I'd need to head to the speakeasy soon for my night as a bouncer.

"Sarah and I are going to a fancy reception up at the Pagoda on Mount Penn day after tomorrow. Hanussen is going to be the guest of honor. Sarah's already put the touch on her Harringworth Coal friends for the inside dirt on the railroad presidents."

"Dr. Ziegler told me that some of the *Völkisch* groups with all of their ritual and falderal also gave honor to the old gods. The *really* old gods," I added. "Veles's name came up. One of his many titles is God of the Underworld. And in case you were wondering, he and Krukis, my patron, don't get along."

West rolled his eyes. "It figures. How much of a problem is this going to be?"

"I'd say if anything, it makes Krukis more invested in our outcome since I imagine he'd enjoy thwarting whatever Veles is doing," I said. I didn't mention my vision on the train. As much as I valued my connection to Krukis, I didn't enjoy feeling like a freak around other humans.

"Pissing matches between ancient gods isn't in my field manual," West replied. "So that's for you to deal with."

"Thanks."

"There's another piece to this," West continued as if he hadn't heard me. "At the top of the Pagoda is a bell the builder brought over from Japan. And etched onto the bell is a prophecy, supposedly about the end times."

"Sarah's going after the bell, isn't she?"

West grinned. "Got it in one. I was hoping you'd be our driver if you can get off from the bar. That way we have backup, and you've got a chance to observe without being seen."

"Because I'll be part of the help, and the help are invisible."

West had the good grace to at least look chagrined. "Yeah."

We'd used that unpleasant truth to our advantage before. Rich people didn't look at the servants, didn't deal with them as individuals aside from the head butler or housekeeper. That made it easy to infiltrate a household or an event. And since they tended to forget the help were around, conversations took place that shouldn't have, making information easy to glean.

"All right. I assume you and Sarah will see to getting me proper clothes?" Sarah especially enjoyed dressing me up.

She kept a tux that was custom made for me at her townhouse, for times when she needed a bodyguard. If I remembered right, she also had a black suit that cost more than I was likely to earn in a year, and a chauffeur's livery, complete with cap. West spent his salary on his flashy Buick and natty clothes. That was out of my league, but I had to admit to preening a bit when Sarah kitted me out like an organ grinder's monkey.

"I think she brought a trunk just for you," West observed drily. "It's a good thing she's a heavy tipper because that poor bellman earned his pay just bringing all her bags from the train station."

I knew for a fact that West didn't travel light unless he was undercover as a blue-collar sort. I'd seen his steamer trunk, although he'd had the good sense not to ask me to carry it for him.

I glanced over at West and realized he had a book next to him. "What are you pretending to read?"

He rolled his eyes. "Not pretending. I had time to kill before you got here. HP Lovecraft. An odd, fabulistic horror tale, with creatures from the depths."

"From the depths, huh? That's Veles's realm, you know. And the mines in these parts go very deep," I replied.

West looked startled. "You think there's a grain of truth to the stories?"

"Don't know. Haven't read them. It just seems like an odd coincidence with everything we're dealing with. How did you pick that book to read now?"

West regarded the novel warily. "Someone left it behind in my train car. I wasn't tired and found it. After I started reading, I couldn't sleep for a whole different set of reasons."

"That good, huh?" It took a lot for a mere book to spook a guy like West. "It *is* horror," I added, letting him off the hook, just a little. Nightmares were nothing to trifle with. I didn't know much about West's history, other than that he'd been in the War, and seen some bloody shootouts against the Mob. We all had our ghosts.

"You think someone left it there for me?" he asked. "That's a bit of a stretch, don't you think?"

"I told you what I heard the ghosts say, at the underpass. Monsters from the mines. Hell spawn from the depths. *Vril-ya.*"

"I have no idea what that last word even means."

"Neither do I, but it must mean something," I countered.

"All right," West relented. "I'll see if I can read through to the end tonight. It counts as work if it's for a case, right?" he added with a lopsided grin.

"I'll see you in the alley behind the Hotel Berkshire Saturday night. Right now, I need to get to work. Wouldn't want to lose my job when I just started."

The night at the speakeasy under Izzy's Market proved quiet. Maybe talk had spread about poor Karl dropping over dead, but since it wasn't the first hex in the neighborhood, I doubted that would slow down the regulars' thirst for beer, camaraderie, and illegal betting.

Now that I had my bearings, it didn't take much to pick up on what was going on. Bathtub gin, bootleg beer, and homemade corn whiskey kept the bar busy. In addition to the wagers on poker games and darts, the clerk at the market's register took bets on horse races and baseball. Fancy girls circulated through the bar late in the evening and left with the most unlikely partners, which told me cash had changed hands. Abe Minker was running his own underground empire, putting Capone to shame. The guy had balls; I'd give him that.

Perhaps my looming presence kept troublemakers in line. West always told me that I was goddamn intimidating. I thought he just didn't like anyone taller than he was.

Whatever the cause, troublemakers went elsewhere, and the regulars were on good behavior. Since I knew more now than I had the first night, I also picked up on little things I'd missed before. Several patrons had the *wolfsangel* lightning bolt tattoo. I spotted a few of the black sun *sonnenrad* marks as well. None of the skull and crossbones, at least not where anyone could see, but that symbol might raise talk. The other designs seemed artistic and could easily be passed off as just an interesting pattern.

I thought maybe Hans or Jakob might be among the speakeasy's customers, but they didn't show up during my shift. Frederick poured me a beer since Minker didn't come out of his office and I clearly wasn't even tipsy.

"Nice job, moving Karl the other night," Frederick said, with a glance over his shoulder. The men at the bar were deep in conversation, unlikely to overhear. "There was a bit of a stir yesterday morning when some *hausfrau* went out to the outhouse and found someone already there!" He slapped me on the shoulder in good-natured camaraderie. "Pays to be able to think on your feet."

As I studied the crowd, I realized that none of them had the look of miners. Factory workers, perhaps railroad men, and common laborers, yes. But not miners.

I had worked among men from the mines too long to not know their type. Always a little hunched, to fit in small spaces. Strong arms from swinging a pickaxe, but not usually big men. Men my size wouldn't fit comfortably in tight tunnels or have room to maneuver. Short, wiry fellows and half-grown boys did better in those places.

And then there was the coal dust. No matter how much a man scrubbed, dark grains always remained beneath fingernails, in the creases of the neck, in hair. The shadow of the mines never left a man, and the dust that didn't mark him on the outside laid its claim in his lungs and the unmistakable drag and rattle of a miner's cough.

"Doesn't look like you get many miners through here," I noted.

Frederick shrugged. "We're not close to the active mines. The ones under the city closed up a long time ago."

I glanced toward the back, where I'd seen Minker down a hallway. "The boss doesn't hang around much out here."

"Doesn't need to. That's what he has me for—and I have you," the bartender replied with a grin.

"Do the hexes worry him?" I said it off-handed like it would worry anyone.

"The boss is a smart man," Frederick said, dropping his voice. "He knows how to take precautions. Old magic. Strong stuff."

A guy like Minker could pay off the cops and the politicians and even the Mob. But if he intended to stay safe with the Free Society nosing around, I hoped he had a powerful witch on his side.

"I heard some guys got roughed up a couple of blocks over." That's what I'd gathered from the gossip I overheard on my walk. Two men had been arguing over whether the ones who got hurt deserved it, or whether it was a warning to those who "didn't belong."

Frederick grimaced and turned away as if I'd hit a nerve. "That sort of thing has gotten worse lately. There are always people who make it their business to decide who belongs and who doesn't." His disgusted tone made his position clear. "The Boss can take care of himself. Watch yourself, Joe. You're not from around here. We had some guys in here tonight who might be trouble."

"The wrist tattoos?" I asked, going with a hunch.

Frederick nodded, worried. "Yeah. Usually means they run with a bad crowd. The Boss makes it a point to serve everyone. I heard those guys talking. Didn't like what they said. I'm worried that they might start taking it on themselves to run off the customers who aren't 'German enough' to suit them."

I snorted, like I found the idea preposterous when in reality, I'd suspected as much. West had warned me about the *wehrwolves*—ruffians who made it their business to "protect" their fortress by running off outsiders, like in that stupid book. Hans and Jakob had proven that the threat was real. "I'm happy to show that sort to the door—the hard way. Just give the word."

Frederick rubbed his temples as if staving off a headache. "Hard to know what to do. If we get rough with them, they might try to bust the place up or burn it down."

I met his gaze. "Not if I'm rough enough. It's never bothered me to take out the trash."

Frederick's eyes narrowed, understanding. "Hope it doesn't come to that, but thanks. Glad you're here."

"I'm glad for the job. You need me to move more barrels?"

Frederick had mentioned old tunnels when we moved the barrels last night. I intended to pay close attention when I went down there the next time to see what might lurk in the abandoned stretches.

"Not tonight, but come back in the morning, and there'll be produce to unload," he told me. I collected my pay for the night and headed back to the rooming house since it was already past midnight.

Tomorrow night I had the gathering on Neversink Mountain, and on Saturday, I'd be playing driver for West and Sarah. My dance card was full, a rarity for me. I wondered how long the meeting would take, and whether exploring in the tunnels afterward might be a good idea. Being undercover made me edgy because it didn't take much for lies to unravel. The sooner we got what we came for and left, the more likely we'd be to survive.

AFTER BREAKFAST, I got an early start on investigating. Since I couldn't ask the living the questions I needed to answer, I figured I would take my chances with the dead. With the "heaven letter" safely in my pocket, I ambled down to the potter's field in Penn's Commons, trying to look like I was just out for a stroll.

I didn't quite know how the document's magic worked, exactly, and I didn't want to walk around talking to myself. Could ghosts read minds? I thought my question and hoped it was "loud" enough to reach the dead.

Were you miners? Did you see monsters in the deep places? Were the mines verhext?

I had been warm in the sun, but now a chill swept over me. The breeze suddenly picked up, cold and damp. When I looked back over the lawn of unmarked graves, three ghosts had answered my call.

Glancing around, I realized that we were alone on this end of the park. Most people were at work, and perhaps the ghosts had their own ways of making sure we were not disturbed.

The spirits were dressed for the hard work of the mines, but their outdated clothing suggested they had been dead a long time.

I saw them just before I died. The speaker was a child's ghost, probably no more than eight or nine years old. Such young workers were common back in the day. *I got sent down to the lower levels in the Eckert mine, to carry a message. Got turned around, went the wrong way. Something grabbed me, pulled me into the old tunnels. The monsters got me.*

What did they look like? I questioned silently.

Not like people, one of the other ghosts replied. He might have been a teenager, still far too young for the backbreaking work of mining. *They were as long as a man, but gray and stretched-looking, and they can walk like us, but they can cling to the walls and ceiling too, like a lizard. And they're fast.*

Damned if that image didn't make my skin crawl. *Did they...eat you?* The three ghosts hadn't appeared with their death wounds, for which I was grateful.

Not with teeth. The third miner's ghost seemed to be the oldest of the three, and he looked ready to defend the younger boys if need be, although the dead were beyond the reach of all but the darkest magic.

How? I asked, and found myself holding my breath.

They touched my skin, and the life drained out of me, the youngest said, and the second ghost nodded in agreement.

Did the...creatures...do any work in the mine? Did they help the overseers? I couldn't imagine what benefit anyone might see in monsters that could suck the life from a person with their touch.

They could make tunnels without digging. Sometimes, we'd break through a wall with our picks and find tunnels already there. But the walls were smooth, not like ours, the third ghost said.

Sometimes they'd move a whole cart from one place to another, the middle spirit added. *It would just be somewhere else in the morning, but no one had done it.*

Did the creatures ever leave the mine? I felt my stomach tighten with the thought of those beings loose in the world.

The last day...we smuggled a braucher *in with us,* the third ghost said. *We feared the creatures, and we'd heard the overseers talking about how if they could be tamed, just a few could do the work of a hundred men. They didn't care that the monsters killed our friends. We had to stop them.*

"How?" I forgot myself and spoke the question aloud.

The witch read from a book that could seal the spirits of the earth. Then we set off dynamite in the lowest tunnels. Broke the lift and caved in the oldest part of the mine. Some of us died there, the third ghost added.

"When?" I whispered, not used to hearing other voices in my head.

The year of our Lord 1828, the year the mine closed, the oldest of the ghosts replied.

Despite my extra abilities and the magic that the *himmelsbrief* conveyed, talking with the spirits left me drained and made my head throb. Whatever questions remained would have to wait for another day.

Thank you, I told them. *I wish you peace.*

The gray things are still in the deep places, the second ghost warned. *Don't let them out.*

With that, the three ghosts wavered and vanished.

I made my way to a bench in the shade and sat down, rubbing my temples to ease the ache in my head. Whatever prowled deep beneath the city could not be allowed to get free. Why either the *Völkisch* groups or the robber barons thought that any benefit they might get from those gray monsters outweighed the risk otherwise escaped me.

When the headache throttled down to a dull roar, I walked to the speakeasy. Frederick had wagons of a different sort for me to unload, this time for the market. Instead of barrels of beer, I hefted cases of rutabagas, cabbages, and potatoes, but they paid me for my work, and Frederick told me he would need me late that night at the bar.

That gave me an excuse to leave the meeting on Neversink Mountain early, in case I needed an out.

To my relief, Hans and Jakob did not expect me to go to the meeting with them. I didn't trust them and preferred to find my own way there and back. I debated whether or not to take my Colt, unsure whether I'd be patted down. My abilities from Krukis were formidable but required being up close and personal, where a gun offered the chance to dispatch enemies at a distance. In the end, I erred on the side of caution and stuck the Colt in my waistband, just in case.

I also made certain that the *himmelsbrief* stayed in a hidden inner pocket of my jacket. Ziegler believed it offered protection, and I'd seen its effect on ghosts. I wanted all the advantages I could get.

The meeting location was in an abandoned hotel, which didn't bode well. Fifteen years ago, Neversink Mountain had been a tourist destination with big lodges and luxury hotels that catered to a well-to-do crowd. A series of questionable fires destroyed some of the most famous lodges, the Centennial Springs Hotel became a sanitarium, and the Highland Hotel, our gathering spot for tonight, sat empty since then. Even the gravity railroad that once ferried guests to the mountain top hotels and made a circuit of the summit struggled to remain in use.

I paid my fare and watched as the city gradually receded beneath the railroad car. The steep slant of the track meant that the car jutted out, providing a spectacular view. The lights made a pretty pattern, and I could spot some of the tall buildings downtown. Ahead of me, the darkness of the mountaintop loomed, far less reassuring.

No good reason existed to meet in the ruins, not for any regular organization. That just fed my concern that this was one of those *Völkisch* groups that did not want to draw attention to itself. Which was exactly what I came to Reading to investigate. But it also reminded me that I meant to betray any secrets entrusted to me by the group and its members, so I'd need to be very careful. I believed Krukis when he told me I would be immortal, but I didn't want to put that promise to the test.

The platform at the top of the incline looked deserted and in disrepair. My heart raced, and I wondered if Hans and Jakob had lured me into a trap. Yet I had done nothing to give myself away, and I realized that scenario was unlikely. I went nowhere without a candle and matches in my pocket, just in case, and I was about to light the wick so that I could see when the headlamps of the incline car went away. A man opened the shutters of a railroad lantern and stepped from the shadows.

"I came for the meeting at the Highland House," I said. "Jakob invited me." I hoped that if I failed to pass muster, the man would just send me back down the mountain. I didn't doubt that I would best him in a fight, but doing so might reveal abilities I would prefer to keep hidden.

He tilted his head and looked me over. I tried not to fidget. Immortal or not, I didn't like the feeling of being judged.

"Alright," he said, jerking his thumb toward the platform exit. "Follow the guides. Mind you stay on the path—it's grown a bit wild up here."

I wasn't quite sure what he meant until I stepped down off the platform and found another man with a partly shuttered lantern at the base of the steps. "There are lanterns along the trail," the man told me. "They'll take you where you need to go."

As my eyes adjusted, I could make out shapes in the moonlight. The dim lights of the lantern trail showed me the direction. Ahead of me hulked a dark shape, a hotel that must have been grand and imposing in its day. It blotted out the stars, identifiable from its silhouette. I made out a large rectangle, four stories tall. How it escaped the flames that claimed most of its neighbors, I wasn't sure. Or perhaps its owners had not been desperate enough to stoop to arson to settle their debts.

I heard the hum of voices as I drew closer, and when I was nearly upon the hotel, I saw glimmers of light escaping from around the edges of the windows. Someone had hung makeshift curtains to cover the openings, and while I suspected it might be in part to keep the wind from sweeping through shattered panes, I felt certain that the true purpose was to keep anyone from wondering about the lights on the mountain and coming to investigate.

A thick-set man with the stance of a boxer blocked the door when I climbed the steps to the Highland House's porch.

"Jakob invited me," I repeated as he eyed me. I tried to look unassuming, but that was nearly impossible given my height and heft. Just when I thought he might turn me away, a familiar voice spoke.

"He's okay." Jakob appeared from the doorway. It didn't escape my notice how the guard immediately deferred. Jakob had some clout with the organization if his word and invitation held that much weight. Despite my advantages, I couldn't help the nervous twist in my stomach.

"Glad you could make it," Jakob said, leading me inside. "Ernst is our best speaker. You're in for a good evening, and be sure you stay for the cookies."

Anarchist cookies. Revolutionaries recruited by dessert. The world was a strange place.

Lanterns illuminated the entranceway and one large room to the right. The bones of the grand old hotel were still intact. Furniture and many of the fixtures had been removed, most likely either sold or stolen. Paint and wallpaper peeled from the walls, floorboards buckled from exposure, and the abandoned building smelled of mildew and disuse. Yet for having stood empty more than a decade, it was in surprisingly good shape.

Rows of folding chairs faced the front of what had probably been a dining room. I eyed the people who had arrived ahead of me. They appeared to be laborers and working men, like I was back in the day. Many of them had probably worked twelve hours today or more, so sacrificing their scant time off indicated interest—or desperation. Hardship and worry had carved their features, making them look older than their years.

A makeshift stage had been erected at one end of the room with boards laid over chairs. On either side, hand-painted banners hung from the picture rails. One had a *sonnenrad*, the wheel-within-a-wheel black sun. The other had the skull and crossbones—*totenkopf*. Emblazoned across the top, it read *"The Free Society of Teutonia."* If I had any doubts about the group's interests, those banners were confirmation.

The organizers urged everyone to take their seats, and the tired men shuffled down the rows. I chose a place where I could make a quick exit, and remain unnoticed, so I found a seat in the last row. Some of the attendees greeted each other with handshakes and backslaps.

"Greetings, my dear brothers!" a blond man said after he climbed onto the wobbly dais. I startled, realizing he was one of the men from my train ride, who had stared at me as if they knew my secrets. "We come together for the memory of the Fatherland, for the glorious history of our native Germany, and for the promise that our homeland will rise again, powerful and victorious!"

That raised cheers from the group, and a few men shouted defiant comments in German.

Ernest broke into *Deutschland Uber Allis*, the German national anthem, and that roused more energy from the group as they joined in, their rough voices deep beneath the leader's clear baritone. After that, he led them through a few folk songs that everyone but me seemed to know by heart, songs that had enough memories associated with them that the men on either side of me teared up.

"We will remember!" Ernst shouted, and the audience echoed his words. "We will not be humbled! We honor the blood of Germany that pulses in our veins, and we will restore the glory of our ancestral home!" They roared in unison.

"Rise to the glory! Rise! Rise! Rise!"

We were all on our feet now, and I mumbled along with the group, watching as anger and wounded pride animated the men who, just moments before, had looked broken and defeated, wearied by life.

The leader basked in their energy for a moment, then gestured for them to sit, and waited out the rustle of clothing and clatter of chairs as they took their seats.

"Great things are in the making," Ernst told his eager audience. "Our goals are nearly within reach. A strong *hexenmeister* is coming to town, and all that we have worked hard to build has almost come to completion. Too long have you been beneath the boot of the railroad barons and the coal kings."

The crowd growled in agreement, and there were shouts of affirmation.

"It's time to show what the men of Germany are made of! You did not come to this country to lick the boots of industrialists. You came to make your fortune, to rise above hardship and bad luck."

"This witch, he is the high priest of the old gods. Of Veles and Morok, the gods of the deep places. And he will call forth salvation from the depths, the lost power of the great kings of ancient Germany, of Charlemagne, of Maximilian. Their magic has been forgotten, and without it, our great land has been humbled. Too many have forgotten our heritage, what it means to be German. But you, you have not. You have kept the faith of your ancestors, of our great kings of old. You will be the rebuilding of the greatness of the German people," Ernst promised, swaying the crowd with his energy and the kind of lies broken men hunger to hear.

"And when our *hexenmeister* calls to those forces from the deep, they will answer. They will follow his voice, and they will rise. And when they do, they will destroy all those who have oppressed you. They will break the bones of the coal kings and the railroad barons, the men who cut your wages and ask for your blood and sinew and repay you with lies and broken promises!"

The young demagogue served up exactly what his audience wanted, dangerous promises and poisonous lies. He'd worked himself into a lather, sweat beading on his brow, spittle flying as he shouted, part street preacher and part snake oil salesman.

I knew his type. They peddled empty dreams from soapboxes and sold hope to the desperate. And part of me remembered being one of those downtrodden men, eager for anything that made me feel strong again, made me feel like a man who controlled my own destiny, the captain of my life.

Maybe Ernst believed what he told his audience. Maybe he didn't. Even now, I didn't doubt the sincerity of the men who organized the strike in Homestead, who believed that we could throw off our shackles and stand proud, that we could wrest what was owed to us from the robber barons and the mill owners. We followed, caught up in a beautiful dream. And we died, wondering where we had gone wrong.

I felt my temper rise. At least the idea of striking for better conditions had worked in other places. But the dangerous delusions this man and his Free Society peddled could only lead to darkness. Nothing that rose from the depths would stop with destroying the rich and powerful. None of the gray monsters from the mine that had killed the ghosts would do the bidding of these dreamers. The creatures would kill, and keep on killing until their hunger was sated.

The men around me were cheering for their own deaths, and they had no idea what awaited them.

"And when that happens, we will show the world what it means to be the men of Germany," Ernst shouted. "We will restore the folkways of our ancestors and bring back the purity of our German heritage. We will raise a movement that will sweep through the communities of those who were forced to leave the Fatherland and send that pure energy back to our true home, where it will scour like fire and remove all that is weak and false and impure. We are the First Wave of the Great Cleansing, and we will not be stopped!"

The men around me were on their feet, shouting and clapping, stamping their feet and lifting their hands, caught up in the emotion. These would-be revolutionaries had been ground down by hardship, had their spirits broken by the mills and the mines, been made to feel that they were less-than-men. Here, they hung onto the hope of redemption—not for their souls, but for their pride.

The Free Society didn't offer to cleanse them from sin like the priests and preachers. It offered something more seductive, promising to restore their manhood, crushed and stolen from them by landlords and bankers, mine superintendents and shift supervisors.

And, gods help me, enough of my mortal self remained that I felt the pull, even though I knew the words were lies and that the promises could only end in blood. And for that, I hated the Free Society and its leaders, because all they could offer these men was ruin, prison, and death.

I clenched my jaw and balled my fists, trying to rein in my temper. These men around me, poor desperate, deluded fools, were not the true enemy. They were pawns, being manipulated by those who needed cannon fodder in a war that, like all wars, would only ever benefit those at the top.

Ernst shared some news from back in Germany for those who didn't have a radio and led the crowd in several more songs and chants before the meeting came to a close. The men's eyes shone brighter than when they came, they stood straighter, reclaiming their tattered pride and wounded manhood. I'd seen preachers work the same magic on their faithful, whipping them into ecstasy, providing emotional release. A hand job for the ego, like twenty minutes with a two-bit whore.

While Ernst talked, someone had put out a tray of cookies on a small table at the back. The men talked among themselves, some in English but most in the Dutchy dialect, a bastardized low German. I tried to listen without looking interested as I munched on a cookie.

"—a better world, without the bosses."

"—get what's coming to them, the greedy bastards."

"—finally be free of the bankers and the landowners."

I had not been immortal for long, but one thing had already become clear—I was doomed to see the same events play out generation after generation since we humans did not learn from our mistakes.

These men didn't really want much—enough pay to keep a roof over their heads, provide food and clothing for their families, have a bit extra to see a show once in a while, buy a beer, or go to the circus. To feel secure. And yet, by cutting wages to enrich themselves, the owners of the mines and the railroads set the workers on edge, made them fear for their future. I knew what violence a man might do to protect those he loved. The men who died with me on that riverbank in Homestead had only wanted to take care of their families, driven to extremes by the remorseless greed of the mill owners.

Yet here we were, fifty years after the Reading Massacre, almost thirty years after the Homestead Strike, with the same tragedy about to play out.

Except that we had not raised monsters from the deep. I doubted the ability of men like Hans and Jakob and Ernst to control such creatures. God help us all because monsters—men or creatures—did not heed orders once their bloodlust had awakened.

"So what did you think, Joe?" Hans asked, coming up and offering me another cookie. I took it, although I did not want anything he touched.

"Very interesting," I replied. "Your leader is a good speaker."

Hans beamed. "He helps us all be proud of who we are and of our heritage. He has a gift."

I'd seen the same kind of "gift" from con men and soothsayers, so I just grunted in response. "I admit, I'm curious about these 'forces from the deep.'"

"It's all psychology," Hans assured me, tapping two fingers to his temple. "Symbolism. Bringing out our inner strength from where it's been hidden. Bringing the working men out of the shadows and into the light. You didn't think he meant real creatures, did you?" He laughed, and I hurried to assure him that I didn't.

I felt quite certain real monsters were exactly what Ernest had in mind.

"Will we see you at the next meeting?" Jakob asked as he joined us and slapped me on the back. "There's much to be done. And we always have cookies."

"I don't always have evenings off," I said. "It depends on when they need me at my job."

"Well, you're welcome whenever you can make it," Hans said. "Just see us at the rooming house, and we'll let you know when. We vary the times, so the cops don't get wise."

Hans and Jakob bid me good night. I turned to go, but as I neared the door, another voice stopped me in my tracks.

"I saw you on the train."

I pivoted to face the speaker. Ernst regarded me warily. "Sorry, don't remember," I lied.

"What are you?"

I kept a frozen smile in place. "German." I knew that wasn't what he meant, but I intended to make him work for any information he wanted.

"You have an aura about you."

"I'm tall, and that makes it hard to miss me," I replied, pretending I didn't understand.

He tilted his head, considering. His talk about "auras" made me suspect he was either a psychic or a witch. Either one could spell trouble.

"I'm glad you could join us tonight," Ernst replied. "Stay in touch. Hans and Jakob said they knew you from the rooming house, so we'll have no trouble finding you." His tight smile showed teeth, like a predator. *Message delivered.*

"I'm not hard to find. I turn up like a bad penny," I replied, holding eye contact just a bit too long, sending a message of my own. "Especially when something catches my interest."

"I understand you're new in town. Do be careful. The streets can be dangerous for outsiders."

"I'll keep that in mind," I assured him, beginning to feel as if we were talking in code.

With a final sweep of his gaze, Ernst silently dismissed me, and I headed toward the rail station. I didn't hurry, but I also had no desire to linger. Ernst's comments made me feel distinctly unwelcome, and I felt watched although I did not see anyone nearby. I hoped that his suspicions wouldn't cause Mrs. Kemmner any trouble, with Hans and Jakob knowing where I had a room. I wouldn't stand for that.

Then again, Ernst could have all the witchy suspicions he wanted, but if he knew my real purpose, he'd make a move. When I made it to the incline railroad without incident, and the car started down the hill, I breathed a sigh of relief.

I was alone in the car, with the lights of Reading stretched out beneath me. With the hotels all closed, the only going concern near the incline was the sanitarium, but I supposed that workers and visitors depended on the incline to come and go.

The trip gave me a few minutes to digest what I'd seen and heard. Were Jakob and Hans earnest fools, or willing collaborators? They wouldn't be the first to be drawn into a dark scheme, willing to disbelieve the horrors for the potential greater good. At the same time, I knew that some men would betray everyone to save their own skin.

I felt certain of one thing—the "forces from the deep" were not symbols. The monsters were coming, and we needed to stop them.

The car jolted and picked up speed. The chain that drew the cabin up the hill had made a steady slow *clunk-clunk-clunk* before, but now it raced like my pulse, as the valley rushed up to meet the car far too quickly.

Ernst had either decided to send me a message or just get rid of me. Perhaps he sensed something "off" about me and chose to eliminate the threat instead of bothering to figure me out.

I had other plans. I called on Krukis and felt his magic sweep over me. Wrenching the door open, I leaned out and grabbed onto the rail beneath the car, holding on with all my god-touched might. The chain creaked and protested, steel grinding upon steel. It slowed the descent enough for me to gauge the distance to the ground before I jumped, landing heavily with a thud that echoed.

The empty car shot down the mountainside and splintered against the lower landing platform.

If I had wondered about Ernst's intentions, I had no doubts now. He'd be disappointed when he looked for my body in the wreckage. On the other hand, when I saw him again—and I'd make sure that I did—we'd have a reckoning he wouldn't forget.

ON SATURDAY, I went early to the speakeasy to unload barrels in preparation for the weekend crowd, finishing the job from the night before. I had begged off playing bouncer, so I could drive West and Sarah to their fancy gathering but promised that I would help handle rowdy patrons on Saturday night. That appeased him but left me chafing at when I might get a look at the mines.

When I came back to the rooming house, Mrs. Kemmner told me I had a visitor. To my surprise, Dr. Ziegler waited nervously in the parlor.

"I had a vision," he blurted, barely waiting until we'd greeted each other. "I saw creatures in the shadows, hideous gray things that had the bodies of men but heads like squid, with tentacles and a sucking maw." Interesting that he had come to me to share his premonition. I wondered again just how much he guessed from seeing me as god-touched.

"Please tell me what this means," he begged. "I have never seen the like. It troubles me, and my books have little to say."

I drew him to the corner, where we would be less likely to be over-heard. "There is a plot afoot to bring something old and evil from deep in the mines. I haven't completely figured it out, but I should know more tomorrow. I came here to stop that plot, and I intend to do so."

The doc drew himself to his full height and squared his shoulders. "I will come with you."

"I'm not sure—"

"No, but I am," he said, in a tone that meant the matter was settled. "There is an old mine beneath the city. My grandfather took me down into it many times when I was young. I know the way, and I can lead you. If there is to be some horror from below, it would make sense to summon it here, in an abandoned mine rather than in one that's working, where there would be more people to see."

He didn't have to say out loud what we both understood. Bringing a monster to the surface in the middle of a city would provide it with more food than at a distant mine. It would feast on the citizens of Reading, and then move on to do the bidding of its masters.

"Alright," I said. "As long as you know it will be dangerous."

He favored me with a tired smile. "I know how to handle a gun. Sometimes, the best way to be a healer is to prevent the injuries from happening." He reached beneath his jacket and withdrew a thin copy of *The Long Lost Friend*.

"This is for you. Carry it with you. It protects those who bear it. You have the *himmelsbrief* I gave you?"

I patted my coat. "Yes. It's an amazing document. I've seen some of its power already."

He nodded. "Oh, yes. I have been looking for answers in my books since we talked. I have searched the *Sixth and Seventh Books of Moses*, powerful spell books, for ways to control the spirits of the earth. I believe we can bind them."

"I have some ideas of my own on how to keep them where they are," I told him. "I'll be happy to have your help."

"You're not going to leave me out of your plans, are you?"

We looked up to see Mrs. Kemmner in the doorway. I glanced around, alarmed, afraid that Hans and Jakob might have heard us as well.

She shook her head as if she guessed my thoughts. "They aren't here. If I help you, maybe those two will leave. I do not like them." She looked at me. "You, I like."

"I'm not sure—" I started. She cut me off with a withering look.

"I lost my Wilfred in those mines," she told me. "Because the men who run them take no heed of the dangers and don't care who lives and who dies. I lost my son to a different kind of monster, human monsters. I don't wish to see those kinds of men become more powerful than they already are." She gave me a crafty smile.

"My nephew runs the Eighth Street Gang," she said. "He's promised to send a few of his boys to watch this house, and Dr. Ziegler's. We won't have any trouble. And if you need a distraction, he will be willing to oblige. He is always looking for a reason to raise a little hell."

"Raising hell" might be exactly the term for what the Free Society and its followers had in mind. I figured we could use all the help we could get.

"Thank you," I told her. "I don't have a plan yet, but I should get some important details tonight." I looked to Ziegler. "I'll come by in the morning, and we can make arrangements."

He nodded. "In the meantime, I will make some plans of my own," he promised. "I'll gather the supplies we'll need and be ready when you give the word."

Mrs. Kemmner headed back to the kitchen, and Ziegler saw himself out as if we had not just been plotting to contain hell spawn raised by *hexerei*. Like this was all in a day's work.

Maybe that was the insight to take from immortality, how these fragile, scarred mortals never failed to amaze with their courage, their defiance, their will to survive. That was a lesson the gods forgot at their peril.

5

T his collar is cutting off my air. I can't breathe."

Sarah McAllen Harringworth clucked her tongue and adjusted my uniform coat to her liking. "I think you look perfect. What do you think, Jack?" She turned toward West, who smirked.

"He looks as good as possible. After all, it's Joe."

"Such a comedian," I muttered under my breath, but I took the ribbing good-naturedly.

I had filled them in on everything that I learned from the Free Society meeting, and on the loose plan to seal the mines. I knew West would want to come with us, and we'd have a fight on our hands to keep Sarah from joining us as well.

Assuming I wasn't strangled by my own jacket.

"The more I hear from my sources, the more I'm sure the Reading Railroad's owners are part of this," Sarah said, taking pity on me and allowing me to remove the jacket until we were ready to leave. We were biding our time in the luxurious adjoining rooms Sarah and West had at the Hotel Berkshire downtown.

The swanky room's marble floors, satin upholstered furniture, and crystal goblets were a world away from my normal experience. The gap between it and my humble rooming house was far more than the dozen streets that separated them. I sat down and settled into the couch. I didn't mind enjoying how the other half lived when the opportunity presented itself.

"Everyone's on edge about labor disputes," West added, sipping a cup of coffee that he'd poured from a silver thermal urn sent up from the kitchen. "Especially with what the Bolsheviks have done in Russia. The anarchists seem determined to make their move, and the industrialists are holding on tighter than ever." He shrugged. "Which means a reasonable solution is probably unlikely."

"I understand what the Free Society is selling to the working men," I chimed in, trying to hold my china cup in large hands not meant for fragile porcelain. "But where's the appeal to the owners of the mines and the mills and the railroads?"

"A good con artist sells the mark his own fantasies," West replied, perching on the corner of a marble-topped desk. "If the miners and workers want to see their bosses laid low, then the bosses want a never-ending supply of drones who will work until they drop, not demand wage raises, and never rebel."

"And since the con artist is the only one who wins, we've got to consider what Hanussen wants," Sarah added, stirring a dollop of whiskey into her coffee from a silver hip flask. "And what he'll repackage to sell back to the palookas he's fleeced."

"Free labor and cheap energy," West replied. "Odds are Hanussen will charge a small fortune for 'access,' then skip out with the money. And you were right, Joe. The ideas were all there in that Lovecraft book I read. A new power source with mystical origins called '*vril*,' and a legion of monsters from the depths, the '*Vril-ya*.' Catnip to the men with the power and purse strings."

"Do you think Hanussen is somehow manipulating the Free Society as well as courting the members of The Order? Playing both ends against the middle?" I asked, wondering why people bothered with cups that barely held a thimbleful of liquid.

"I think it's possible," West replied. "But what's keeping them from unveiling the whole thing?"

"Maybe they were waiting for their *armanenschaft*," I said. "Their high priest, to summon the *Vril-ya*. Hanussen."

"The bigwigs at Reading Railroad have to be drooling at the prospect," Sarah added. She sat opposite me on the couch, with her legs drawn up beneath her. Sarah looked svelte and classy in a black, slit-to-the-hip sheath that covered daring wide-legged pants. Others would see her outfit as a fashion statement. West and I knew it served for her to climb to the bell tower and retrieve the prophecy. Or make a quick getaway.

"The railroad is losing money. Several of the executives are in debt. The coal and iron mines are even worse. Most likely, it's general incompetence coupled with the very high operating costs of three large businesses," Sarah went on.

Anyone who mistook her for just another pretty face was sorely mistaken. While she had sold the coal company she inherited from her late husband for a handsome profit, she understood its inner workings and balance sheet as well or better than most of the executives. The only daughter of James "Barron" McAllen had been raised from birth to play a man's game and win.

"So the idea of free labor and free, unlimited energy would have been a siren call to them at any time," she went on, "but now? They're likely to ask even fewer questions than usual. Investors are wary. There's talk that the Market may not be solid. Those executives will pounce on an opportunity that would give them the advantage to weather a bad economy."

"So who ultimately wins?" I asked, carefully setting my fragile cup aside before I broke it. "Who's pulling Hanussen's strings? He doesn't seem likely to be the mastermind."

West chewed his lip, a sure tell that he knew more than he was supposed to say. "There are troubling voices rising in Germany, angry young men who have gained a following. Hanussen's known to have admirers among them."

"America spoiled the plans of the Kaiser, coming in on the Great War at the end. If monsters from the deep were unleashed in America, it might keep us too busy to intervene the next time someone in Europe got ambitious," I suggested.

West shot me a sharp glance, telling me without saying a word that I'd cut to the chase.

"Good thing we're on the job," Sarah replied with a grin. "Let's go climb a bell tower."

I don't know where Sarah got the cherry-red Duesenberg Model J when I knew for a fact she and West came into Reading by private Pullman car. No doubt, her infinite network of friends came into play, from boarding school, university, country clubs, and family by blood and marriage. I'm good behind the wheel, but driving a car that cost far more than I could have earned in my entire mortal life made me nervous. Fortunately, to Sarah, it was just a car.

I knew the plan. I'd pull up at the front of the Pagoda so Sarah and West could make a high-profile entrance. The invitation-only gathering wouldn't be covered by the press or photographers, but Sarah knew the value of making a memorable impression. People would remember where they were, so they would be less likely to recall later where they weren't.

After I dropped them off, I took the car around back and parked to make a quick getaway. I hoped that wouldn't be necessary, but I didn't trust our luck to last. Once I stashed the car, I'd made my way in through the servants' entrance and unlock as many of the doors to the bell tower as possible.

Sarah drew the short straw of going up to the top of the building to examine the prophetic inscription on the bell since the space was too tight for the likes of West or me. Fortunately, the bell tower was accessible from inside the building. Unfortunately, Sarah had no plausible reason to be there if she were discovered.

A burly guard stood watch over the back door. I knocked him out as gently as I could and dragged his body into the shadows. It didn't take me long to pick the lock.

The dark entranceway was deserted, so I headed for the door to the stairs. It, too, was locked, and I felt tempted to just rip the door from the frame, but that would be noisy. With a sigh, I made quick work of the lock and headed up the first flight of steps.

At the top, I paused to listen and heard footsteps on the other side of yet another locked door. Someone must have heard me because two bullets ripped through the wood right where I'd been standing only seconds before.

I pulled my gun and yanked the door open, tearing it loose from its hinges, and seized the moment of surprise to fire on the guard, who died with a look of utter shock on his face. The noise drew another goon watching from the upper level, who tried to shoot down the stairwell at me. He hit the plaster wall. I didn't miss, and his body came tumbling down the steps, leaving a bloody trail.

I dragged the two corpses away from the stairs and took a moment to pat them down. Where one man's sleeve rode up, I saw the *wolfsangel* tattoo. A death's head mark on the other goon's neck showed beneath his collar.

That confirmed that the bruisers weren't the usual Pagoda security. The bell itself weighed hundreds of pounds, so no one was likely to be worried about it being stolen. Whatever the inscription was on the bell, it had to be important if Hanussen was going to this much effort to keep it a secret. That told me that the prophecy might reveal a weak point we could use to our advantage.

By the time Sarah had made it through the social gauntlet and excused herself to powder her nose, I was at the base of the stairs, waiting for her.

"All clear?" she asked when she slipped through the door.

"Smooth sailing, all the way to the top," I assured her. "Don't mind the mess." I handed her the hard wax and special paper she'd need to do a rubbing of the bell's mysterious inscription. She headed up the steps, and I leaned back against the door, effectively blocking it should anyone else decide to go exploring.

Sooner than I expected, Sarah hurried down, handing off the wax and paper. "I hope it's readable. I pressed as hard as I dared. Didn't want to make it ring by accident and draw attention." She dragged the soles of her high-heeled shoes across the floor a few times to clean away any traces of blood.

"Nice work," she said with a wink. "Although the housekeeper probably won't approve."

I tucked the items back into the interior pocket of my coat and checked the corridor before waving her through. Once Sarah headed back to the big party, I wound back through the service hallways until I found a quiet place to the right of the stage. If I positioned myself carefully, I could see through the crack between the two swinging doors, while not drawing attention to myself. The other drivers would either wait in their cars or huddle around the employee doors having a smoke and sharing a flask. I knew West and Sarah would report what happened, but I felt the need to see for myself.

I startled when I spotted the night's speaker. He was the other man on the train, the well-dressed one who kept looking at me, the one I suspected of being a witch. A sinking feeling hit my gut. I wished for a way to signal to West and Sarah, but I couldn't think of anything that wouldn't make it even more likely we'd be caught. I kept my gun in hand and waited for the shit to hit the fan.

Hanussen cut a striking figure in his tuxedo. Thick dark hair and heavy black eyebrows gave him a dramatic appearance, as I remembered from the train. Not a handsome man, but memorable, less because of his features than for his manner. Whatever else he might be, for good or ill, Hanussen was a consummate performer. He didn't overplay his part, like a cut-rate vaudevillian, or bore the crowd with a lecture.

Hanussen's showmanship transfixed the room as he spoke of ancient mysteries, translated ciphers, and arcane lore. His dark eyes gleamed with passion, and perhaps more, as I recalled his reputation as a mesmerist. I could see the audience leaning forward to catch every word, following his movements with rapt attention.

From where I stood, I couldn't tell where West and Sarah were in the crowd, although I knew they'd be toward the back, on an end, where they could make a quick getaway if things went south. Whatever cover story they'd used had bought them entry among Reading's elite. Men in tuxedos and women in gowns filled the audience. Expensive jewelry gleamed beneath the electric chandelier, one of the modern luxuries the Pagoda boasted of as a promise of things to come with the planned hotel expansion.

"…gateway to hidden knowledge, the wisdom of the ancients," Hanussen said. He sounded educated and cultured, which would appeal to his audience, and this being Reading, they would not be put off by his German accent.

"The wonders of King Tutankhamen's tomb are nothing compared to what we will learn when we engage the secrets of the Elders. In my visions, they have shown me glimpses so that I may share those insights with you. You are worthy of being among the first to hear these truths, which have not been uttered lo these many millennia."

He had them eating out of the palm of his hand, shills willing to be fleeced, and as much as I despised Hanussen on principle, I had to admire his skill as a con man.

"Not everyone has the mental fortitude to appreciate this information," Hanussen continued. "It is not for the weak-minded or the weak of will. But for those who are superior, who do not shrink from what is difficult, who are foreordained to lead, the secrets I am about to share with you will be invaluable."

I'd expected parlor tricks from Hanussen, a bit of high-class mumbo jumbo—putting volunteers into trances, a bit of "mind reading" that depended on hidden advance research, a little sleight of hand.

But the longer I watched him stride back and forth across the dais, the more I felt a prickle of warning that he was more than just an excellent performer. My intuition, grown stronger after my deal with Krukis, told me that Hanussen had a bit of real magic, either of his own, or gifted by an entity who used him for its own purposes. I remembered Krukis's warning in my vision on the train and repressed a shiver.

"Think of the possibilities for unlimited energy," Hanussen urged his audience. "Energy to power factories and railroads, mills, and steamships, without worry about its cost or the need to transport the bulk of wood, coal, or oil. Imagine what you could achieve with a superior workforce that asks for nothing except purpose, that cannot comprehend insubordination, that lives only to serve."

"This is the future I have glimpsed, ladies and gentlemen. The future that is just now within our ability to grasp." Like a spider, Hanussen had woven a beautiful web, and now came the time to invite the fly to dinner.

"I have no doubts," he proclaimed. "And before I ask for your help, before I present the ways in which you might become involved in making this glorious future come true, I wish to offer you proof. Proof, so that, like me, you will also have no doubts."

The warning prickle grew stronger. Perhaps the magic that bound me to Krukis sensed Hanussen's ability, or maybe I'd just been fucked over enough times in my life to see it coming, but my gut clenched, and I knew we needed to leave.

But we couldn't, not yet, not until we saw what we came to see and heard what Hanussen planned to offer the elite of Reading in exchange for their souls.

Two black-clad stagehands rolled a table and chair out onto the dais. On the table's dark covering lay something, but from my angle, I couldn't see what. Those in the audience strained for a look, and Hanussen chuckled, promising he would reveal all very soon.

"I propose a demonstration! I will show you just a bit of the *Vril* power that lies, untapped, beneath us. Power that cannot be withdrawn with shovels and picks, or with machines and steam. No, this power is called forth by mind and will, and only those suitable to the task—like you—can wield it."

Hanussen walked around the small table and sat, managing through the gracefulness of his movement and the fluttering of his hands to keep every eye on him, riveted. He lifted the artifact on the table, and I realized it was a *sonnenrad*, the lightning-spoked wheel-within-a-wheel. The relic he held looked to be about a foot wide, large enough for him to see the crowd over it, but big enough for them to clearly see it as well.

"I present the Black Sun, one of the most potent ancient symbols of the *Vril-ya*, the People of the Power," he said, voice dropping as if he conveyed information of the gravest importance.

"This rare artifact amplifies my natural mesmerism, my psychic talent, so that I can channel the ancient energy, to settle any doubts you may have."

He slowly scanned the audience. "I do not want you to harbor any doubts, any concerns, that what I am sharing with you is real. I give to you my whole truth, holding nothing back."

Hanussen gripped the Black Sun with one hand on each side. It began to glow from within, emphasizing the double *wolfsangel* bolts that formed the dark rays. A hush fell over the audience, and Hanussen's baritone voice rose in a chant, in a language that did not sound like anything spoken on this world.

I figured it was time to call in the big guns. *Krukis, I call on you. Lend me your strength and spirit so that I can protect and defend. Make me your instrument!*

I felt the shift, as Krukis's power filled me. My skin warmed, as the old god's magic made it into thin, flexible metal, and my bones took on the strength of steel. I could pull with the power of a mule team and run with the speed of a racehorse. Enhanced by an extra touch of the divine, my senses sharpened, as did my intuition.

I knew we were all in terrible danger.

Light flared from the relic Hanussen clutched. It did not burst forth toward the audience, like a sunbeam. Instead, a deep violet glow suffused the black sun, and then outlined the mesmerist in its otherworldly radiance. Hanussen raised his head, and even where I stood, I could make out that same purple light shining from his eyes. The audience gasped, but I caught my breath as my heart pounded.

Hanussen channeled Veles, the god of the underworld. He went by many names, Chernabog, Morok, the Horned God. All of them spelled trouble.

Why is Veles screwing around with a guy like Hanussen? I didn't doubt that it was borrowed power from Veles and not the *Vril* that gave Hanussen his fancy glow. But as soon as the question formed in my mind, so did the answer.

Veles is the god of the underworld. Death and destruction make him more powerful. War, riots, marauding monsters, all increase the death toll. If Hanussen is raising money to help a new angry power rise in Germany, a few parlor tricks would be nothing compared to the deaths Veles could reap.

An assistant brought out an electric lamp, making it clear that the fixture was not plugged in. Hanussen stretched out his hand, purple light arced, and the lamp glowed brightly. The crowd clapped and cheered.

Two more assistants brought out a small electric motor on a board, also unplugged. They set it on the table in front of Hanussen, who repeated his parlor trick. The purple glow surrounded the entire motor, which roared to life as if by "magic."

This time, the crowd surged to its feet, applauding Hanussen as if he were an inventor and not just a conduit. He'd have their cash and be safely back in Germany before they realized how easily they'd been bilked.

The "free energy" Hanussen promised was a pipe dream, but the monsters that The Order and the Free Society wanted to raise were real. West and Sarah and I needed to close down this deadly game before it turned bloody.

The mesmerist turned in his seat so that his eyes seemed to see right through the doors that hid me. "We have a traitor in our midst! One who could seek to prevent our victory. He hides there! Seize him!" Hanussen cried out, pointing right at my hiding place.

In that split second, I had a choice to fight an ancient god in a room full of breakable mortals, or run and hope the plans we'd made would bottle up the creatures before Hanussen could complete his scheme.

Sarah screamed a bloodcurdling shriek, which I was sure was intended for distraction. A shot fired, and its bullet hit the chandelier, plunging the room into darkness.

I ran.

Before my pursuers could even storm the stage, I was out of the service hallway and past the kitchen. I didn't know where Sarah and West were, and I wasn't about to leave them as hostages to the Horned God, but I knew we would all do our damnedest to get to the car, so that's where I headed.

Once I'd cleared the doorway, I hauled a heavy wagon in front of the door, blocking it from opening. That would hold, even if several men at once tried to force the door open. But it only provided a delay, since the mob would quickly reverse course and come through the front doors, then around the side.

I pulled my handgun and sprinted toward the Duesenberg, not surprised that I had beaten my friends to the mark. Voices and foot-steps carried on the night air as pursuers came around on the Pagoda's right-hand side, and I drove them back with shots meant to warn, not wound.

Sounds from the other direction made me fear that I'd been flanked.

Instead, more gunfire helped to send the mesmerized mob scrambling away from the road, and I knew West and Sarah had caught up.

"Get in!" Sarah shouted, already behind the wheel of the Duesenberg. West and I both squeezed off warning shots to force the mob back, and for good measure, I hit a front tire on each of the two closest vehicles to slow down pursuit.

We dove into the back seat, nearly crashing into each other, as Sarah took off with a squeal of tires.

"Hang on!" she yelled, and I did, because I had ridden with her before and knew that she could challenge any Grand Prix driver for skill and daring.

I braced myself but managed to twist enough to look out the back, expecting gunshots to shatter the glass or the headlights of pursuers. I saw only darkness.

"Whatever spell Hanussen put on them, I don't think the hoi polloi of Reading are going to chase us down the mountain," West observed, flinging out a leg and an arm to keep himself from being tossed around as Sarah slalomed the Duesenberg down the curves of Duryea Drive.

I fought the urge to close my eyes as Sarah took the bend wide, hoping we would not plow into oncoming traffic. I never doubted Sarah's grit, or her ability behind the wheel, although at this moment, I had second thoughts about her sanity. On the way up the mountain, I had noted the sheer drop along one side, and the guard rails that seemed unlikely to restrain a car from plunging into the forest.

"Veles," I said, holding tight to keep from being thrown against West as we took another curve at breakneck speed. "Hanussen channeled Veles. The Horned God. God of the underworld. Sworn enemy of Krukis."

West raised an eyebrow in surprise. "That's how he sensed you."

I nodded. "I felt Veles's presence right before everything went to hell. Or, rather, Krukis did."

West cleared his throat. "Is he…still with you?"

"No. He left me when the car doors slammed." Bulletproof skin would have been a big help had we needed to stand and fight, but I knew from experience that Krukis only lent me his magic when what I needed surpassed what I could do for myself. Apparently, the heavy steel body of the Duesenberg was shield enough.

"Good. Because I wouldn't know what to say to a god," West replied. "I'd have to be polite."

"Perish the thought."

Sarah slowed as we reached the foot of the mountain. By the time we pulled out onto the main road, we matched the speed of the vehicles around us. Still, a bright red Model J wasn't exactly designed for blending in, and I didn't know whether any of the mob at the Pagoda had phoned accomplices in the city to hunt for us.

"Did the other guests know who you were?" I asked West. I felt certain he'd given an alias, but I wasn't sure whether Sarah was acquainted with any of the attendees.

He shook his head. "No. Our names were as phony as our interest in underwriting Hanussen's crazy scheme. And we registered under yet another set of names at the hotel."

West and I might butt heads now and again, but he's good at what he does.

I glanced out the window and realized Sarah had taken us downtown. Before I had my bearings, she gunned the engine, and we slewed into a darkened parking lot in the shadow of Pomeroy's Department Store.

"I'll have someone get the car tomorrow," Sarah said, switching off the ignition and jumping out as if it had all been a planned romp. "We can leg it to the Hotel Berkshire from here—it's only a few blocks."

West and I exchanged a glance, then shrugged, neither of us able to fault Sarah's impeccable plan.

"Don't dally—we have a visitor waiting for us," Sarah admonished, striding off in her black opera cloak like a creature of the night. How she managed to do that in heels, I'd never know, but I'd seen her turn stilettos into weapons on more than one occasion, so I had no intention of arguing.

To my relief, we reached the well-appointed lobby without incident. Neither hell spawn nor bewitched scions of industry tried to stop us. The doorman nodded to Sarah as she swept by, gave a deferential nod to West, and eyed me like I might make off with the silverware. I held my head high and followed Sarah as if I belonged in such a swanky joint.

If the elevator operator wondered why West and Sarah had their driver accompany them upstairs, he was too well-trained to ask. I couldn't wait to get out of the wool uniform and back into my own clothing. We reached our floor, and West poked his head out to assure the way was clear, then motioned for Sarah and me to follow. I didn't want to guess what sort of clandestine affair the elevator operator might imagine, but it would be a less fantastic tale than the truth.

Sarah opened the door to her room, while West and I entered into his adjacent room, for propriety's sake. We quickly unbolted the connecting odor and joined Sarah and a slightly built, dark-haired stranger in her suite.

"This is Mrs. Yoshida," Sarah said. "And these are my colleagues, Mr. West and Mr. Mack." If Sarah introduced us by our real names, I figured Mrs. Yoshida could be trusted.

She and our visitor took seats on the sofa in the sitting area, while West and I each appropriated an armchair. The scale of the graceful furnishings felt all wrong for my bulk, but I did my best to wedge my large frame into the seat and hoped it wouldn't snap beneath my weight.

"Mrs. Yoshida is well-known for her bonsai trees and her work with the Reading Garden Society," Sarah explained. "She knew my mother because of their shared interest in saving rare varieties of flowers, and we've kept in touch over the years."

Sarah's personal network of connections was vast and varied, ranging from mobsters to millionaires. More than once, her social circle had saved our asses, so I wasn't about to complain.

"It is very good to see you," Mrs. Yoshida said, and Sarah clasped the woman's thin-boned hand between both of her own.

"Thank you for meeting us on short notice," Sarah replied. "I trust they took good care of you while you waited for us?"

Mrs. Yoshida smiled and patted Sarah's hand. "Oh, yes. They brought me all the tea and cakes I wanted and tried to feed me dinner. I am very happy."

Sarah gave me a look, and I pulled the parchment with the rubbing of the bell's inscription from its safe place inside the jacket. Sarah passed it to her visitor.

"I'm hoping you can translate this," she said. "I apologize for the poor copy, but we were rather in a hurry."

Mrs. Yoshida lifted the reading glasses that hung from a gold chain around her neck and shifted to get better light. She studied the paper, then frowned.

"Where did you get this?"

"It's the inscription on the bell in the tower of the Pagoda," Sarah replied. "We think it may have something to do with a...situation we're trying to resolve."

Mrs. Yoshida sighed and shook her head, but with a fond expression. "Always the sleuth, like in those Christie books you read."

If Agatha Christie had ever tackled Lovecraft's Cthulhu, it was news to me, but I remained silent.

"Can you read it?" Sarah leaned forward, eyes bright with excitement.

"I will do my best," her guest replied. She murmured under her breath in Japanese as she made out the characters. After several moments, she looked up.

"It's a very odd inscription. Not exactly a poem. *'Down in the valley the gong resounds low and deep...with the moon on high it sounds clearly in the heavens...with the flowers into the land of the dead.'*"

I felt a shiver go down my spine. The words sounded more like prophecy than poetry, and eerily applicable to our current situation.

"Yes, I think that sounds exactly right," Sarah replied. "Thank you so much. I'm sorry to have brought you out from your home for this."

"That's quite all right," Mrs. Yoshida assured her, handing back the parchment. "I can use a bit of excitement from time to time. Keeps me young."

West and I retired to his room while the ladies chatted for a bit and changed back to normal clothing. He poured us both a slug of scotch from a decanter on a sideboard and raised his glass in a toast.

"To getting out in one piece," he said, and I lifted my glass in salute.

Moments later, we heard Sarah and her guest leave their room; I figured Sarah intended to see Mrs. Yoshida safely to a cab. Before long, she returned and came through the unlocked connecting door. West pressed a glass of scotch into her hand.

"I thought we made a hell of a team tonight," Sarah announced, toasting us. "This was so much fun; I can't wait to see how the next part goes!"

6

Sarah's admirable enthusiasm aside, I felt like tonight had upped the stakes.

"Veles knows I'm here—and that Krukis knows what's afoot," I said, peeling off my jacket. I withdrew the parchment, the *himmelsbrief*, and the copy of *The Long Lost Friend*, and put them with my coat, not wanting to chance leaving them behind. "That's going to force his plans. I think we need to go to the mines tonight."

"I agree," West said.

"And we're coming with you." Sarah had a defiant look I knew from past experience made it futile to argue. I glanced at West, who shrugged.

"We need different clothing," I pointed out.

"Not a problem. We packed for every possibility," Sarah assured me. I didn't doubt her.

"What do you make of the prophecy?" West asked. "And how does Veles play a part in this?"

I leaned against the wall, feeling more confident in it holding my weight than I did any of the furnishings. "Veles likes conflict," I explained, "conflict kills people, he gains more souls in his realm. So he'd be willing to nudge guys like Hans and Jakob and the Free Society to raise the *Vril-ya* from the depths because when blood runs in the streets, he wins."

"Lovely," Sarah remarked drily.

"With Hanussen, I've got to figure that Veles has some purpose in wanting his ideas to gain traction—or maybe, it's the money he raises here that will set something in motion back in Germany."

"Why didn't he come after us at the Pagoda?" West questioned, swirling his scotch.

"Veles is an instigator, not a hands-on kind of god. Not like Krukis. Hanussen isn't Veles's champion. He's just the schmuck Veles is manipulating to get what he wants," I replied. "The Free Society sees him as their high priest, but I doubt Hanussen is courting the rabble and the swells at the same time. I don't think he'll want to be in town when the *Vril-ya* rise. So I'm betting he isn't part of their scheme and that Hans, Ernst, and Jakob thought it up all on their own."

"Do you think Veles will try to stop us?" Sarah asked, sounding remarkably cool about going up against a god.

"I get the impression that Veles is constantly running around lighting fires, figuring that a couple of them will blow up into something big, but not caring which ones. We all go to him in the end." Or at least, everyone who wasn't immortal would. I had already seen far too many friends age and die. I thought vengeance would balance my grief, but it never did.

"I need to go rouse Dr. Ziegler. He's our guide. If his abilities are as good as I think they are, he's probably already waiting at the rooming house," I told them. "And we're going to need some dynamite."

West grinned. "Never travel without it. We've also got extra guns and ammunition. The benefits of traveling by private rail car."

"Then let's get changed. We've got a busy night ahead of us."

I FELT BETTER JUST WEARING my own clothes again. I carefully tucked away the items I didn't dare lose and slipped my Colt into my waistband. West changed into a dark shirt, black work pants, sturdy boots, and a heavy canvas coat, looking more like a second-story man than a secret agent. Sarah joined us, dressed in boots, practical pants, a dark shirt, and a short black wool coat. Her hair was pulled up in a sensible knot beneath a close-fitting knit cap, and all traces of makeup were gone, along with her jewelry. She looked like a spy. I probably just looked like a common ruffian.

"Ready?" West had already distributed some of the useful goodies he'd brought, which we stashed in the small rucksacks we all wore. Matches, candles, helmets, miners' lanterns, fuses, and explosives, plus other handy items.

"It's only a few blocks. We can walk. The fewer people who see us, the fewer who can remember us," I said as we slipped down the back steps of the hotel and out the delivery door into the alley.

When we reached the rooming house, we came around to the kitchen side, slipping from a dark alley through the gate. I tapped on the window to get Mrs. Kemmner's attention. She hurried to the door.

"Hans and Jakob aren't here. They never came back, although their things are still in their rooms," she told me. I beckoned for Sarah and West to join me. She gave them the once-over, locked eyes with Sarah and seemed to approve because she gave a no-nonsense nod.

"Dr. Ziegler has been fretting in the parlor for at least an hour. I haven't been able to get him to stop pacing," she told me, leading us toward the front of the house. She offered us food, but we declined. I didn't know about the others, but my stomach was too tight with worry about the night's work to be able to keep anything down.

Ziegler brightened a bit when he saw us, as much as his hound dog countenance could. "Joe, I was worried. I have seen things that must not come to be." He looked past me at Sarah and West, uncertain.

"You can trust them. This is Sarah and Jack."

I noticed that Ziegler was dressed differently than I had seen him before. Gone was his jacket, starched shirt with stiff collar, and dress shoes. His worn and stained pair of miner's overalls with a work shirt, sturdy woolen jacket, and boots meant he was dressed for action. I wondered what amulets or relics he might have hidden about his person and saw that he had the good sense to bring both a helmet and a Colt 1911 like my own.

"We need to get into the mines—the old portion, under the city," I told him. We gave him a bare-bones recap about the allure of *Vril* power and the *Vril-ya* race of "servants," and I could see that he was quick to understand where it would all go terribly wrong.

"The section beneath the city is the oldest and deepest of all the shaft mines in the area," Ziegler told us. "There are miles of closed and abandoned tunnels. But the original part of the mine is below Eckert Avenue. We can get there through the mechanical room for the fountain in Penn's Commons."

West did a slow blink, absorbing that fact. "Through the mechanical room?"

"It goes down pretty far to connect to the water mains," Ziegler replied with a shrug. "Some of the brewery tunnels connect, and the oldest sewer and stormwater lines run through spaces that were originally mining tunnels."

"So if they summon the *Vril-ya* from the deepest point, it has a ready-made subway to go pretty much everywhere in the city?" I said, horrified.

Ziegler nodded, managing to look more glum than usual. "Yes. If these creatures escape the deep pit, we won't be able to bottle them up again."

"Once we're inside the old mine, under the fountain, where do we go?" I asked. The idea of wandering around a long-abandoned mine full of monsters didn't sound like a good idea to me.

Ziegler pulled out a large sheet of paper that had been folded many times.

"I found this map. It was made when the fountain and the sewer lines were run through the top level of the old mine. It's not a map of the entire mine, but it wouldn't be wise to try to go down into the depths—for a lot of reasons. Aside from any monsters, I wouldn't trust the steps or the lifts. But...there are two shafts that go down to the very heart of the mine," he added, looking up with eyes alight. "The sections above the cave-in that shuttered the mine originally."

I remembered the ghosts telling me how they had set off that blast intentionally to seal the monsters inside. Over the course of a century, the *Vril-ya* had worked their way loose. Maybe we could seal them up for another hundred years, if destroying them was not a possibility.

"One is the main elevator shaft that brought up the loads from each of the horizontal corridors. The other is the western air shaft. As far as I can tell, they both go nearly all the way to China." Ziegler went on, not appearing to notice that I'd taken a mental detour along the way.

I felt better realizing that we had an option to avoid rickety stairs and deathtrap elevators. "What's at the bottom?" I asked.

"The original mine," Ziegler replied. "They sank the shaft a little farther than they expected to dig. Then they worked their way up, digging out tunnels that ran perpendicular to the shaft. No one's had reason to be down there for a very long time. The mine closed after a cave-in when the city expanded, so it's been abandoned for around a hundred years."

"There are mines all through this area. What's special about this one, that the *Vril-ya* are here?" Sarah asked, leaning over the map.

"I fear it has to do with my vision about the 'black spot' on the mountain," Ziegler said. "Long before Reading became a city, the tribes and traders who passed through here spoke about a 'darkness' that haunted the mountain. Some said it was bad luck, or an ill omen, while others claimed they had seen creatures or heard screaming from inside the mountain."

"So someone decided to dig a mine," I muttered. "How could it go wrong?"

"The mine wasn't open long," Ziegler said. "This was before mining was a big business. Two men bought the land, hired the miners, and dug the shaft. It had bad luck from the beginning. Miners quit, saying it was haunted, or cursed. Men died or disappeared. Stories went around about there being 'something' down in the mine. The miners went on strike, the owners of the mine went bankrupt, there was an explosion, and then they sealed off the entrance. They sold it to the city. And here we are," he added with a shrug.

"That's very much the same story that I heard from the ghosts at the potter's field," I said and recounted what the three spirits had told me. "Proof that the creatures are real. If sealing the mine back then has kept them bottled up all this time, then we might be good for another hundred years if we can keep Hans and Jakob from blowing it wide open."

Mrs. Kemmner cleared her throat. "There's one other thing," she said. "Before they left, I heard Jakob talking about working some kind of ritual in Penn's Commons, over near the potter's field. They didn't say what it was supposed to do, but it didn't sound like the kind of thing Pastor Schmidt would have approved of."

I doubted very much that any man of the cloth would approve of the activities planned for tonight. "Do you know when?" I asked.

"After midnight," she reported. "That's all I heard."

It was already just past nine in the evening. I had no idea how long it would take us to deal with the problem in the mine. We'd deal with Jakob afterward—assuming we made it out in one piece.

"I, um, took it upon myself to meddle," Mrs. Kemmner said with a hint of a smile. "Spoke to my nephew, asked him to round up his boys and give anyone who showed up at the potter's field some trouble. That should slow Jakob down if nothing else."

"Bless you," I told the landlady, who blushed at the praise but tut-tutted about it being nothing. With the help of the Eighth Street Gang, we might be able to derail both rituals, stop the Free Society's mad plan, and save the world.

But first, we had to break into the fountain.

Ziegler said something in German to Mrs. Kemmner, and she nodded, patting her bosom beneath her apron. I picked up enough to know he had given her a *himmelsbrief* and a copy of *The Long Lost Friend* for protection, and that the landlady knew enough about hexes to work some spells to safeguard herself and the house.

We followed Ziegler through the back alleys, keeping to the shadows. The weather had turned cold, and a light rain fell. While it made walking unpleasant, the shift in the weather meant fewer people were about, making it easier to slip undetected toward our destination.

On the way, we passed Penn's Commons, and a missing piece clicked into place in my mind.

"As above, so below," I murmured.

"What?" West's head came up sharply.

"The potter's field in the park, it's right above the mines," I said. "Want to bet that whatever ritual Jakob and his Free Society pals are planning is a 'part two' for freeing the *Vril-ya* in the mines below?" If I'd had any doubts that it was urgent to deal with the matter tonight, this sealed the deal. Even without our misadventure at the Pagoda, tonight was meant to be the night.

"I believe you are right," Ziegler said. "Which is why I have the *Sixth and Seventh Books of Moses* with me. They have instructions on how to bind the spirits of the earth. Cover me while I work the incantation, and if Heaven wills it, we will prevail."

I wasn't counting on heaven to rescue us, but I placed what remained of my battered faith in Krukis and said a prayer to let him know I'd be calling on our arrangement again soon. He was a god, so maybe he already knew what I needed, but I figured it was best to cover all my bases. Trust didn't come easy to me.

We reached the nondescript maintenance building without incident, which just made me more nervous, since I figured our luck was due to run out at some point, and the longer it took, the worse it would be when it happened. If Jakob intended to preside over a dark rite at the pauper's cemetery, it didn't look like he or any of his cronies had arrived yet. I wondered if Hans and Ernst meant to summon the *Vril-ya* down in the mine. If so, we needed to be extra cautious, since I wasn't sure how much magic Ernst had.

The small, solid stone fountain building had been built at the turn of the century, and it reminded me of a mausoleum.

"Do you have a key?" I asked Ziegler. He shook his head.

"Oh, for heaven's sake," Sarah huffed, pushing to the front. Her lock picks made quick work of the old tumblers, and Ziegler raised an eyebrow but said nothing of her unorthodox skills.

Once inside, we looked around. The stone held damp, and despite my layers of clothing, I shivered. The main room held a metal desk piled with papers and a control panel for the fountain. The streamlined console couldn't possibly hold all of the actual equipment, just the wiring and relays for the controls. Which meant that the true workings of the fountain had to be below us.

"Do you think Hans and his Free Society buddies would have come this way?" I asked.

Ziegler shook his head. "Doubtful. There are other ways in, although they are farther from the old section. This route is not as well known."

"Why didn't someone brick up the connection years ago?" Sarah asked.

"The way I heard it, when the fountain was built, the engineers took advantage of some of the uppermost mine corridors to save on excavation costs," Ziegler said. "They ran water pipes through the old mine and brought them up to the basement of this mechanical house. But in case there was a problem beneath the fountain or with the pipes, they left the connection to the mine—just put it behind a locked door. Over time, people pretty much forgot it was there."

West had somehow obtained four electric miner's headlamps for us, and before we headed down the metal steps to the basement, we put them on and made sure they worked. To keep us from being beacons to give away our position, he had smeared a clear blue gel over the lights that dimmed the glow but also made it more difficult to see from a distance. The light bobbled as we walked, but it was safer than carrying an open flame into mines where the air could be questionable at the best of times.

"If the mines have been closed for a long time, how do we know the air is safe to breathe?" I asked. I'd heard stories of firedamp and other noxious gases that could easily explode, or suffocate a man in minutes.

"Because the old pipes ran through the upper levels, and workmen needed access, vents were installed to circulate the air," Ziegler said. "I checked—they're still in place, and most looked operational. They're just located in out-of-the-way places, so no one notices them."

West handed a thick piece of red chalk to Sarah. "Use this to mark our turns with an arrow pointing in the direction we're going. I'd hate to get lost down here."

The maintenance building had a basement and a sub-basement, and we clomped down the old iron circular staircase, going deeper below the park. The main valves with their big twist wheels filled the upper basement. Though the top floor appeared to still be in regular use, the dust down here suggested it had been a while since anyone had bothered with this area.

"Give me a hand," Ziegler said, eyeing an old set of metal shelving against one wall. West and I maneuvered it so that we could slip behind, where a metal door obviously hadn't been used in some time.

Sarah picked the lock like a pro, and we pushed the door open into darkness. The air smelled stale, but I could also pick up the scent of wet rock and damp dirt. Our headlamps barely put a dent in the darkness, and I tried not to think about being underground.

Ziegler led the way with his map. I followed, then Sarah, with West taking up the rear. In the distance, I heard water dripping.

Our lamps illuminated old iron pipes that extended into the darkness and connected to the mechanical room behind us. Other pipes appeared to be for sewage and water, and they led on past the pump room, down another darkened tunnel. From the cobwebs, I knew no one had been this way in a long time. If Hans and his buddies were going to make their move, they hadn't entered here.

"This way," Ziegler said, with the old map as his guide. We took a branching tunnel. Sarah dutifully marked the turn with a large chalk arrow. Becoming lost down here worried me more than whether Hans would be able to follow us.

We followed the tunnel for half an hour, according to the glowing hands on my wristwatch. Then, Ziegler came to an abrupt halt, and we dug in our heels to keep from crashing into him.

"It's blocked," he told us, and our headlamps revealed a tumble of rocks and dirt that filled most of the passageway. Perhaps, if there were no alternative, we could wriggle through, but I didn't like the idea of tempting the ceiling to collapse further, trapping us on the other side.

"Now what?" Sarah put her hands on her hips and turned in a circle, with a look of annoyance as if the tunnel had thwarted us on purpose.

"The top level was a large square," Ziegler replied, consulting his map. "We took the most direct route. We should be able to go around the long way and get to the shaft."

I really didn't like the idea of wandering around down here. Our lamps would only work for so long, and without them, we would be help-lessly lost. I wanted to get in, get done, and get out.

"Maybe we can find a guide." I remembered how the spirits of the Reading Railroad Massacre had shown themselves to me. We weren't far from the potter's field, where I'd found helpful ghosts before.

Ziegler met my gaze and nodded, understanding. I laid my hand over the pocket of my jacket that held the *himmelsbrief* and closed my eyes, concentrat-ing. I thought about what we needed to find—a safe path to the place where the *Vril-ya* rose from the deep places so we could destroy them. I pictured the consequences if the hell spawn were to be loosed on the city. I spoke a silent prayer to Krukis, and a plea to the restless ghosts of the miners to help us.

"Joe, I think they heard you," Sarah said, bumping my elbow.

I opened my eyes and saw the same three ghostly figures who had appeared to me in the park. Now, they stood just a few feet away. I could make out their features and their clothing, but they were insubstantial, like an image from a black-and-white movie.

"Thank you," I said, hoping they could hear me if I spoke aloud for the benefit of my companions. "We want to find where the monsters are, stop them, and then get out safely. Can you help us get around the blocked tunnel so we can blow up the main shaft?"

The three ghosts regarded us in silence, and I hoped they weren't angry about being roused once more from their slumber, even though it was for a good cause.

"Some bad men want to let the monsters out. We're trying to make sure that doesn't happen. But the tunnel is blocked. Please, show us how to get to the elevator shaft," I added. They'd been done wrong by the men who owned the mines and railroads, just like my friends and I had been betrayed by the steel barons and mill owners. I couldn't save them, but perhaps together, we could stop the bastards who had caused our deaths from claiming more victims.

The mine grew even colder than before, and I saw Sarah wrap her arms around herself. West stared at the ghosts, looking a bit poleaxed. Ziegler seemed to take it all in stride.

"Are there others in the mine tonight?" I asked. "Other living men?"

The ghost boys nodded. That meant the race was on, between us and Hans's Free Society, with the fate of the city—and more—hanging in the balance.

Dripping water and the crunch of rock beneath our boots filled the tunnels as we followed Ziegler's map and our ghostly guides. I wondered where Hans had found another entrance, and whether he and his cronies had unsealed the original mine mouth.

We went back the way we came and passed the machinery room doorway, then kept on going down another long, dark corridor. After a while, I realized that the air had grown colder, and a foul smell filled the air.

Despite what Ziegler's map showed about the upper level being a large square, in the dark, the reality was more confusing since little spurs extended frequently from the main corridor. I wondered how much light the miners had to work with, and how much they learned the navigate their underground world by feel. I was grateful for our ghostly guides, who moved through the tunnels confidently.

The tunnel widened. I wondered if we were coming up to what had originally been the mouth of the mine. My guess proved right when we turned the next corner and saw the remains of a flat road used for horses or mules to drag out the heavy wagons. The road ended abruptly in a wall of stone blocks, held solid by cement.

The air felt different here, fresher. If I squinted, I could see where a few of the uppermost blocks had been pushed out of the way. Far enough for a few thin men to wriggle through. Hans and his crew, no doubt.

"Someone has broken the binding," Ziegler said.

"What do you mean?" West glanced sharply at the *braucher*.

Ziegler held his hands palm out and moved them over the blocked entrance. "When the mouth of the mine was sealed, someone had a witch with strong magic add a binding spell. Whoever broke the seal also broke the spell."

"Wonderful. Let me bet—that also helped to contain the *Vril-ya?*" I asked.

"Yes. But it's not the only magic in the mine," Ziegler replied. "I can feel another strong protective spell that permeates the whole site. That's what I think the men came to break, to let the monsters loose."

"Wait," I said before we moved on. I pulled out my slim copy of *The Long Lost Friend* and handed it to Sarah. "Keep this close. It'll protect you." I kept the *himmelsbrief* so I could communicate with the ghosts.

"What about you?" Sarah asked, reluctantly accepting the book.

"I'm going to put my money on Krukis," I replied, and said a silent prayer to my patron.

Ziegler's map led us deeper into the mine, away from the entrance. As we moved, the blessed letter in my pocket made me aware that we were surrounded by ghosts, although they did not make themselves visible to us. I had an eerie feeling as if moving farther away from the old mine entrance moved us somehow back in time as well.

"What's that smell?" West complained.

The urge to retch nearly overpowered me, all of a sudden. The air, which had been dank and stuffy, now stank of rotted fish. Then I realized that buckets hung from brackets along the path, and their contents glowed, a faint blue-green light.

"In the old days, before electricity, candles and flame-lit lanterns could set off mine gas," Ziegler said in a hushed voice. "So they brought down buckets or rotting fish because they glow as they decompose."

"That fish hasn't been down here for a century," West noted.

"Want to bet Hans and Ernst brought it down with them?" I asked. I wasn't sure the light was worth the smell.

Bong. The peal of a bell resounded from somewhere in the darkness. I jumped at the sound and saw the others flinch as well. It rang again and again, and old habit made me count the rings.

"Seven," I said when silence shrouded the mine once more. A memory I hadn't thought about in years came to mind. "That's the danger signal." Seemed like the mine's ghosts were active tonight.

"And what the hell is that?" Sarah turned her flashlight on an odd cluster of blue crystals that cascaded down a wall like something from beneath the sea. Ziegler walked over and stared at the crystals and then the wall. To my surprise, he smiled.

"I've seen this before. They're called 'coal flowers.' Children make them with ammonia and some other ingredients, for something pretty at the holidays." He gestured toward the wall, which glistened with moisture in the glow of our lamps. "I'm guessing rainwater with a high ammonia content seeps in here and reacts to the coal."

"So I'm thinking we're in the right place," I said, remembering the riddle-like prophesy engraved on the Pagoda bell: "*Down in the valley the gong resounds low and deep...with the moon on high it sounds clearly in the heavens...with the flowers into the land of the dead.*"

We'd heard the alarm *gong*, and the rotting fish gave off something of a moonlight-type glow. The coal flowers were definitely the only kind we would find here, in a mine with a high death toll—the "land of the dead."

Although Ziegler had described this upper level as one floor, that hadn't prepared me for how large it was. Gradually, I realized that we were walking the outline of a huge square, with deep shafts in the center that descended to the abyss. We didn't know for certain how far down the mine went; those records had been lost long ago. Far enough that no mortal would survive hitting the bottom.

Far enough that inhuman creatures had survived for thousands of years in the deep places.

"Dim your lights," West ordered. We complied, then stood completely still for a moment as our eyes adjusted to nearly complete darkness. "Do you hear that?" he whispered.

"There!" I kept my voice low and pointed.

Across the depthless darkness in the center, I could just make out the shapes of several men on the opposite side of the pit. As I strained to hear, using my god-enhanced senses, a familiar voice reached me, chanting an incantation.

"It's Ernst and Hans," I told them. "Some sort of incantation. Maybe from a grimoire? It looks like one of them is holding a book."

"Then we're already almost too late," Ziegler said, barely hiding a note of panic. He set down his bag and rummaged through it, rising with an old tome in his hands. The leather had peeled in places, rubbed smooth in others from frequent handling.

"I need to see to read. If they notice us, there's no helping it," Ziegler said. "We're almost out of time." He looked up at the three of us. "Cover me. I'll do my best to bind the creatures. No guarantee."

Not what I wanted to hear.

West, Sarah, and I drew our guns. I worried that if we had reason to shoot, we might get more than we bargained for. Gasses built up even in active mines, pockets of bad air that could suffocate a man or, in the case of firedamp, explode.

If Ernst and his buddies noticed us—and I felt certain they had to have known we were there—it didn't slow them down. The speaker kept on chanting, and I felt a chill that had nothing to do with the temperature of the air around me.

I glanced back the way we came. Now that I knew what to look for, I could make out a faint light where the entrance to the fountain's mechanical room offered us our way to escape.

Whether or not it would be too far depended on what might be chasing us.

Skittering noises, claws on rock, sounded in the darkness. We glanced at each other in horror. Either the creatures were close enough for us to hear them or had massed in the depths so that the noise was amplified by a horde. Neither option was good.

"Hurry up!" Sarah urged. Ziegler kept on reading, as I saw the shadows of the pit begin to move.

A dark gray wave of movement swelled from the deep mine shaft and spilled over onto the opposite side, where Hans, Ernst, and their friends called forth the *Vril-ya*. I stared, horrified and entranced at the pulsating movement as the creatures moved in silent coordination, flowing up over the lip of the shaft and then rising before the dark witch who summoned them.

It all went wrong when the gray horde set on the witch and his followers, and the screaming began. Ernst cried out to Veles to save them, his voice filled with terror. As I had suspected, no salvation came. Veles had left them on their own, and when Ernst realized the betrayal, he cursed the god of the underworld with his dying screams. His friends shrieked in pain, as the gray monsters from the deep swept over them like a riptide and pulled them under, silencing them forever.

"Sarah—keep your gun trained on the pit and shoot anything that comes out of it," West snapped. "Joe—I need help with the dynamite."

The bark of Sarah's gun, firing shot after shot at creatures scrabbling over the edge, told me we were nearly too late.

Ziegler kept on reading the binding spell as more and more of the creatures spilled over the edge of the pit, a rising, writhing mass that made it impossible to tell where one began and another ended until they stood on elongated legs and stretched out long, slender claw-tipped arms to snatch their prey.

Sarah never stopped firing, switching guns rather than pausing to reload. I ran to help West, who had bundle after bundle of dynamite tied on a long rope, each with long fuses. With shaking hands, I passed him one after another to be lit, sure that I would either feel claws rip into my back any second or that the explosives would misfire and send us all to perdition.

I wasn't entirely sure either would kill me, but it would be the end of Sarah, West, and Ziegler without a doubt, and our failure would set the scourge loose on the world.

"Come on!" West urged, taking one end of the rope. "We've got to get to the edge."

"I'll make it happen." Krukis's magic filled me, and while I was no match by myself for the hordes of *Vril-ya* scrabbling up from the shaft, I could clear a path through the ones in front of us.

I swung my metal-skinned fists like sledgehammers, knocking the slender creatures out of our way, sending their thin bodies flying. Claws tore at my clothing and screeched against steel, able to do no worse than scratch me when they would have flayed a mortal. West stayed right behind me, carrying the lit-fuse dynamite bundle that threatened an entirely different death if we weren't fast enough.

Gunfire punctuated every breath, and the smell of gunpowder hung in the air. Ziegler kept reading, although I had no idea what the German words meant. West and I made progress toward the lip of the chasm, but moving just those few feet took longer than it should—longer than we had—every inch hard-won as I kicked and punched and hurled bodies out of my way.

Some of the creatures nearly got past me. I brought my boot down hard, squashing an elongated head with a crack of bone. Ahead, the gray wave surged, and I felt despair swell up inside me.

Too many. Too far. Too late.

We were nearly at the edge—and nearly out of time. The slow-burn fuses glowed, growing relentlessly shorter, never meant for this kind of delay. It was likely to go off in West's hands, killing him and the creatures near the blast, leaving me damaged and overwhelmed and insufficient to the task of saving the world.

I stumbled as a creature pulled hard on my leg, then realized that the onslaught of scrabbling monsters had turned like the tide. Some power sucked it back into the darkness, relentlessly dragging the horrors over the lip and down into the mine shaft, back into the abyss.

"Throw it!" I yelled to West as Sarah kept on firing at the stragglers, and Ziegler's voice, harsh and raspy, never faltered.

West hurled the explosives over the edge, after the creatures still retreating down the sides of the pit. I felt a surge of triumph at the unexpected win.

Then West lurched, falling as one of the *Vril-ya* wrapped its claws around his ankle and pulled him with the tide toward the depths.

I lunged forward, grabbing West's wrist and wrapping my hand around it in an unbreakable grip. Bone would shatter before my steel fingers would loosen their hold. I saw the terror in his eyes as the wave bore him over the edge—and me with it.

Krukis gave me inhuman strength, for one man. But the weight of the massed creatures that pulled West toward the bottom of the shaft was far more than even I could counterbalance. I dug in my toes and my free hand, plowing grooves into the rock as I tried to free West without pulling him into pieces.

He cried out in pain and terror. I could see him kicking at the claws that held his ankle, trying to free himself. I'd probably dislocated his shoulder, but I refused to let go. West slipped over the edge, fingers scrabbling for a grip as stone crumbled beneath the weight of the receding horde.

I started to tip over, head-first, into the darkness. I might survive the fall, maybe even the explosion. Perhaps I could even crawl back out if Krukis didn't abandon me. But West couldn't.

I'd almost forgotten about the dynamite.

The rope-chained bundles of TNT had fallen deep into the shaft, sucked down among the retreating *Vril-ya*. A loud blast reverberated in the mine, shaking the ground. The explosion sent a force upward, and I used it to haul West over the lip of the pit, then protected him with my steel body as chunks of rock and pieces of creature rained down on us.

The whole cavern trembled, and it sounded like the dynamite set off other explosions farther down. Pockets of explosive gases, maybe even old stashes of dynamite, reacted to the sudden, consuming fire.

More rock pelted us from above, as I climbed to my feet and yanked West to stand. He looked surprised to still be alive but recovered from his shock quickly. Since the *Vril-ya* hadn't grabbed bare skin, I hoped he hadn't been weakened from their touch.

"We've got to get out of here," he said, as Ziegler grabbed his pack. Sarah stood amid a pile of spent casings, with two guns shoved into the waistband of her pants and two more in hand.

"Go!" I ordered. "I'll bring up the rear." That way, if the roof fell in on us, I was the most likely to survive the cave-in.

We ran back the way we came, glancing only to make sure we followed Sarah's careful markings, aware of the black pit in the center. Booms and crashes echoed from far down the shaft, telling me that we had set off more than we'd bargained for.

As we neared the door to the mechanical room, I heard a crack like thunder, and the roof of the mine split in two, collapsing under its own weight. I swept Sarah and West up in my metal arms, hunching over them as I used my immortal speed to keep us ahead of the destruction, pushing Ziegler along in front.

So close, yet I feared we wouldn't make it as the stones that pelted us grew larger, big enough to do real damage. The temperature plummeted, and a faint glow flared all around us. For the few seconds it took to reach the safety of the steel-reinforced mechanical room, I saw the spirits of the dead gather around us, shielding us with their presence, protecting us as the rock skittered harmless down their backs.

I pushed the others inside and stayed in the doorway, unable to tear myself away from the sight.

Part of Penn's Commons fell through a gaping hole in the mine roof, bringing down chunks of turf, splintered wooden caskets, old bones, and the screaming members of the Free Society who had accompanied Jakob to work his part of the ritual by the potter's field.

Our ghostly protectors had vanished once we reached shelter. West and Sarah pulled at me to come inside. I could not take my eyes off the scene in front of me. The Eckert mine crumbled in on itself, a sinkhole that peeled off level after level until the doorway where I stood opened onto empty space, and the old tunnels collapsed into the abyss. Maybe to Hell itself, if such a thing existed.

I finally yielded to West and Sarah and felt Krukis's power leave me. No longer steel, I felt bruised and spent as we hurried up the metal steps, not slowing until we slammed the upper door behind us and locked it tight.

"Holy shit," West muttered.

"Hot damn," Sarah echoed.

"*Gott In Himmel,*" Ziegler breathed.

"Fuck," I said.

One end of Penn's Commons had vanished into the yawning darkness, with a fringe of grass and a few sheared-off bushes to show where the lawn had been. Sirens wailed, and the first police on the scene were trying to keep back onlookers since the margins of the hole could easily crumble. Off to one side, a group of rough-looking young men lounged, out of reach of the cops. Their cigarettes glowed in the darkness, and I figured that was the Eighth Street Gang, hanging around to watch the excitement. Of Jakob and his followers, I saw no trace.

"I think it's time to leave town," West said as the four of us ambled away from the park as if we were just out for a stroll. "Get your things and meet us at the train station. You can ride back with us in Sarah's private car."

West favored his arm, the one I had grabbed, and I wondered how badly he'd been hurt. As we fled, I hoped the darkness kept anyone from noticing the coal dust that smudged our skin and clothing.

"I'll be there as fast as I can grab my bag at the rooming house," I replied.

"Joe…thank you. I thought I'd run out of luck, there for a few seconds," West said, and for once, his face was open and candid, without the usual bravado.

"I thought we had, too, for a few seconds," I replied with a lopsided smile. "Thank Krukis. He hauled both our asses out of the fire."

Sarah and West headed back to the Hotel Berkshire, while Ziegler and I walked back to Ninth Street.

"You really did it," I said, still barely able to believe we were alive. "Whatever spell books you used did the trick."

Ziegler gave a self-conscious smile. "The magic flowed through me. I was just a conduit. I am grateful I could be of help."

I walked him to his door since it was on the way. "Thank you for everything. I hope you don't mind—I gave my copy of the book to my friend. I have my own deal."

"The book and the letter were yours to keep and do with as you will," Ziegler assured me. "You do good work, Joe Mack, whatever god you serve."

He waved goodbye, and I hurried to the rooming house. Mrs. Kemmner waited at the window and rushed over when I came in the door.

"I heard what happened. Are you okay?"

I might be immortal, and the champion of a god, but I wasn't immune to being mothered now and again. It felt good. I took both of her hands in my big paws. "I'm fine. Dr. Ziegler is fine—and he's the real hero of the night. My friends are fine. And you won't have to worry about Hans and Jakob anymore."

From the look she gave me, I wondered if her nephew had already given her the scoop about what happened in the park. She gave my hands a squeeze and stretched up to land a peck on my cheek.

"You're a good man, Joe. I don't know what you did—and I don't want to know. But…thank you."

I couldn't remember the last time I blushed. "Couldn't have done it without all your good cooking," I joked to lighten the mood.

She sighed and looked up at me. "So you'll be leaving."

I nodded, honestly a little sad about it. "Tonight. My friends are waiting. I just wanted to say goodbye and grab my things."

Mrs. Kemmner waited by the door until I came down again with my suitcase. She handed me a package tied up in a piece of cloth and bound with string. "For the trip. There are ham sandwiches and homemade pickles, and some of my cookies. So you don't go hungry." She patted me on the arm, and I figured maybe she needed a chance to mother someone since her own boy was gone. I thanked her and gave her a hug as I went out the door.

Private Pullman car or not—I had no intention of sharing my homemade goodies with Sarah and West.

7

I thought you said that Hanussen was working with Veles," Sarah said as we reclined on the sofas of her private railcar. A butler served drinks from the stash of high-class hooch. West and I enjoyed a fine stogie, while a cigarette burned at the end of Sarah's long ebony and silver holder.

"He was," I replied, savoring good scotch and the Cuban cigar while I could. Both were perks of working with Sarah. "I definitely sensed his presence at the Pagoda, and he recognized me."

"I'm not looking a gift-horse in the mouth," West said, "but why didn't he do something to help at the mine?"

"For the same reason Hanussen bolted out of town like his tail was on fire," I replied and took a sip of my drink. Sarah's liquors had names and were old enough to have their own driver's licenses. My liquor at home had been brewed in a bathtub and aged for a whole week.

"Veles is an instigator. He doesn't stick around to face the consequences. After all, he can always find another chump to do his bidding," I added.

"I've alerted authorities that Hanussen will be trying to get back to Europe, but I suspect he'll slip over into Canada and probably has the help of one of his admirers to return to Germany," West said. I could tell from his tone that it galled him not to be able to wrap up the case with a bow.

"What about The Order and the Free Society?" I asked.

West cleared his throat. "Thanks to an anonymous tip, the police raided the Free Society's base in that abandoned old hotel on the mountain. They are officially disbanded, so that should drive them underground for a while."

"As for The Order and the Thule," Sarah continued, "they're going to be lying low too, I suspect. Especially if Hanussen's European contacts prove unseemly. The railroad executive who hosted the reception at the Pagoda was taken by a sudden fit and had to be hospitalized. So I doubt he'll be dabbling in the occult until he's on the mend."

West raised his crystal tumbler in a toast. "Here's to living to fight another day." We murmured our agreement and knocked back the scotch faster than such a fine whiskey deserved.

The butler poured another round of drinks. Sarah and West chatted about the case, then moved on to other news. I looked out the window as the scenery flashed by, pensive despite our win. I identified with the ghosts of the railroad massacre, and the dead miners. I belonged among them, not here in a millionaire's private compartment. Sometimes, it seemed harder and harder to remember the Joe Magarac I'd been before Homestead, before Krukis.

"Did you catch that, Joe?" West asked. "I got a lead on a problem in Chicago that I'm going to need your help on."

I turned from the window and raised an eyebrow. "Mob?"

He shrugged. "Werewolves and vampires are muscling in on Capone's territory. We need to stop them before it gets bloodier than usual."

Sarah smiled. "I do love Chicago. The Berghoff. Marshal Field. And a clever little gin joint down in Greektown. Did I mention that Edna, a dear friend of mine, is marrying a Federal agent there, Elliott Ness? I dare say, I can be of assistance."

Here we go again.

The Joe Mack Files will Continue

PART III

CHICAGOLAND

1

I hate wendigos. They're fast. They've got sharp teeth, bad breath—
and they stink like roadkill.

This particular wendigo looked and smelled like he'd been
sleeping in a Chicago dumpster. For all I knew, he had. Fighting one of
these creatures isn't easy under the best of circumstances. Add holding
my breath so I didn't puke while having my eyes water from the stench—
which made everything blurry—and this wasn't my best day.

"Watch out!" Federal agent Jack West yelled. I knew he wasn't shouting
to warn me. But our new buddy, Eliot Ness, had stepped a little too close
to the monster's long arms and wicked claws. Neither of us wanted the
guy to survive sending Al Capone up the river only to get gutted by a
shaggy-assed monster with a taste for human flesh.

Ness jumped back out of the way, and the wendigo's claws swiped
close enough to rip the buttons off his shirt.

"Hey, asshole!" I yelled in my usual, subtle way, and while I wasn't sure
the creature remembered enough about being human to understand the
insult, the noise drew his attention off West and Ness and right onto me.

That would have been a dumb move—if I were still mortal. But those
days were long gone. I said a silent prayer to Krukis, god of blacksmiths,
and felt his power wash over me, making me stronger, faster, and nearly
impossible to kill. The wendigo slashed at me with his claws and then

howled in pain and fury when they splintered against my temporarily metallic skin.

While he cried over breaking a nail, I moved in for the kill, with a flare gun I'd modified just for times like this. I shot the creature nearly point-blank, and the flare set its matted, filthy pelt on fire, turning him into a crunchy critter and a pile of ash right there in the alley.

"Everyone alright?" I didn't see blood, but that didn't guarantee safety. The wendigo had ambushed us, and we'd danced around those claws for too long before I could get a good shot.

Ness stared at me. Then I realized that my shirt had been slashed by the wendigo's razor-sharp claws, and my "skin" had four long gouges that looked more like creases in a piece of sheet metal than gashes in a human body.

Because I wasn't completely human anymore either.

"What are you?" Ness asked, wide-eyed. It figured that I'd managed to spook the guy who nabbed Capone.

Then again, West mentioned Ness was still a bit wet behind the ears at the tender age of twenty-seven. West had a decade on him. I looked about the same age as West, but looks were deceiving. I just hadn't aged since I died and called on an ancient Slavic god to make me his champion.

"Tired and grumpy," I replied, sidestepping the question for now. "And I really want to know how that wendigo got to downtown Chicago. They're a Canadian monster, usually from the far north woods."

I didn't feel like getting into the whole story of my death, although I figured Ness would pry it out of me at some point. Obviously West hadn't spilled my secrets, which I appreciated. Besides, I didn't want the government taking an interest in me. Been there, done that—which is how I ended up dead in the first place.

Blame it on the Pinkertons. I had been a steelworker in a small town outside of Pittsburgh, where I'd come to start a new life with my wife and son, fleeing our native Hungary. Fever took Agata and Patryk from me, leaving me alone. I stood on the riverbank beside my friends, neighbors, and co-workers in the Homestead Strike, cut down by government agents who far outgunned us. As I lay dying, I called out to the Old Gods, wanting vengeance. Krukis heard my prayer, and now I fight on his behalf for the little guys and take out supernatural monsters.

Trusting West is a stretch, but he's made it clear he disavows the Pinkertons. He vouched for Ness. I hoped his trust wasn't misplaced.

Ness's eyes narrowed slightly, enough to let me know he hadn't missed my non-answer. "Capone had plenty of Canadian 'business' partners. It's not a stretch to think that Rocco Perri or one of his other rum-running pals either sent the creature as a 'present' or meant for it to get rid of Capone."

West kicked at the pile of ashes, like he expected the wendigo to spring to life. "You knew a monster was loose in the city. That's why you reached out to me and wanted me to bring in Joe. This isn't a surprise to you."

Ness blew out a breath like he was trying to figure out what to say. I got that he didn't like having to ask for help. I vaguely remembered being his age, young and strong, full of myself, thinking I was always going to have luck on my side. That was a long time ago for me, and life had made a point of proving me wrong. I hoped Ness didn't have to learn his lesson the hard way like I did.

"We think Capone was controlling the wendigo somehow, using it as a weapon," Ness said. "That hit against the North Side Gang that the press loves to call the 'Valentine's Day Massacre'? We let the reporters assume they were killed with bullets, but they were clawed to shreds. Same with the murder of Ben Kerr, one of Capone's Canadian connections who had a falling out with him in the same month. Shredded." He looked a little green around the gills at the memory, and I figured it must have been really bad.

"And now, with Capone in jail, the pet monster got loose?" West didn't look happy, and I agreed. It would have been nice to know some of these details going into the fight.

"That's our working theory," Ness admitted. "Which is why I hope you two gents can help us sweep up the mess."

I glared at him. Ness had the good sense to look nervous. "You want our help? Then you level with us. Secrets get people killed. We're either full partners and you share what you know—everything you know—or we get back on the train and go home."

Personally, I kinda hoped Ness decided to be an asshole about it so we could leave before someone got hurt. We'd come up from Cleveland in Sarah McAllen Harringworth's private Pullman car, and I'd be just fine going back home without getting bloody.

It didn't help that Ness was a hotshot wonderboy as well as a Fed. I'd seen that sort get everyone around them killed, and while I wasn't worried about myself, I didn't dislike West as much as I pretended. West could be a real prick, but he was honest, smart, loyal, and a damn good shot. I could do worse for a partner on cases where I needed his government connections as much as he needed my monster know-how.

"I'm sorry." Ness looked like the words tasted bad, but I was so surprised that he managed to say them that I let it slide. "I should have told you everything. You're right. It's just...I've had to play things close to the vest for a long time, not trusting anyone except my team...keeping secrets becomes second nature."

West and I exchanged a look, and I saw that he was as dumbfounded by Ness's unexpected change of attitude as I was. Maybe Ness wasn't a *complete* asshole, after all.

"How about we go back to my office, and I'll fill in the blanks," Ness said, a peace offering. "It's the one place in Chicago that I know for sure isn't bugged. And since Capone's boys want my head on a platter for sending their boss to prison, and the rest of the Mob wants to off me so I don't come after them, it's likely to be better for our health than standing around yakking in a back alley."

West and I followed Ness, feeling more like bodyguards than partners. I intended to change that, fast, since I wasn't kidding about hopping the next train to Cleveland if this didn't shape up to be an equal investigation. I'd stopped being anyone's lackey when I died at Homestead, and I wasn't about to pick up where I left off.

I had no idea what to expect Ness's office to look like, but I had a vague thought that it might be a posh place like a mansion's drawing room, all wood-paneled walls, shelves of antique books, and leather club chairs.

Ness led us into a fairly new brick high rise, the Transportation Building. This was the headquarters for the team the press nicknamed "The Untouchables," Ness's hand-picked men who were immune to the Mob's attempts at bribery and intimidation.

We rode the elevator to the third floor, and West looked as on edge as I felt. Ness might be a real hero, but I'd been disappointed in heroes before, so I reserved judgment.

The doors opened onto a floor with a small vestibule guarded by two heavily armed officers and a wall that closed off the rest of the space from easy access. A steel door made it clear that casual visitors weren't welcome. The lobby's gray walls and nondescript white floor tile epitomized government bureaucracy, completely devoid of decoration or personality.

The guards stepped aside, and Ness unlocked the door, ushering us on ahead, then closing and locking it behind him. I noticed the keyed dead-bolt, presumably to keep Capone's goons from getting in. I hoped Chicago managed to avoid having another epic fire because we'd never make it out in time. Fire was the one thing that could destroy me, and I didn't want to find out whether a high rise burned as hot as a steel mill's crucible.

Inside, standard-issue metal desks sat row on row, a dreary bullpen for Ness's team who were part secret agent and part drudge accountant. Only three men sat at their desks, absorbed in their tasks, and they barely looked up when Ness entered.

Ness headed for an office against the wall, which showed no more hint of personality than the rest of the floor. His desk was the same gray-green steel as those in the main area. A diploma hung in a plain black frame on one wall. The functional blotter and desk surface devoid of clutter or personal objects made me suspect Ness was compulsively organized and probably equally good at compartmentalizing his emotions too.

He waved us toward two cheap wooden chairs and went around to sit behind the desk. The only touches that might indicate higher status were a high-backed swivel chair and a classy fountain pen, which I guessed might have been a long-ago graduation present.

"I used to think that catching Capone would be like grabbing the brass ring," Ness said, with a note of weariness in his voice that was too strong to overlook. "Turns out, it's more like slaying the hydra. Cut off one head, and more grow from the stump. Capone's organization is tight. He's in jail, but his lieutenants aren't, so the machine carries on without him."

Ness sighed, and I had the impression of a man who couldn't abide loose ends. "My team might be incorruptible, but Eastern State is a big prison, and we all know there are guards who can be bought. Capone will find a way to remain in control of his operation from the inside. It galls me, but nothing's a surprise anymore. I'm resigned to a long, messy mop-up. But I don't know how to deal with the monsters he left behind."

"The wendigo wasn't the only problem?" West asked. He wore the "evaluating" expression normally reserved for witnesses who might or might not be hiding something.

Ness hesitated, then shook his head. "No. It's just the one we'd gotten a good enough look at to guess what it might be. Down in the coal ash tunnels, the ones the garbage collectors use to cart waste away without clogging street traffic, there've been disappearances. Only one body was found, but something had ripped out its heart."

"You think someone wanted to make it look like a monster?" West asked. "People can kill other people in monstrous ways."

Ness shrugged. "Possible. But I don't think so. The workers' union pays kickbacks to Capone's men for protection. It would be a pointless attack by the other families—high risk and low payoff."

"Wendigos eat flesh, but hearts aren't their thing. A werewolf, maybe," I mused. "Or a rougarou."

Ness gave a bitter laugh. "Werewolves *belong* in Chicago, along with vamps. They've been part of the Mob since there's been a Mob. They don't really count as monsters here anymore. The families keep them on a tight leash, and they have a place, a purpose. They would be stupid to risk everything to snack on a few sanitation workers."

I'd already decided that Chicago wasn't my kind of town, but Ness's admission removed all doubt. Cleveland had its Mafia witches—I counted one of them as an almost-friend and sometimes ally. But the Lavecchia family was strictly human. Still monsters, but human ones.

"So you think it's another creature Capone was using to do his dirty work?" West asked.

Ness nodded. "Yes. And I think he found a way to bend the ghosts of Death Alley to do his bidding too. There've been several suspicious deaths there, all people Capone was known to have a beef with."

I'd heard of Death Alley. When the Iroquois Theater burned more than two decades ago, killing over six hundred people—many of them children—the bodies were stacked in the alley behind the building until they could be identified. Many spirits never left. It's been one of the most haunted places in Chicago ever since.

"I knew there were ghosts. Never heard they were violent," I said.

Ness met my gaze. "They didn't used to be. Then all of a sudden, Capone's enemies started turning up dead there, not a mark on them. No traces of poison. Just some strange gray goo leaking from their ears and eyes."

Ectoplasm. Linked to high-energy hauntings, it was the slime-trail of a dangerous ghost, one that had enough juice to harm the living and interact with the material world, like poltergeists.

West looked to me. "What can power up ghosts like that?"

"Nothing good." I could think of a few possibilities. Necromancers. Demons. Dark magic. Ness definitely hadn't been forthright with West when he dragged us into this.

"What else?" I growled. I could afford to take my chances, but West and Sarah were all-too-human and, therefore, breakable.

Ness gave me a look, and all of a sudden, I understood. Eliot Ness wasn't afraid of Capone or his enforcers and hitmen. He could go up against the Chicago machine—vamps, weres, and all. They were normal in his mind.

But this other stuff…scared him. Big, bad, ball-busting Eliot Ness was afraid. He didn't know how to handle that or how to ask for help. It wasn't all vanity. He needed the Mob to fear him in order to clean up the rot in Chicago. Ness might have a team for fighting criminals, but he sensed that they might not believe him about supernatural threats, and he couldn't afford to undermine his authority.

It must have cost him to reach out to West, and to bring in a stranger —me—to a volatile situation and potentially jeopardize everything he'd worked for. But he did it for Chicago, and I could respect that. Maybe I could bend my own stiff neck, just a little, for a good cause.

"The only thing I've ever run into that could affect ghosts like that is bad magic—powerful and very dark," I said. "Did Capone have a *strega?*"

"Not that we've ever known," Ness replied. "But he's been obsessed with the occult for a long time. It's strange because these mafia guys are normally so superstitious. But Capone never shied away from using any weapon that served his purposes. He's a very practical man."

That was the other missing piece I needed to hear. Ness could loathe everything Capone stood for, hate his methods and his crimes, but only a fool underestimates his opponent out of disdain. Ness was nobody's fool. He didn't admire Capone—I'd seen lawmen seduced by the appeal of the outlaw before, and it always ended badly. But Ness also didn't write his nemesis off in a bout of hubris, and he was willing to step way outside his comfort zone to do the right thing, to protect the city he had sworn to serve.

I could work with him.

"We might be able to get some inside information on those tunnel deaths," I said, glancing at West, who gave me a barely-there nod to continue. "An associate of ours invited us to dinner with Jonathan Kirkpatrick."

Ness's eyebrows rose. "The CEO of Kirkpatrick Mining?" I could practically see the wheels turning in his brain, trying to figure out how West and I were possibly connected.

West cleared his throat. "Our associate, Mrs. Sarah Grace McAllen

Harringworth, is a friend of the Kirkpatrick family. We may be able to get an unguarded reaction about the disappearances—which could be...informative."

"Well fuck me sideways," Ness said, rolling his eyes. "Damned if you don't walk right into the access my team's been trying to get for over a month. Normally I'd say that the goings-on in the tunnels were beneath the bossman's notice, but Kirkpatrick has a reputation for immersing himself in the details. On top of that, the ash removal contract with the city puts a pretty penny in his pocket, so anything that threatens his workers threatens that revenue."

I felt kinda bad for him if he'd been chasing that lead without success, but it wasn't something West or I planned in advance. Sarah had insisted on joining us, and having her along never steered us wrong before. She's good with a gun, her connections are legion, and if there are any doors her name alone won't open, she's fast with a lock pick.

"We'll let you know what we hear," West assured him. "Did you have any other questions you want us to ask if he's in a talking mood?"

"The disappearances are the main thing," Ness replied, mollified at being asked. "We've gone up the chain of command from the shift supervisor to the vice president of the company, and they either don't know or are scared to talk about it. At first, we thought it was a gang war, but it's gotten worse since Capone's been locked up, and he doesn't benefit from disrupting operations."

"So either it's a rival gang muscling in on his turf and faking the cause of death to scare people, or it's a monster who slipped his leash," I mused.

Ness nodded. "Yeah. And it's a toss-up which is worse."

"I can't breathe in this thing." Monkey suits always bring out the worst in me. Tight collars, made even tighter by a bowtie, and a perfectly fitted bespoke jacket tailored to make room for my gun made me feel claustrophobic.

"Poor baby."

Sarah McAllen Harringworth tut-tutted as she finished tying my tie. West had taken care of his own tie in the mirror on the other side of the parlor that separated our shared room from hers in one of The Drake Hotel's luxury suites. That's another perk of traveling with Sarah—she believes life is too short not to have the best of everything, which she can afford, and she is generous enough to take West and me along for the ride.

Since Sarah likes to have me accompany her to events—either as a bodyguard or a mysterious male companion—she has her late husband's tailor whip up the latest style of tux for me when the whim strikes. She makes sure the tuxes are in one of the steamer trunks she travels with when we go on a job, and I do my best to be gracious about looking like an organ grinder's pet.

I'd feel like a kept man, but the relationship—at least between Sarah and me—is strictly professional. My Agata was the only woman for me, and while I don't look it, I'm a good seventy-five years older than Sarah. If there is or was anything between her and West, it's mutually casual and none of my business. On a job, they're all business.

"You do clean up well, Joe," Sarah said with a teasing glint in her eyes.

"At least until something *blows* up," West observed. "I've lost a lot of good suits that way." Our ventures did have a habit of ending in explosions and blood.

Sarah wore a navy blue beaded silk dress in the most fashionable cut, which I knew because she had mentioned it several times. West and I might not be married men, but we were savvy enough to nod and smile at comments like that. She was a beautiful woman—blond, trim, athletic, and thoroughly modern. I might not be interested—she was far out of my league—but I had eyes.

The good thing about walking into any room with Sarah was that everyone looked at her. West and I weren't noticed, a benefit in our line of work, although I knew it irked West a bit since he enjoyed being in the spotlight much more than I did.

"Here's a quick history, so you're not completely lost at dinner," Sarah said as she powdered her nose and touched up her red lipstick. "Kirk's father went to Northwestern with my late father-in-law."

"Kirk?" It took me a moment to realize she meant Jonathan Kirkpatrick, the coal baron.

She chuckled. "He hates 'Jon' or 'Jonathan.' Anyhow, the two fathers stayed friends, and the families often vacationed together—hunting or skiing out in the Rockies, hiking and fishing in the Adirondacks...that sort of thing. So when I married Henry, Kirk was always around. We've stayed in touch, and we have dinner together if we're in the area. I'm widowed, and his wife left him for a ski instructor in Jackson Hole, so we can be seen together without a scandal." She grinned. "Which, of course, is also where the two of you come in."

"Chaperones?" West teased.

Sarah looped her arm through his. They made an attractive couple. "No, silly. Arm candy."

I knew my job—be quiet and look dangerous. This wasn't the first time I'd played bodyguard. I didn't mind. The food was good, and I got to see how the other half lived.

Too bad we were here at the behest of Chicago's staunchest defender of Prohibition. I'd have to wait until I got back to the room and Sarah's illicit stash for an after-dinner slug of bathtub gin.

"Kirk" sent a car for us, which happened to be a sleek black Maybach Zeppelin. I held the door for Sarah and West to get in the back, then rode up front with the driver. Light traffic made the ride even shorter than I expected, and we pulled up in front of the stone exterior of The Standard Club before I'd barely had a chance to settle into the comfortable leather seats.

Sarah thanked the driver, I got out to open the back door, and the club's doorman stepped forward to check credentials.

"Guests of Jonathan Kirkpatrick," Sarah said, slipping into the role she had been raised to play.

I was as fascinated watching Sarah recreate herself to suit the situation as I was when West shed his flashy image to go undercover. Mostly, it intrigued me because I was pretty much the same wherever I went. I'd never needed to be anyone else, and now I generally didn't give a damn. Other than using what my mother would have called "company manners" on nights like this, I was just me.

Of course, "just me" included owing my soul to an ancient god. Maybe I wasn't quite as uncomplicated as I liked to think.

The Standard Club didn't disappoint. Inlaid floors, wood-paneled walls, leather furniture, and fancy ceilings with gold accents screamed wealth and privilege. Crystal chandeliers glittered overhead. Formally dressed servers moved swiftly and silently beneath the watchful gaze of the old men immortalized in large oil paintings along the walls.

Sarah moved through the club like she'd been there before. We headed into the dining room, where the maître d' showed us to a table in a private room where we could talk undisturbed.

Jonathan Kirkpatrick looked to be a decade older than Sarah, with dark hair accented by flecks of gray at the temples. I'd expected him to have a softer look since he wasn't a working man, but Kirkpatrick had a rugged, almost craggy appearance that reminded me of the men I once knew who worked in mines like his.

Kirkpatrick pressed his lips to the back of Sarah's hand in greeting, and she bussed an air kiss beside his cheek. He faltered a bit when we came to the table, unsure who should pull out Sarah's chair, silently speculating about West's role. While the two top dogs tried to figure it out, Sarah pulled out her own chair and sat down, smoothing her skirt beneath her. I tried to hide my smirk.

"It's been too long," Kirkpatrick said, looking genuinely pleased to see her and managing to exclude everyone else in his focus. "Maybe two, three years?"

Sarah nodded, returning his attention in a way that wasn't exactly flirting but bestowed the force of her charisma on him, like a gift.

"At least," she agreed. "You look well."

Kirkpatrick shrugged, and I could see he was trying not to look overly pleased. "I've been too busy to notice, but that's kind. You're as beautiful as ever."

"Charmer," Sarah deflected. I thought again that she would have made a good spy. She loved the game, and while Sarah broke plenty of restrictive, old-fashioned conventions, she also knew how to use them to her advantage when the situation warranted.

Still, I picked up real friendship between her and Kirkpatrick, or maybe just the warmth of shared history and a survivor's appreciation of moving past loss.

Our server stopped by and recited the menu for our order. Everything sounded good. Since he didn't rattle off the prices along with the descriptions, and since I figured Kirkpatrick was paying, I ordered what I wanted, which was a steak. West did the same. Sarah chose trout, and Kirkpatrick picked lamb.

The wine master followed with a bottle Kirkpatrick must have chosen ahead of time and poured for all of us. Apparently Prohibition didn't count in the rarified spaces of Chicago's clubs for the wealthy and influential. The interruption seemed to have broken the flow of conversation, telling me that Sarah and her friend were a bit more awkward with each other than they initially let on.

"So," Kirkpatrick said, clearing his throat. "What brings you to Chicago...with bodyguards?"

Sarah sipped her wine. "Still cleaning up some of the loose ends from Henry's affairs. Money's involved, so I figured I shouldn't travel alone."

The lie seemed to satisfy him. After all, she could hardly say she'd come on a lark to help Eliot Ness with his monster problem.

"Sorry to hear that's dragged on, but any excuse to catch up is a good one," Kirkpatrick said.

He's not okay. I wasn't psychic, but I'd gotten good at reading people. I believed Kirkpatrick was genuinely happy to see Sarah, in part because I had the sense tonight took his mind off weightier things.

Then again, he was the head of a big mining company. He could be worried about all kinds of things—labor strikes, the price of coal, competitors. It struck me how odd it was to find myself dining with a coal baron when I had known so many men who toiled and died in the mines beneath the Pittsburgh hills. In my mortal life, I had raised a pint at the pub when miners wished death and damnation on their bosses, silently toasting their ruin just as I had nothing good to say about the Carnegies and the Fricks of the world.

"And you?" Sarah inquired, with feigned polite detachment. I knew she had an agenda, but I was more than willing to sit back and watch her work.

Kirkpatrick gave a wry chuckle. "Nothing tremendously interesting. I'm sure you recall the tedium of managing a large enterprise."

Sarah had taken control of Harringworth Coal when her husband died, and by all accounts ran it much better, increasing its value before she sold to a rival and cementing her place among the independently wealthy.

"Things should be quieter in Chicago, with the infamous Al Capone in jail," Sarah said.

"Crack down on one, and there's always another to take his place," Kirkpatrick replied, sounding world-weary. "It can actually be worse for a while, as all the underlings jockey for position once the boss is gone. As bad as Capone was, he might have kept a lid on others who were just as bad."

Is that his worry? Better the devil you know? I didn't envy any business owner navigating Mob politics—payoffs, protection money, bribes, always wondering when the price would go up or the demands would grow.

"There's always something," Sarah agreed.

The food arrived, as well as a second bottle of wine. No one seemed concerned that the club might be raided for alcohol, and I knew no cop who valued his badge would dare try to cart the club's wealthy and powerful members off to jail.

The conversation turned to movies and the weather. West chimed in on occasion, especially when the topic shifted to baseball. I stayed quiet, as befitting hired muscle. *Ears open, mouth shut.*

"So is it true?" Sarah asked as the cheesecake arrived for dessert. She leaned forward, dropping her voice confidentially. "You've still got the ash contract with the city, right? Are the stories they tell true about the monsters in the tunnels?"

Kirkpatrick flinched. Barely, but I caught it, and I knew the others did too. He hesitated, and I figured he was trying to decide whether to lie.

"We don't know what's going on yet," he said, carefully choosing his words. "Some of the workers are fairly transient. That makes it hard to know if they've really gone missing or if they just up and left. Of course, we hope they left on their own. But their sort is hard to trace, even for the police." He licked his lips, a sure tell that he was nervous.

Sarah sighed. "And here I thought I was going to hear a ghost story." Her acting skills were excellent, and I knew that she was enjoying herself.

Kirkpatrick relaxed a bit, and the fondness in his eyes warred with his set jaw. In the end, not wanting to disappoint her won out over his reluctance to discuss the situation. "This can't be repeated," he said, dropping his voice even though we were in a private room and the servers had gone elsewhere.

Sarah leaned in, favoring him with a conspiratorial smile. "Our lips are sealed," she said, pantomiming locking her mouth and tossing away a key.

"We think there may be some kind of feral animal down there. Maybe a big dog or some exotic pet someone let loose, like those alligators in the New York sewers," Kirkpatrick said. "A body turned up, one of the maintenance men. Clawed apart. Awful. But the strangest thing…whatever killed him didn't gnaw on the bones. It just took his heart."

Sarah gasped in horrified fascination. I bit my lip to keep from laughing because I'd seen her in a fight and knew that blood didn't faze her at all. I sometimes suspected she had the potential to be the most ruthless of the three of us, hidden beneath Paris fashions and a perfect manicure.

"His heart? Are you sure?"

Kirkpatrick nodded gravely, but I could see how much he relished her attention. *Does he have a crush on her?* If so, he was doomed to disappointment because now that Sarah had both wealth and freedom, I knew she would never trade it for marriage again.

"We took pains to keep it out of the papers, of course, which is why you mustn't say anything to anyone," he replied. "But it's not the only strange thing down there. They didn't find the others who went missing, but now and again, there've been bloodstains, too much to be a rat or a raccoon. The police, however, didn't seem worried."

Of course not, since they work for Capone.

"Are there ghosts? You know I've always loved ghost stories." Sarah played to a willing audience, and Kirkpatrick grew more talkative. I wondered if anyone listened to the man outside of his work.

"I'm not sure about ghosts, but there's a stretch of tunnel under the Lexington Hotel that the men go out of their way to avoid. Of course, they don't think I know, but I run a tight ship," he said with a tentative smile like he was out of practice. "Now you have to take what they say with a grain of salt. They're a superstitious lot."

Probably recently come over from the Old Country, where people still believe in the supernatural. Where they know that fairy tales are based on ancient warnings, and the stories definitely aren't meant for children.

Kirkpatrick's gaze flicked to the side, giving me to suspect that he paid more attention to the tales than he wanted to let on.

"And then there's the secret chamber." He stopped as if perhaps he had said too much.

"Secret chamber?" Sarah's eyes widened. "Kirk, you can't leave me hanging. Go on!"

I could see the instant when vanity won out over common sense. "It's probably nothing," Kirkpatrick said. "But one of the maintenance teams accidentally broke through an old wall that went into some sub-basement of the hotel, I guess. A workman stuck his head inside with a lantern and said it was covered with scribbling. Strange marks painted on the walls, nonsense words scrawled everywhere."

"What did the police say?" Sarah asked, doing a good impression of being breathless.

"It wasn't a matter for the police," Kirkpatrick assured her. "Since it was on private property and there was no lasting harm done. I arranged to have it plastered over, and that was the last of it. Probably vandals or some nutter off his rocker with a can of paint. But it gave everyone a bit of a scare until we got things calmed down."

Charming as Kirkpatrick was to someone of his class, I knew how his kind operated in the wild. I didn't doubt that the workmen had been ordered to secrecy, threatened with losing their jobs or worse. The fact that word hadn't reached Ness told me that the CEO's threats must have been dire enough to gain full obedience.

My gut tightened, and suddenly that fine steak and cheesecake didn't set as well.

"Oh my," Sarah replied. "Do you think it might have been a witch's workplace?"

Kirkpatrick chuckled, but this time his humor had a condescending edge that rankled me. "You've been reading Poe again, haven't you? He always was your favorite." He shook his head. "A witch might make for an exciting explanation, but I imagine that a madman on the loose explains both the violence and the odd room."

We lingered over coffee while dessert settled. Just as we were about to take our leave, Kirkpatrick leaned in and met Sarah's gaze. His expression was open and vulnerable. Scared.

"I heard a rumor that you helped stop a dangerous problem in Reading a few months ago." He took in West and me with a glance before returning his focus to Sarah. "I won't ask you to confirm that, but if you did, and you have some way of knowing what's really going on in the tunnels, I would be very grateful to find out how to make it stop. I don't believe the police report. I saw the body. The workers down there deserve better, but I don't know who else to ask."

I wanted to dislike Kirkpatrick. I wanted to believe his concern was merely posturing to impress Sarah. I had experienced the disregard industrial barons had for the lives of "replaceable" workers. Hell, I'd been killed by them. But my instincts told me Kirk was on the level. Maybe he wasn't a total asshole, after all.

"I'll keep my eyes and ears open," Sarah promised him. "And if we find out something helpful, I'll let you know."

I loved how she gave him an honest answer without actually admitting to anything. And I knew for a certainty that as soon as we changed out of our fancy dress clothing, we were going to have a look at those tunnels.

2

T his is impressive." West swiveled his head to take a gander at the freight tunnel as we headed inside. Bare bulbs overhead lit up the depths, and we walked carefully, mindful of the track for the electric trains that carried coal, ash, garbage, and freight to and from all of the buildings on the street above us. Telephone and telegraph cables ran along the ceiling, and handcarts dotted the loading docks where the sub-basements of buildings opened into the underground network.

"Sixty-two miles of tunnels," I said, having spent some time chatting with the janitor at our hotel while I waited for West and Sarah. He was happy to share what he had learned from talking to the garbage collectors who gathered the hotel's trash.

"That's a lot of places to hide," Sarah murmured.

We were dressed in black, each with a miner's hat left over from our adventure in Reading. The gear bag I carried had flashlights and lanterns, an extra shotgun with shells filled with rock salt, and plenty of knives. West and I both had machetes. I had a shotgun; he carried a pistol. Sarah had a gun and a smaller—but equally wicked—knife. I hoped we didn't run into the cops because we'd be hard-pressed to explain ourselves.

Then again, this was Chicago. Maybe they'd buy "monster hunters" after all.

We did our best to melt into the shadows when a train went by. The man in the control booth never noticed. People tend to see what they expect to see, and that worked in our favor.

"Look." Sarah pointed to the wall at the nearest juncture. The names of the streets above us were painted onto the concrete walls, giving us a way to navigate. That saved us from having to mark our path with chalk, although I had some in the bag. Never know when things will come in handy.

"He said the secret room was under the Lexington Hotel," West said. "This way." We followed him through the maze of tunnels, marveling at the underground complex. My janitor acquaintance had confided that rumor held the tunnels weren't profitable. I also knew that there could be a big difference between the money reported to the IRS and the money actually changing hands.

I didn't doubt that bootleggers moved cargo through here, disguised as other types of freight. The complex had multiple openings to the surface as well as into the buildings they served, which were probably put to good use by shady players who needed to make a fast, discreet getaway. Trains ran day and night, so vagrants picked somewhere else for sleeping off a bender, but there were enough darkened nooks—especially near the tunnel mouths—that were probably utilized for quick trysts by Chicago's streetwalkers and their customers. Just in case this trip went sideways, I said a prayer to Krukis and hoped he heard me. If there was a rogue were-wolf—or some other heart-eating monster—down here, I didn't want to wait until the last minute and find out my patron deity wasn't answering the phone.

Kirkpatrick said that the Chicago Mob families had their own vampires and werewolves, like in Cleveland. So whatever monster was running amok down here was either acting on a plan by one of the families or had gone completely rogue. I didn't like either option, but at least a monster following orders might have rules about what could and couldn't be done. A rogue monster was a complete wild card and thus even more dangerous than usual.

"We're here." West's voice cut through my musings, and I looked up to see a blank concrete wall ahead of us, unremarkable except for the newly patched area that stood out by its lack of grime.

"Kinda hate to bash it in since they just got it patched," Sarah said, but I could see the eagerness in her eyes to look inside the mystery room.

"I'll try to bash gently," I told her with a smirk. Sarah and West stood back when I grabbed the sledgehammer out of my bag and took a big swing. The patched concrete crumbled, opening a dark hole and sending up a cloud of dust.

We froze, listening to hear if anyone was coming, but after a few moments of silence, we decided to go on. The hole wasn't large enough for my big shoulders to fit through, but Sarah and West wouldn't have any trouble. I insisted on sticking my flashlight and my head in first, to make sure there wasn't a creature waiting for them.

To my relief, no monster stirred inside. What I could make out of the interior validated Kirkpatrick's report, except that I recognized the "nonsense" words and symbols as having occult meanings.

"Go on in," I said. "I'll keep watch." West went in first, gun drawn, followed by Sarah. I handed her my flashlight. A moment later, the electric lights flicked on. I knew West had his Nikon, a fancy toy provided for the Supernatural Secret Service, and one he'd been eager to try out.

If anyone happened by, I'd tell them that someone had obviously broken through the patch, and I had reported it, then agreed to stand guard until the police arrived. In this clothing, I looked enough like a dock loader that people were unlikely to question my presence. I just hoped that I didn't need to use my phony cover story and that West and Sarah wouldn't take all night collecting evidence.

To my relief, they emerged after about half an hour. "I got the pictures," West reported, tucking his camera back into his bag. "Let's hope they turn out. I have the stuff to develop them back in the room."

"I sketched as much as I could and took notes, just in case," Sarah added. "Certain symbols repeated, and so did some words."

"Looked like a ritual room for dark magic," West said, dusting himself off. "Candles, dried plants, bowls, goblets. The door was locked or sealed from the outside—where it connected to the Lexington."

The hotel where Capone had his headquarters. That couldn't possibly be a coincidence.

"Did Capone have a secret *strega*?" I wondered aloud. It sounded like we had two issues now—the heart-eating creature and a dark witch. Then again, I've been wrong before.

"No idea," West replied. "But they sure weren't holding Sunday School in there."

I heard faint rustling down a nearby tunnel, too large to be a rat, too quiet to be a train. Nothing had changed, but now the electric lights seemed to leave far too many shadows pooled at the edges and corners. Some of the branching tunnels looked completely dark. There were too many access points, making our position indefensible if something chose to attack.

My gut said we were being watched, and even before I swore my soul to Krukis, I had learned that my intuition was rarely wrong.

"We need to go." I didn't make it a question. "Now."

I'd expected pushback from West or Sarah, but to my surprise, they both agreed, packed up, and hurried out, making me wonder if at some level, they sensed a threat as well.

The clatter of the small trains seemed distant, reminding me we had veered off the more populated route. I felt hyper-aware of every sound—the drip of water, the scrape of our shoes on concrete, and the clinking of the gear in our weapons bag. And just at the edge of my enhanced hearing, I could make out the faint sound of movement, stealthy but not too far away.

Something knew we were here—and it stalked us.

"Hurry," I urged, dropping my voice so it didn't carry beyond the three of us. "We're not alone."

We picked up the pace, not quite running but close to it. Our steps echoed in the tunnels, sounding like they came from everywhere at once. Human hearing wouldn't have caught the faintest scuff that kept pace, not closing yet, but not veering away. Following us.

Up ahead the lights grew brighter as we came back to the more frequently used tracks. If our stalker meant to do us harm, he'd move on us before we reached witnesses.

"Go," I ordered West and Sarah. "Wait for me somewhere with a lot of light, people, and traffic."

"Joe—" Sarah protested, as West tried to steer her by the elbow.

"I'll catch up. Now go!"

All those supernatural enhancements from Krukis included speed as well as strength and metal skin, and so far, I hadn't run into anything I couldn't match or better. Catching up wouldn't be a problem. But if a creature from the depths of the tunnels stalked us, then I intended to be the wall that stopped it from following West and Sarah.

I waited until their footsteps receded before I addressed the tunnels. "I don't know who or what you are, but I'm your match. You don't want to fight me. Go away."

I caught a whiff of old blood and rotted meat and felt the creature's gaze raking over me, sizing me up, trying to decide if I was worth the risk. Then as quickly as it appeared, it vanished, and I felt relief like the sudden lifting of pressure before a storm.

Even so, I stayed motionless for several minutes, in case the withdrawal was a trap. Finally, I hurried to meet West and Sarah, glancing over my shoulder at intervals until the hubbub of the busy portion of the tunnels surrounded me.

"What was that?" West asked as we hurried toward the exit. I felt sure we were all equally eager to be above ground.

"I don't know," I replied. "But I'm sure it's at least part of the reason there've been disappearances and deaths."

"Part?" Sarah asked, cautious but not overly spooked.

"Yeah. Because I think we might have more than one monster."

I hadn't realized how tense I'd been until we emerged from the tunnels, safe and sound. We caught a streetcar back to the hotel and made our way up the back stairs to avoid notice.

West and I unlocked our room, Sarah let herself into hers, and we met in the shared parlor in the middle.

"If we can manage with just one bathroom for a few hours, I can set up my darkroom in ours and get these pictures developed," West said. Since I had gone my entire mortal life without indoor plumbing, the possibility of needing to share one marble-tiled washroom for an hour or two didn't seem like a hardship. "Don't wait up for me. I'll have the prints ready in the morning."

"Make yourself comfortable, Joe. I need to get all this rock dust out of my hair, and then I'm going to turn in," Sarah said, heading for her room. "If you want a drink, the flasks are in my valise," she added, pointing to a leather Gladstone bag on the table behind the couch.

I was never much of a drinker before I died, and now that I'm immortal, I could probably drink all the hooch in Chicago and barely get a buzz, but sometimes I enjoyed taking the edge off. Not to mention the social aspect, which makes me feel a little more human on nights when dark dreams haunt me.

Prohibition made drinking the biggest shared secret in America, and while part of me admired Ness's resolute pursuit of justice, I still thought banning booze was a bad idea. The ban obviously didn't work, it made criminals out of regular folks who just wanted a beer, and since contraband always came at a high price, the new laws fueled the rise of the Mob and guys like Capone. All in all, it seemed to prove what they say about the road to hell and good intentions.

I poured myself a glass of whiskey. It had a raw, smoky taste that reminded me of the liquor back in my native Hungary, made in hidden stills by friends and neighbors. Potent and rough, the liquor took men's minds off their troubles.

I settled in on the couch and turned on the radio. Seems I had my pick of channels—news, music, drama, and sports. I flipped back and forth until I found one playing some of the songs I'd heard the last time I saw a vaudeville show at the theater. I sipped at my drink and leaned back to enjoy a safe momentary respite. Much as I loved spending time with West and Sarah, I needed quiet to gather my thoughts.

Unfortunately, at this point, I had too many questions and not enough answers. I knocked back the rest of the whiskey, set the glass aside on the side table, and got ready for bed. I hoped things seemed clearer after a good night's sleep.

THE NEXT MORNING, I found that the hotel had delivered coffee and pastries to the parlor of our suite, a luxury I intended to fully appreciate. West woke me up before dawn whistling in the bathroom while he developed more photos, so I dressed, ate, and slipped down to the men's room in the lobby to clean up. I had just returned when the bathroom door swung open.

"You're going to want to take a look at this." West bustled into the room, holding prints of the photos he and Sarah had taken down in the tunnels.

"You have the pictures already? Let's see them!" Sarah came in from the other side, wearing a comfortable outfit with black wide-legged lounging pants and a red silk kimono-style top.

West spread out the photos on the coffee table and leaned over them. The secret room looked as if it had been set up as a bedroom or perhaps a cell since the only door was locked from the outside. I wondered who had stayed in that windowless room and why. Did the person escape through the hole in the wall or leave because the hole made the room unusable?

"I sent off a couple of telegrams to my contacts regarding the words and symbols I didn't recognize," West said, and I remembered the boxy "suitcase" he had brought with him, which served as a mobile station. I wondered if West had slept at all. "They'll probably get back to me tonight. But some of these we've seen before."

Over the years, I'd run across a lot of runes, sigils, and spells. There were too many for anyone to know them all, but certain symbols were more common than others, especially when it came to protection against evil.

"I've seen this before, and these," I said, pointing. "They ward against the devil. Or more specifically, vampires."

West nodded. "Yeah. That's my thought too. So did the person in the room particularly fear vamps? Or did Capone's gang keep a vamp prisoner down there, and more to the point—where is he now?"

I studied the words and phrases scrawled across the walls in black paint. Kirkpatrick might have dismissed them as nonsense, but I knew better. "They're in a lot of different languages," I said, squinting to see better. The light hadn't been great for photography, and the pictures were rather dark.

"That one looks like English, sort of," Sarah said, pointing to a line up near the ceiling. West dug through the prints and found an enlargement.

"Old English," he surmised. "Like Chaucer. Not something you usually find outside a museum."

I recognized the word, though I hesitated to say it aloud or to pronounce any of the words painted on the walls. Such things had power. "It's giving an order for someone—or something—to 'remain confined,'" I said, drawing on knowledge I'd gained on another case.

"It repeats here, and here—oh, and here," Sarah noted, and as soon as she said that, I saw several other places where the word appeared as well.

"Not just that word," West mused. "The same five lines, over and over."

"Maybe they all mean the same thing," I said, with a strong hunch that I was correct. "A binding spell to keep whatever was in the room imprisoned, reinforced by wording in different magical traditions, maybe even invoking different kinds of power. It would explain the repetition."

West stood, arching his back to stretch. "I think you're right. We'll wait and see what my sources have to say, but that would make sense."

"If that's the case, then when the workmen knocked a hole in the wall, it also broke the warding," Sarah said. "And provided a way to escape. Is that what's ripping out hearts and leaving pools of blood? A vampire—or something else?"

"I guess we'll have to go back down and figure that out," I replied, figuring I'd need to do that anyhow. "But this morning, I want to have a look at Death Alley."

"I'll come with you," Sarah replied.

I shook my head, bracing for a fight. "The ghosts probably can't hurt me, and I need Ness and West riding shotgun, but there's no reason to drag you into it. Let me go see what we're up against, and then bring you in if there's a way you can help."

I saw the stubborn glint in Sarah's eyes and the set of her jaw. To my surprise, she gave in. "Okay. I'm supposed to meet a friend at the Field Museum for coffee. I went to the gala when the museum first opened a few years back, and I can't wait to see what they've added since then."

Neither West nor I believed Sarah's visit was a purely social call, and I suspected she knew that we knew. Still, we all maintained the polite fiction because she'd tell us what she was up to in her own time.

We went through the rest of West's pictures. West and Sarah made short work of the coffee, but a call downstairs sent a server up with more.

"Let's have a look at the photos again when we get back," I suggested. "Maybe we'll see new details once we've had a chance to think about them."

"I can play with the developing," West offered. "I did the quick-and-dirty version to get us started, but I might be able to tinker a bit and lighten them up, enlarge them, so we can see better. Those lights were pretty dim, but I didn't want to risk using a flash bar. That would have gotten us caught for sure." The blinding white light of the magnesium flash might make a photographer happy, but it played merry hell with being able to see afterward, not good when something might be waiting in the shadows to attack.

"Do you mind if I take one with me to the museum?" Sarah asked, although she had to be pretty sure that West wasn't going to turn her down. "Something reminds me of an exhibit I saw there, and I want to see if there's a connection."

"Be my guest," West said. "Just have a good story in mind if someone asks where you got it."

Sarah flashed us a grin that made it clear she relished the intrigue. "Always!"

I went into the bathroom to get the pastry icing off my hands. I heard the phone ring and figured West would handle it. When I came back, West was finishing another Danish and washing it down with coffee.

"Ness said he'd meet us at Death Alley," West said by way of greeting. "I told him to bring a shotgun and salt rounds."

I nodded, taking a Danish for myself and refilling my coffee cup. "Our shotguns are ready to go. Made sure we had plenty of rounds last night while you played in the bathroom in the dark."

West rolled his eyes. "It's called a 'darkroom' when film's developing."

I snickered. "It's a 'dark' room when the light's out too."

We headed down to the lobby and hailed a cab from the swarm that waited near the hotel's front doors. If the cabbie who drove us wondered what was in the army surplus duffel bag, he kept his mouth shut. After all, this was Chicago. At least it wasn't a violin case.

Ness was waiting by the entrance to the alley in a black Buick, and I'd have bet money it had reinforced steel doors and bulletproof glass. He got out and held his shotgun down along his gray topcoat as if that made it less noticeable.

"Salt rounds?" he said by way of greeting. Chatty bunch, him and West.

"Dispels ghosts," I replied, pulling an iron knife out of our bag and handing it to him. "So does iron. If the ghosts attack, shoot them or slice them. I want the two of you to bottle up the alley so the ghosts don't come out and people don't go in. I'll take a little stroll and see what's got them riled up." I grabbed my shotgun and a knife. I didn't think the ghosts could hurt me, but they could be damned inconvenient, and I didn't want to find out what it felt like to be mobbed by hundreds of angry spirits.

I probably didn't need Ness and West for backup, but in case I had to blast the ghosts, I wanted guys with Fed badges to vouch for me with the local cops. Gunfire draws unwanted attention, even in Chicago.

I'd made West stop on the way so I could buy three canisters of salt. I handed two of them to West and Ness and kept one for myself. "Ghosts can't cross a salt line. Lay down a solid line across the entrance to the alley, and don't let it get broken. If you have to come in, step over the line —you're safer out here," I told them. Then I walked into the alley and glanced behind me to make sure they followed through.

The Iroquois Theater had touted itself as the most modern showplace in the city back in 1903, claiming to be absolutely fireproof. That turned out to be like the *Titanic* being unsinkable. As it turned out, the theater skirted most fire safety requirements, locked gates kept those in the balcony from escaping, and the doors opened inward. When stray sparks ignited a blaze, the standing-room-only crowd was trapped inside. Over six hundred died, and more were injured. The Iroquois was renamed and remained open for a few years before being torn down and another theater built on the same lot.

The ghosts never left.

I felt their presence as soon as I entered the alley. Even in daylight, the air felt cold, and shadows shrouded the space. I thought I could hear voices, just far enough away to not quite make out their words, although the malice in their tone was unmistakable. It didn't surprise me that I was alone here. No one mortal—or sane—should enter.

After Sarah left for the museum, I'd spent the rest of breakfast talking with West about the strange deaths in the alley. While everyone agreed that the back street had been haunted since the fire, there hadn't been reports of the ghosts causing injuries. That had only changed recently, and all the victims had ties to Capone.

Since the Mob boss wasn't a witch—as far as we knew—then he had to have some kind of supernatural help to turn regular spirits into killers. That meant the ghosts had been forced into murder after they had already suffered a tragic death. I needed to stop the killing. But more than that, I wanted to let these spirits finally rest.

This had to end.

The idea of Capone taking advantage of the ghosts made me angry, and I was, after all, the instrument of Krukis's vengeance, the champion of the powerless.

I could feel the charge in the air, like static electricity before a storm. The ghosts were all around me—I didn't need to be able to see them to know that in my bones. I said a prayer to Krukis before I entered and felt his magic wash over me, making me nearly impossible to kill.

A shotgun fired from Ness's end of the alley, and moments later, from West's side. I didn't know whether that would rile up the ghosts or put them on notice. As long as they stayed the hell out of my way, I didn't much care.

My fight wasn't with the ghosts. They were pawns, press-ganged to serve a bad master. I brought what I needed to set things right.

The air stirred in warning, in an alley where it should be still. A prickle of foreboding ran up my spine, and I was sure if I hadn't invoked Krukis's power that the hair on my arms would have stood up.

I don't have magic of my own, but when I borrow Krukis's power, I'm much more aware of the energies around me, magical and natural. I focused on those energies, trying to tune them in like a scratchy radio station, looking to get a fix on why the ghosts were riled up.

It wasn't hard to picture the scene after the theater tragedy. A snowy day just before Christmas, smoke thick in the air, weeping survivors, and the fire barely under control. Bodies everywhere, many burned beyond recognition. Whole families perished. Then the final indignity—bodies stacked like cordwood when they could finally be retrieved because the morgues were full.

No wonder the ghosts were pissed.

Shotguns fired again. I wondered if the ghosts had gone after Ness and West because they were mortal. Did the spirits believe me to be one of them, instead of *merely* immortal? That wasn't something I wanted to think on too hard.

Instead of draining their energy, the shots seemed to make the ghosts even angrier. Shadows in the alley began to move, and out of the corner of my eye, I could see gray wisps flitting back and forth. The temperature continued to drop until I could see my breath. This definitely wasn't good.

Last night after Sarah went to bed and while West was busy developing pictures, I'd called a sorta-friend, Ben Lavecchia, a Mob *strega* back in Cleveland. I carefully didn't mention any connection to Ness or Capone—after all, Benny's old man, Vincent, runs the Cleveland *Cosa Nostra*. But I did get his "professional" advice on what would turn regular ghosts into killers, and he gave me some ideas on how to fix it. So I put that knowledge to use, looking for a way to set the ghosts free and stop the murders.

"Look for the old bits," I muttered under my breath. That's what Ben told me to do. It wasn't hard to find part of the original theater's back wall. The new owners claimed they tore all of the old building down, but they kept part of the rear wall and also reused the salvageable brick from the Iroquois, figuring no one would ever know.

Soot still darkened some of the bricks like ash from a crematorium. No wonder the spirits lingered. I examined the old section closely, aware that the swish and swirl of spectral presences had grown thicker around me, wanting and watching—or maybe, preparing to attack.

I wheeled and found myself facing down a row of gray ghosts, dressed in the Sunday finery of a by-gone era, sunken-eyed and pallid.

Get out.

You are not one of us.

Not human. What are you?

Leave!

I leveled the shotgun at them, and they stayed where they were. "I'm trying to help you," I told them. "But if you mess with me, I'll blow you to smithereens. So back the hell up."

Of course, that's when they rushed me, hands like claws, mouths open and wailing, throwing pebbles and going full-on poltergeist.

I blasted them, and they vanished. But I knew they'd be back.

Whatever bound them had to be somewhere in the old section of brickwork. Thanks to Ben's advice, I spotted the sigils that were carved into the wall. From the descriptions Ben gave me, I recognized their purpose: to bind the ghosts to this location and torment them. A third sigil matched what Ben said might be a way to control the ghosts and manage who they attacked. With Capone gone, my guess was that no one was controlling the ghosts anymore and the switch had been left "on."

The ghosts drew closer, losing their fear of me. I couldn't keep blasting them and still break the spells, so I put a salt circle down to buy myself a little elbow room since the ghosts couldn't cross the salt to get their clammy spectral hands on me. That didn't stop them from hurling themselves against the barrier while Ness and West blasted them like it was a shooting gallery.

"Hey! Watch where you're aiming!" I yelled as a few stray pieces of rock salt pelted me, pinging off my metal skin. It didn't hurt, but I had no desire to have welts and bruises when this was over, even if Krukis's magic protected me from worse injury.

I'd brought a chisel with me and a hammer, as well as some protective items Ben said might help. The first blow of the point against the brick caused a flare of green light and a surge of power that threw me across the alley. Fortunately, it also blew the ghosts' images away like a strong wind, so I didn't get mobbed.

I climbed to my feet unhurt, went back to the wall, and laid down the salt line again. Before I took up the chisel once more, I pulled a flask from my bag and doused the wall with a mixture of salted holy water and a few other ingredients good for neutralizing magic. When I struck the wall again, the green light dimmed substantially, giving me a shove that I easily ignored.

The ghosts regrouped but kept their distance, more curious this time than angry. Maybe they got the idea that I was trying to help them. It took time to chisel away the sigils, which had been carved deep into the brick. Every so often, I stopped to soak the wall again, hoping to avoid being tossed around.

When the sigils were completely obliterated, I turned toward the alley and the crowd of gray specters that watched me warily. It seemed like a lot of ghosts, but I knew they were only a fraction of the number that haunted the street. The others might not have chosen to make themselves visible, but I felt sure they could still hear me.

"Ghosts of the alley—you're free!" I called out to them. "The magic that bound you and tormented you is broken. Be at peace, and do no more harm."

One by one, the spirits blinked out. I wondered if the magic had twisted them beyond saving or if, now that they were freed of the sigils' control, they would be able to remain peacefully or move on. Ben had warned that the next step, if they remained vengeful, was banishment and exorcism. I hoped that wasn't necessary.

Ness met me at the entrance to the alley. "You think that took care of them?" he asked, looking past me down the short, shadowed street.

"If it didn't, we need a priest," I replied. "Actually, that wouldn't be a bad idea, regardless. Have him come say Last Rites and do a blessing. With luck, we won't need more."

Ness shrugged. "Not hard to find a priest in Chicago. That, I can manage." He hesitated. "Nice work. I knew West's department handled the weird stuff, but I guess I never really realized just how weird it got."

"Gee, thanks," West quipped, joining us with his shotgun slung over one shoulder. He glanced at me. "You okay?"

Krukis's magic had faded, and I was just me again. West knew about my extra abilities and protections, but I appreciated his concern. "Yeah, although I might have some bruises from that salt you fired. You two ever think of aiming?"

"Sure. We can hit the broad side of a barn," West joked back. "Hit you, didn't we? It's pretty much the same thing. I thought nothing got through that hide. Gonna have to buff out some dents?"

"Very funny," I replied in a droll tone. I was used to West's style of humor. Annoying the hell out of someone meant West cared. If he didn't give a damn, he just ignored the situation. Ness watched us, and I knew he was trying to figure out the rather unorthodox relationship between West and me. I wished him luck with that because after all this time, I still hadn't.

"Are we done here? I need to get back to the office," Ness said. West and I automatically bracketed him like bodyguards as we walked him back to his car. "It'll be good to have this piece wrapped up, but we've still got more to fix. Let me know if you get any leads."

With that, the car roared away, leaving us in the exhaust.

"Let's head to the hotel," West said. "I want to show you the enlargements I made of some of those secret room photos and see what you make of them. Maybe by now, Sarah will be back from her mysterious museum outing."

"You thought it was mysterious?" I was used to Sarah doing as she pleased when she pleased, so having her take off to meet up with a friend at the last moment didn't seem odd to me.

"I don't think it was a social call," West replied. "Especially since she took some of my photo prints with her. My bet—she's got a friend on the museum staff; hell, maybe the curator is an old admirer. There's no telling when it comes to Sarah."

I could hear the admiration in his voice and shared the sentiment. Sarah was a force of nature, and we both respected the hell out of that.

"Ben said I could call him back if I had more questions," I offered. "I wish we could send drawings over the telegraph. Some things are hard to put into words."

"Maybe someday," West replied. "Now, we're just lucky I've got the portable telegraph rig, so we don't have to explain ourselves to the man at the Western Union office."

WE FOUND Sarah already in the parlor of the suite. Room service had delivered a cross between afternoon tea and an antipasto spread. Tiered plates with bite-sized pastries and itty-bitty sandwiches sat beside a butcher block cutting board heaped with sliced meats and cheeses, plus olives, peppers, and crusty bread. A pot of tea and several carafes of coffee completed the bounty.

"Figured you might be peckish," Sarah said, looking up from her spot on the couch. She had several of West's photos laid out on the coffee table.

West and I heaped our plates and came to join her, me in the nearby wing chair and West on the couch. "Find out anything interesting at the museum?" West asked.

Sarah grinned. "How'd you guess?"

West rolled his eyes. "You are the least sneaky person I know. Because you've never had to be sneaky."

"Not true," Sarah challenged, reaching over and stealing one of his olives, then popping it into her mouth. "I can be very sneaky. You don't know about it because...that's the whole meaning of sneaky."

I sighed, enjoying their banter. Sarah had the soul of an international spy and the instincts of a cat burglar, which had saved our hides many times. Both West and I knew that when she wanted to, she could out-sneak anyone.

"Some of the symbols reminded me of the ones from King Tut's tomb," Sarah said. "My father was a huge fan of Howard Carter, the archeologist, and became one of his patrons. That's how he got chummy with the Earl of Carnavon, who bankrolled most of Howard's expedition."

West and I exchanged a glance, noting that Sarah and Carter seemed to be on a first-name basis. Nothing really surprised me about Sarah's wide-spread connections anymore.

"Anyhow, I rang Howard last night, and we had a lovely chat...then I brought up the symbols that were in that sealed room." She shifted on the couch, tucking her legs underneath her as she cradled a cup of tea.

"He's spent his whole life studying Egypt, including all the stories about gods and monsters. Now obviously, I couldn't show him a picture, but I described the symbols in detail," Sarah went on. "And he felt certain that at least some of those symbols were used to bind a vampire."

I felt a prickle at the back of my neck. Sarah's comment confirmed my suspicion since the first time we laid eyes on those strange markings. West didn't gape in surprise either.

"On my way out, I wandered through a temporary exhibition of sacred relics and art," Sarah added. "Thought it wouldn't hurt to know what they had on display, in case we needed to nick a piece or two for the case."

Only Sarah would make a museum heist sound like snatching an apple from a street vendor. Then again, we'd broken into some high-class places with her once or twice before.

"We know the Mob families have vampire and werewolf factions in Chicago like some do in Cleveland," West said as he took his empty plate to the side table and poured himself a drink from a flask in Sarah's valise.

The other crime families in Chicago might not object to de-throning Capone for his excesses, but if Ness decided to go against all of them, he couldn't win. I hoped he was smart enough to have figured that out.

"What was Capone doing with a vampire captive?" I mused. "Or was it just a windowless room for the vamp to sleep in and not a prison?"

West shook his head. "When Sarah and I were inside, the door into the hotel didn't have hinges on the inside. It was steel. Sounds mighty unfriendly to me."

"Harold wanted me to show the pictures to a friend of his at the museum who curates the Ancient Egypt exhibit. We had a nice discussion, and of course I didn't tell him where the pictures came from," Sarah added, with a look at West as if she could read his thoughts.

He raised his hands like she was about to shoot. "I didn't say a word."

Satisfied, Sarah continued. "The curator could be more detailed, since he examined the photos instead of having me just describe them. He recognized some of the languages that those 'nonsense' words were from —mostly ancient and rather obscure. Hardly something Capone would just happen upon in a thriller novel." She held out her cup for a refill, and I brought her more tea, eager to hear the rest of her story.

"His impression was that the vampire prisoner was old and very strong. The words and symbols were meant to bind his power and weaken his strength so he could be...used," Sarah went on, choosing her words carefully.

"Interrogated?" West asked. "Used—how?"

Sarah leaned back, smiling like a cat with cream. "Drained...maybe of blood, possibly of power. There were other words and symbols that meant 'hidden' or 'cloaked,' which he interpreted to mean helping to hide the prisoner so others couldn't sense him."

I took a drink from the too-small porcelain coffee cup that looked dwarfed by my big hands, then set it aside before I broke it. "That sounds more like a prisoner than someone Capone was protecting," I said. West nodded, apparently thinking alike.

"Would Capone be ballsy enough to nab a vamp from one of the other Mob families as a hostage—or a 'battery' for someone's dark magic?" I asked, then glanced at Sarah. "Pardon my language."

She laughed as I knew she would, but old habits die hard. "Not a problem, Joe."

"And the answer is...yes," West replied. "Especially if he felt confident that he could keep the vampire under control." He cleared his throat. "Which plays into something I was going to tell you. I'm meeting a contact at a speakeasy downtown tonight—you're welcome to join me. He's a shifter...more Irish Mob than Italian. He's likely to have some insight or have heard rumors no one would mention to Ness."

"Let me guess—and because his family runs the joint, we can also get good booze?"

West grinned. "That too. So we don't drink all of Sarah's stash."

She waved a hand toward the valise. "Have at it. Not hard to find good hooch in Chicago, no matter what your buddy Ness thinks."

West's mouth firmed. "I wouldn't say Eliot is my 'buddy.' Colleague? Source? Occasional backup? Yes. A little too hardline for me—obviously," he added, waggling his glass of bootleg whiskey.

"And if we get raided?" Sarah asked, raising an eyebrow.

West patted his jacket where he kept his badge. "We'll hope that having friends in Federal places will keep us out of the slammer," he replied with a grin that said he relished the challenge.

SARAH TOOK us to one of Chicago's legendary chop houses for dinner, and the food lived up to its reputation. I had a huge prime rib, done just right, and a baked potato that was nearly the size of a football. West went for a Porterhouse, rare, with mushrooms and onions, and ate half my potato because neither of us could polish off a spud that size by ourselves. Sarah ordered a petit filet mignon, with asparagus and a side salad, but she stole bites of potato from my plate when she thought I wasn't looking.

We had dressed to look good and still be able to move quickly if the night required it. West and I got by with black slacks, "Fed" shoes—dress shoes with rubber soles in case we had to run—dark shirts, mine black, his burgundy, and black jackets. Easy to blend in, and room enough to hide a few weapons.

Sarah wore a midnight-blue outfit with flowing, wide-legged pants and a matching top, wrapped up in a chic, drop-waist black velvet coat over low-heeled shoes. Stunning, as always, and carrying at least half a dozen weapons that I knew about.

After cheesecake for dessert, I checked the time—fashionably late enough to go looking for trouble. Sarah paid the bill, and we walked out with her between us, taking an arm on each side. Knowing Sarah, she loved the attention of being escorted by two brawny guys—even better since the joke was on the audience if they drew unseemly conclusions. "Let's Misbehave" was Sarah's motto long before it became a hit song.

"So where's this mysterious nightspot?" I asked West as we headed out. If anyone else found the speakeasy's name, "86," a little ominous, no one mentioned it.

"Right around the corner," he replied. West led us down the kind of dark alley smart people avoided in the big city. It took me a minute to realize he was whistling *Mack the Knife*. A few guys my size or larger lounged against the walls and gave us the eye, but they nodded to West as he whistled on past them, and I realized the song was a code.

The alley looked cleaner than others I'd seen in Chicago, without any piles of smelly garbage or skittering rats. More to the point, it didn't stink like a latrine. That alone was a tip-off this wasn't just another side street. West stopped in front of a dented steel door which was in the middle of a brick wall. Nothing identified the building, but *86* stood out in black paint against the steel, and below it, a narrow opening with a sliding panel.

West stopped whistling and rapped in a precise rhythm on the door. My brain caught up a moment later, recognizing the pattern as Morse Code. *Dash-dash-dash-dot-dot, dash-dot-dot-dot-dot.* Code for "8-6"—clever.

The sliding panel drew back. "We're closed. Whaddaya want?" The voice sounded like it belonged to someone who was big, hairy, and bad-tempered.

"Just lookin' for my melancholy baby," West replied with a straight face.

The slide slammed back into place, and for a moment I thought West had gotten the password wrong. Then the door creaked open, and a bouncer who made me look tiny opened the door, stepping back to let us in. Given his size, we all had to shuffle past sideways toward steps that led to a lower level.

After all the theatrics with the whistling, tapping, and password, I was expecting a secret handshake, but apparently we'd passed muster.

"Whoa," I muttered under my breath when we got to the bottom of the stairs because I'm classy like that. For as questionable as the alley above had been, the downstairs rivaled the opulence of the Standard Club if it were crossed with a fancy brothel. Dark wood, rich emerald- and ruby-toned wallpaper and stage curtains, accented by the glitter of polished brass and the glint of huge mirrors with beveled edges.

Over-the-top luxury, exemplifying the belief that too much is not enough.

Cigarette girls tottered past in short skirts and high heels with their trays of smokes. A blue fog hung in the air, proof that the patrons were enjoying a cigar with their bootleg bourbon. A jazz band played on the stage, and a few daring souls did the Charleston and the Lindy Hop on the minuscule dance floor.

Like with Ben Lavecchia's speakeasy back in Cleveland, the customers came from all walks, united by their love of a good time, a good drink, and the chance to thumb their noses at the government. As long as they minded their manners and followed the dress code, the social restrictions of the street-level society proved flexible here.

The musicians were Black as well as the bartender—but so were several couples in the audience, dressed to the nines. Two women in flapper-style dresses sat a little too close to be best friends, as did some fellows at a back table, sitting shoulder to shoulder and no doubt hip-to-thigh. I was almost-but-not-quite sure the band's torch singer was in drag. If anyone tried to make an issue, I felt certain that "Tiny" at the door would give them the bum's rush out. I was still in the early days of immortality, but I'd already lived long enough to decide that most of the rules people made each other miserable over were a bunch of bunk.

"Where's your friend?" Sarah asked as West slowly pivoted to scan the room. He was looking for his contact while I sized up the place for escape routes and possible threats.

"Sarah?" a voice asked behind me. We turned to see a tall man with angular features and chestnut hair approaching us.

Sarah looked surprised, then pleased. "Lassiter? My god, what are you doing here?" She gave him a warm hug, then stepped back and shook her head. "You haven't changed at all."

"You two know each other?" West sounded surprised. I, on the other hand, just assumed Sarah knew everyone until proven otherwise.

"Saranac Lake, 1926," they said, almost in unison, and laughed. It must have been quite the memory, whatever it was.

"Friends of friends are married to friends," Sarah replied, turning to West and me. "That's the short version."

"C'mon—I've got a table in the back." Lassiter Davis waved us toward a circular booth in a back corner where we could all sit with our backs to the wall and see the door.

I remembered what West had told us about Davis being a shifter and bet that was news to Sarah, although she played it cool. The name rang a bell with me, and I searched my memory, trying to place it.

Lassiter Davis. Davis Stockyards. One of the biggest meatpacking companies in the Midwest tied into the railroad barons and mobbed-up to the hilt.

Now that I knew, I could see the wolf in him. His light brown eyes were an odd color for a human, with the glint of a predator in them. Davis knew Sarah and West, but he eyed me cautiously, clearly sizing me up to decide whether I was a threat or an ally. I stared back, unintimidated.

The leather cushioned corner table might as well have had Davis's name on it. Clearly, he held court here, and he ushered us into his space with the kind of entitled confidence that came with wealth and being an apex predator.

"What brings you to Chicago, Jack? As I recall, you don't like the cold." Davis gave West an assessing look.

"Cleaning up Capone's mess," West answered with an honesty that surprised me. "Dark magic, and some creatures he's controlling that go way beyond 'muscle.'"

"Shoulda figured you'd get pulled in," Davis said, signaling to a tux-clad waiter to bring over a crystal bottle of dark liquor and three more glasses. He poured for us and slid the drinks to their owners before taking a sip of his own. "You working for Ness?"

I felt the tension rise, despite Davis's friendship with Sarah and his history with West.

"*With* him, not *for* him," West replied. "And while he knows about a couple of the incidents, I'm not of a mind to tell him more than he needs to know."

That seemed to appease Davis, whose shoulders loosened and jaw relaxed. "And you think I know something useful?" Those gold-brown eyes held a shrewd light in them.

"You always do," West replied, and I wondered what the story was between them because they knew each other well enough to telegraph entire conversations with just a few words.

Davis sighed and leaned back, taking another sip of bourbon. "The Families survive because there are *rules*," he said. "Limits. Boundaries. When the rules are broken, it's bad for business, bad for everyone. Capone is a hotshot. Thinks the rules don't apply to him. There've always been witches. But bringing in creatures beyond the vampires and the werewolves who are part of the Families...that's been off-limits."

"I heard the Delacroix family cooperated with the Feds to put Capone away." West's voice stayed neutral like he was discussing the weather.

Davis nodded. "They did. Because they believe Capone destroyed their patriarch. Their *maker*."

Well, shit. Wars have started over less.

"Did he?" Sarah asked, leaning forward intently.

Davis shrugged. "That's what a lot of people believe, which matters more than whether or not it's true."

A powerful vampire prisoner might explain the sealed room in the basement of the Landmark Hotel, but I wasn't going to bring it up if West didn't.

"I imagine you heard about what the papers are calling the Saint Valentine's Day Massacre," Davis went on. "Even Ness's people couldn't mistake bites for bullet holes. Something ripped those men to shreds—and it wasn't one of ours."

"Werewolf?" West asked. I knew that in the supernatural community, shifters believed themselves to be better than weres because they could change at will and weren't governed by the cycles of the moon. Shifters were born to their abilities, not turned by a bite, another thing they saw as a mark of superiority.

Davis shook his head. "Not anyone from the local Families. But Capone had connections with the Canadian bootleggers—and their wendigos and rougarou are a bit more...feral."

"Why would the Canadians meddle?" Sarah asked. I was wondering the same thing myself.

"They had a lot of business dealings with his organization," Davis said with a shrug. "If he's out of the picture, they'll want to protect their interests, and that usually begins by knocking off the competition."

"Why are you telling us this?" West asked. We'd tried to keep a low profile, but just being seen with us put Davis at risk.

Our host leaned back against the upholstered seat, looking weary. "I'm tired of the fighting. It's a drain on all our resources and energy that, frankly, we could be putting to better use. When the Families have equilibrium, the killing stops. We can all focus on business. Capone broke the rules, and he's left a mess for the rest of us. I don't trust Ness at all. I trust you more," he said to West.

I noted the shades of gray in that statement. Davis trusted West more than Ness, which still fell short of real "trust." At least he was being straightforward, and I could respect that in a man.

"How did Capone get involved with the occult?" I asked.

Davis looked at me for a moment before he answered, as if he were second guessing his assumption that I was just hired muscle. I get that a lot, and it doesn't usually bother me. While they're busy dismissing me, I've got my eyes and ears wide open.

"Capone's grandmother was said to be a witch who could put the Evil

Eye on someone," Davis answered. "That sort of thing gets taken very seriously around here. But Capone got obsessed. I hear he read everything about magic and the paranormal that he could. Even went looking for ghosts, if you can believe that. He was a regular down at that occult bookstore, picking the owner's brain about things long before he built his organization. Couple of authors wrote books on witchy stuff, and Capone was their new best friend. Even went looking for Pat Quinlan's errand boy to learn all the secrets of the murder house."

"Murder house?" I frowned, knowing that the phrase was familiar, something from long ago, something that made the headlines…

"H. H. Holmes. Built a rooming house for the World's Fair that was really designed for him to be able to murder the guests in their rooms. Quinlan was his manager, got off scot-free claiming he didn't know anything about all the people who checked in and never checked out," Davis added with a derisive tone.

I wondered if the shifter was older than he looked. The Chicago World's Fair was in 1893, the year after I died in the Homestead Strike. When the Holmes scandal broke, it made all the papers, too sensational to ignore. I remembered it, but of course, that was too long ago for Sarah and West to recall.

"The house is still standing?" West looked horrified and surprised. Then again, he was law enforcement, so he had probably studied the case.

Davis nodded. "It's been burned, vandalized, and had more than its share of squatters and thrill-seekers, but it's still there."

"But why would Capone want all the occult stuff?" Sarah gave him that charming look that tended to make men forget their filters and tell her everything she wanted to know.

"Insurance?" Davis replied. "It's another case of disturbing the balance. Every Family has a witch. Since we all know that, it makes everyone behave. What's the good of me turning you into a toad if your people are just going to turn me into one too? Magic becomes a deterrent because it's a zero-sum game."

"Unless someone changes the rules with a one-of-a-kind weapon," West muttered.

Davis's lips twitched in a half-smile. "Right you are. Give the man a kewpie doll."

West rolled his eyes. "Cute. Who was Capone's witch, and where are they now?"

"Capone is a do-it-yourself kind of guy," Davis replied. "Must have inherited some power from his grandmother, and he taught himself what he thought he needed to know. But that's Capone, overconfident bast— jerk," he said, glancing at Sarah, who just smiled.

That explains why everything we're finding seems cobbled together, words from all different languages, symbols from a hodgepodge of sources. Capone was making it up as he went. No wonder it started to unravel as soon as he wasn't here to keep an eye on things.

The most dangerous witch is one who's untrained.

"Lassiter. We need to talk." The stranger strode up to the table like he had a right to confront the club's owner in his own space. Two of Lassiter's bodyguards closed ranks from the side, cutting off the newcomer. The stranger had his own goon behind him, although he was sizable enough to bounce the bouncer. I wondered how he managed to get by Tiny at the door.

"I have nothing more to say, Jules." Davis sounded pissed. "The answer is still no."

"If you're playing coy, I can't hold the opening for you forever," the man warned.

Davis looked at him with annoyance. "When have I ever played coy? Seriously, Jules. I'm not changing my mind. Leave now. Or I will make it happen." His voice veered from weary impatience to dangerous steel by the end, a shift that the newcomer seemed to register.

Jules's expression tightened, and his eyes narrowed. The effort at goodwill he'd mustered for his attempted negotiation dropped like a discarded mask, and his lips thinned with anger.

"I'll be interested to see how that works for you, Lassiter," he said, threat clear in his voice. He gave a dismissive look to Davis's bodyguards. "I can see myself out." He turned and headed back across the club with his goon in tow. Davis nodded to his guards, and one of them followed.

"Sorry about that," he said. "Some people just don't know when to quit." He paused as if debating with himself about how much to say.

"The Canadians I mentioned? Jules Duval is one of them," he went on. "He's Rocco Perri's man—Capone's counterpart in Toronto. We can't figure out whether he was sent to spy on Capone or make deals behind his back. He didn't waste a day after Capone got taken away before he was moving in on all of his partners, offering them better terms, trying to cut his organization out of the deals. That's not how business is done," Davis said, reproach clear in his voice.

"Just one guy? I'm surprised someone hasn't come after him," I said.

Davis shrugged. "He's slippery. And Capone's organization is in chaos right now. That's the problem with a strongman—doesn't trust their lieutenants enough, so there's no one to hold everything together."

Davis, like Sarah's friend Kirkpatrick, struck me as a new generation of mobster. More educated and refined than the guys who had clawed their way up from the back alleys and never quite left that brass knuckles attitude behind them. Still all shark, but wrapped in expensive suits and pricy haircuts. That made them even more dangerous in my book because no one would mistake Capone for being an upstanding citizen, but these slick guys could pull it off, which made them a lot harder to deal with.

After that, Davis and West talked shop for a little while, with Sarah chiming in when someone she knew came up in conversation. I fell back into being a bodyguard, scanning the room for threat, making note of faces, paying attention to who was with whom. Never knew when that might come in handy.

At a certain point, Davis seemed to disengage, and West realized we'd been dismissed. We left amid promises to stay in touch, which I didn't know whether West meant or not.

No one had paid us any attention when we walked in since we hadn't been of importance. But after spending most of the evening with the big man in private conversation, it was clear others had noticed and regarded us with an evaluating gaze, sizing up our threat level. I gave them a dead-eyed glare, suggesting I'd shoot them and step over their bodies without thinking twice about it, and the room parted for us as West and Sarah swept through like the homecoming king and queen amid their court.

Once we were back in the alley, we didn't need to discuss wanting to put distance between ourselves and 86. The big guys still loomed in the alley, and although seeing us leave the club meant West's defiant whistle wasn't necessary, we felt a little more welcome coming than going. A stray dog followed us, probably looking for a handout. I didn't relax until we were back in the safety of The Drake Hotel.

It was well after midnight, and the night clerk gave us a bored once-over. Since he didn't summon security, we must have passed his scrutiny.

We gathered in the suite's parlor to make plans for the next day before turning in for the night.

"I'm going to chase down the murder house angle," I said before anyone else could claim it. Holmes had been executed decades ago—his tomb encased in concrete to deter grave robbers—but that didn't rule out dangerous energies. I'd be less vulnerable than either of them, which is why I claimed the task and hoped we didn't have to argue.

"I think a discussion with the owner of this 'famous' occult bookstore is in order," West mused. "If Capone was a regular, maybe he knows what topics interested him. That could help to point us in the right direction, narrow the field."

"I'll take the authors," Sarah volunteered, sounding excited. "A friend of mine from boarding school, Juliana, runs a long-standing book club here in the city. The topics of those occult books might not appeal to her crowd, but I bet she knows the authors—and probably all the gossip about them."

West let me clean up in the bathroom first since he wanted to poke around with his photo developing stuff before he turned in, and I wasn't going to fight about the chance to get some shut-eye.

I had the feeling that we'd learned something important tonight. I just wasn't sure what it was. With luck, tomorrow would help to narrow that down because I couldn't shake the impression we were on borrowed time.

3

Finding Pat Quinlan's errand boy, Eddie Durant, wasn't as hard as it sounded. He held court on a park bench a block from Holmes's "murder castle" and offered to take passers-by on a tour if they'd just buy him a drink.

Eddie was probably in his early forties, but he looked like he'd taken the long road to get there. Jaundiced skin and bleary, bloodshot eyes gave the short version of his story, along with the way clothing hunt off his gaunt frame.

I peeled a few bills out of my wallet and held them out. Eddie reached for them with a shaking hand, and I pulled back, just enough to get his attention. "I want a tour. A real tour," I said. "Not just walking around the block. Take me in the basement."

A shudder ran through Eddie, and I saw his lip twitch. West and Lassiter Davis had dismissed him as a drunk and a con man, and I didn't doubt that both were true. But Eddie had the look of a man who saw horrors he could never outrun, and I suspected he'd been trying to drown those images in alcohol for a long time.

"I can't—"

"I think you can," I replied. "You took Mr. Capone there." It was a gamble, but I knew from the way Eddie flinched that I was right.

"Nobody tells Mr. Capone no," Eddie replied, and his gaze flickered between the money and my face.

"I can be very persuasive." I knew that the money I held out was far more than Eddie's normal fee, enough to feed him a few good meals, buy a bottle or two of rotgut, and a cheap room to sleep it off in.

"You sure? A man can't un-see what's in that place," Eddie asked with a shiver.

"I'm a history buff," I replied. "And I've got a strong stomach."

"Don't say I didn't warn you," Eddie muttered, leveraging off the bench. He led the way to the infamous building and stopped on the opposite side of the crosswalk. A black and white stray dog eyed us from its spot near the park fence.

"Place used to have two more floors," he said, gesturing toward what was now a one-story brick building of storefronts at street level. "Always had the shops on the bottom, but the third floor was for the hotel and the second floor was for bad things." His expression darkened. "And the basement was for real bad things."

We crossed at the corner, and I tried to picture the building as it had been before a fire—most believed it to be arson—gutted the top two floors. Given the building's horrific story, I was surprised there'd been an effort to save it at all. Would have thought the city fathers might have been glad to be rid of such a notorious reminder.

Here and there, I could still see scorch marks on the bricks, as I had back in Death Alley from the theater fire. I wondered if the place was haunted and figured it had to be. Holmes had confessed to twenty-seven murders, but most people thought there had been many more. I suspected they were probably right.

"I was ten years old when Mr. Quinlan hired me to fetch things for him," Eddie said without looking back to see if I had followed him. "Thought I'd hit the jackpot, what with this being such a fancy place and all. I just wanted enough money to buy me a ticket to the Worlds' Fair and get something to eat when I got there," he added.

"Did you ever go upstairs?"

Eddie shook his head. "Not back then. Mr. Quinlan used to meet me at the back door to tell me what he needed and take what I brought back for him. Later though, after it got shut down, but before the big fire, us kids used to go in and explore." He licked his lips nervously. "Creepy damn place."

I knew the basics from the accounts in the newspaper, although I couldn't say so without revealing my real age. The third floor had appeared to be normal, with the hotel office and guest rooms. Even so, hidden passageways, trap doors, secret chutes, and elevators made it possible for Holmes to dispose of bodies without being seen.

The second floor held many of Holmes's most fiendish additions. Airtight rooms piped with gas to asphyxiate those trapped inside, dark rooms with no light fixtures, a maze, secret doors, and other oddities designed to trap and kill his guests. In the basement, he could clean up the corpses and dissect them to sell to medical schools. A crematory furnace and an acid bath helped eliminate the evidence. Reports said he even owned a medieval rack.

"Did you meet Holmes?" I asked, trying to gauge how crazy Eddie was. I had the feeling that he'd seen more than he could handle, even if that compelled him to keep returning to the scene of the crime. Although he'd only been a kid at the time, I wondered whether some errands seemed less innocent in hindsight and if the alcohol he clearly overused helped to blur both memories and guilt.

Eddie's gaze slid away. "Only once. Near the end. Mr. Quinlan always seemed nervous if Mr. Holmes was around, like he might get in trouble for asking me to help. He didn't seem to want Mr. Holmes to know who I was."

My mind supplied darker reasons since Holmes had killed several children who became inconvenient, in addition to the many women he murdered. If Quinlan had been protecting Eddie, it was one of the hotel caretaker's few admirable actions.

"And?"

Eddie squirmed. "He had cold eyes, even when he smiled. Like he could put on being nice, but he really wasn't. My dad was like that, so I knew the type. I thought Mr. Quinlan seemed afraid of him. To be honest, kinda reminded me of the way my mum used to tell my dad anything he wanted to hear to keep him from getting mad."

I didn't doubt that Quinlan had gotten himself in way over his head with Holmes and did whatever he could to keep from becoming one of the many victims. That didn't excuse turning a blind eye to the goings-on at the hotel.

"And Mr. Capone? What did he want to see when you took him inside?"

Eddie looked both ways as if to make sure he wouldn't be overheard. "He kept asking if I'd ever seen odd markings or symbols around the place," he replied, dropping his voice. "Or if I ever got sent to pick up items from witches. Whether I'd seen either of the men work magic.

Weird stuff. I mean, who believes in that kind of thing?" The nervous laugh told me that Eddie did, even if he didn't want to say so.

"What did you tell him?"

Eddie bit his lip. "Mostly the truth. That I hadn't gone inside when Holmes lived there, and that I only got to explore later, when the place was pretty damaged. But even so, there were some weird things—weird even for here."

Eddie jimmied a lock on a basement door while I kept lookout. As I waited, I called on Krukis's power. Holmes might be dead and gone, but evil stains the places where it has been welcomed and fed. Ghosts were the least dangerous of the entities such dark power might draw to a site like this. I felt the ancient god's magic change me and thanked him for his gift.

Eddie flipped on the lights as we went inside, and he led me down a worn set of wooden steps into the large basement. He didn't seem concerned about the owner of the store above us finding out we were here, and I wondered if he had a kick-back arrangement on his fee that benefitted both of them. Or maybe the store manager just rented the space and didn't give a damn about the basement.

"Don't worry. Mr. Pasarella, the store guy, never comes down here," Eddie said as if he had read my mind. He gestured toward the wide-open space. "Well? What do you think?"

Bare overhead bulbs didn't fully light the cavernous cellar, leaving shadows that clung to the edges and corners. Odd stains marked the concrete floor, dark enough to have been blood. The furnace with its wide door large enough for a human body remained in place, cold and empty. A glass trough sat to one side, and I guessed it was the acid bath Holmes used to get rid of bodies.

"You ever find any of those symbols down here?" I asked, trying to sound casual.

Eddie looked nervous like he hadn't been expecting me to want to actually poke around, just take a quick look and leave. My suspicions grew that he had glimpsed more horrors as a child than he let on, although playing dumb had probably saved his life.

"Yeah, a couple," he said, probably figuring that if he made me happy, we could leave all the sooner. He led me to spots on each of the walls, not a surprise since marking the four quarters is common in magic. I recognized the symbols from the research we'd done as a variation of a binding sigil—not quite the same as for Capone's vampire, but similar. I made note of the differences to look into later. A friend in Charleston knew all about this stuff, and he'd help me sort it out.

Other than carting off the bodies and tidying up the crime scene, it didn't look like much had been done in the basement. No surprise—even if it wasn't haunted. Tools and other evidence had been seized, but that left shelves full of bottles filled with odd powders and liquids and bins whose contents hadn't disintegrated too far to be recognizable. I recognized them as ingredients for dark magic and figured if anyone else had made the connection, they also knew enough not to mess with a witch's stash.

As I moved carefully around the room, I spotted other symbols carved into the walls that Eddie either hadn't noticed or didn't want to talk about. "You said you went through the upstairs after the fire, once Holmes was long gone. Were symbols there too?"

Eddie shivered and squeezed his eyes shut for a few seconds before he answered me. I suspected that he'd found more than he'd bargained for exploring those places.

"Yeah. In the wallpaper pattern, in the borders, carved into the wood. All over the place. I think...I think they kept the souls from leaving because we heard voices and saw things."

In the park, Eddie had been willing to put on a show for some drinking money. The pale, gaunt man in front of me wasn't acting. He'd seen and experienced things that had shattered him to the core, making him Holmes's final victim.

"What other questions did Capone ask?"

Eddie scrubbed a hand over his grizzled jaw, either trying to remember or not wanting to say. "He asked about who did the killing for Holmes, whether he did it himself or had someone who worked with him. And then he wanted to know about how Holmes got people to trust him —because he could be a charming bastard—that's how he got close to those women. I said I didn't know, couldn't help him. He looked around a little after that and then left."

Capone had been thinking of outsourcing his murders long before he trapped a vampire and enlisted help from a wendigo and werewolf to kill his rivals. He'd seen something in Holmes that he admired and went looking for a blueprint for dark magic and occult power. As for the interest in Holmes's charisma, charm was the stock-in-trade of every con man, so I figured Capone wondered if there'd been spells involved to help Holmes work his will on his victims and those around him.

The idea of one madman seeking inspiration from the dark, twisted mind of another sent a chill down my spine.

"I think we should go," Eddie said, almost stuttering with nervousness. "Before, you know, the cops notice or something."

The basement had grown colder. I didn't doubt the ghosts knew we were here, poking around in a room no sane people wanted to visit, the place where the last indignities had been done to the bodies of the victims. But I sensed something else as well, something evil that wasn't a ghost—and probably had never been human.

"Hey, Mister? We need to go," Eddie urged, his voice gone higher with fear. He was smart to be afraid because something very wicked was heading our direction.

"Go," I said. "Get away. I need to deal with this."

I expected to hear Eddie's running footsteps and the slam of the door. Instead, I turned to see him standing with his shoulders back, head raised. "Not leaving you in here. I'll stay."

Even pale with fear, Eddie stood his ground, and I respected that. "Here," I said, handing him an iron poker from next to the oven. "Anything comes at you, swing this." Then I put down a circle of salt around where he stood, as he watched me, puzzled. "Don't step outside the circle," I told him. "You're safe inside."

Eddie gave a curt nod. "What about you?"

I felt the hum of Krukis's magic and knew I was protected. "I'll be okay. Someone needs to settle this."

A wisp of dark smoke curled from the vent of the oven, though its fires had long gone cold. The column of smoke swayed, growing more substantial, taking on the rough shape of a man. Naked, hairless, with glowing red eyes and crimson lips framing sharp white teeth, the creature glared at me and smiled.

"Leave," I ordered. I suspected from its appearance that it was an imp and not a full demon, but still very dangerous.

"And miss dinner?" it replied in a dry rasp. The creature rushed toward me in a blur of movement like a dark storm, enveloping me. I could feel it trying to force itself inside, hoping to possess me, perhaps sensing my strength and coveting that for its own use.

"Leave him alone!" Eddie stammered, mustering his rage despite his fear. He held up the poker like a baseball bat, ready to do battle. I wondered if he'd glimpsed this creature before.

With a hideous chuckle, the imp tried again, evading my blows with the iron knife I'd pulled from my belt, intent on forcing itself on me.

I could hold the imp off, thanks to Krukis's magic, but I didn't come prepared to exorcise a demon, and I feared I wouldn't be able to protect Eddie. I shouted a banishment spell in my native Hungarian, knowing that the infernal spoke all languages. It pushed the creature back, but only for a moment.

Funny thing—you can't be possessed by an imp if you're already the champion of an ancient god.

And apparently, ancient gods don't like to share.

Sparks flew and a flash of lightning—indoors—struck the roiling black cloud as a tendril of power also zapped Eddie like a live wire and sent him flying back against the wall. The entity shrieked loud enough to rattle glass and vanished.

Thank you, I silently told my patron. Then I ran to help Eddie, who had shaken off the power surge and climbed to his feet.

"What was that? And how did you make that happen?" he asked, wide-eyed.

"I'm afraid that's a long story."

"It's gone," he said in a wondering voice. I figured he meant the black smoke imp.

"I don't think it'll be back," I told him. "And to help make sure, I'm going to break the sigils on the walls."

He shook his head. "No, I don't mean that *thing*, although it's good to have it gone too. I mean, in here." He laid a hand over his chest. "I think there's been a bit of that darkness in me since the first time I ever came to this house, and it wouldn't let me go. But now...it's gone. For the first time in all those years, I'm free."

Eddie still had the gray-flecked stubble and unkempt hair, disheveled clothing, and worn boots as when I met him. He still smelled of alcohol and sweat. But his eyes now held a clarity they lacked before, and he stood straighter, his own man instead of an owned creature. If he'd had that imp's influence riding him nearly all his life, no wonder he'd sought to drown it out however he could.

He refused to leave while I made a circuit of the room, watching me cut through the sigils and douse them with salted holy water from a flask in my pocket. If the store owner above us heard anything, he chose not to investigate. That made my job easier. If the store weren't still occupied, I'd have had no hesitation about burning that cursed building to the ground.

"I'm never coming back here," Eddie swore as we left the basement. I believed him. The thing that kept him tethered was gone, and I suspected that Krukis had destroyed the imp rather than merely sending it away. Even so, I meant to talk to Ness about sending a priest to do a thorough cleansing—along with Last Rites for the ghosts and an exorcism too. Now that the imp was gone, maybe the spirits were free to rest as well.

We parted ways across the street, where that same stray dog hadn't moved from its place by the fence. "I don't know who you are or how you did that, but thank you," Eddie said.

"Take care of yourself," I told him. "Good luck."

NEITHER WEST nor Sarah had returned to the suite yet when I arrived, so I took off my jacket and my shoes, helped myself to hot coffee and some cookies from the freshly stocked goodies in the parlor, and thought about what I'd seen at the murder house. It didn't surprise me that some kind of infernal taint afflicted Eddie. It probably sank its claws even deeper into Pat Quinlan, and no doubt the imp played a role in keeping Holmes's victims from escaping. I wondered what effect it had on the storekeepers and their staff in the first-floor rental and how much that kind of evil might have polluted the entire block and the land beneath it.

I didn't have that kind of expertise, but I had a contact in Charleston who was an even older immortal than myself, and he had knowledge of such things. I glanced at the time and knew he was still asleep in his safe place until sundown, so I promised myself I would give him a call once night fell.

Sarah arrived next, cheeks flushed from a brisk walk in the cold autumn air. Room service followed on her heels with a tray of sandwiches, crudités, assorted nibbles, and mini cheesecakes. Another server made a new batch of coffee and refreshed the creamer, sugar, and cups. Life with Sarah meant never going hungry.

"Oh, you're here. Good," Sarah said as she swept into the room, tossed her coat over a chair, and stepped out of her shoes. She washed up, then came back, made herself a plate, and plopped onto the couch to eat with such unapologetic glee I couldn't help smiling.

"I'm famished," she announced, and took a bite of a ham and Swiss sandwich, then crunched through a couple of carrots. "Go ahead—fix yourself a plate. I hope West gets here soon—I had a good morning, and I want to tell both of you all about it."

I fixed lunch for myself and sat across from Sarah in the wing chair. Fancy furniture made me nervous since it rarely looked sturdy enough for my bulk. I'd already tested this chair, but even so, it took me a moment to let it take my whole weight.

"This hotel has good food," Sarah enthused, jumping up to get a fresh cup of coffee and then curling back onto the couch, this time with a plate of cheesecake bites as well.

"Excellent food," I agreed. I'd been hungry at times in my life and made do with much less fancy fare. That just made me all the more grateful when a good meal came my way, especially when it was shared with allies and close friends.

"You're not going to believe what I found out," West announced as he strode through the door. He stripped off his coat and hat, carried them to the bedroom, and tossed them on a bed—hopefully his and not mine—and then came back to retrieve a sandwich in one hand and a cup of coffee in the other, foregoing the plate. Sarah just shook her head and chuckled.

"Go ahead," Sarah said. "I'm going to savor this cheesecake."

West finished his sandwich in record time. "I met with the man who started the occult bookstore. I hadn't been sure what to expect—thought he might be walking around in wizard's robes or something. Turned out to be a rather mousy guy in a three-piece suit who looked like he might be a professor. He's a Spiritualist, like those table thumpers up in Lily Dale, but the store goes far beyond that…I felt a bit like I'd walked into a witch's lair."

"What do you mean?" Sarah asked, clearly fascinated. The glint in her eye made me wonder if she'd be paying the store a visit herself before we headed back to Cleveland.

"Crystals, candles, oils, and all kinds of powders and dried plants… thought I might get hexed just looking around," West recounted, only partly kidding.

Sarah gave him a measured glance. "You don't look like a toad to me. Well, more than you usually do," she added with a twitch of her lips.

"I managed to skip that part," West replied in a dry tone. "Anyhow, the man remembered Capone—younger at the time—being a regular. He would riffle through the books and ask questions, mostly testing the owner's thoughts on whether he believed all of it was true. Later on, Capone asked about how to use the magic for his own gain. That started to make the owner uncomfortable, but he knew even then Capone was mobbed up. So he told him as little as he could and tried to steer him away from the sources that had spells of any real power. He definitely thought Capone was trying to teach himself to be a witch."

Sarah ran her finger around the rim of her coffee cup as she thought. "He must really have had some talent. Anything else?"

West shrugged. "More of the same. Toward the end, Capone asked a lot of questions about demons. The bookstore owner swore he didn't give Capone any real information, but that's worrisome."

"Did you get any input on the symbols or the words from the hidden room?" I asked.

West nodded. "Yeah. I took a few of the pictures, blown up enough that no one would know where they were taken. Made up a story about where I found them. What he said matched a lot of what we'd already worked out. He did say that some of them weren't just for controlling ghosts or vampires...they were also ways to summon and master a demon." He gave us both a pointed look. "And he swears Capone didn't learn the marks from him."

"Fits what I heard," Sarah said, and set her cup aside, then stretched. "Both of the occult authors I talked to were more like professors than something out of *Macbeth*. But they were very willing to expound." Her smirk suggested that Sarah had gotten all the answers she'd been looking for.

"And?" West asked, voice muffled a bit with cheesecake.

"They said Capone sought them out, invited them to dinner at his private club, and plied them with questions all evening about the rules of magic and how ghosts and spirits functioned. He wanted to know how to summon ghosts and control them and how to make binding marks and banishing spells."

"So he pieced his magic together bit by bit, do-it-yourself, instead of having an actual mentor," I said. "That's about the most dangerous way he could do it."

West shrugged. "Capone had a different tolerance for danger, or he wouldn't have ended up running a major Mob operation." He glanced at me. "How about you?"

"I banished the imp that infested Holmes's murder house—with some help from Krukis."

West choked a little, and Sarah didn't try to hide a chuckle at his reaction. "You what?" West asked, eyes wide.

I told them the whole story, leaving out nothing, even Krukis's dramatic appearance. I don't usually talk much about the whole servant-of-a-god thing because I like at least pretending to fit in with normal people some of the time. I know Sarah and West don't hold it against me, but it always makes me feel...different. Which I am. But sometimes it's nice not to be reminded.

"If that darkness affected Eddie, do you think it touched Capone too?" Sarah asked when I finished.

"Why wouldn't it? Especially when Capone wanted to tour the house because he actually admired Holmes's ability to get away with his crimes for so long," West pointed out.

I nodded. "Capone certainly wasn't pure of heart when he got Eddie to take him through the place. So whatever touched him just made him worse."

"A demon, huh?" West mused. "Not exactly part of the standard playbook."

"Thought you boys in the Supernatural Secret Service didn't follow the normal rules," Sarah teased.

"We don't," West retorted. "But this whole case is going off the rails. Rogue vampires. Werewolves or wendigos carrying out Mob hits. Vengeful ghosts as hitmen. And now demons? I'm never going to be able to show my face at headquarters after I turn in this report. No one is going to believe me."

"Yeah, but you'll have the best stories in the bureau," Sarah joked. "Think of the bragging rights."

"If they don't fit me for one of those jackets where the sleeves wrap all the way around and tie in the back," West said, rolling his eyes. "This is a lot to take in—even for me."

"I think we need to go see Capone's old floor at the Landmark Hotel tomorrow," Sarah said. "I want to see how that secret room fits with the rest of it, and find out if Capone had other hidden places. If he liked that murder house as much as you say, he could have had the Landmark retrofit his place to suit him. Who was going to tell him no?"

Now that we knew a little more about what was going on, I agreed. "Sounds like a plan. We just need to get access."

Sarah smiled. "Leave that to me."

4

W e stacked the dishes on the sideboard and cleared off the parlor table so we could each work on research from the books we'd brought with us and a few that West purchased at the occult shop. As soon as the sun went down, I excused myself and called Sorren, my contact in Charleston. A servant answered the phone, asked my name, and said he would inquire whether Sorren was available. I waited in silence, trying not to be impatient.

"Joe. Good to hear from you. How can I help?"

I'd only met Sorren once. He looked like a well-off young man in his twenties, but I knew he was a vampire who was more than five hundred years old. Although he could pass for American, I'd heard he had been a jewel thief in Antwerp before he was turned. For the last several centuries, Sorren had headed up an alliance of mortals and immortals who kept the world safe from supernatural threats.

I laid out my concerns and described the symbols and spells we'd found, and Sorren listened without interrupting. That gave me confidence that we hadn't truly imagined the whole thing.

"What you're describing is entirely possible—and very dangerous. If he really has bound a vampire to his will and kept him imprisoned—especially with those sigils—then it's very possible his prisoner has gone mad. I'm glad you're handling this, Joe. With your protections, you're probably one of the few who can."

That validated my concerns but didn't make me feel any better. "How do I stop him?"

"Beheading is the only sure way," Sorren replied. "I'd suggest burning the body as quickly as possible. You wouldn't want to run into one who had a resurrection spell in place."

No, I definitely wouldn't.

"Thank you," I told him. "Any advice on the werewolves?"

"Just make sure you know what you're dealing with. Werewolf, shifter, wendigo, rougarou. Under certain conditions, they can be similar enough to confuse a hunter, but the differences matter," Sorren replied.

"Davis felt sure it wasn't a shifter, although that might have been his pride talking."

"Shifters see themselves as more human than the others, and to an extent, they're right," Sorren told me. "They're not compelled to shift, either by the moon or a curse. They could go without shifting for a long time if they needed to, although it's not good for them. It's easier for them to pass among humans without raising suspicion, and they aren't as prone to violence. Not to say a shifter isn't just as capable of murder. But when they do kill, it's their own choice."

"What's your hunch?" I knew Sorren had been playing this game longer than I had.

"You know I'm not psychic," Sorren said with a chuckle. "But I think your shifter was telling the truth. If the werewolves are tied to the Mob families, then I'd think they would know of an unaffiliated newcomer and deal with it themselves. That leaves wendigos and rougarous, the more feral cousins."

I asked everything I could think of on how to kill those creatures, and Sorren shared his knowledge and experience. When I finally hung up, I still felt uneasy, but at least I had a better idea of how to handle the situation. He'd also shared a contact, Father Michael Kinsella, at Holy Name Cathedral, who he suggested might be receptive to helping with occult matters. I decided I'd give the good father a call to cover all our bases.

I mulled over the information we'd read and the additional details from Sorren. What we knew seemed to point to one conclusion—and a pretty strong suspicion.

"I think we're dealing with a rougarou," I said when I came back to the parlor where Sarah and West were still working. Sarah had tuned the radio to symphony music, and while I suspected West would have preferred a ballgame, I didn't mind at all.

"How do you figure?" West asked, glancing up from his book.

I told him what Sorren had said and why that probably ruled out shifters and werewolves. Then I went on to the answers I'd come up with. "The people the creature killed were clawed apart, but not eaten. A wendigo is a cannibal. That doesn't fit with the evidence or with the kind of creature Capone needed under his control. A witch can curse someone to be a rougarou though," I added.

"Can they pass for human?" Sarah asked.

"That depends on the version of the legend," I replied. "But most say it's possible. What if Capone laid a curse on someone and controlled when he could shift?"

West gave me a horrified look. "So the person wouldn't have a choice or be able to stop the shift?"

I shrugged. "Again, there are different versions of the story, but I'm inclined to believe that Capone would want a 'secret weapon' that he could turn on and off at will."

"And what about the cursed person?" Sarah asked, looking fascinated and repelled in equal measures. "Can they be cured?"

"That was one place where the lore was consistent. No—not after they've killed their first human."

West looked like he was about to ask another question when the phone rang. He went to answer it and returned looking decidedly unhappy.

"That was Ness. Duval wants to meet up—said he had information we'd want to hear," West said as if he had a bad taste in his mouth.

"Wanna hear my theory on who the rougarou is?" I asked, pretty sure West and Sarah had already guessed.

West whispered a curse, although I knew Sarah wouldn't object. Hell, I'd heard her say worse in a dire situation. She could curse like a sailor when the occasion warranted.

"Duval?" he said as if daring me to disagree.

"Uh-huh. Both the wendigo and rougarou are Canadian monsters. Duval fits the bill—he's on loan from Capone's partner-slash-rival in Toronto, he had a beef against Capone as soon as the man got sent to jail, and he's the new guy in town," I replied.

West nodded. "Glad we're on the same page. The question is—does Ness know?"

I thought about it for a minute and shook my head. "Doubtful."

"He's walking into a trap." West didn't even make it a question.

"That's my bet." Shit. I had figured we'd need to deal with Duval, but I hadn't meant right fucking now.

"Do you know how to deal with a rouga-yoo-hoo or whatever Duval is?" West asked.

"Yeah. We've got all the stuff I need," I replied, glad for the conversation with Sorren. "Damn, I just wanted to set it up so it was on our turf instead of Duval's."

"It is what it is. Better hurry. We'll need to catch a cab to get there in time."

If this situation ended up going our way, I'd be spattered with blood on the return trip, so I hoped Ness could give us a ride home because no cabbie in his right mind was going to stop for us. "Take your machete," I told West. "I've got salt, a lighter, and a flask of alcohol to torch the body afterward."

"You think Ness will go along with that?" West's eyebrows rose.

"The man's a little naive about supernatural things—he's not stupid."

"Have fun," Sarah said. "I'm meeting a dear friend in the private bar downstairs for illegal cocktails and the inside scoop on the Lexington Hotel. Her father was the general manager. We did the Grand Tour of Europe together, right after boarding school." A mischievous glimmer came into her eyes. "Had ourselves quite a good time on that trip. Forget Paris—hello, Prague!"

I most definitely didn't want to know. West just rolled his eyes and shook his head. "C'mon," he said to me. "Probably not a good idea to be late and leave Ness to the wolves."

Sarah wished us luck, and we headed down to catch a cab. We couldn't talk with the cabbie listening in, which left me with my thoughts. My head felt overstuffed with everything we'd discovered, and I tried to sort out my impressions and make a plan.

If this was a trap, Duval was taking a hell of a chance because it wasn't even full dark yet, and the meeting place he'd suggested was on a busy street filled with restaurants that would be filling for the supper crowd. Gutsy place to make a hit, but wouldn't be the first Mob kill in plain sight, not in a town like Chicago. Anyone who knew what was good for them would find they hadn't been paying attention, didn't remember, had been doing something else when the deal went down. Witnesses would be nowhere to be found.

Still, it would be awfully brazen to pull something like that unless Duval was desperate, and as far as we knew, he didn't know West and I were onto him. Unless he thought he could take all three of us and just rid himself of the nuisance.

He'd shown plenty of arrogance making a move on Capone's territory so soon after the mobster's arrest, so maybe Duval figured he was invincible. Lassiter Davis hadn't seemed worried about Duval, but clearly no love was lost between the two.

The cabbie dropped us off. I noticed a dog lurking by the lamppost, the fourth or fifth I'd seen today, starting with one outside the hotel and two in the park where I met Eddie. Someone needed to do something about all the strays. Then again, as long as the dogs weren't hellhounds, it wasn't my problem.

I sized up the area. The cold evening meant no one lounged at outdoor tables along the row of restaurants, but from what I could see through the big plate-glass windows, the tables inside already looked packed. I didn't mind the cold as much as I used to when I was mortal, but the wind off the lake was something else entirely, worse here than in Cleveland.

A garbage truck sat parked or broken down across the street, without its crew at this hour. Cars lined both sides of the curb. One of those was Ness's bulletproof Buick. He must have been keeping watch because he got out when he saw us, and West and I once again closed ranks on either side like a security detail.

"Duval say what he wanted?" West asked as we walked toward the restaurant.

"Said he had something to hand off to us, something that would help us put Capone away for good," Ness said. The turned-up collar of his coat and slouched angle of his hat made his face difficult to see—no doubt exactly what he intended.

"You believe him?" I asked.

"No. And even if he does have the goods, it's because he's seen a way to advance his own cause, not because he's an upstanding citizen," Ness replied.

"Could be a trap." From the stiff way West held his shoulders and the slight turn of his head as he scanned for danger, I guessed he and I were on the same wavelength as far as anticipating trouble.

"Of course it's a trap," Ness snapped. "Either the contents are bogus, or there's an agenda behind giving them to me. Or he wants to kill me."

I wondered if he wore an armored vest beneath his topcoat. That wouldn't protect him from a head shot, but it ruled out a slug to the chest. I thought about praying to Krukis and decided to wait. If Duval really was a rougarou, he might sense my "otherness," and I didn't want to spook him. I didn't know what Duval's agenda might be, but I had my own—plenty of questions that needed answers.

Duval looked cool and collected as he loitered outside Tivoli, a classy sit-down restaurant that probably had good food if the aromas filling the air were any measure. He held a dark leather briefcase, just another businessman to the eyes of passers-by.

"Wasn't sure you'd come," Duval greeted Ness. He eyed West and me, and without him saying a word, I might have felt unwelcome if I actually cared. "Didn't need to bring your troops."

"Mutual interest," Ness said in clipped tones. "What do you have for me?"

Duval's gaze flickered from side to side, making sure we were still alone. "Copies of invoices, ledgers, bills of lading. Cooked books. What you've got has him iced for now, but it won't hold him long. Prove he cheats on his taxes, and you might keep him locked up a while longer."

"And what's the price?" Ness clearly didn't like Duval. I suspected the feeling was mutual, but Duval did better hiding his animosity. Or maybe he just wanted something.

"Capone's unstable. Dangerous. He's upset the balance. Take him out of the equation peacefully, and we can all get back to business as usual."

Ness snorted, making it clear that he didn't hold much with Duval's idea of "business as usual," but I was reminded that the enemy of my enemy was my ally, if not actually my friend.

Still, something struck me as off about Duval. For all that he feigned being unhurried, his body looked ready to spring. I saw the tightness at the corners of his eyes and mouth, the way his breath was shallow and fast. He knew something we didn't.

"You want the papers or not?" Duval growled. "I'm sticking my neck out here helping you, not to mention being seen."

I could see the calculation in Ness's features, trying to figure out Duval's angle. He knew this would come back to bite us on the ass in some way, but the allure of finally finding something that would put Capone away for good was nearly irresistible.

"Give 'em here," Ness said, holding out his hand. Duval offered the briefcase, and Ness took it.

"You didn't get it from me," Duval warned. "Now beat it before someone sees us."

Duval turned and strode off in the opposite way we'd come. He moved a little too quickly as if trying not to run.

Shit. The briefcase is a bomb.

I shoved West in the direction Duval had gone. "Go! Get him!" In the same breath, I called on Krukis and prayed he was listening and felt speedy.

I felt the old god's power shimmer over me in the same second that I launched myself at Ness and slammed him to the pavement beneath me. If that case went off, not only would Ness die, but it would blow out the restaurant windows, and a whole lot of civilians were likely to get badly hurt, or worse.

Ness groaned as I landed on him, and I hoped I hadn't broken his ribs, saving his life. I pinned his body while I tried to rip the handle out of his grip. Stubborn to a fault, Ness didn't let go, and I feared I'd have to break a finger or two. I had no idea how long of a timer was on the bomb, but Duval sure had seemed in a rush to be elsewhere.

I finally had the case and sent it spinning on its side beneath and beyond the car nearest me. I knew the heavy steel of the wall of parked cars would shelter us, although broken glass was still a hazard. I trusted my magically metallic skin to protect us.

The stray dog that had been following us bolted from where it had been lounging near the corner. I saw running paws beneath the car's chassis, and for an awful moment, feared it intended to retrieve what I'd thrown in a deadly game of fetch. I couldn't see what happened next, but the case didn't come sailing back over the car, and the explosion, when it came, sounded muffled along with a heavy *thump* and a weird echo.

Ness tried, unsuccessfully, to push me off, probably wanting to breathe. Krukis's power left me, taking about thirty extra pounds or more with it. I rolled to one side, and Ness gasped for air.

"What the hell?" Anger flashed in his eyes, and I figured he was one of those guys who covered his fear with bluster.

"Saving your life. You're welcome," I replied, getting to my feet and dusting myself off. The restaurant patrons wisely stayed inside, obviously native Chicagoans.

Ness's cheek had a nice scrape, and he might have a black eye. One arm curled around his chest, and I felt a little guilty about the ribs. With luck, he wouldn't have a concussion too. Then again, if I hadn't gotten the bomb out of his hands, he'd have been confetti, so it was still a win.

West came running up. "I lost him," he admitted. "I looked back, and that stray dog grabbed the case and pitched it into the garbage truck. What in the name of God is going on?"

Stray dog. "Oh, shit. The dogs. Lassiter Davis probably put a literal 'tail' on us. I wonder if he was curious or if he suspected something from Duval."

Ness had gathered his wits enough to speak to the beat cops who came to investigate, and flashing his badge made our departure quick and uncomplicated. "I'll drive you back to the hotel—then I want to know all the stuff you haven't told me."

"That might take a while," I replied.

"I've got all night," Ness said in a voice that didn't allow for leeway.

He pulled the Buick into the lot behind The Drake Hotel. Night had fallen, and the lot looked a little too dark for my taste. It didn't register with me until we'd all gotten out of the car that the overhead lights had been shot out.

Duval was waiting for us. This time, he didn't waste time on human weapons like explosives. He raced from the well of the loading dock, transformed into his beast. Coarse gray hair covered his too-long arms and gaunt body. Clawed hands and feet posed a distinct danger, as did the big fangs prominent in his lantern-jawed face.

Ness and West had their guns out and firing while I sent up a plea to my patron. I didn't wait to feel his power this time, knowing that my regular immortality protected me from the worst Duval could dish out, short of ripping off my head. Krukis could probably fix even that if he thought I was worth the effort.

"Joe—stay back!" Ness yelled. I ignored him and rushed Duval, putting on the kind of speed no one expects from a guy with my bulk.

Colliding with Duval's rougarou felt like hitting a hairy wall. He was solid muscle and strong as a bear. Claws raked down my arm, raising bloody gouges and hurting like a son of a bitch. Ness and West yelled for me to get out of the way so they could resume target practice, but none of their shots had slowed down the creature. Maybe if they'd put one between his eyes, but both G-men went for center mass, just like they were trained to do.

The rougarou wrestled me to the ground, and I planted my feet and flipped us, trying to shift my grip so I could get to the machete on my belt. West knew what I was fighting, but he'd never seen one before. From the stream of profanity coming from Ness, the Fed had no idea what was going on.

Finally, I felt Krukis's power kick in. I rammed my elbow into the rougarou's chest and then launched an uppercut that shattered his jaw. A well-placed back kick with my boot broke a leg. That bought me time to roll to my knees, pull my machete, and scythe it right through Duval's neck, sending the head tumbling as blood fountained.

"What the everlasting *fuck*?" Ness roared.

West had already holstered his gun and went to retrieve the monster's head, carrying it by the hair like I'd seen in a painting somewhere. An empty barrel on the loading dock caught my eye. I jogged over for it as the adrenaline of the fight left me, and Krukis took back his magic for what I hoped was the last time tonight. Thanks to him, the gashes in my arm were already healed.

Neither of us answered Ness until we'd crammed Duval's body and his head into the barrel and gotten the lid on. I wondered if he'd stay in his rougarou form, or if whatever poor bastard opened the barrel would find a naked, headless man inside. I didn't much care. One part of our problem was out of the way.

"Rougarou," I finally answered Ness, as if that was sufficient, and among the right people, it would have been.

"What?"

"Rougarou," I repeated slowly. "Kinda like a Canadian werewolf, only not really. That was Duval, trying to finish the job since the bomb didn't work."

"That creature was Jules Duval?" Ness looked at me like I'd lost my mind, but the occult was my territory, and so I had home-court advantage.

"Yep. And most likely the one who Capone controlled to kill the North Side Gang in the Saint Valentine's Day Massacre. You said they'd been shredded."

West nudged me. "We should leave before anyone notices the blood."

I felt bad for the custodian, but not enough to stick around and clean up the mess. Ness was our stay-out-of-jail ticket, and if he couldn't handle this, we were going to be in trouble.

Ness had a blank look, but I figured he was processing what had happened tonight, squaring it with the missing pieces and theories. He'd called West and me in to find and kill Capone's pet monster, and we'd done exactly that—while uncovering a few additional threats along the way.

"I think we need to talk," Ness said finally.

West gave me a once-over. I looked like I'd come from a battle, covered in blood with my jacket sleeve hanging tattered from the rougarou's claws. "Go get a shower, Joe. I'll take it from here. Get some rest."

I figured that was West saying he would handle Ness Fed-to-Fed. Fine with me. A hot shower sounded heavenly to get clotted rougarou out of my hair, and I wouldn't turn down a slug of Sarah's bootleg whiskey either.

West and Ness stepped carefully around the pool of blood, and I went up the service stairs, hoping I didn't run into anyone. I took off my ruined jacket, turned it inside-out, and used it like a towel to scrub away the worst of the mess. That way I merely looked like I'd been hit by a bus instead of bathing in the blood of my enemy.

Today had already lasted an eternity, and I couldn't wait to get clean and grab some shut-eye. Relief settled over me when no one came to knock on the suite door after I let myself in, meaning Sarah was still drinking with her friend in the hotel's secret bar. I really wasn't up for conversation. I didn't want to alarm her, and I didn't feel like giving a play-by-play recap just yet.

Once I had stripped out of my blood-streaked clothing and stood under the shower, I started to feel human again. Getting the gore out of my stiffening hair took time and a lot of soap, but by the time I finished, my skin was pink from scrubbing, and every trace of the rougarou was gone.

Something pinged in the back of my brain, meaning an overlooked tidbit, probably important. It would have to wait. I pulled on pajamas, tossed off a slug of whiskey from Sarah's stash, and nearly face-planted on my bed, utterly done with saving the world for at least a solid six hours.

5

S arah's friend, the daughter of the Lexington Hotel's former general manager, had spent part of her childhood living in a suite at the property long before Capone took over two floors for his headquarters.

"I hadn't seen Louise for years, although we kept in touch through our boarding school network," Sarah told us at breakfast the next morning.

It was far too easy to get used to having a hot breakfast made to order and delivered to our suite, along with all the coffee we could drink and pastries to top it off. I fully intended to enjoy every moment, and nothing seemed to deter West, either. I had no idea how Sarah indulged and still stayed trim, but then again, her boundless energy probably burned the food off as soon as it was consumed.

"Of course, when she lived at the Lexington, she and her friends went exploring," Sarah continued, licking the icing off her fingers. "Found all kinds of secret passageways and hidden rooms—and that was long before the Mob. Some of the corridors went down to the coal and ash tunnels…and to other places underground most people have forgotten about."

I knew that at one point, parts of Chicago had been "mudjacked," raised above the flood levels, and that often left streets and what used to be the first-floors of buildings permanently buried and eventually lost to memory. A perfect place for a rogue vampire to hide. My chances of finding him in all of that were nil, even with all of Ness's G-men at my beck and call.

She grinned conspiratorially. "Louise was always a rule-breaker. She had a regular little explorer gang going, pretending they were archeologists, completely fearless. And she kept in touch with some of her friends whose fathers stayed with the hotel when hers moved on. Got an earful about Capone's time there, and all the juicy rumors about how he used the rooms and passageways and made some additions to suit his lifestyle."

"Are you going to keep us on tenterhooks, or tell us?" West asked, fondly vexed.

Sarah couldn't help loving the spotlight. I had no trouble forgiving her excesses because she always came through in a pinch and had some of that fearlessness herself that she admired in her friend.

"She says Capone had a secret vault hidden in a room off the hotel basement. No one was allowed in the room except him, and whenever he went inside, the maintenance staff who caught a glimpse said he was wearing weird robes like some kind of priest."

West and I exchanged a glance. "Or ceremonial robes to do magic," I said. The true practitioners I knew weren't into the costumes and folderol unless ritual required it. They didn't swan around in velvet robes or wear pointy hats or call attention to themselves. But Capone had pieced his knowledge—and probably his grimoire—together on his own. That made it likely to be cobbled together from Lovecraft's horror tales and Aleister Crowley's mad ramblings—with just enough real information to be extremely dangerous.

"We had quite a nice evening," Sarah said. "Polished off a couple of bottles of wine in the hotel's hidden bar, reminisced a lot—and found out everything Louise could tell me about how to navigate the secret parts of the Lexington." She had a cat-that-ate-the-canary grin again.

"Ness and I were in the very dry restaurant," West observed. "Glad you and your friend didn't happen to pop out at the wrong time. The Drake wouldn't be happy if we brought his Untouchables down on them."

Sarah shrugged. "That's why I gave the maître d' your description and asked him to send me a note if he spotted you."

I didn't try to hide a snicker. Lucky for us, Sarah chose to use her many talents for good instead of evil, or the world would be out of luck.

"You didn't happen to get a map, did you?" West asked.

Sarah produced some drawings on the back of the daily specials menu insert. "It's been years, but she remembered most of it. What she couldn't draw, she described. We need boots because some of the oldest tunnels hold rainwater, and we should take lots of flashlights."

"I'd suggest bringing whatever we need to handle a rogue vampire because if Capone's ex-prisoner is still on the loose, old abandoned tunnels are going to be where he's hiding," West warned, echoing my thoughts.

"Do we tell Ness?" I asked, although I felt sure I already knew the answer.

"Hell, no!" Sarah replied before West could open his mouth. "This is our adventure. Besides, I don't want Louise's name to come up. She's married to a dreary banker who has absolutely no sense of humor."

West and I gathered the weapons and the supplies we'd need for exploring and vampire hunting from our gear. Sarah sent the concierge to buy Wellingtons for all of us and had them delivered with extraordinary speed. Charm, wealth, and being an extravagant tipper will get those kinds of results.

We headed over to the Lexington Hotel, and Sarah took a suite on one of the former Capone floors. That gave us a reason to hang around and explained the trunk of equipment we brought with us. Of course, we kept our real base at The Drake as a fallback when we were done.

I threw our boots into my gear bag so we didn't have to tromp through the hotel in them, and we headed out. Capone's people had only recently been cleared out, so with the help of a master key West pick-pocketed from a housekeeper, we started with the rooms the mobster had inhabited personally.

"I imagine Ness and his boys picked this place over pretty well," West mused as we fanned out through Capone's suite. I feared he was right. Beds were stripped down to bare mattresses, upholstered furniture slit open where the Feds had looked for contraband, small personal items gone except for a few crumpled papers. In one corner, flush against the outside wall, stood a lead safe. The thick door hung open, but I eyed the vault as my mind worked out possibilities.

"Looks like they beat you to whatever was in there, Joe." West stood beside me, then took a few steps and bent down to do a futile double-check and came up shaking his head.

"Betcha they didn't look behind it or under it."

West looked at me in disbelief. "Probably because they couldn't get a mule team in here to drag it out."

I shrugged. "Good thing you've got me." I had better than normal strength without calling on Krukis, and I didn't want to wear out my welcome with the god, so I figured I'd do this on my own. I inched the big safe out, "walking" it first one way and another until we had enough room for West to see behind it with a flashlight.

"Yeah, there are a couple of things. Can you tilt it so I can see under?"

I obliged, although I grunted at the weight. Fortunately, West moved fast. "Got it!" he said, coming up dusty but triumphant.

I shoved the safe back into place, and then Sarah and I clustered around West as he laid the treasures out on an empty desk.

"A red pair of dice, a carved ivory elephant, some saints' medallions, and a pocket watch," Sarah observed. "Maybe they were on top and got knocked behind."

"Or maybe they were pushed behind as a last-minute hiding place if the Feds surprised Capone," I theorized. "They could be ritual items."

"There's also this." West added an old-fashioned key to the pile. "What are the odds it opens the locked door to that ritual room with the busted wall?"

I wasn't a bookie, but I figured that was a safe bet. "Okay, Sarah. You're the one with the map. Where do we go now?"

"Louise said there were eleven secret staircases—counting the two Capone added when he was living here—and ten different tunnels out of the hotel, not including the coal and ash passageways," Sarah replied. "Supposedly, some of Capone's new additions led to his favorite brothels and speakeasies."

"Let's have a look at that ritual room, and then that secret vault," I replied. "We're burning daylight, and we don't know if the rogue vamp even needs to sleep during the day down in the passageways."

We gathered our equipment, and West pocketed the loot from behind the safe. I had a funny feeling about the seemingly meaningless items like they weren't random at all. They'd been hidden for a reason; I felt certain of it. I just wasn't sure what it all meant.

The Lexington was a much older hotel dating from before the turn of the century, while The Drake was not quite a decade old. The age showed, mostly in the behind-the-scenes passageways Sarah led us into, following Louise's directions. While the guest areas had been refurbished, the service hallways showed water stains on the plaster, peeling paint in places, scuffs, and dinginess that came with age and hard use.

We found the "hidden" room more easily than I expected. "Easy to ignore" was more like it, a locked door in an off-jog in the hotel's sub-basement. From the location, I guessed it was initially a storage room. Although with the secure door and heavy lock—neither of which looked new—I suspected whatever had originally been stored was valuable or dangerous—or both. Capone had certainly made good on that with his latest "guest."

"This looks even weirder the second time," Sarah murmured as we walked inside, and she flicked on the lights. Now that we had translations for the words scrawled across the walls and the symbols interspersed between them, I could imagine Capone keeping a vampire imprisoned here. Someone had patched up the outer wall after our minor vandalism.

"Davis said the vampire Mob helped to catch Capone because they blamed him for killing their maker," Sarah said. "What if he didn't kill him? What if he kept him prisoner?"

"Why?" West asked. "He had to know the vamp would get away sooner or later."

"He might have been a hostage to ensure the rival Mobsters would do as he wanted," Sarah replied.

I felt the pieces of the puzzle fall into place in my head. "He didn't want the vampire—he needed his blood." They both looked at me, trying to figure out where I was going with this. "He didn't just bind a vampire. He also bound a demon. Maybe he started off controlling the wendigo and then Duval and his rougarou, so he took the vampire and increased his power. But I think the demon was what he was after all along."

Remembering the conversation with Eddie and what happened at the murder house made me certain Capone had decided he needed a demon of his own, one that served him, not the other way around.

"So where is it? And why haven't we run into it?" West asked, making a slow circle of the room as if mentally matching the scribbling on the walls to the photographs we had all studied long enough to memorize them.

"Whatever you do, don't say the words out loud," Sarah warned. "That never goes well in the fairy tales."

I could almost feel the tumblers turning in my mind, *thunking* into place. "Didn't you say Capone had another vault? A secret one?"

"Louise wasn't entirely sure where it was—because, you know, secret. But she narrowed it down to a couple of possibilities," Sarah replied.

"Were any of them near here? Because if Capone needed the vampire's blood to bind the demon, he probably didn't want to be traipsing all over the hotel with it," I said.

Sarah consulted the notes she'd made and the rough map Louise had drawn for her. "Yeah—this one," she said, pointing to the picture. "It's on this level. I think he took another heavy-duty storage room and sank a vault into the concrete. I doubt the staff come down to this area anymore —all this old-fashioned equipment isn't in use and probably hasn't been for a while."

If the staff had any intuition at all, they'd have steered clear of the area. Between the vampire and the bound demon, it should have given anyone with the least bit of sensitivity to the supernatural the heebie-jeebies.

"We need Father Kinsella," I said. "Handling a vampire is one thing. But taking on a bound demon—it would be good to have backup."

West looked askance at me. "I thought you and your ancient god sent the demon at the murder house back to hell?"

"That was an imp, a minor infernal creature. We have no idea how strong the demon is that Capone bound."

"Won't your patron think you're cheating on him?"

That was a good question. Then again, I'd worked with priests before, and Krukis had still heard my prayers. Krukis had been worshipped long before a virgin gave birth in Bethlehem, before Rome, before Catholicism. He and the old gods had nothing to fear, nothing to prove. Those meant to follow them found their way to where they belonged.

"Krukis will be fine. The priest might be a little confused, but the friend who made the referral wouldn't steer me wrong," I said. If Sorren thought Father Kinsella was okay with our kind of problems, I trusted his advice.

"If Capone had a bound demon, how did the Feds catch him?" West asked.

"Something must have happened to weaken his protections," I said. "Maybe it was the vampire escaping. Duval seemed to slip his leash pretty quickly too. It might also be that with Capone far away and unable to keep up his end of the bargain with vamp blood, the demon doesn't feel like making good on his promises."

"What about the items we found behind the other safe?" West reached for his pocket as if to jangle them, then stopped himself.

"We figured out the key," I replied. "Spells often require objects that mean a lot to the caster as a focus or as ritual items in the process itself. Just because the knick-knacks look like junk to us doesn't mean they're worthless. They might have held a lot of meaning to Capone."

"What now?" Sarah asked. "Stop and get your priest friend, or go looking for that vamp?"

It was just after lunch, so we could do some exploring and still get back to the room in time to call Father Kinsella and invite him over for dinner and demon banishing.

"Let's explore a bit," I replied. "That rogue vampire is around here somewhere, and if he's got a nest nearby, I'd like to get him out of the way before we try to deal with the demon."

I pulled the boots out of my bag and handed out flashlights. Many of the hidden passageways led from the upper floors of the hotel, one of them from Capone's own bathroom. We could deal with those later, if need be, and not need our boots. I doubted the vampire had been rattling around behind the walls. Too much risk of discovery. He'd go where it remained dark, down in the lower tunnels, places that had been abandoned even by the desperate.

The coal and ash tunnels had working electric lights, although with enough distance between the fixtures that dark pools stretched between the glow of the bare bulbs. From the rust on the tracks, it didn't look like this section saw a lot of traffic. The farther we walked from the Lexington's secret exit, the more deserted the tunnels became.

"I think I read something about some of the above-ground businesses no longer needing the ash removal when they changed over their furnace systems," West said quietly. "Guess that included the ones in this stretch."

We stayed close together, flashlights slicing into the shadows. Several areas had puddles, making me glad for the boots and suggesting another reason why this stretch of tunnel might no longer run trains. With a lake and a river close by, Chicago was known for wet basements and flooded first floors.

I halted, and the others nearly ran into me. "Look." My angled beam showed footprints emerging from a darkened side tunnel, preserved in the skim of sediment on the floor.

"Not fresh," West remarked, crouching for a better look. "But recent."

There'd been a big rainstorm the night before we arrived. That probably left damp walls and wet floors in the tunnels. It also provided a rough idea of when our quarry had passed this way since the muck most likely remained soft for several days.

"If he escaped right about the time we got here, then he hasn't gone far," I replied.

"Why not leave? Go back to his people?" Sarah asked, her voice just above a whisper.

"We don't know the toll Capone's rituals took on him. He might not be sane," I said. *Just what we need—a vamp that's crazy as well as rogue.*

I peered into the darkness of the side tunnel. Either the wiring had failed, or someone intentionally put out the overhead lights. Much as I wanted to find our missing vampire, I wasn't suicidal enough to go in there, even with Krukis's magic. A moment's concentration focused sharper-than-human senses. I picked up the stench of old blood and a smell that mixed flop sweat and spoiled meat.

"Let's go," I said sharply. I didn't doubt that the vampire had its nest down that godsforsaken tunnel, but we needed to be gone before he picked up our scent as well. I suspected that Sarah and West came to the same conclusion, as we made our retreat as silently as possible.

Out of curiosity, we poked around a few more of the older tunnels, all of them well-lit even if largely abandoned. We saw plenty of rat tracks but no footprints, nothing to suggest anyone had come this way in a long time. I felt simultaneously relieved we hadn't happened upon a pile of bones and annoyed we didn't have more evidence to show for our wandering.

We came back up through the passage in the Lexington, and Sarah huffed as she kicked off her boots. "I'm thoroughly disappointed," she said. "I was counting on finding one of those brothel tunnels." The mischievous gleam in her told me she was only partially kidding.

I cleared my throat. "Well, while you ponder the possibilities, I'm going to go talk to a priest." It seemed to me like this sort of thing was better done face-to-face. I couldn't quite imagine how it would go on the phone. "I should be back before dinner."

The walk to Holy Name Cathedral let me clear my head. Crisp fall air and the never-ending breeze off the lake felt like a slap of astringent on my face. It stung my eyes and made my nose run, but I felt alive. I tried to hang onto the little things that reminded me of being mortal: the taste of food, the smell of flowers, and the feel of sun and wind on my skin. I needed to remember so that I didn't end up adrift.

Capone had ordered a hit on a member of the North Street Gang in front of the cathedral several years ago, before he gave up and just wiped out the entire group earlier this year. Four bullet holes from a machine gun pockmarked a corner of the church. Not long before Ness's Feds swooped down on Capone, the senior priest had met with a messy end as well. I wondered what Father Kinsella might have to say about that and whether he'd be willing to help.

I'd given up on the Christian god the night I buried my wife and son, long ago. My soul was sworn to Krukis. Yet I respected that most churches, even the cathedrals, kept their doors open at all hours as a waystation for those who needed a shelter from the storm. And despite my beef with a god who hadn't answered my desperate pleas, the beauty of the architecture, the glow of stained glass, and the glimmer of candles still spoke to my battered soul. The air smelled faintly of smoke and incense, and my footsteps echoed between the stone floor and the soaring arched vaults over my head. I found that I'd genuflected and crossed myself out of habit without even realizing it.

I hoped Krukis wasn't paying attention.

In my phone call, I'd mentioned Sorren's name and that I had an urgent need to speak with him. Father Kinsella had told me to come straight away and said he'd be in the sanctuary preparing for tomorrow's Mass.

Too many memories rose to choke me as I made my way toward the chancel. This cathedral was far fancier than St. Michels in Homewood, the little parish where I'd worshipped with Agata and Patryk long ago. Candle smoke reminded me of their funeral Mass, of the way it burned in my eyes, already red from sobbing. I recalled the rumbling voice of the priest who tried to comfort me with promises of a Heaven that I didn't think either of us really believed.

For the first time in a very long while, I was back in that awful moment, cold with shock, numb with grief, barely able to draw breath, heart aching with every beat.

There was a reason I avoided churches.

"Can I be of help?" A warm hand lightly gripped my shoulder. I looked down at a slightly built, shorter man with thinning red hair who wore a black shirt and priest collar. He seemed honest in his compassion.

"I'm looking for Father Kinsella."

"You've found him."

My surprise must have shown on my face. I wondered if the man could possibly be old enough to have finished seminary, and I wondered why Sorren had sent me to this...child.

"I'm older than I look," Kinsella said, fortunately finding humor in my momentary flummox. "Shall we talk in my office?"

If he sensed that I'd been overwhelmed by memories here in the heavy atmosphere of the sanctuary, he didn't mention it. I felt glad to leave the place behind, knowing I'd most likely revisit the memories in my dreams.

He led me to his office, a cramped, overly full room that smelled of books and cigarettes.

Kinsella sat behind his desk and motioned me toward the only other chair. "Sorren doesn't call to chat," he said, giving me an assessing look. "So when he does call, I listen. He said he had a friend in town who needed a hand. Something about demons."

"We think Capone bound a demon with a shoddy patchwork of rituals and incantations he came up with himself. Now that he's not here to tend it and feed it vampire blood, we think the bindings are starting to unravel. My colleagues have some training, but they're not exorcists."

Kinsella sobered at the word and looked away. "Our senior priest, Father Callahan, was targeted by the Capone Mob because he was a powerful exorcist. We knew when that happened that Capone had an alliance he didn't want broken."

"Sorry for your loss. I guess I'm a day late and a dollar short." Why the hell had Sorren sent me here if the exorcist was already dead?

"Which is why we've kept my training at the Vatican quiet," Kinsella went on. "I showed an aptitude early in seminary, and they sent me for field studies with members of the Occulatum. I downplayed what I could do to keep another, dodgier group from recruiting me. I assure you, I have both training and experience."

He stated the information plainly but without arrogance, factual but not bragging. Despite myself, I liked the guy. "We think the demon is locked in a vault. I'd like to have you there when we open it."

Kinsella watched me closely. Assessing. "You're not exactly as you appear. If we're to battle the powers of Darkness together, I should know who I'm fighting beside."

I figured this was where I might get thrown out on my ear, but what the hell. The short version of my sad story didn't take long to tell. When I got to the part about Krukis, I expected the priest to hold up his crucifix like I was a vampire and order me from holy ground. Instead, he listened intently, tenting his fingers as he hung on my every word, and I felt antsy being the object of his sharp focus.

"The Slavic gods," he said when I finished. "I wondered since their touch was not familiar to me. We have something in common then, you and I. You are pledged to a blacksmith, and I to a carpenter. Hands-on men, both of them, doing honest work."

I blinked, beyond surprised. "And you're okay with that?"

"We serve a common goal," Kinsella said. "The alliances made in the 'shadow business' of the Church are untraditional but effective. You come with Sorren's endorsement. That's enough for me."

"Yeah, same here," I replied. "If you're game, I have some more information." I filled him in on what happened at the murder house, what we'd learned about Capone's fascination with the occult, and mentioned that Capone had controlled a rougarou, although I didn't confess to having had a hand in ending him. I'd brought some of West's photographs of the ritual room and mentioned the items we'd found behind the first safe, as well as the issue of the missing, possibly mad, vampire.

"You ever think of moving to Chicago, Joe? Because your kind of crazy fits right in here," Kinsella said, with a warm teasing that made me chuckle in spite of myself.

"Too damn...er, darn...cold, Father. But thanks anyhow."

Kinsella reached for a pair of reading glasses and examined the photos in silence for a while, occasionally asking questions about the occultists from whom Capone had sought advice. He reached behind him and took down two very old leather-bound volumes from his overstuffed bookshelf and consulted the yellowed parchment pages. His brow furrowed, and his lips firmed as he read, neither of which seemed like good signs to me. Finally, he closed the book and crossed himself with a murmured blessing.

"You're right—he's made hellish hash of the symbols and incantations," Kinsella said. "For the record—Lovecraft and Crowley weren't originally mad. What they saw and summoned drove them beyond what the human mind is meant to process without protections. I'd heard Capone's eccentricities blamed on syphilis, but I think that a more demonic origin is likely, given what you've told me."

Interesting.

"If the demon was bound using the vampire's blood, then I suspect that when we deal with the demon, the vampire will feel compelled to attend," Kinsella said.

"Lovely."

He shrugged. "Better than having to chase it through the streets and underworld of Chicago. Are your companions capable of dealing with a vampire?"

I thought of Ness, West, and Sarah. Ness didn't know the occult, but he understood how to kill. West had what the government considered to be training in the supernatural, which was better than nothing. Sarah was a civilian with dead-eye aim and remarkable calm in a crisis.

"Yeah, I think so. Is it really gonna take the both of us to wrestle this demon back to the Pit?"

Kinsella nodded. "We're going to need some materials. Some of them I have here, just in case," he added with a knowing smile. I had no doubt that he'd been sent as the Vatican's man against the Mob-fueled powers of Darkness.

"I brought some of the harder to get items with me," I told him, rattling off what was in my bag back at the hotel.

"That's good. We can work with what we've got. Those items you found behind the first safe are definitely part of Capone's binding ritual—he would have needed them every time he refreshed the spell."

"What would you like to have, to tip the odds more in our favor?" I asked.

He laughed. "I wouldn't turn down a shoe buckle from St. Theresa of Avila or the rosary of St. Anthony the Great. Our relics here at the Cathedral may help heal the sick of heart and frail of body, but they are of little use against the demonic."

"If we could borrow relics like that, would the exorcism destroy them? Or would they just lend power?"

"It might drain them for a while, but a true relic's power comes from God," Kinsella replied. "They would not be destroyed."

"We'd like to get this done as soon as possible. What's your calendar look like today, Father?"

Kinsella chuckled. "I'd like a few hours to pray, make ready—and eat dinner. But I can be good to go by about seven tonight? That soon enough?"

"You bring the holy water; I'll bring the salt. We're in Room 434 at the Lexington Hotel."

I STOPPED at a payphone and called our room at the Lexington. West picked up and handed the receiver to Sarah. I explained what Father Kinsella had said about the saints' items, and Sarah promised to see what she could finagle from her museum friends.

"Don't worry—I'm due to make a generous donation to the museum. They won't mind doing me a favor," she assured me.

"Hey, I don't know if this matters, but St. Michael is sometimes claimed as the patron saint for mobsters," I told her, remembering something I'd read. "That could work for or against us, but it's something to keep in mind."

"I'll see what I can do." Sarah passed the receiver to West.

"Ness brought some fun new toys for the party," he said, giving me a head's up that we had company. "And just so you know, there've been a bunch of 'stray' dogs outside the hotel—watch where you step."

So Lassiter Davis still had his shifters watching us. Interesting. Since one of those dogs had saved our lives, I didn't mind the extra help, although Davis's people wouldn't be anywhere close to the action at the vault if things went bad. Then again, not all of Capone's "family" had gone to jail, so maybe Davis's real goal was to make sure we weren't interrupted, although how he might have guessed our plans, I didn't know. Maybe he didn't need to know the details—he just intended to keep the Capone goons off our ass. Either way, I wouldn't turn down help.

By the time I got up to the suite, Sarah's valise with the bootleg hooch was tucked out of sight. Ness might be an ally, but he wasn't a friend, and there was no point in testing our luck. I found both men chatting in the parlor over coffee and cookies.

"Any luck with the priest?" Ness asked.

"He'll be here at seven. Had some preparation he needed to take care of," I replied, scoring a cookie for myself and pouring a hot cup of java. I didn't feel like squeezing into the armchair again, so I just leaned against the wall.

Sarah came back half an hour later, good timing since we'd nearly exhausted our capacity for small talk. She glowed with triumph and pulled a couple of worn wooden boxes out of a Marshall Field shopping bag.

"I need to bring these back by close of business tomorrow," she said. "Undamaged, if at all possible—or I'll have to write a much bigger check." Sarah was good for the money, but I respected the history of the pieces and hoped we didn't have to sacrifice them to stay alive.

"The icon of Saint Marcellus—known for slaying a vampire—is said to contain part of his finger bone," she said, placing a small but beautiful painting in a thick frame on the table. It was done in the Russian style, with gold leaf and vivid colors, and showed an old man in red and white robes.

"A relic from Saint Roche," she added, laying a small box with a glass lid beside the icon. Inside lay a rosary made of stone beads. "He was a plague saint." Since vampires were often linked to plagues, the connection seemed solid.

"And a medallion sacred to Saint Hubertus, patron of hunters." A silver disk with a crucifix and a stag's head joined the other items. She grinned. "Not quite the shoe buckle of Saint Theresa of Avila, but not too shabby either."

"They just let you take those from the museum?" Ness asked, eying her haul like he might need to arrest her.

"They let me *borrow* the pieces," Sarah answered coolly as if she had picked up a note of suspicion in the Fed's voice that irked her. "And I wrote them a check that had a lot of zeroes after the number. Consider it collateral."

Ness blinked first, which didn't surprise me. Sarah can be tough as nails.

We ate dinner in the suite, a concession to avoid attracting attention. The three of us might not be known locally, but Ness was a celebrity of sorts these days. We didn't need anyone speculating about what we might be doing together.

A knock came at the door, exactly at seven. Father Kinsella carried a black valise and had changed into a full cassock with a purple stole appropriate for exorcism. "Ready when you are," he said, and his lips twitched into an almost-smile that made me think he was enjoying this.

We headed down to the room Sarah's friend had pointed out to us. West picked the lock after letting Kinsella and me check for magical protections. What I sensed felt distant, making me think that the real protections were on the inside.

I said a silent prayer to Krukis and felt his power flow through me. Kinsella glanced at me as if he sensed the shift but didn't say anything.

West flicked the lights on, revealing pale blue walls, a color said to repel evil. Many of the words and symbols painted on the walls were the same as in the vampire room, but there were some new ones I had seen in the lore that were specifically to bind demons. Kinsella took it all in silently, but I saw recognition in his eyes.

"There's the vault," West said, pointing to a rectangle on the floor where the concrete was notably newer than the rest of the area around it. He opened our gear bag and pulled out two sledgehammers, while Ness took up a machine gun, and Sarah handled a Colt 1911 loaded with silver bullets like a pro.

We each took a few swings at the concrete, but I realized after the first round that with my god-touched abilities, I could probably do this on my own. I just needed to find a way to point that out without damaging West's ego. Fortunately, he came to the same conclusion.

"Don't you have some kind of super strength? Why am I bothering?" If he saved face by noting it himself, I was fine with that.

Goggles protected my eyes as I put my whole unnatural strength behind a swing with the sledgehammer, but shards still flew. They didn't cut me since my skin had gone metallic, and I hoped everyone else had the good sense to stay well back. The force of the strike reverberated up my arm, but since my bones were temporarily steel, it didn't hurt.

That one full-powered swing did twice as much damage as West and I did together. Two more swings shattered enough of the concrete, and West could start using a folding camp shovel to remove the rubble. A couple of taps and the door of the safe was revealed.

"Hey Padre," I called to Kinsella. "Are you ready for this?"

Out of the corner of my eye, I'd noticed the priest chanting and carefully placing candles and the borrowed relics around the room. He didn't seem to need any help translating the obscure words and phrases painted on the walls, which deepened my suspicions that he was some kind of Vatican super badass.

Finally, Kinsella turned back to us. "Alright, it's as warded as I can make it. Let me check the safe for traps."

By the time we shoveled out the debris, the actual safe was a foot below the level of the floor. West sent a coating of salt across the lead door, then climbed out, letting Kinsella take his place. I stepped aside as well since I take up a lot of space.

Kinsella ran his hands just above the surface of the safe, palm down, hovering about an inch over the metal. Suddenly a tangle of symbols and sigils flared to life, glowing like fire, covering the entire surface.

"Protections," he said. "Warnings against evil. Bindings on demons. Some of these are obscure and…it's a strange juxtaposition."

"Capone was a do-it-yourself witch," I supplied. "I think he was making it up as he went."

Kinsella grimaced. "It worked—to a point. But they're weakening. He must have been doing something to continually refresh them."

"Would blood from a powerful vampire be a component in a spell like that?" I asked.

Kinsella's eyes widened for a fraction of a second. "Yes. It would." He shook his head. "Shit. That's some very dodgy dark magic."

West cracked his knuckles loudly. "You ready for me yet?"

"Yeah," Kinsella nodded, hopping out of the vault-shaped hole. "Have at it."

We stood back and made sure West had silence and plenty of light. I didn't realize that safe cracking was part of the Fed training program, but West obviously had talent. Moments later, he hauled the heavy door open.

"Don't touch anything," Kinsella warned. "There's something with real power in there."

I could feel it, a frisson of tainted energy against my skin. Krukis's magic reacted instinctively, creating a barrier and pushing back.

A box with intricate carvings blurred in my vision, pulsing with other-worldly power. I'd lay my bets it imprisoned the demon, especially when I saw the mess of symbols that covered its surface, painted on and carved into the wood. Next to it were several bags of yellowed linen, bulging with their contents. They didn't look like much, but I felt the power rolling off them. Finally, I saw a clay tablet with strange markings, stained with what I feared might be blood.

"What do you make of it?" I asked Kinsella.

"The demon is bound in the sigil box," he replied. I nodded since that matched my assessment. "The pouches are gris-gris bags. If Capone did them right for this particular usage—and I think he did—they're made from a shroud that was wrapped around a corpse nine days in the ground."

That sent a shiver down my spine, despite Krukis's magic.

"And the tablet?" West asked. I would have laid my bets that this part of the adventure hadn't been included in his training.

Kinsella bent closer to get a better look without touching. "Can't say without examining it, but my best guess would be a binding spell. Probably immersed in the lake water and written in dove's blood."

Damn. Self-taught or not, Capone showed potential.

"Do you have the items you found—the ones from behind the other safe?" Kinsella asked. West took them out of his pocket and handed them over carefully. The priest received them like they were a ticking time bomb. He looked up to meet my gaze. "It's exactly as we suspected. He turned these into ritual items for his spell casting. They must have had a very deep resonance with him."

"How do you want to play this, Padre?" I asked.

"I'd like you to assist me since you have some additional protections," he said. "And that leaves the rest of you on guard to keep us from being interrupted. Once we start, don't let anyone inside, and don't break the salt line."

"And the demon?" Ness asked as if he couldn't quite believe he was saying those words.

"If my hunch is correct, the demon didn't want to be bound," Kinsella replied as he unpacked items he had brought with him. "It might rather be back in the Pit than stuffed in a box and buried, so it could go back willingly. But demons are opportunists, and if it gets away from us, it might decide to stick around and cause trouble. If that's the case, I will happily send it back to Perdition."

"What about the other items?" Sarah asked. "What do they do?" She pointed at the gris-gris bags and tablet.

"They're a first line of defense for the box," Kinsella said. "So we eliminate them right away."

We took our places. Kinsella laid down a thick line of salt from a container in his bag along the doorway and locked the steel door. Then he set a silver chalice on a table that we dragged to be near the safe. He put down another salt line around the edge of the broken concrete surrounding the safe so that all of us were between the two protective barriers.

Clearly, none of us wanted to touch the items inside the vault. Kinsella took the dice, pocket watch, medallions, and carved elephant and placed them in the chalice. Then he added enough holy water to cover the pieces and added sacred oil from a separate vial. The priest withdrew a wafer of the consecrated Host from a portable monstrance and held it carefully between his palms as he folded his hands in prayer. His lips moved silently, and his brow furrowed with concentration. With a whispered "amen," he gently placed the wafer on the surface of the water.

"I abjure the powers of Darkness and cast out all traces of the infernal. By the blood of Christ, the breath of the Holy Spirit, and in the name of the most holy and Almighty God, you have no dominion here. Get thee hence!"

Kinsella struck a match and cast it into the chalice. It caught in the oil and sent up vivid blue fire. At the same instant, the fragile linen of the gris-gris bags burst into flame, and the tablet split with a crack like gunfire and turned to powder.

Ness crossed himself. West's eyes went wide.

"Son of a bitch," Sarah muttered quietly.

Kinsella drew a deep breath and rolled his shoulders, proof that he wasn't as unflappable as he appeared. "With those out of the way, we can get to the main event."

He glanced at each of us in turn. "I'm going to say Last Rites for any spirits trapped here or for any ghosts who might have been sacrificed to the demon. Then I'll say the Rite of Exorcism, but I'll pour the elements directly into the vault rather than trusting the transference of power from the chalice."

Kinsella licked his lips in what I guessed to be a nervous tic. I couldn't blame him for being edgy. "There will be a moment when the boundaries between realms may thin, and the demon may show himself. It can't hurt us—so long as the protections remain unbroken."

Otherwise, those thin boundaries might not hold the demon at bay.

The priest made a careful circuit of the room, checking the candles, saying a short prayer for protection to the four archangels—Michael, Raphael, Gabriel, and Uriel. He returned to the center and began to slosh salt liberally into the vault, each time with a prayer for deliverance from evil. He followed that up with a drizzle of holy water and then sufficient sanctified oil to set the remaining contents of the safe on fire.

I felt waves of energy coming off the demon box. The entity inside might be bound, but its anger and malice transcended its fetters. Despite my protections from Krukis, I took a half step back, a gut reaction to the embodiment of evil.

Father Kinsella gripped a silver crucifix and began to say the Last Rites. The temperature in the room dropped. My heightened senses picked up chaotic energy, as if the demon hurled itself against the confines of its prison, sensing that it had been unearthed and had a shot at freedom.

This felt different from the imp at the murder house, a matter of scale between a light summer breeze and a fierce, deadly storm at sea. I thought of the mayhem Holmes had been able to achieve with the help of his minor spirit and shuddered at the thought of what this full demon could enable Capone to do.

Father Kinsella faced the adversary with a grim expression, jaw set and eyes hard. His wide-legged stance and squared shoulders made it clear that he would not be moved.

Krukis didn't offer any suggestions in my mind, but I knew that his eternal enemy was Veles, god of the underworld, so his sympathies would be with us, which was clear in his assent to share his magic with me.

Despite being god-touched and nearly immortal, fear bloomed in my belly. Only a fool faced a demon without apprehension.

As Father Kinsella transitioned from the Last Rites to the exorcism, a loud crash somewhere close by shook the room. I put myself between the priest and the doorway, staying within the salt circles. West, Sarah, and Ness readied their weapons and faced the entrance.

The steel door groaned as an unstoppable force ripped it free of its hinges from the outside, bending the metal before tossing it aside. The violent opening broke the salt line, scattering the grains.

Capone's rogue vampire stood in the doorway. Despite the disappearances and bodies in the coal ash tunnels, the creature looked starved, corpse-white skin drawn tight over the bones of its face, fangs protruding over pale lips, eyes sunken and wild.

A barrage of gunfire echoed deafeningly in the small room as silver bullets tore into the vampire at close range. In seconds the creature's chest was a mess of black blood and ribbons of dead flesh. That didn't stop the monster from sending West sprawling with a backhanded blow, hurling Ness across the room and shoving Sarah hard enough to send her tumbling.

They all aimed for center mass instead of splattering the vampire's skull into pieces.

Kinsella never faltered, keeping up the cadence of the Latin as he neared the end of the exorcism. The energy in the demon box roiled within its confines, and I sensed that if the spirit broke free, it would slaughter everything in its path.

Which left me as the last redoubt against a crazed and starving bloodsucker.

I drew my machete, intent on keeping the vampire away from Father Kinsella. The vampire bared its teeth and lunged, moving too fast for the human eye to track.

But I wasn't human, and I saw him just fine. Sharp nails screeched against my metallic skin. I heard the snick of teeth, but they couldn't pierce through. I reached out and grabbed the vamp with one hand, struggling to hold him even with my god-granted strength. The monster fought with the power of madness, but it was weakened from hunger and age, and I was the instrument of a deity.

I swung my machete, and it sang through the air, cleanly lopping the head from its shriveled body. The jaw continued to snap open and closed, and the corpse twitched, making me fear that for once, decapitation might not be sufficient. I brought my boot down squarely on the vampire's face, crushing the bones and breaking the jaw. Thankfully, the rest of the creature stilled. Ichor and gobbets of dead vampire spattered me from head to toe, and I wanted to lose the contents of my stomach.

Instead, I turned my attention back to Father Kinsella and the vault. The air had grown thick with tension and straining power, and from the concentration on the priest's face, the demon put up one hell of a fight even with its bonds. The wooden box shook, juddering back and forth as if it might blow apart. Green light, like blinding foxfire, blazed from the sigils and markings, forcing me to avert my gaze. Kinsella narrowed his eyes but didn't look away, as if he were staring down Lucifer himself.

"...*Ut Ecclesiam tuam secura tibi facias libertate servire, te rogamus, audi nos!*" Father Kinsella shouted the last of the Latin rite triumphantly, with his arm outstretched and fingers splayed, palm out, as if to shove the demon back to Hell.

The demon shrieked a sound that conjured nightmare images and would forever haunt my dreams. Its infernal voice held the peril of the Sirens and the banshee, sharp like talons scoring against my bones. Kinsella's eyes blazed with fevered intensity, pitting one man's will and his unwavering belief against an agent of damnation.

Kinsella lit a match and dropped it into the vault. It caught with a small explosion, and in the crimson fireball that rose toward the ceiling, I saw the leer of a demonic face and the contorted form of its body, right out of the most tortured Medieval paintings. The strange fire rushed upward, spreading across the ceiling, and for an instant, I feared we would all burn. But the demon flames didn't catch in the concrete ceiling and vanished between one breath and the next, although my ears nearly bled from the demon's keening.

The fire died as quickly as it had risen, leaving nothing but black ash in the vault and the lingering smell of sulfur and smoke.

Father Kinsella crumpled in slow motion, eyes rolling back in his head, body slack, sinking to his knees, boneless.

Fearing the worst, I caught him, relieved to see the rise and fall of his chest and watched the steady beat of his heart in the pulse at his neck. Only then did I have the chance to check on my friends, worried that the vampire had hurt them. To my relief, they looked dazed but not seriously injured, though they would probably have spectacular bruises.

"Is it over?" West asked as he dragged himself to his feet with the help of the wall. "And how the hell did the vampire get in here?"

I lifted the priest in my arms like he was a sleeping child. Krukis's magic left me, but I remained easily strong enough on my own to carry the other man.

"They re-patched the plaster and concrete hole in the wall of the ritual room, but no one replaced the words and symbols," I replied, berating myself for overlooking the obvious, a mistake that could have cost lives. "The vampire had a connection to the demon through the blood ritual. Or maybe the demon called to it, hoping to kill us and get away. But without the wardings in place, the vampire broke through the wall and found its way here."

Ness helped Sarah to her feet. West glared but said nothing. After all, we three would be leaving in a Pullman car together in the morning, while Ness stayed in Chicago to finish his mission.

"What do we do with the vault?" Ness asked.

"I vote we close it up, spin the lock, and pour new concrete over it," West said. "Leave it buried and out of reach."

"Sounds good," I agreed, as Ness and Sarah nodded. "Although someday, someone is bound to find it and dig it up. They'll be mighty disappointed to discover that Al Capone's vault is full of nothing but ash."

"It would serve them right," West replied.

Ness let out a long breath and ran his hand back through his hair, looking young and exhausted. "Thank you. It's just going to take a little while to process all this. It's...highly irregular." His smile wavered, but I admired his effort to keep himself together. "And the more I think about it, the more I like the idea of going after Capone for his taxes if we can't make the other charges stick. Two monsters down, one to go."

"What are you going to do with the priest?" Sarah asked, nodding toward Kinsella, whom I still held in a bridal carry.

"Carry him to our rooms and let him sleep it off while we all get showers," I said. "I really need to get the vamp guts out of my hair."

"I'll help Ness finish things here and seal the vault," West said. "You and Sarah go on to the room and clean up."

We took the service stairs again since I looked like a butcher who'd been on a rampage. Sarah checked to make sure the hallway was empty and then opened the door to our rooms so I could lay Father Kinsella on my bed to let him recover.

"Go shower," Sarah told me. "I'll bring him some hot tea and cookies."

She didn't need to ask again. I scrubbed with soap until my skin turned pink, under the hottest water I could get, and washed my hair twice. *Do they make special soap for people who work in slaughterhouses? How about soap to remove the stench of Hell?*

When I'd gotten as clean as I could manage, I changed into fresh clothing, thinking how this trip had gone hard on my limited wardrobe. I should have known better than to worry since I found two stacks of fresh shirts and pants neatly folded on my dresser, courtesy of Sarah and her helpful concierge.

Father Kinsella wasn't on the bed anymore, and it looked like he had taken his teacup and plate of cookies with him. I found him perched in the wing chair, chatting with Sarah, who really could strike up a conversation with absolutely anyone.

"Joe, thank you for your help back there," Kinsella said. "I have to admit—it was one thing to have you tell me about your abilities, and another to see them in action."

I shrugged. "Yeah. I hear that a lot. I'm just happy we all lived through it."

Sarah looked up at me from her place on the couch. "Is it really over?"

I thought for a moment and then nodded. "We did what we came to Chicago to do, and then some. Freed the tormented ghosts in Death Alley, handled a wendigo, a rougarou, and rogue vamp, and dispelled the bound demon—with your help," I said, nodding at the priest. "Bonus points for the imp at the murder house."

"You've gone above and beyond," Ness said as he and West came into the parlor, setting down their bags of gear and weapons. "You all have my gratitude and the unofficial thanks of the city of Chicago."

I figured Ness would have to adjust what he wrote in his report, as would West. Sarah and I were independent, and the Vatican wouldn't bat an eye if Kinsella recounted the whole truth, although I doubted he needed to do so.

"Then I think this calls for a celebration," Sarah declared. "The concierge gave me the name of another steakhouse and said we absolutely must try it. Shall I make reservations for five?"

Father Kinsella smiled indulgently. "Thank you, but I have left some things unfinished back at my church, which I should take care of." He glanced to me. "May I have a word, Joe?"

"Sure," I replied as the others gave a questioning look. I walked the priest to the door. "What's on your mind?"

"You're aware that there are several different groups operating with the backing of factions at the Vatican to handle the occult?"

"Uh-huh," I replied. "Not really my business."

"It may become your concern. My group, the Occulatum, is pretty moderate, all things considered. The Sinistram, a group that lives up to its name by being the secret 'left hand' of the Holy Father, takes a harder line with perceived supernatural threats." He met my gaze. "Be careful, Joe. So far, the Occulatum has tried very hard to stay out of the Mob's affairs. But we think the Sinistram may see an affiliation with whoever emerges as the strongest Family to be advantageous to their purposes. Which will pull us in as a counterbalance."

"Sorry to hear that, but it's still not my business."

"The Sinistram judges everything supernatural not in its employ to be a monster and gives no quarter," Kinsella warned. "That would include creatures like you and Sorren, your witch friends, even helpful ghosts. Cross Cotton Mather with Torquemada, and you'll get the idea."

Shit. "How do we stop them?"

Kinsella shrugged. "I don't know yet, but watch your back. If we don't find a way, we'll have gang wars that become a new Inquisition, and it won't be good…that's for sure."

"Thanks," I said, as worry roiled in my gut. "I'll keep my ears open. Let me know if you hear anything." He nodded and slipped into the hallway.

"Something wrong?" Sarah asked when I came back to the parlor. Ness and West had washed up, and everyone was getting their coats on for dinner.

"No," I fibbed, not really a lie. "He just wanted to make sure you sent the relics back to the museum." The dire future Kinsella warned about hadn't happened yet, and there was nothing I could do right now. If and when things changed, I'd lay all the cards on the table.

West, Sarah, and Ness had risked their lives to tie up this case. They deserved an evening to celebrate.

Hell, so did I.

I grinned. "Let's go eat some steak."

THE END

PART IV

SPELLBOUND

1

1929

A shady medium is bilking my cousin." Edmund Harrison looked defiant as if daring me to mock him. "I hear you're good at fixing supernatural problems. I've got one, and I'd like you to fix it."

I had to give Harrison credit for guts; he put what he wanted right out there and led with his chin, as they say. Whether or not I was the right person to help with his problem remained to be seen.

"There are a lot of fraud busters." I sat back in the diner booth. "Why me?"

"You helped a buddy of mine in Cleveland. He said I could trust you," Harrison answered, again with the implied dare. "And Archie Dunning, a private investigator I know, says you're okay."

Harrison's case was part of the reason that brought us to Pittsburgh, a tip-off from a couple of informants here in Pittsburgh that the spate of supernatural-themed entertainment events that were touring the area might not be harmless thrills and chills.

Even though I liked to come off as aloof, I cared—probably more than I should. Coming to me on a friend's recommendation carried a lot of weight, even if I couldn't recall the particular acquaintance who might have suggested me to Harrison. We'd learned that Archie Dunning was one of our informants, and he'd set Harrison up with us seamlessly.

I'm Joe Mack, and as I lay dying in the Homestead Riots back in 1892, I begged Krukis, the god of blacksmiths, for vengeance. He made me immortal as well as extra fast and super strong, and when I call on his name, he lends me his magic to make my skin metal and my bones steel. In return, I'm his champion, protecting the underdog. Fortunately, my skin doesn't look metallic, which saves on explanations.

"Cousin Amanda lost her husband, Vincent, in a railroad crash a few months ago. She's mad with grief, inconsolable. Amanda is certain that if she can just find the right medium or Spiritualist, they can let her talk to Vincent again," Harrison said. "We've all counseled her to be cautious. I know there are some people with real ability, but there are plenty of frauds. I'm afraid Amanda would be a prime target since she inherited a great deal of money from her father and then from Vincent. I don't want to see her be taken advantage of," he added, looking glum. "She invited me to go with her to a session, and I did, although the medium didn't seem happy to see me. This is going to sound odd, but I had the feeling that the ghost was real—but it wasn't Vincent."

"Interesting." My mind began to conjure up likely scenarios.

"The temperature dropped, items flew through the air or hung without falling, and a misty figure mostly took shape."

"What's in it for the medium?"

"Aside from a lot of repeat visits that aren't cheap? I'd say 'influence' if I had to guess," Harrison answered. "The medium she sees has a high-end clientele. Extremely wealthy widows and bereaved family members flock to him. All he has to do is nudge them into asking their dead loved one for financial advice, and he could divert a tidy amount into his pocket."

I knew what it was like to lose people I loved—over and over again as the years went by. Taking advantage of that grief was a special kind of evil.

"Do you know anything about the medium? If he's as good as he claims, there should be a trail of happy customers and newspaper interviews," I said.

"I asked Archie, he's a retired private eye, to do me a favor and look into it." Harrison slipped a folder across the table. "Everything he found out is in here. The medium goes by the name of Nathaniel Radimore and says he's from Boston. Only Archie couldn't find any trace of him in Massachusetts—not a birth certificate, passport, or diploma."

"Was he from anywhere else between Boston and Pittsburgh?"

Harrison shook his head. "Not under that name. But Archie got suspicious, and he started looking into high-profile mediums. He found several who could be Radimore under different aliases. He never stays in one place longer than a year. Won't give interviews, although that doesn't stop the media from raving about him. The photographs that exist are blurry, or he's wearing a hat that shades his face."

"Convenient."

"If this guy has some magic, it wouldn't be hard for him to mess with cameras," Harrison said. "So I've heard."

I opened the folder of the investigator's findings and flipped through it. "Aside from being rich, do the marks have anything else in common?"

Harrison thought for a moment, then shook his head. "They're not even all female—he's worked with widowers and grieving parents too."

A suspicion teased at the back of my mind. "How did they make their money? Even if they weren't the ones who earned the fortunes, what industries did they represent?"

Harrison frowned. "You think there's more to this than just a fancy grifter?"

I knew how things worked—there were schemes within schemes and always a money man or larger group in the shadows, pulling the strings. Several government and Vatican organizations existed with connections to the supernatural. So when someone like Radimore showed up, I couldn't help wondering whether he was working on his own.

Harrison sat back and took a sip of his coffee. "I was so concerned about Amanda, I hadn't thought about the possibility of a bigger issue, but you make a good point."

"Do you think your cousin is in imminent danger? Because I have a plan, but it could take a couple of days to pull it together," I asked.

"I don't think she's supposed to go back to see Radimore for another week. Is that enough time?"

"Should be. I'll keep you posted. Radimore won't know what hit him."

THAT EVENING, I sat in a suite in the William Penn Hotel with two of the most dangerous people I'd ever met.

Jack West looked the part of a government secret agent—dashing, debonair, and dickish. Fortunately, he's a good guy underneath the attitude. West could be mistaken for a hotshot gambler or a hitman instead of a Fed with his slicked back hair, fancy suits, and movie star handsome good looks. He knows that I'm not completely human, and he's okay with that. As a Supernatural Secret Service agent, he also has the kind of connections that could find out just about anything through classified channels.

Sarah Grace McAllen Harringworth was also scary good at ferreting out information, but her networks were social, not official. The daughter of a steel magnate and the widow of a coal baron, Sarah's wealth bought her independence and information.

"Do you know whether anyone else besides Archie Dunning tipped off the Supernatural Secret Service about the questionable paranormal events?" I asked West. "Since you're the one who got the assignment."

"I suspect tips came from someone else as well, although I don't know who," West replied. "I heard whispers that someone very well connected fed them enough evidence to kickstart an investigation. Dunning's information corroborating that tip might have pushed them to move on it. I don't have any details beyond that."

"I really don't like the idea of a fake medium bilking his clients. I'd offer to play the grieving widow, but I could do without seeing my late husband's ghost," Sarah said in a dry tone. "Other than that, count me in—this sounds like fun." She rubbed her hands together, and I figured she was excited to be back in the game.

Sarah and I were West's frequent accomplices when it came to stopping a cataclysm in unexpected—and unofficial—ways. Despite her blue blood and blue sapphires, Sarah could pick a lock—or a pocket—with disturbing skill. She had wicked aim, enough money to grease a lot of skids, and nerves of steel. Jack was good in a fight, clever, and loyal, even if his smart mouth could be infuriating.

I was an annoying son of a bitch on my good days, so maybe it wasn't a surprise that we all got along just fine.

"From what I got out of the case file, Radimore's picky about his clients," West sat back in his wing chair and sipped the bootleg whiskey Sarah brought in her valise. "They're not only very wealthy—they also come from families with strategic value."

Which was what I'd suspected. "How so?" I toyed with my glass. Having a drink was part of being sociable, even though alcohol had little effect on me anymore.

"Steel, coal, banking, shipping, international trade." West gestured with his crystal glass. "Over the course of his consults with the clients, I don't doubt that they share all kinds of private information, as well as asking their departed loved one for advice on personal—and business —decisions."

Just because the wives, mothers, and sisters might not run a business outright, that didn't keep them from being privy to all kinds of sensitive information or serving as secret advisors. Sarah was proof of that, having taken over the reins of her late husband's failing coal company and turning it around before stepping back from management with an extremely generous retainer—while remaining on the board.

"There's more," Sarah said, curled up in the corner of the couch like a cat. "The clients are all very well connected socially. Their opinions carry a lot of weight, even if unofficial. So any organization that wanted to influence the powers that be would see Radimore as a very valuable ally."

Sarah nursed her drink from the stash of good bootleg liquor she always brought when she traveled. The topic seemed to make her pensive. While she came from a purebred Robber Baron background, Sarah had a conscience. After she discovered that her family had been part of the South Fork Rod and Gun Club—whose devastating earthen dam collapse caused the Johnstown Flood and killed more than a thousand people—she committed herself to stopping the oligarchy from making world-ending mistakes.

"So Radimore doesn't have to steal their money." I was getting a feel for what we were up against. "He betrays their confidence." To me, that was worse. "If your people sent us after him, does that mean they aren't working with him?"

He shook his head. "Not officially, and not off the books either, as far as I can tell—and I have my sources."

"Department of Supernatural Investigation?" Sarah questioned.

"Not their style," West said. "They're straight shooters. So's the Occulatum. A rarity."

"So that leaves Sinistram—or some group we haven't heard of yet."

"My money is on Sinistram," West replied. "But I've heard whispers about 'Operation Ferryman'—nothing more than the name, but I don't know their angle."

Most people didn't believe the supernatural was real. That didn't change the fact that it was. Several government and Vatican organizations handled those secrets, in theory, to make the world a safer place. In reality, they acted like all the other government entities that played political games and constantly battled for turf. Some, like Sinistram, were particularly renowned for their underhandedness.

"You're going to need bait," Sarah said. "I made a few calls to friends. Told them I wanted to reach my father's ghost. Asked if there was anyone especially good at séances." She grinned. "I'll hear back with a connection to Radimore by morning. Guaranteed."

"Let me guess—I'm the bodyguard." We had done this kind of infiltration before. No one would mistake me for a wealthy heir looking for spiritual guidance, but they might believe I was Sarah's favorite goon.

"Very good," she teased.

"Meanwhile, I'll see who's helping Radimore in Pittsburgh and where they've been before," West said. "That might give us an idea of who expects payback."

AT LEAST SARAH didn't make me wear a tux this time.

On previous outings, we've had to go formal. I shouldn't complain, because Sarah bought me a custom-tailored monkey suit so I fit in. It wasn't comfortable, but I had to admit that I cleaned up better than expected.

This time, a nice suit sufficed. Sarah was dressed to the nines, as usual, understated but expensive. She chose muted colors, not exactly mourning black but subdued.

"Mrs. Harringworth. Welcome." Radimore completely ignored my existence, which gave me a clue about his character. "Please, have a seat."

We were at the Monongahela Club, one of the city's invitation-only old social clubs. Of course, Sarah had access.

I stood next to the door, out of the way, but where I could see the whole room. Radimore had done a good job of stage dressing what was probably a small meeting room. He hadn't gone full carnival fortune-teller—that would be too tacky for his clientele. Instead, he appropriated elements from a variety of cultures, mashing them together in a Hollywood tableau of "strange and mystical."

Odd and macabre artifacts decorated the flat surfaces. A yellowed skull, ritual candles, carved statues, and bone sculptures from a dozen unrelated cultures and traditions crowded together. Propped against the wall atop a side table, a dark painting channeled medieval canvases about the torments of hell. Beside it was a large sculpture of a vengeful goddess and a crude poppet that I felt certain was cursed.

Radimore's hair, longer than proper, gave him the look of a professor. His custom clothing passed for a business suit with elements borrowed from the looser formalwear of Asian countries, adding a dash of mystery and mysticism.

I assumed he was as much a thief of magic as he was of decor and fashion.

"I miss my father," Sarah told the medium with a convincing hitch in her voice. Some days I was convinced that the theatre was her true calling. "I've heard you're the best. I hope you can reach out to him for me."

Sarah sold the con by not going overboard. She didn't claim to need help with stocks or dangle the desire to find a missing safe combination. Just a bereaved daughter wanting word from her father. Easy enough to fake and a way for Radimore to gain her confidence.

"Of course, my dear. Tell me his name, and I will put out a request for my spirit helpers to find him and bring him to us."

I felt like I was watching a private performance by two consummate actors. Radimore had mastered faking sincerity and compassion, a requirement for a successful grifter. His good looks and exotic styling made him particularly appealing to women, as did his ability to make his client feel the full power of his attention—a heady drug for the lonely and bereaved.

"First, we must ready the ether." Radimore did not ask for payment up front—he knew his clients would pay. He needed to set the stage, make them comfortable and relaxed—and quicker to accept his suggestions.

I swallowed a laugh at how demure and harmless Sarah managed to appear since I knew the truth.

"Take a deep breath and relax. Place your hands flat on the table, and think happy thoughts about the person you wish to contact. Remember the best moments, and picture your person in detail," Radimore coached.

Sarah closed her eyes, and her smile reminded me of the statues of the Virgin Mary I'd seen in my youth—peaceful and filled with graciousness. Definitely not the real Sarah.

"What is the name of the person you wish to speak with?" His soft, gentle voice coaxed.

"James McAllen," Sarah replied, sounding like she was in a trance. "Friends called him 'Baron.'"

She's not taking this seriously, is she? But I knew better—Sarah was the most clear-eyed person I knew and the least likely to be hoodwinked.

The room grew chilly, then downright cold. I could almost see my breath—a clear indication that spirits were present.

Okay, he can gather real ghosts. But are they the right ones?

"The spirits are receptive," Radimore said, in the kind of soft, calming tone people tended to use on children and spooked horses.

Something knocked on the table, and moments later, the noise repeated on a cabinet in the back of the room. Easy enough to do with wires and some theater tricks.

I silently called on Krukis's power, which lets me access his magic. It's mostly good for fighting, but it heightens my senses.

I didn't have a gift for summoning or communicating with ghosts, but if they made themselves visible, I could see them maybe a bit better than some people. I also had good intuition about them being present, and right now, I was certain that spirits were in the room.

Fairly strong ones too. I watched as a large scrimshaw seashell levitated from its resting place and hovered in the air before slowly crossing several feet of open space to land gently on the table in front of Sarah.

I knew for a fact that Sarah had seen much more fearsome and impressive signs and wonders, but she gasped and regarded the traveling seashell with appropriate awe.

Next, a handful of decorative glass pebbles rose from their vase, swooping and darting through the air until they finally stilled and dropped, single file, back to their resting point.

A fine mist formed, swirling and dancing but never quite forming a recognizable figure.

"Papa?"

A bell chimed, distant and muted.

"It's Sarah. I've missed you."

The bell sounded again, louder this time.

The mist formed the vague outline of a man. His features weren't defined, so there was no way to confirm that it was the ghost of Sarah's father.

"He says that he knows you're anxious," Radimore said in a low, reassuring voice. "Worried. He didn't want that for you."

Sarah's startled sob told me that Radimore's guess was close to the truth. *Does he have a bit of telepathy? That would certainly come in handy.*

"Oh, thank God! It hasn't been the same without you," Sarah gushed, addressing the ghost. "We've had a run of bad luck. The head housekeeper broke her ankle, the apple tree in the garden got blight, and there was trouble down at the mill. I would feel so much better if I could talk to you about everything."

She was handing Radimore the perfect opening, and I wondered if he'd take it.

"He says that he's here now, and he would like to help however he can."

"Oh, Papa! Thank you." With that, Sarah launched into a tale of woe no less remarkable for what I was sure was an utter fabrication. She didn't let slip any "company secrets," but her story confirmed enough wealth for a household with servants and grounds and her active role in managing a troubled steel company.

Along the way, Sarah also filled her "papa" in on gossip about his friends, and while she didn't mention their full names, it was clear to anyone who kept track of the hoi-poloi who she meant.

Radimore kept her talking with soothing, generic comments supposedly from her father. As she added to her story, I took a better look at the "decorations." Now that my eyes had adjusted to the dim lighting, I noticed sigils and patterns marked on the walls and woven into the table-cloths that had an occult origin. The skull looked real, the candles were colors used in divination, and one small black box covered with runes sent a shiver down my spine.

Whatever paranormal abilities Radimore had, he certainly plumbed supernatural resources for lore and relics. I suspected the items enhanced his natural abilities and might deter unwanted spectral visitors.

If his ghosts are just playing a part for the client, what does he do if the real spirit shows up?

"Your father worries that you are shouldering too much of the weight. He hopes you are seeking wise counsel and listening to advisors who have your best interests at heart." Radimore planted the seed that I suspected he would return to over future consultations until he became one of those "trusted advisors." Even if he avoided the usual table-thumper grift of making off with stock certificates and insurance money, he was likely to come by valuable inside information in the course of his counseling sessions.

"I try," Sarah sobbed and dabbed at her eyes with her handkerchief. "Milton and Isaac are supportive. Carl and Ben hang back—I think they wish you'd named a man as your heir. I fear they'll look for ways to find fault with anything I do." I'd never heard her mention those names before, so I assumed they were fictional.

Radimore closed his eyes, and I suspected he was trying to look like he was communing with the spirit of Sarah's dead father, but I thought he just looked constipated. Then he opened his eyes and smiled at Sarah, still with a distant, dreamy look as if he were in a psychic trance.

"He agrees that is a worry and has asked for time to consider options to share at another visit."

And there's the hook, I thought. A reason to return, baited with the information the client needs most desperately.

"Yes, of course. I want to return," Sarah told Radimore, then turned to address the misty figure that had grown more translucent. "It's so good to hear from you, Papa, and know that you're well."

"He says that he can't hold this shape much longer and needs to leave," Radimore told her. "And he says that he has missed you and hopes you will come again. He's out of practice since no one has tried to communicate with him before this."

I noticed the little touch of guilt to make the client more willing to return soon. Radimore was scum, but he had the game down pat.

I felt the ghosts notice me, brushing against me like frozen fingertips. A subtle power pressed against my mental defenses, testing me. I slammed my psychic protections into place, and the energy pulled back. I didn't like the intrusion and wondered what might have happened if I had been a regular person.

Like Sarah. For all her sass and bravery, she's only mortal. Money goes a long way, but it's not true magic. Now I worried that I had endangered her if this fortune teller turned out to be the real deal in a wrong way.

The dim light and my location near the door made it difficult to get a good look at Sarah's face. She seemed drawn and distracted, but I couldn't tell whether she was just playing her part.

"Your father wants me to tell you that he only desires the best for you and that he's very proud of the woman you've become," Radimore added.

Sarah's smile only looked pleasant to the unwary. "Thank you. You've taken a great weight from my mind. I will definitely be back."

She removed an envelope from her purse that was stuffed thick with bills. "Today's payment. Thank you for setting my mind at ease."

Radimore didn't grab for the packet or count the bills. In what I assumed was a show of massive self-control, he rose to escort Sarah over to where I waited at the door.

"Please let me know when you would like to return," Radimore said. "Now that the channel to the Other Side has been opened, a longer conversation with your father should be possible."

Sarah sniffed demurely and dabbed at her eyes with a linen handkerchief from her purse. Her performance was never overdone and entirely believable—for someone who didn't know what a fierce warrior Sarah could be when the chips were down.

"That's such a relief. Thank you."

I fell in behind Sarah and Radimore as they walked to the outside door. He said his farewell with a deep bow. I nearly expected him to kiss her hand, but he didn't go quite that far.

Sarah and I didn't speak until we were in her Duesenberg.

"Well?" I asked, holding my opinion back because I was curious to hear hers.

"Unless my father suddenly decided to take more notice of me after he died than he ever did in life, Radimore's a sotting fraud. For one thing, he insisted on being called 'Father.' He would have gnashed his teeth at 'Papa.'"

"Well, that answers one question."

"I could use a cigarette—and a drink," Sarah grumbled. The incident had put her in a bad mood, and I was sorry for asking her to play a role that bothered her.

"Did you pick up on anything else? Strange feelings, a presence?"

Sarah frowned. "I'm pretty sure there were ghosts around—just not my father. Can't say that I'm disappointed about not seeing him, but that means other people who did want a reunion are getting bilked."

Her comments echoed my thoughts. "Anything else?"

Sarah got a faraway look, and I guessed she was taking stock of everything that happened. "I'm a lot more tired than I should be. Yes, I was nervous going in, but not like when we've faced a fight, so there shouldn't have been an emotional crash. I wasn't looking forward to seeing my father, so I'm not crushed that it wasn't real. It wasn't a socially difficult interaction. I didn't do anything physically demanding. So there's no reason for me to be this tired."

She looked over to me. "Unless Radimore did something? Is that what you suspect?"

"That's my theory. I think he's draining energy—how? I'm not sure yet. Lots of creatures can do that. He might not even be keeping all the energy himself. Don't know where the ghosts come in, either, but I'm more certain than before that gathering sensitive information is the goal. Maybe West came up with some ideas while we were busy."

"It's a type of hungry ghost," West said as we ate at a diner that evening.

"A hungry ghost?" Sarah asked in between bites of her burger.

We had changed after our meeting with the fortune teller and dressed comfortably before going out again. West and I got rid of the suit coat and tie. Sarah's simple, flattering dress probably still cost a pretty penny but didn't scream money. Somehow, we blended in enough that no one gave us a second glance.

West sat back and chewed on a toothpick. "Hungry ghosts show up in pretty much every culture, under a lot of names. We're more likely to call them psychic vampires."

"Are they really vampires?" Sarah asked, setting down her burger. I kept eating because life is uncertain, and it was a good burger.

West shrugged. "In a manner of speaking. They take sustenance from what sustains other people without asking permission. It could be blood, flesh, or energy."

"Is it Radimore or his ghosts?" I asked, still trying to make sense of what I'd seen and felt.

West twirled his pen as he thought. "Maybe both." He leaned forward. "I think Radimore is a wraith. The energy he steals helps him look human. Wraiths live to eat. It's possible that he's bound spirits to him like hunting dogs."

"Why bother with the séances for the rich if any human with energy would do?" Sarah asked, licking her fingers as she finished the last of her burger. "And why would a medium want to gather data for Sinistram—or whoever?"

"Even wraiths like to live comfortably. Maybe wealthy people's energy tastes better. Or perhaps it enjoys putting one over on the big wigs. As for the data gathering—he might have expensive taste. Or it's possible that the buyers have something on him. I'm very interested in following the money." West took a sip of his coffee, then held the cup out for a refill when the server walked by.

"I did some checking while you were getting your palms read," West said with a smug smile. "Radimore's other identities left a trail of sick clients. The symptoms were a lot like consumption—pale, weak, anemic, no energy. Sound familiar?"

"Did people die?" Sarah asked as if she feared the answer.

West nodded. "A few. Others never fully recovered. The authorities never suspected their fortune teller."

"If he passes on information to Sinistram or someone else, then Radimore must have notes on all his customers," Sarah said. "We need to retrieve those so they don't just get given to a third party."

"I didn't get the sense that Radimore is a strong enough medium to force the ghosts to do his bidding on his own," I mused. "I'm also not sure that he cared about connecting with the ghost his client wanted as long as a ghost showed up."

"Then he's got some way to make 'his' ghosts do what he wants," West said. "Is that possible?"

I thought about what I'd seen with charms, spells, and relics. "Yes—if you have an object of power and know how to control it. Radimore's decorating taste certainly leaned toward the occult and bizarre. And we know at least one or more of his knick-knacks packs a punch."

Sarah took a long sip of her drink and then looked up. "Once Radimore's done flimflamming in Pittsburgh, he'll move on and do it again. Unless we stop him."

West flashed a crafty grin. "Then I guess we'd better get right on that."

WE WENT BACK that night after the Monongahela Club closed, armed with weapons of steel, iron, and silver. West had his gun while I had a shotgun loaded with salt shells, and we each had a length of iron rebar. Sarah had a purse Derringer, a shiv or two tucked away, and a couple of tricks up her sleeve.

Sarah picked the lock, which saved me from breaking it down. I had released Krukis's magic while we were at the diner, but now I gathered it around me again like a cloak. I had the feeling that the wraith had more abilities than we'd seen.

Radimore's séance room looked creepier at night than it had by daylight. We all carried flashlights, but they didn't brighten the whole area, leaving pockets of shadows along the walls.

The temperature in the séance room dropped rapidly until my breath clouded. The ghosts knew we were here.

"Find the files," West told Sarah. "We've got your back."

When we came for Sarah's meeting with Radimore, I thought we'd been able to see the whole room. Now I realized that his artwork and sculptures created a partition that hid the rear corner.

West caught Sarah's eye and motioned toward the hidden space, and she nodded, moving in that direction.

Two ghosts flickered into view right in front of West and me a second before they charged us. The glimpse suggested they were working men who had been down on their luck, but I didn't get a good look before the brawl started. I swung my iron bar, and the ghost vanished with a screech. *So much for stealth.*

West slashed through the spirit that rushed him, sending it away in a tangle of mist and confirming that he could see the ghost too. We were both holding off on using the shotgun to keep down the noise, although I didn't expect we'd avoid facing off with Radimore before the night was through.

Sarah slipped behind the partition while West and I blocked anything from going after her. I saw her flashlight bobbing and hoped she could find what we wanted quickly. I had no desire to pay Radimore a visit at home looking for the files.

"Behind you!" I hissed as the second ghost manifested next to West and shoved him hard enough to send him staggering. Before I could react, the first ghost appeared so close we were toe to toe. He tried the same trick that had worked on West and discovered that with Krukis's magic active, I was an immovable object.

"Don't crowd me," I muttered as I stabbed the rebar through him like a sword. I don't imagine the ghost liked the taste of my steel skin either. It vanished in a puff of mist, but I felt it solidify behind me in the next breath and wheeled, bisecting the ghost at the waist with the iron bar.

"Anything?" West called in a stage whisper to Sarah as he battled his ghost. We didn't give the spirits time to fully form before blowing them to smithereens with the iron, but my initial impression of two down-on-their-luck workers seemed valid from what I saw.

These were Radimore's ghostly prisoners—or allies. I still hadn't figured out the connection and whether he bound them to his will with a spell or relic. There didn't seem to be a reason for the ghosts to stick around of their own will, but I didn't have time to ponder right now. Krukis's magic didn't give me special powers to see ghosts unless they could make themselves visible to everyone, so I figured West and Sarah could see them too.

"Why do you help him?" I asked in the breath between the ghost taking shape and me making him disappear.

"The reliquary." The words came from thin air, barely audible.

"Did you hear that?" I called to West, who was still whacking at his ghostly opponent like the world's worst tee-off on the back nine.

"I'm a little busy here," West replied. "But yeah."

Before I could answer, Radimore appeared seemingly out of nowhere. Since he'd been solid when we met him, I bet that there was a door hidden behind one of his tapestries or paintings rather than magic.

"You have no right to be here," he snapped. Instead of the debonair medium we had met before, Radimore looked gaunt with sunken eyes and hollow cheeks, like a mummified corpse. I wondered if siccing his bound ghosts on us drained him.

Sarah picked that moment to emerge, holding a small file box.

Radimore's face twisted with rage, and he lunged to grab her. As soon as his fingers closed around her sleeve, he recoiled and screamed in pain.

"Everything I'm wearing was soaked in saltwater," Sarah told him with a malicious grin.

I blasted Radimore with the shotgun, throwing him back several feet. West was doing a good job keeping the ghosts off us, but he wouldn't last much longer.

"Watch my back," I said as I headed for the table where Radimore kept many of his unusual objects—perhaps items of power. Radimore moved to follow, and Sarah grabbed him from behind, locking her arms around his waist and pressing her salt-infused clothing against him.

"Do it!" she yelled.

I brought my rebar down on the rune-covered box I'd seen before as I realized it was a wooden reliquary. I kept my steel-clad body between the relics and my friends in case breaking them caused some kind of physical blast. For good measure, I smashed the skull, candle, and other objects and ran my rebar through the creepy medieval painting. I thought that smashing the reliquary would release the ghosts, but all hell didn't break loose until I crushed an unimpressive little jar that I nearly overlooked.

A pain-filled, ear-splitting wail filled the room, and the shrine flashed with a blinding violet glow.

The ghosts battling West suddenly vanished, leaving him off balance as he swung and hit only air. They appeared with a feral growl in front of Radimore, faces twisted with hate and hands grasping.

"Sarah—move!" I shouted. She backed away and grabbed the file box as the ghosts stalked their tormentor.

"Get away from me!" Radimore commanded, panic threading through his voice. He took a step backward and the ghosts pressed toward him, hedging him in. Their mouths were moving, but I couldn't hear what they said. From the terrified look on the wraith's face, he understood their threats just fine.

Which is why he never noticed West behind him until the silver bullet tore through the wraith's back and heart an instant before my shotgun took off most of his head.

What remained of Radimore's body sank to the ground in a spreading puddle of blood.

"You're free," I told the ghosts. "Get lost—and don't bother the living, or I'll come looking for you."

They didn't need to be told twice and blinked out of sight.

"Let's go—someone had to have heard that." West remained calm, cool, and collected despite being spattered with wraith ichor and having gone nine rounds with a couple of ghosts.

"This way." Sarah motioned us toward the side door Radimore had used, which led to a service corridor. At this time of night—in between the last bleary-eyed revelers and the first bushy-tailed bakers—the hallway was empty. That didn't guarantee we hadn't been heard by a diligent security guard, but it boded well for not ending the night in jail.

I led the way, just in case a trigger-happy cop saw us slinking out the back door and decided to take a shot, but no one was in sight as we emerged in the alley behind the club. Those thick stone walls provided more soundproofing than I'd expected.

We piled into Sarah's car and hung on as she pulled away. If anyone saw us, we figured the cops would be less likely to stop a Duesenberg Model J than West's Buick. Fortunately, my theory didn't get put to the test.

"Now what?" Sarah asked as she drove. For the moment, she kept the speed down, but I knew she could handle a car like a race driver if needed. She enjoyed driving and had given her usual chauffeur, Steven, a few days off.

"Go back to the hotel, clean up, and get some sleep," West replied, doing his best to wipe off the blood spatter with a towel Sarah had thought to throw in the back beforehand, probably anticipating the night's events could get a bit messy.

"We can go through the files in the morning and see what kind of information he was passing on," I added. "Maybe get a clue about who was getting his updates." I had released Krukis's magic when I got into the car, and now my yawn reminded me that it was the wee hours of the morning.

"I just want a shower," Sarah said as she pulled smoothly into the hotel parking garage. "Salt itches."

2

I think you know my private investigator friend, Archie Dunning," Harrison said with a nod to the older man who sat on his side of the table. "He needs to hear what you've got to say."

"We've corresponded, but it's nice to meet in person, Mr. Dunning." I extended my hand.

"Archie, please."

We met in the basement speakeasy at the William Penn Hotel because after what happened with Radimore, I needed a drink. Apparently, Harrison and Archie figured some Dutch courage wouldn't hurt since they'd already acquired glasses of whiskey.

I walked up to the bar. Back home in Cleveland, my favorite speakeasy was run by Ben Laveccia, the son of the head of the Laveccia Family and its only mostly-honest businessman. I'd wager one of the Pittsburgh families had a similar interest here.

"I'm looking for a blind tiger," I told the man behind the bar. "Seen one around?" It was a joke, of course, a fiction that allowed speakeasies to skirt the law. Patrons paid for the chance to see a tiger that didn't exist and were served a "complimentary" beverage while they waited for the spectacle that never happened.

"Caribbean or Tennessee tiger?" he asked, meaning rum or whiskey.

"Tennessee sounds good." He slid a glass with amber liquid toward me in exchange for my money. "Keep a hold of those tigers," I told him. "I'll be back for another look."

I sat across from Harrison and Archie. Jack and Sarah were upstairs in our suite of rooms going over the records we'd retrieved from the wraith-medium. I needed to find a way to assure Harrison that he didn't have to worry about the predatory fortune-teller without admitting to making the man disappear.

"We scared Radimore off and destroyed his files," I told them, hoping they'd buy my story and not press for details.

"Bullshit." Archie's glass thumped on the table. "You don't need to hide the details from Harrison. He knows the score."

I eyed Archie, taking in details. I guessed him to be in his late sixties, with a trace of a Scottish burr to his voice and white hair that still held a reddish cast. His lined face was most generously described as "craggy," but his blue eyes didn't miss a thing.

"What—aside from a predatory con man—do you think we dealt with?" I had the feeling Archie knew more about the situation—and maybe me—than I'd first thought.

"I brought you in on this because we already figured the ghosts and magic were real," Archie replied. "Otherwise, any big guy could have been hired to put the fear of God in him. You and your friends deal with the supernatural. You know it exists, and you've got skills. Thirty years ago, I handled some very unusual cases," Archie said, still glaring at me. "Just before the turn of the century. Stopped some horrors that would have made the Great War look like a walk in the park. So don't play games. What was he, and how did you deal with him—and what became of his files?"

When I got back to the suite, I intended to have West tell me more about this not-so-retired private eye. "Alright. Radimore was a wraith. He used necromantic relics to control two unwilling ghosts. The ghosts pretended to be the customer's 'dearly departed' relative, while Radimore drained his guest of energy and also compiled potentially valuable information."

Neither of them blinked. *Son of a bitch. I guess this isn't their first rodeo after all.*

"Was?" Archie asked, raising an eyebrow.

"We broke the relic that let Radimore bind the ghosts. They reacted badly." I kept my face blank and my voice impassive.

Archie nodded. "Good." Harrison didn't seem upset either. "Reclaim any purloined information?" Archie toyed with his glass.

"We think Radimore might have been part of a bigger game," I replied, trying to decide just how much to tell them. "His files may reveal that."

"I saw something like this happen once before," Archie said. "What we were able to stop was tied to forces that came to a head in the Great War. That we're seeing such things again, along with the troubles in Germany, makes me worry those powers may be rising once more."

I looked hard at Archie, wishing my borrowed powers included reading minds. I'd fought dark magic in the deep places beneath Reading and stopped supporters of German authoritarians from drawing on forbidden lore to help their cause. I did not want a rematch.

"I've dealt with such things myself and would prefer not to do so again," I replied. Archie's lack of surprise made me wonder again how much he had studied up on *me*. He might have tipped off the Supernatural Secret Service to get an agent looking into the situations, but might not have expected to get Sarah and me as part of the bargain.

"I'd like to introduce you to some friends of mine," Archie said offhandedly, although I could read from his body language that the suggestion was anything but. "I think they could be helpful. Let me see what I can set up—if you're willing."

I allowed a hint of a smile. "Definitely curious."

"I'll take that for a yes." Archie licked the last of the whiskey from his lips. I wrote the phone number of our suite down on a napkin and passed it to him, keeping up the pretense for Harrison's sake.

"If your friends want to meet, give me a call."

Our case here involved five traveling events that had supernatural themes and were suspected of being connected to a larger, nefarious purpose. Archie Dunning had been one of the tipsters who alerted the Supernatural Secret Service to the events and their possible connection—and larger danger. Whether he'd been an agent himself back in the day, I didn't know, but he definitely had a bigger picture view than the average private eye.

Harrison laid a hand on my arm. "Thank you," he said with fervent sincerity. "You've saved my cousin and, I'm sure, many other people from ruin."

We get so busy saving the world that sometimes I forget that for most people, saving one person *is* their world.

"Sure thing. Glad to help," I replied and meant it.

Harrison left, and Archie motioned for me to stay. I took the bartender up on that second blind tiger and sat back down. "What's up?"

"I've got intel on that second problem—the fights," Archie said.

"I'm listening."

"Big guy like you—know anything about prizefighting?" he asked.

Yes, I'm a large, solid man, and I can handle myself in a fight. That was true even in my mortal days. But I never liked fisticuffs, and while boxing was a popular sport, I didn't care for it. After getting beaten to death by the Pinkertons, my dislike for watching people throw punches for fun or money deepened.

"Not a fan," I replied.

"My grandnephew died under what I consider suspicious circumstances," Archie went on. "Good kid. Fought in the Great War, came back in one piece but...shell shock. So he had trouble finding work. My sister, she worried a lot. Especially when he started coming home with bruises and black eyes. But he said it was temporary, that he'd won some money prizefighting to pay off debts."

On any given night, I knew there were fights going on, some legal and others not so much. They were an outlet for young, angry men with nothing to lose and nothing to offer except blood and bone. Some won enough to walk away without too much damage. Others didn't.

"Then he started to beef up—muscles like Charles Atlas. He said he'd been working out at a gym, and Sis believed him. But he got real moody. Sometimes he scared her. That was not who Freddie was," Archie said, pausing to get control of himself. "He was a kind boy, took good care of his mom and his grandma. I wasn't sure he'd take to soldiering—so for him to go looking for fights and fly into rages? I smelled a rat. So I started digging."

Archie's instincts were spot on, and I could see how his personal connections through friends and family would be powerful motivation to want justice—and vengeance. Archie was turning out to be a valuable asset, and if his insider knowledge could save us days of legwork and dead ends...

"What did you find?" I asked and sipped my drink.

"I found out which gym he boxed for, and it didn't take much to get them to believe that a guy with a mug like mine might be a fan," he said with a crooked smile. He had a point. Archie's nose looked like it had been broken a time or two and not reset quite right, and he was missing a front tooth. Scrunch a fedora on his balding head and he'd look like most of the guys I'd ever seen at the betting track or in line for a bookie's payout.

"The starter rounds were normal. Seemed to attract ex-soldiers—both the fighters and the audience. They played that up in their matches. As the night wore on, they started bringing out guys who had a lot more bulk. They pounded on each other until I thought someone was going to die, but they didn't. That was the first thing that seemed weird." Archie took a long slug of his whiskey. I could tell that the story bothered him.

"When I went to place another bet, the guy at the window asked if I wanted in on the 'freak show.' I said 'sure.'" He tapped his nose. "Don't need to be a bloodhound to smell something wasn't right. So I got a ticket, and he told me to go to the basement when the last fight was over. Asked me if I had trouble sleeping—because if I didn't now, I would later."

Archie looked off into the middle distance, silent for a moment. I guessed that the man's prediction had proven true. The PI didn't seem easily rattled, and I didn't think I'd like finding out what gave him nightmares.

"They were monsters," Archie said quietly. "The men were bad enough. The warm-up fight had two unnaturally burly guys beating on each other like a back alley fight. The loser died." He swallowed hard. "Then they brought out the first 'freak.' I've been in this business a long time, seen a lot of weird stuff—I know what's out there in the dark. And I swear he was either a shifter or a werewolf."

I leaned in, suddenly more interested. "Fighting a human?"

Archie nodded. "Well, an 'altered' human, one of those too-muscled guys. And he held his own for longer than I expected—bare fisted—until the claws came out."

My head spun. We had heard rumors about trafficking—capturing cryptids for hunts or experimentation or snatching humans to sell to monsters for blood or organs. That might be part of the prizefighting ring, but the whole angle with ex-soldiers and too-fast body changes made me wonder if there wasn't something even worse going on. The reasons the SSS had sent us to check out the fights—and the other paranormal traveling events—were becoming clearer and clearer.

Maybe the Operation: Ferryman people aren't stopping with sensitive information. If they think there's another Great War coming, super-soldiers would come in handy. The thought sent a shiver down my spine.

"What's your plan?"

"Get you in as one of the first-round fighters, if you're willing. See what you learn on the inside. Come back with reinforcements when we know who's in charge, so we don't just shut them down for a night—we put out their lights permanently," he replied.

Archie didn't know about my "extra" abilities from Krukis. I might have been able to hold my own as a mortal, but with metal skin, steel bones, extra speed, and strength, I could handle a werewolf—or a vampire. I was the perfect ringer, even though I hated the idea.

"I need to talk to my team," I told him.

"Of course," Archie said. He slid three tickets across the table. "There are fights every night, although I think the 'freak' fights are only on certain days. Have a look, and let me know."

He looked away. "Freddie deserved better. When I said 'suspicious circumstances,' I mean that he looked like he'd been clawed by a wild animal, even though they found his body over on the North Side." Archie took a savage swipe at his eyes. "I owe it to him and my sister to get the bastards who did that to him."

I couldn't fault his logic. And if the prizefighting really was part of something larger, avenging Freddie might prevent something a whole lot worse.

"Call me," Archie said, adding his business card to the tickets. "I'm technically retired, but the phone number is the same."

I promised that I'd be in touch, finished my drink in one slug, and shot the bartender a salute as I left.

When I went up to our suite, it looked like a filing cabinet had exploded in the parlor.

West had his tie off, and the sleeves of his white shirt were rolled up, as casual as he ever got if he wasn't undercover. Sarah wore a silk blouse and a pair of wide-legged trousers and still managed to look elegant, even with a pencil lodged behind her ear.

Papers and files covered every surface. As usual when we traveled for a case, West and I split one room while Sarah had the other, with a sitting room in between. Traveling with Sarah meant the best of everything, including room service, hot tea, coffee on demand, and of course— bootleg gin.

"What happened?" I noticed that a bottle of liquor was open, and the level was lower than it had been last night.

West looked up. His usually-perfect hair looked mussed, a sure sign he'd been running his hands through it in frustration.

"This is worse than a needle in a haystack. It's like looking for the *right* needle in a stack of needles."

Sarah sat curled up on the couch with a sheaf of files in her lap. She glanced in my direction. "What he's struggling to express is that Radimore was scamming the upper crust, who have so many incestuous connections that we aren't sure *which* incestuous connections are the important ones."

Her mischievous grin softened her jibe, and West just rolled his eyes. I never quite figured out if there was anything between Sarah and West or if they just enjoyed the sexual tension. There hadn't been anyone for me since my wife Agata died when I was still mortal, and there never would be.

Even though I'd had a shot of rum at the speakeasy, and despite the fact that liquor didn't really affect me much, I figured a little gin wouldn't hurt.

I poured myself a drink, pulled up a chair, and rolled up my sleeves. "Might as well hand me some files—there's got to be a 'needle' in here somewhere."

"How did your 'client' take your recap?" West asked without looking up. I took the bundle of files Sarah handed to me and got comfortable.

"About that. He brought his gumshoe friend—who called my bluff and didn't bat an eye about Radimore being a wraith. Archie Dunning—our informant."

"Interesting." West frowned, thinking. "I'd heard of him before he tipped us off. Not recently—his heyday was thirty-some years ago, but he was involved in pretty high-profile cases. Ones that got played off as being mundane and definitely weren't."

"Think he's on the up-and-up? " I took a swig of the gin and felt the burn. If I concentrated, I could pretend a little buzz followed. I wanted to hear what they'd learned before I dropped the new case in their laps.

"Maybe. I'd like to get a look at what we're dealing with before we trust him for more than information," West said. "And then there's this." He gestured at the piles of paper.

"Radimore's clients were rich, well-connected, and influential. They have ties to the biggest companies in Pittsburgh—and the US," West vented. "They're a Who's Who of the Social Register, so they're related by blood or marriage to everyone's who's anyone. Being able to manipulate these people into disclosing or distributing information could help any number of nefarious purposes. Collectively, they are fabulously wealthy and control patents, trade secrets, and corporations. More than a few of them have judges and politicians in their pockets. They intersect *everywhere.* But where does it count?"

"Guess that's what we're here to find out," I said. "First the wraith-medium, now the cryptid prizefights. And after that, a creepy circus."

"The word from HQ is that their tips from highly placed sources included a questionable theatre group and a malicious mesmerist," West added. "All of them traveling independently, yet often landing in the same city or area at roughly the same time—and choosing locations where there's money, technology, and trade secrets." He wrinkled his nose. "Like that's not suspicious at all." West leaned back, half-sitting on a side table. "The trick is spotting the connection and knowing that's what it is."

"Spotting the circus isn't difficult—not with full-page ads in the news-paper." Sarah held up today's paper with a graphic—some might say lurid—advertisement for Macabre Menagerie.

"Thrills and chills galore," she read from the large-type headlines. "Enter the nightmare realm if you dare. Once in a lifetime chance to experience the circus and freak show that will haunt you forever!"

"They've either got a real gift for overstatement, or it's a deadly vortex of dark magic that will doom the city," I remarked, sarcasm thick in my tone.

"Quite possibly," West replied, not specifying which he thought to be likely.

"My bet is on doom, personally," I remarked. I've found that counting on things going wrong leaves me pleasantly surprised on the rare occasions that they don't.

"I think you're right," Sarah agreed. "They're hiding in plain sight."

I cleared my throat. " Before we take on the circus, I think we should check out Archie's intel. He's an inside man for us on this. Illegal cryptid prizefighting—and maybe souped-up super-soldiers."

"Fuck," Sarah muttered.

"Please tell me you're kidding," West said, knowing I wasn't.

Sarah and West listened as I recounted what Archie Dunning had told me. It didn't escape my notice that they both refreshed their drinks. "So, what do you think?"

West rubbed his temples like he had a headache. "I hate to say it, but I think you're right that we need to look into the fights before the circus—they could be related. The cryptid angle is definitely our thing. And the presto-change-o scrawny kid to muscle-man element worries me. Super soldiers. I can think of too many government ex-military types who might love to get their hands on something like that."

"I agree. Let's do it." Sarah set down her gin glass with a thud. "Haven't watched a decent fight since Dempsey's last match."

I called Archie to let him know we were in. He gave me the address of the gym, the man to contact to get a spot on the right roster, and offered to help however he could.

"I'm going to dress down and then go to the gym to see a man about a fight," I said. "Figure I need to look a little rougher than usual around the edges."

Sarah looked delighted. "This will be fun. I'll take care of getting our outfits squared away." West gave me a look of resignation because we both knew Sarah was a force of nature.

Even though I was going to be the one in the ring getting hit, I thought I might have the better end of the deal.

THE GUY at the gym took one look at me and signed me up for the next night, which is how I ended up in the ring surrounded by a cheering, catcalling crowd awaiting my opponent. I wasn't crazy about being given the fight moniker of "Joey the Bull," and I figured West would never let me live it down, but no one asked my opinion before adding it to the broadsheets.

I wasn't a boxer. I'd died in my first and only fight as a mortal, but since then, I'd been in plenty of brawls with a lot of creatures, human and not. From watching the previous fight, I got the impression that bare-knuckled enthusiasm mattered more than technique since the crowd came to see a show. With my prayer to Krukis, I was protected, on top of being damn near immortal.

Maybe that was cheating. I doubted it was the only rigged game the gym had ever seen.

While I waited to be announced, I bounced on the balls of my feet, nervous. I knew the general plan from seeing a couple of matches before mine. They had looked pretty normal, with two rather average guys duking it out. From the reaction of the guy who signed me up, I had the feeling he had something "special" planned for me. Still, it wasn't a late night "freak fight," so odds were good my opponent was at least mortal and passingly human. I hoped.

"Tonight we've got a treat for you! A newcomer and a wild card, welcome Joey the Bull!" the announcer crowed through his megaphone. I bounded in and rolled under the ropes, striding around the ring like an idiot to get the betting public to back me as the dark horse fighter.

West and Sarah were somewhere in the crowd, undercover in the get-ups Sarah had managed on short notice. Archie Dunning was our driver, borrowing a Hudson Super Six so we could show up in style, like proper bootleggers. I didn't ask where he got it, and he didn't tell.

"And in the other corner, we've got a crowd favorite—say hello to Clobbering Clyde!"

On cue, my opponent came in from the opposite side, and I stifled a groan. If I'd doubted Archie's hunch about souped-up fighters, Clyde removed all question. He had the face of a boy in his early twenties and the muscles of a bodybuilder a decade older. Even worse, he took one look at me, and I saw terror in his eyes.

He thinks I'm going to kill him. So does the crowd. Shit. I've got to get both of us out of here alive.

Clyde must have channeled his fear into action because he swung first. I let the kid get in a few hits, and watching him in action reinforced my suspicion that he had no real fight training. So when I grabbed him in a headlock, I tightened it enough to make him stop squirming so I could warn him.

"If you want to live through this, stay down when I put you down, and I'll get you out."

I pushed him away from me, sending him stumbling. When he turned, I saw wary trust and a flicker of hope in his eyes—right before I KO'd him.

The referee grabbed my arm and pushed my fist into the air. Someone else shoved an envelope full of money into my other hand. I picked up Clyde to the consternation of the ref.

"I'll drive him home. Least I can do, considering." Then I breezed past the flabbergasted ref as the announcer kept sputtering something I ignored.

The guy who had signed me up tried to block my path. "We'll handle Clyde."

"Nah, we're gonna take the kid home." West swaggered up, channeling Pretty Boy Floyd with slicked-back hair, a double-breasted suit, and spats. His long coat hung over his shoulders like a cape, with a suspicious bulge that might have been a Tommy gun. Sarah shimmied her beaded flapper dress like a true gun moll, completely distracting the referee and the organizer, who barely kept their tongues from hanging out.

Before they could gather their wits, we were out of the building. Archie was waiting for us in his bootlegger car. Sarah and I got into the back with Clyde, who was still out for the count. I almost expected West to stay in character and ride on the running board, but he ducked into the front seat as the Hudson roared away from the curb.

Clyde groaned but didn't open his eyes.

"We need to get him to a hospital." Sarah gave the kid a worried once-over.

"No can do, lady," Archie said as he drove like a maniac through the Pittsburgh streets. "Too many questions. But I got us covered. I know a retired doc who helps out Hunters. Already gave him a heads up that we'd need some help. I'll have us there real quick—hold on."

We left the gym in Penn Hills and wound through neighborhoods heading north to Plum. By the time we pulled into the driveway of a modest house, Archie had slowed to a reasonable pace.

Someone inside switched off the back light, making sure we couldn't be seen entering, and the door opened. "Get him in here," a rough voice commanded.

I had let go of Krukis's magic, so West and I half-carried, half-dragged Clyde into the house while Sarah and Archie kept watch.

Our host had set up a makeshift medic's office in the kitchen, complete with an IV rig and a clean sheet thrown over the kitchen table. West and I maneuvered Clyde onto the table and stood back, trying not to crowd the doctor or block his light.

"This is Doc Porter," Archie said. "He's a good guy. I'm gonna ask Joe and the lady to step into the living room, give us some space."

West and I exchanged a glance, knowing what was coming.

"The *lady* volunteered with the Veterans' hospital as a nurse's assistant when the doughboys came home from France," Sarah noted tartly, referring to the Great War. "How about I stay and lend a hand, and you fellows all go drink some whiskey?"

Doc Porter snickered. "I'd welcome the help, ma'am. Archie—go to my room and get her one of my work shirts so she doesn't get blood on that pretty dress."

The rest of us knew when we'd been dismissed. Archie seemed to know his way around, so after he brought Sarah both a shirt and a carpenter's apron, he followed West and me into the snug living room and rummaged up a bottle of bootleg whiskey and three glasses.

"Better make that four," West cautioned. "Sarah's going to want some when they're done."

I hadn't taken any damage in the "fight," and Krukis's power would have healed me by now even if I had. I felt guilty about having hurt Clyde, even if I'd pulled my punch as much as I could.

We sat quietly, listening to a variety show on the Crosley radio in the corner, and tapped our toes in time with popular songs.

Before long, Doc Porter came to the doorway. "He's awake. He's got a mild concussion, but I gave him something for the headache. Didn't need stitches—seemed okay otherwise." He looked to Archie. "You got somewhere to stash him?"

"Yeah. There's an Amish guy who owes me a favor. He can always use a new farmhand, and Clyde can put those big muscles to use."

Sarah joined us, sans extra shirt and apron, and West held out a drink to her, which she accepted gratefully. She took West's place on the worn couch while he and I headed for the kitchen to get what we could from Clyde before he passed out again.

"Where am I?" the kid asked, looking a little glazed.

"Somewhere safe," West told him.

Clyde's eyes widened as he took in West in his gangster get-up. "Are you in the Mob?"

West rolled his eyes, and I laughed. "No, he isn't. We're the good guys. Which is why I got you out of there. We can take you somewhere the fight people won't find you—but we'd like you to answer some questions first."

"Sure. Shoot." Clyde looked alarmed. "I don't mean—"

"You're safe," West repeated at the boy's panic over his word choice.

I didn't know whether Clyde agreed because he thought we'd make him talk or because he wanted to rat out the gym, and right then, I didn't care.

"What did they do to bulk you up?" I cut right to the chase.

Clyde glanced down at his overly buff body with an expression mixed with pride and chagrin. "I went to the gym because I was on the scrawny side. I put some muscle on in the Army, but it was hard to keep without all the drills and marches. After I'd been there for a couple of weeks, the owner asked if I was interested in some new pills that would help me get bigger faster. He swore it was legal."

"He lied," West replied. "Although the pills probably did come from a shady government group. How did it work?"

"At first, I took the pills and that made it easier for me to gain weight and get bigger," Clyde replied. "Then the gym boss—Mr. Costa—told me that if I wasn't afraid of needles, he could do more for me even quicker. I liked the results I'd gotten so far, so I said yes."

"And then?" I asked. Clyde seemed like a good kid, and my anger focused on guys like Costa, who lured vulnerable young men into what I strongly suspected was a government agency recruitment effort.

"I bulked up, fast enough that it hurt, like I could feel the muscle stretching," Clyde admitted. "That's when he offered to let me fight. I needed the money—I bus tables at Valente's Restaurant, and they let me sleep in their storage room and mostly pay me in food."

Clyde looked down, and I could sense his shame. "The first couple of matches were easy. I tried not to hurt the other guy too much, but I won both times. Then I lost a few, and Mr. Costa told me I could win more if I took bigger doses. I didn't start questioning until I found out about the 'freaks'—things that aren't human. When I said I wanted to be done, Costa laughed and said there was only one way out."

Which confirmed my suspicion that Costa expected me to kill the kid. Now, I really wanted to take my anger out on Costa's hide.

"Lucky for you, I was your next match," I told him. "Did Costa ever say where he got the magic pills and stuff he shot you up with?"

Clyde's sheepish expression gave us the answer before he spoke. "No. I didn't even think to question because he was the professional, and I was the new kid."

"Did Costa ask you about your time in the Army?" I figured I'd go out on a limb, and for once, I wasn't disappointed, given Clyde's reaction.

"Yeah, he asked a lot of questions about that. I didn't want to talk much about it because my platoon saw some action, and people who haven't been there don't really understand," Clyde mumbled. "But Costa had all these questions about what would make a good soldier even better. I thought we were just shooting the breeze."

"Do you have people who are going to worry about you if you don't go back to the gym and your job?" West asked, although I feared I knew the answer.

Clyde shook his head. "No. Mum died while I was overseas. Dad's new wife doesn't want me around, and my sister passed away when we were kids. I came to the big city for a fresh start," he added with a derisive snort as if he was appalled at his hopefulness.

"If you stay in Pittsburgh, I wouldn't put it past Costa to hunt you down and drag you back to the ring," I told him. "He doesn't want you to tell anyone what you just told us. The next guy you fight might punch for real."

Clyde looked young and scared, despite the hulking body from what I suspected were experimental drugs. "I don't have anywhere to go."

"Our driver has a friend with a farm who could use a strong guy like you," I told him. "The Amish don't talk to strangers, so if Archie tells him to make sure you're 'invisible' to outsiders, no one will know you're there. You'll work hard, but they'll take good care of you—and the food is pretty damn good. Archie can let you know when we've shut Costa down and when—if—it's safe to leave. Who knows? You might just like it there."

Clyde nodded enthusiastically. "Yes, sir. Thank you, sir. I'll make sure to earn my keep." He paused. "Will you…can you…stop Costa from doing this—" he motioned to indicate his overly-developed body, "to someone else?"

West gave a dangerous smile. "We'll take care of it. The less you know, the better."

Dunning promised Doc Porter cigarettes and bathtub gin, and West slipped the good doctor some cash. He dropped Sarah, West, and me off where we'd left Sarah's car parked and then went to give his borrowed flashy gangster car back before he drove Clyde to the farm.

Once the three of us were back in the suite and changed into regular clothing, we all collapsed in the parlor with generous portions of gin.

"This has to tie into the big case." I tilted my head from side to side to crack my neck.

"Yep." West had a worried expression. "I don't know what's worse— the medium who milked desperate, grieving people for information, or pumping some young kid full of God-knows-what to make him a killing machine."

"How are we going to stop the gym from making more hulky soldiers?" Sarah asked.

"Even with Archie's help, I don't think the four of us can take on their whole 'freak fight' crew," I added, wondering the same thing.

West grinned. "Good thing we're not on our own. After we handle the other iffy events, I'll notify our field office here—they'll be glad to swoop down on the gym and be thorough enough to give anyone pause about picking up where Costa is going to leave off."

3

The Macabre Menagerie was the main reason we came to Pittsburgh, and the other four questionable paranormal events got tacked on because they seemed to be related. The traveling circus had gained an ominous reputation as it moved through the big cities of the Northeast—areas where the military, technical, and engineering industries happened to be concentrated.

Maybe it was coincidence that over the last six months, a string of deaths had occurred among people who possessed different kinds of sensitive knowledge. And the only thing they had in common was having visited the circus a few days before they died from unusual circumstances.

"That's why the FBI was so quick to hand these cases off to the Supernatural Secret Service," West said, attempting to inflict some order on his piles of paper that littered our hotel suite parlor as he sat in the other armchair and sipped his drink.

"Any luck narrowing down the possibilities?" I didn't believe the deaths were a coincidence, but there were too many possible supernatural explanations, and finding the best weapon depended on picking the right reason.

We were still going through the files taken from the wraith-medium and trying to find connections and suss out secrets. Since we all believed there was a nefarious power behind the cases, we had to be careful about asking for help, because we didn't know who on the official end of things could be trusted. That meant doing all the research ourselves until we knew what was going on.

The idea of a new, secret government organization focused on leveraging supernatural abilities for intelligence or military uses was scary as hell. I'd seen the Pinkertons in action—I knew how immoral an organization with powerful backers and plenty of guns could become. "Paranormal Pinkertons" chilled me to my core.

"Dark magic is almost certainly involved—but I'm not sure how yet." West swirled the liquor in his glass and watched the light catch it. "If the performers and the creatures they parade as 'attractions' aren't bewitched, then they're something other than human."

"I'm still trying to figure out how the deaths are related," Sarah replied, setting aside her files for now. "Thousands of people have attended the circus and not died. How did it target the people who did? Why them? And how did going to a show turn fatal?"

"Guess we'll find out when we go tomorrow night," I said, and despite the certainty that attending was dangerous, I'd have been lying if I'd claimed not to be curious. Back when I was mortal, my wife and I took our son to the fair once. That had been a day filled with joy and laughter. I felt certain that our visit tomorrow would not be.

THIS PLACE GIVES ME THE CREEPS," Sarah murmured as we bought our tickets. The circus styled itself more like an amusement park fun house—lots of red and black, ominous music, and paintings of scary demonic creatures. It surprised me that there weren't church folks protesting, but maybe the event paid off the right people, or the holy-rollers figured it would move on soon.

"I think that's the whole idea," West muttered. He and Sarah played their part as a couple, and I was the third-wheel friend.

The creepy circus had set up in the large parking lot for Burke Glen, an amusement park in Monroeville, just east of Pittsburgh. Since the park was closed for the season, the circus attracted fans who wanted one more thrill before winter set in.

I hadn't called upon Krukis's magic yet, wanting to get a sense of the place on my own. Turned out that I agreed completely with Sarah and West—the place gave me a bad feeling.

Cartoonish paintings of ghosts and monsters lightened the undertone of danger. While some of the costumed characters were menacing clowns and grim, caped figures out of *Dracula*, other silly sheet-covered spooks and odd-looking creatures reassured patrons this was all in fun.

I didn't believe that for a moment. Something evil lurked beneath the carnival atmosphere. My instincts screamed a warning, and I'd learned the hard way to trust my intuition.

The majority of the costumed cast members seemed to have acquired a wardrobe courtesy of Edgar Allen Poe, with dark clothing and high-collared shirts. They looked like a gathering of funeral directors. Even the more upbeat music played in a minor key, but the lively trend-setters who had swarmed to the city's newest attraction laughed and joked with their dates or their clusters of friends and didn't notice or care. I feared that for at least some of them, that might change before the night ended.

"Come on—we want to get seats," Sarah urged, tugging at West's arm like they were a real couple.

I let them lead the way and hung back, observing everything around us. Red tents, crimson banners, carnelian flags—everything was the color of blood and hell, set off by the black of midnight, shadows, and the grave. Even the long cords of bare electric lights seemed dim by normal standards, enough to light the way but not sufficient to drive away the darkness.

A barker dressed like a somber Victorian attempted to entice us into a "haunted" fun house. Thankfully, West and Sarah had the good sense to refuse. Even without fully activating Krukis's gift, I could sense a low level of magic permeating everything here, like the rumble of distant thunder.

Next we passed a hall of mirrors, which had a line of giggling customers waiting for their turn to enter. People exiting the attraction laughed and talked excitedly, proving that it wasn't a one-way portal to hell. Still, it set off my intuition, and I hoped we wouldn't find it necessary to go inside.

"Oh my God!" Sarah exclaimed, pulling at my sleeve to get my attention. I looked to where she pointed and saw a huge carousel. At first, her surprise didn't register since I had seen such things at fairs and amusement parks before. Then I took a closer look at the theme of its decorations.

Instead of the usual happy calliope music, the songs were dark and brooding. Where pastel-toned paintings of peaceful scenes usually adorned the center panels, the artwork depicted famous paintings of war, doom, and destruction.

Then there were the carved animals. These were monsters, not horses or zoo favorites. Griffins, hippogriffs, dragons, and coiled snakes had been captured by the wood carver in mid- strike, along with hellhounds, kelpies, and a giant spider that gave me the willies.

"Why would anyone want to ride those things?" West muttered, and I agreed. Suspicious bastard that I was, I didn't trust the dark undercurrent of magic not to awaken those monstrosities and bear their riders off to somewhere extremely unpleasant.

We watched the carousel stop and start three times, and I could tell from the expression on my companions' faces that they were also awaiting some horror to reveal itself. I noted the riders and counted the people, careful to assure myself that everyone who got on also got off. None looked worse for the wear, and they joked among themselves like they had done something daring and gotten away with it.

"Maybe the rides are just rides," West said with a sigh.

I understood. While I wasn't looking for trouble, I knew in my marrow that something about this place was evil and unnatural. The longer it took us to figure out the source of the problem, the more my battle-trained reflexes thrummed with pent-up energy, ready for the fight.

"Let's go see the show," Sarah suggested, linking her arm with West's and leading us to the big top.

We got in line, and I listened to the excited whispers of the people around me. They speculated on what might be inside or what lurid thrills the local gossip had promised them. No matter what supernatural forces lay behind the circus, I doubted we would see outright murder or bloodshed. I didn't think this outfit had the mojo to hex the entire Pittsburgh police department. I expected to see performances enhanced by subtle magic, and "wonders" to make the audience gasp and thrill but which they could rationalize away once they left.

What we don't know is what killed those people and what's in it for the circus.

Music swelled like a force of nature inside the big top. The calliope gave way to the blare of trumpets, then the insistent beat of drums. I felt the impact on my emotions, soaring and crashing, building fear and tension, then matching and speeding past my heartbeat. I suspected that the musical manipulation contributed to the crowd's excitement and worried about what darker emotions might be evoked as the show moved to its climax.

West, Sarah, and I had agreed to watch the main show and wander the grounds before trying to uncover the circus's secrets. We turned down popcorn from the wandering vendors and sat where we had easy access to an aisle in case we needed to make a quick exit.

West and Sarah made small talk since we would probably look odd if all three of us just sat silently and stared. I replied if they lobbed a question my way, but otherwise, I constantly scanned the crowd, trying to figure out the circus's secret.

Despite the macabre tone of the music, costumes, and decorations, the guests looked pretty normal. Given the ticket price, it didn't surprise me that the event drew a crowd who might not be rich but were clearly well-off. I'd been around long enough to know that mid-level folks often knew more secrets than those at the top because they were tasked with tracking and organizing information. They wrote the briefings the big wigs heard and forgot.

I wanted to know more about the people who had died. Somewhere in the glut of information there were crucial details we were missing.

A face in the crowd caught my attention. An older man with a push broom swept the sawdust from the aisle, but he didn't seem like the janitor type. His shrewd gaze also seemed to be searching for something, sizing up the crowd. I felt sure that the coveralls he wore and his broom were props, like a costume for a play.

Is he a performer in disguise? Or maybe we aren't the only ones who realize something in this circus isn't what it seems.

The janitor ducked into a backstage corridor and out of sight, and I resumed my scan of the audience. Another patron drew my curiosity. He looked to be in his mid-sixties, with a long face and thinning gray hair. Unlike everyone else who was surrounded by family and friends, this man sat alone. What I could see of his suit appeared to be good quality but not unusually expensive, something I might expect from a senior office worker. The bulge beneath his coat made me frown. *Why would someone bring a gun to a circus?*

Actually, that wasn't a hard question—West, Sarah, and I were all armed. *Okay, why would anyone else be carrying a gun?*

His age made him an unlikely bodyguard or undercover security. Where the fake janitor's expression suggested street smarts, the man in the suit regarded everything around him with what I could only think of as an accountant's obsession with detail.

I took a good look at the crowd once more and let my gaze roam to the cheap seats at the top. A stocky man dressed all in black stood in the last row. Since no one was behind him, he wasn't blocking the view, but it struck me as odd that he hadn't taken a seat.

Maybe he's a stagehand. That was possible, but my gut told me that the man in black had a different—possibly more sinister—role.

"Joe—it's starting." Sarah tapped on my arm to bring me out of my thoughts, and I smiled because, despite our ruse, she looked genuinely excited.

Trumpet fanfare silenced conversation. The calliope started off with a merry tune that quickly segued to minor and discordant. Drums shifted from a dance rhythm to an ominous call to battle.

Clouds of colored smoke billowed into the center ring—brilliant hues of red, yellow, and orange lit from within like fire. Shadowy shapes ghosted through the haze. Their silhouettes and the way they moved did not look human.

Torches flared as the smoke thinned, reflected from huge mirrors that hadn't been there moments before. The band played a march transposed into a minor key. Dancers in tattered shrouds of gray and white led the procession, and while their fluid movements weren't conventional, they didn't defy the limits of human motion.

A collective gasp rose at the next entrants. Five soldiers marched amid the smoke and torch light. Their pallor and their white, unseeing eyes made me certain that whatever they were now, they were no longer alive.

Zombies. I shuddered and called on my patron's magic, figuring that if we were treated to such horrors at the beginning, things would only get worse.

"Are you seeing what I think I'm seeing?" West whispered. Sarah and I both nodded, looking a little sick.

"The show's just starting," I reminded him.

Long wires manipulated the mirrors to keep shifting the views and reflections. New colors of smoke billowed, and the torches flared, sending flickering shadows. The eerie music and constant drumbeat added a level of tension and expectation. Everyone around me was sitting on the edge of their seats.

An ornate, horse-drawn hearse came next. Black Percherons with inky plumes and full regalia drew the wagon, emerging from the smoke like something from dark legend. It stopped, and half a dozen figures came tumbling out, cartwheeling, somersaulting, and flipping through the air in ways that seemed to defy physics.

"Now I know why people have nightmares about clowns," West muttered. Sarah nodded, wide-eyed, and I suspected that her grip on his arm was more for reassurance than show. He might have bruises by the end of the night.

These weren't regular clowns. Their face paint mimicked grave rot, and their torn and tattered clothing suggested the risen dead. All around us, the crowd watched in horrified fascination, scandalized in ways they had only hoped might happen when they bought their tickets.

Since they think it's all just a stage play, they're not scared. They don't think anything can hurt them—that it's all what it seems, smoke and mirrors. I wish I could believe that, but we know better. How do we keep more people from dying?

The hearse moved across the center ring and disappeared backstage, leaving its clown-ghouls positioned at the four quarters as a cavalcade of monsters slithered and roared into view.

A few shrieks rose from the crowd, quickly drowned out by cheers and clapping for the spectacle. I recognized four of the same infernal creatures from the carvings on the carousel and wondered for a second if they had somehow been brought to life.

"Do you think they're real?" Sarah whispered, looking as simultaneously intrigued and repulsed as the crowd.

"I'm hoping they're not since I really don't want to fight them," I replied.

The ghoul-clowns played beast masters, snapping whips to put the creatures through poses and tricks. My stomach twisted. I hated to see anything coerced into performing for the amusement of others against their will, even monsters.

Over the decades, I'd faced down a lot of supernatural threats, including my fair share of true horrors. I'd never pitied them before, and I wondered what dark magic bound them and how fragile the bonds were that kept them from breaking free and slaughtering us all.

A sudden crescendo drew our attention to the center of the ring. Flames, smoke, and light burst upward, and when our eyes adjusted, we saw a man gracefully descending from the tent's peak.

"There aren't any wires," Sarah whispered, eagle-eyed as always.

The ringmaster landed without a stumble, like floating through the air was the most natural thing in the world. Maybe for him, it was. For an instant, I thought I saw a glint of red in his eyes, which left me staring and questioning what I'd seen. *Was that a trick of the light, or is he something more than human?*

The creatures all sat in deference, and the clown-ghouls bowed low. *So this is the big boss. Good to know.*

"Ladies and gentlemen. Welcome to Macabre Menagerie! I trust you have enjoyed your visit thus far?" The ringmaster's question drew thunderous applause, and I wondered if Sarah, West, and I might be the only ones who thought his smile seemed nefarious.

The three of us...and the long-faced stranger. I caught a glimpse of him in the crowd now that the smoke had cleared. He leaned forward, holding a pair of opera glasses to see the action in more detail. The circus seemed like an odd choice of entertainment for a guy I thought might be more likely to enjoy a horse race or a concert.

When he lowered the binoculars, I caught the determined glint in his eyes and the set of his jaw—and I remembered the bulge of a gun beneath his jacket. Perhaps his interests weren't as intellectual as I first thought.

He's studying them, watching for a clue. Question is—are we looking for the same things?

"You've thrilled to fantastic creatures and seen some of our amazing performers—but be prepared to have your ideas about reality completely shattered because the best is yet to come!"

The ringmaster vanished in a flash of light and smoke, and the ghoul-clowns led their monsters on a final promenade before they exited center stage.

Acrobats and contortionists took the spotlight next, pushing the boundaries of what human bodies could endure. Krukis's magic heightened my senses, and I felt ripples of dark power beneath the outward reality of the circus, with tendrils that snaked and slithered among the patrons, probing for...something.

Character flaws to be exploited? Hidden weaknesses that might be exposed? Or perhaps it's scanning minds, looking for valuable knowledge or connections?

The next act featured an illusionist, a magician who did far more than pull rabbits out of hats. I felt certain that magic enabled his amazing feats and thought that the phantoms he conjured for the thrill of the crowd looked all too real to be entertaining.

I glanced toward the top row and saw the man in black still standing. His hands were raised to waist level, kept close to the body, but I could make out motions as if he were conducting an orchestra.

A witch? Maybe. Enhancing the effects to make the show more thrilling? Lending a little magic to the performers so their "tricks" are more impressive? Those explanations were plausible, but something didn't set right with me. *I'm missing something—but what?*

Halfway through the show, I caught West's nod. Time to move out. As I rose, I cast a last look toward the accountant—who was gone.

No time to think about that now. West led the way, and we found the circus office tent hidden away from the public areas in a back corner, not far from the wagons that transported the creatures and housed the performers.

As we neared the tent, I heard a noise and froze. West and Sarah did the same, but when no other sounds came, we moved forward cautiously, guns drawn. I hung back, letting West take the lead with Sarah between us. They could pillage the office. I'd watch the door.

Light from the park grounds' many strands of bulbs bled through the tent canvas to shed a dim glow inside. I entered behind them since it would draw attention for me to stand outside.

The office looked a mess—or like it had just been trashed. On a battered desk sat a large microphone, probably to make announcements over the public address system. Files, tablets, and papers were everywhere.

My prayer to Krukis had turned my skin to metal and increased my senses. Which meant I knew we were screwed a second before a dark form rose from behind the desk, gun pointed at West and Sarah.

"Freeze," the stranger ordered.

"You freeze," West barked back. "Jack West—Supernatural Secret Service."

"Ellis Lawrence—Department of Supernatural Investigation," the intruder snapped.

"Put your damn guns down," I drew down on the man in the shadows as I heard steps behind me and the barrel of a pistol pressed into my back.

"Lower your weapons right now," the newcomer said in a tone that didn't allow for argument.

I knew his bullet couldn't penetrate my magically metal skin, but it could ricochet. Or the shadowy stranger might take a shot at West or Sarah.

"Sorry to interrupt the standoff, but let's do the badge thing," I said, annoyed more than afraid. "He'll show you his if you show him yours," I couldn't resist adding.

The guy in the shadows lit a cigarette lighter and held up a badge that looked official. "DSI," he huffed. I wasn't surprised to realize he was the janitor I'd thought seemed suspicious.

So the accountant is probably the one holding a gun on me.

West pulled his badge from his suit coat and brandished it in the flickering light. "Good enough?" he challenged. "Because there'll be hell to pay and way too much paperwork if we shoot each other."

That made the guy behind me snicker, and the gun barrel stopped poking me. "Isaac Daniels—DSI."

"Whatever you're looking for, it's not here," Lawrence said. "I've gone over everything. Let's get out of here and talk."

"Like we're going to take your word for it." West could be territorial.

"Unless you want to explain why we're here to the creep show boss and his monsters, I don't think we've got a choice," I said.

"Too late." Lawrence's lighter flickered and went out as the temperature dropped and our breath clouded. Half-formed ghosts swirled around us, moaning and wailing and then growing bold enough to shove Sarah and knock Lawrence's lighter from his hand.

"Shit," West muttered.

Lawrence grabbed for a rectangular box on the desk, but invisible hands knocked it to the ground. His partner dove for it, rolled, and came up with the box clutched at chest height.

"See how you like this," Daniels growled as he wrenched a dial to one side.

Nothing happened—at least, nothing I could see or hear. The ghosts, on the other hand, howled in pain, and their misty shapes began to flicker and then wink out.

"What the hell?" West stared at the box.

"Later," Lawrence snapped. "We'll have worse company coming once they figure out we drove the ghosts off."

Daniels slung the box's long strap over his shoulder and exchanged a look with Lawrence, who pulled a sawed-off shotgun and a machete from beneath his coat. Lawrence handed the shotgun to his partner and kept the blade.

"Better get ready—this is gonna go south six ways to Sunday," Lawrence warned. "You know how to fight demons?"

"Demons?" West echoed. "Seriously?"

Lawrence regarded him coolly. "Just because you haven't run into them doesn't make them unreal."

"We've run into similar beings," I said, thinking of the ancient crea-tures we'd battled in the deep tunnels. Demons had nothing to do with Heaven or Hell, God or Lucifer. Those concepts didn't really apply in our business. For us, a demon was an evil spirit because it was malicious, not because of dogma or old myths.

"We were hoping to find some kind of anchor object—a relic or an altar maybe—that would break the ringmaster's hold over the spirits... and the people they've possessed," Daniels added. "But either someone sicced those ghosts on us, or they were the alarm."

"Come out, come out wherever you are," the Ringmaster's eerie voice sing-songed. "We know you're in there. You come out—or we send our pets inside."

I glanced at the box that had dispelled the ghosts. "Will that work on monsters?"

Lawrence shook his head. "No. Just spirits. But while we've got it cranked up, the ghosts won't be back." He grinned. "If we crank it the other way, it summons ghosts. Handy."

"Don't make me wait," the Ringmaster warned. "I smell three humans and...something else. Don't be shy. We're *dying* to meet you."

"Cover me," I told the others.

Daniels grabbed my arm. "You can't go out there."

"Long story—no time to explain, but I'm your best bet," I told him as I shook free. "Follow me, and hope we don't have to shoot too many of them." I glanced at Sarah. "See if you can find the anchor."

I strode through the tent's doorway with West and the two agents behind me. The ghoul-clowns and their beasts formed a half-circle, cutting off our escape. The Ringmaster stood in the middle, making no effort to hide his glowing red eyes.

"You shouldn't be meddling," he said, in a low growl that reminded me of a big cat stalking its prey.

"You shouldn't be topside with your demon scum," I shot back, running with Lawrence's theory.

We stared down the ghoul-clowns, an infernal ringmaster, and four slavering creatures with big teeth and sharp claws. I didn't think the beasts could hurt me, but my companions didn't have metal skin or immortality. And if the Ringmaster and his accomplices were demonic, I didn't have a lot of faith in our shotguns and blades being enough to get rid of them.

"We weren't planning to stay here forever—just long enough to gather what we needed," the Ringmaster said. "Now, you've complicated our plans."

"Boo-fuckin'-hoo," I muttered. "Pack up and get out, and we won't burn your show to the ground."

The Ringmaster's malicious smile showed pointed teeth. "With all those innocent people inside? I think not."

The loudspeakers on a pole nearby crackled to life. "Attention, customers!" Sarah's voice boomed. "This is an emergency. Don't panic, but please move swiftly to the exit. You must leave *now.*"

I couldn't stifle a smile at Sarah's ingenuity, but the Ringmaster's smarmy grin twisted to a snarl. "Get her off the speakers!"

And just like that, we had a brawl.

As Sarah repeated her warning, the ghoul-clowns sent their monsters bounding toward us. We opened fire, greeting the creatures with a hail of bullets and lead shot. The Ringmaster drew back, content to let his underlings face the gunfire.

We stood blocking the entrance to the tent, giving Sarah time to repeat her warning and clear the park grounds. I don't know what she could hear from outside, but her voice never wavered, and I gave her credit for staying cool under pressure.

I got a good look at the creatures as they lunged toward us, teeth bared. Two hellhounds, a huge cat that didn't look like anything I'd seen in a zoo, and a massive snake. I'd been afraid that all the monsters on the carousel might come to life. If there were only four, we could handle that.

Beyond the ghoul-clowns, I saw the five zombies from the big top show. We didn't have a battle—we had a war.

Lawrence and Daniels worked together like a well-oiled team, despite their age. They stood back-to-back, firing round after round, covering each other as they reloaded. The two of them went after the hellhounds— massive wolf-dogs with red eyes and humped backs.

West stuck with me. He took aim at the cat-creature while I kept my attention on the snake. If those fangs held venom, I had better odds with my speed and metal skin than my all-too-mortal companions.

The snake struck, but I moved faster, putting myself between it and West. I didn't dare pay attention to the battles going on around me. All my focus stayed on the snake, bobbing back and forth to match its move-ment. It lunged again, and this time its fangs hit my arm, skidding harm-lessly down the steel with a shrill squeal.

I seized on its momentary confusion to launch myself at it, moving faster than it could strike. I brought my gun up under its head and pressed the trigger, putting a bullet through its skull.

That slowed it down, but its continued attack confirmed my fear that these beasts weren't really alive. Whether they were magically animated or pulled through some rift by a dark witch, they weren't of our world. That meant killing them was going to be a real bitch.

I didn't like these odds. Once the beasts finished with us, the ghoul-clowns would attack, and then the zombies. The Ringmaster might be waiting for them to weaken us before he used his magic, or perhaps he'd enjoy the sport of calling in reinforcements.

I smelled blood and feared for my allies. We couldn't fight the monsters forever.

"*Exorcizamus te, omnis immundus spiritus, omnis satanica potestas...*" a new voice boomed over the loudspeaker, starting a version of the Latin exorcism. Since I was soul-sworn to a different god, that invocation wouldn't work for me, but I lifted my voice in an ancient banishment rite as I struggled with the snake-thing.

"Be gone, all foul and tainted creatures," I shouted. "Get thee from this place, and never return. I cast you out. I abjure you. By all that is holy and sacred, get thee hence!"

Howling, hissing, and shrieking, the beasts convulsed before turning on their masters as the exorcism and banishment broke the Ringmaster's control over them. The ghoul-clowns lost their smug expressions as they fought the creatures and the zombies' reanimated bodies were no match for the monsters once the bonds of magic had been released.

When the ghoul-clowns and undead monsters had been ripped apart and lay in pieces, the creatures gave a last howl and the spirits that animated them separated from their bodies, leaving them dead on the ground.

"What have you done?" the Ringmaster screeched, turning his ire on me as the combination of the exorcism and the banishment forced the unnatural energies from his body. Sulfurous yellow smoke streamed from his mouth, nose, and ears, leaving an emaciated corpse behind.

"Get the others out of here," I yelled over my shoulder at West. "I'll see if the rest of the creatures are dead."

"To hell with that. We stay together. But who the fuck read the exorcism?" West countered.

"That would be me."

We turned to find the man in black, the guy I'd spotted high up in the bleachers inside the tent. He didn't wear a clerical collar, but now I could see that the black coat resembled a cassock more than an overcoat.

"Father Kawalski," the man introduced himself. "I slipped in under the tent during all the distractions. I'm with the Logonje."

I must have startled at the word because I'd heard of the Eastern European priests who could do magic as well as perform exorcisms. They specialized in dealing with the supernatural, so creatures and demons were likely all in a day's work for Kawalski.

"I saw you in the big top tent. You were making strange motions with your hands," I said, still suspicious.

"Trying to ward the audience to protect them, as best I could," Kawalski replied. "Each of the circus acts sent different tendrils of dark magic into the crowd, searching for people with special characteristics. I did what I could to shield them and keep the magic from finding what it wanted."

That's when I heard a groan that sounded like Lawrence.

"Don't be a stubborn ass," Daniels chided as the two men came into view, although his own jacket bore slashes and his shirt was bloodied. "You're hurt. We need to get back to base and deal with that."

"I'm fine."

"I'm dragging you, not carrying you, if you pass out," Daniels threatened, and I got the feeling this was an old, complicated dance.

"Fuck you," Lawrence muttered, but without heat, as if he knew the battle was pointless and that he'd already lost.

"I'll go with the newcomers and check to make sure the threat is gone," Kawalski said to Lawrence, meaning West, Sarah, and me. "Take Ellis back and patch him up. Then meet us at the diner in an hour."

Daniels nodded and helped Lawrence toward where I guessed their vehicle was parked, as the injured man grumbled until they were out of earshot.

Sarah walked out of the tent carrying a burlap sack covered in runes. "The good father told me this was what we were looking for," she said, eyeing the bag as if it might bite. "Can we go now?"

West and Sarah burned the ringmaster's corpse and the rest of the bodies while Kawalski and I made the rounds of the circus grounds. The exorcism and banishment had pulled the spirits out of all the infernal creatures within the sound of our voices, which meant the circus was now officially kaput. We burned the additional corpses we found and went back to join the others.

"Do we burn the bag too?" Sarah asked. By the time Father K and I got back, she and West had cleaned out the files in the circus office to take with us.

Kawalski shook his head. "Won't do any good. Fire alone won't hurt it. I need to take a look at the relic and figure out which magics are being used so I can destroy it."

"What about all the others?" Sarah asked, and I knew she was thinking of the performers and stage hands who might have paranormal abilities and likely were not completely ignorant of the circus's true purpose.

"I tipped off the local office of the SSS that we were moving on the circus tonight. They've already got the perimeter cordoned and a dragnet in place—and they'll handle the human police," West said.

We heard sirens in the distance. "That's our cue to get the hell out of Dodge," West said.

"Dewer's Diner, Murrysville," Kawalski said, naming a small town west of Burke Glen, where we were now. "Give us an hour." He disappeared around the back of the office tent while we jogged toward where we had parked.

No one tried to stop us, but I didn't release the breath I was holding—or let go of Krukis's magic—until we were safely inside West's Buick and on the road. A string of police cars with the lights flashing passed us going the other direction.

"Are we going? To the diner?" I asked as West drove.

"Do you believe that those guys are really Federal agents?" Sarah asked. "Shouldn't they be retired?"

I'd wondered that myself, but then again, I've become a bad judge of mortal's ages.

"Not if they've got desk jobs," West replied, sounding grumpy. "Section chief, division head, senior partner-in-charge. It's possible, although most people don't want to hang onto the job that long."

"I spotted all of them in the big top," I told them, recounting my impressions. "I think they're legit, and I'm in favor of meeting with them. We might be on the same side."

"I'm not letting them claim jurisdiction," West warned. "We were assigned this case. Federal. I don't care where those guys are based, this one's ours."

"Down, Tiger." Sarah chuckled as she patted West's shoulder. "It's just coffee and talking. Maybe pie if we're lucky. No need to flex those muscles."

"Very funny," he grumbled, but he unclenched his jaw, which was progress.

"I ran across the Department of Supernatural Investigation years ago. As I recall, they had a reputation for being the good guys—as much as Feds can be," I needled.

"We spun off from the Secret Service, and they were an offshoot of the FBI," West replied. "It's the usual alphabet soup federal proliferation. Why have one department when you could have half a dozen, all fighting for turf and resources?"

"Do we all agree that the Menagerie was beyond creepy?" Sarah asked.

"Yeah." West and I spoke in unison.

"There's more going on than just a single witch—or the Ringmaster," I said. "He might have been running the day-to-day, but I bet he wasn't the big cheese who created the Menagerie. It took a lot of mojo to bewitch all the performers and creatures, keep control, and have the money to set up the circus in the first place. Especially if there are other versions operating elsewhere."

"I agree," West replied, without taking his eyes from the road. "That means there's a money man and a puppet master somewhere higher up. I don't like the possibilities."

Neither did I, but for once, I kept my mouth shut.

Dewer's Diner looked like it had been around forever, a true local's joint. West's Buick seemed out of place next to the hard-worn trucks in the lot. We parked off to one side, unwilling to be the first to arrive.

While we waited, we tossed out theories to explain how the supernatural forces in the Menagerie might have been brought under control and what the bigger picture might entail. We kept circling back to the idea of government interference and a dangerous official interest in people and creatures with supernatural abilities. None of our scenarios envisioned anything good.

Father Kawalski arrived first in an Oldsmobile. If he noticed us, he didn't give any indication and walked inside. I could see through the window as he spoke to the server. He must have asked for a table in the back because she gathered menus and led him to the far end of the dining area.

A few minutes later, a three-wheeled motorbike that didn't look like anything I'd seen before rumbled into the lot. Two leather-jacketed riders dismounted and removed their helmets to reveal Lawrence and Daniels. Whoever these guys were, they didn't believe in aging gracefully.

"Guess it's our turn," West mumbled, sounding grumpy.

"Well, let's see how this goes," I muttered under my breath. "Play nice," I warned West.

"I always do," he replied with a shark-like grin that gave me no reassurance.

The priest and both DSI agents looked up as we approached. We sat down with Sarah between us, and for a moment, our two groups faced each other with awkward silence.

"Is the pie here good? I'm starving." Sarah reached for the menu in a clip in the middle of the table, and her comment broke the ice.

I cleared my throat. "We haven't been introduced. I'm Joe Mack. Consultant."

"Sarah Grace McAllen Harringworth," Sarah added and gave them a dazzling smile. "Patron." The long-faced man gave her an appraising look. Anyone from the Pittsburgh area would recognize McAllen Steel and Harringworth Coal.

I looked at Lawrence and Daniels and frowned as the names jostled a memory. One problem with an unnaturally long life is how bloody much there is to remember. "Wait a minute. They called you two 'Double Trouble' back in the day."

West startled. "Seriously?" He stared at the sedate men in their sixties who sat across from us. "You were legendary—for all kinds of crazy exploits you managed to survive."

Daniels shot a dour look at his partner. "Those were mostly Ellis's fault."

"As if," Lawrence muttered, looking none the worse for his injuries from tonight's escapades.

Sarah cleared her throat and tapped a perfectly-manicured nail against her menu. "Explanation, please."

We paused to order dessert and coffee and waited until the server was out of earshot.

"My partner and I have handled cases in this region for over thirty years," Daniels replied, his expression softening as he spoke to Sarah. She had that effect on people. "Some of those involved very... unusual...scenarios."

"Don't beat around the bush," Lawrence broke in, clearly the bull in a china shop of the pair. "We helped save the city—and the world—a couple of times. Broke plenty of rules along the way, ticked off powerful people, took a few chances that paid off."

I couldn't remember specifics, but the bits of memories that tugged at the edge of my brain suggested that Ellis drastically understated the risks.

"Aren't you a little old for field agents?" West never went to charm school.

"We moved into management twenty years ago," Daniels answered, and I wondered if he'd stepped on Lawrence's foot under the table to keep him from a retort. "But on occasion, we look into situations that warrant our attention. In this case, a deadly threat to an old friend."

"We got assigned the case because it was weird, and we were close—Cleveland's home base," West replied. "'Weird' is kinda what we do."

Daniels chuckled. "You can't imagine how familiar that sounds."

The server returned with pie and coffee, and we called an unspoken truce as we polished the food off in record time. Sneaking around always gave me an appetite, and great coffee was one of the joys of living.

Once the cups were refilled and the dishes cleared, West leaned forward. "Why were you at the circus tonight, and what did you see?"

The two DSI agents exchanged a glance, a whole conversation born of long experience that didn't need words, no doubt deciding whether to trust us. They seemed to come to a conclusion since Ellis sat back, looking less likely to bolt or fight. Father Kawalski spoke first.

"Our bet going in was on something demonic," Kawalski replied. "That would explain the creatures and the 'tricks' that required powerful magic. From what happened in the fight, I think we guessed right—up to a point. The Ringmaster might have been running the show, but I don't think he was the big boss. And the real question is, why was the circus created, and what is its true purpose?"

"And the zombies?" I was pleased that they seemed to be thinking along the same lines we were.

Lawrence flinched. "We've seen those things before. All it takes is an insane witch and some twisted magic. Unfortunately, creating them isn't as difficult as you'd think."

I didn't want to think about those horrors, although I felt certain I'd see them again in my nightmares.

"Those spirits always have a weak point," Daniels jumped in. "A relic, spell book, altar—something that binds and focuses its power. The real question is—do we have a human trying to compel a demon, or a powerful demon trying to compel humans?"

"Bigger question—who was using them to draw a crowd, and what was that dark magic they sent into the crowd supposed to do? And what's the end game?" I added.

That was the crux of the problem because depending on the answer, the response could take very different forms.

"The ringmaster had red eyes," Sarah spoke up. "And he *hovered*. Was he controlling the demon—or was he possessed?"

"That was what we hoped to figure out when we went to search the office," Daniels replied with a glare in West's direction. Clearly, the friendly rivalry wasn't settled. "The relic box had power—but once again, it was more about maintaining control—not creating the situation in the first place."

"We need to follow the money," West returned. "And we want to know if the circus is related to two other cases we just handled as part of a larger investigation. We shut down a fake psychic with ties to the upper crust who siphoned off sensitive information, and once we're done here, we'll pull the plug on a prizefighting ring that's trying to create super soldiers. The deaths that occurred at the Macabre Menagerie's prior stops all involved people who knew important—classified—details."

"That's what pulled us into the field again, hands-on," Lawrence answered, looking pensive. "We've got a friend who was quite the *wunderkind* in his younger days. Genius inventor. Attracted the attention of the biggest companies—and government agencies. Patrick stepped away from all that years ago, and since 'the powers that be' confiscated his supernaturally-inclined inventions and Westinghouse owned the patents to the others, now he just putters for his own amusement."

I bet they didn't get all his gadgets—like that handy box that scared away the ghosts.

"Except that he obviously didn't forget everything he knew," Daniels stepped in. "So we've made sure he's always got a security detail to keep anyone from thinking they'll kidnap him and make him invent for them. Trust me—we've foiled more than a few schemes."

I felt bad for their genius friend who couldn't even retire to anonymity.

"We'd heard about the Menagerie, and we had people tracking them. So when they came to Pittsburgh, we had our agents gathering intel," Ellis picked up the story. "There are assets here in the city that can't be compromised."

I hated when any of them slipped into what I thought of as Fed speak. *"People,"* I said, not hiding my grouchy tone. "Those 'assets' are *people*."

Daniels cleared his throat. "Yes. Of course. And one of them is our friend, Patrick. We worried when we found out about the deaths. We were even more concerned when Patrick received a personal invitation and a free ticket to attend."

"Hunting the demonic is part of the Logonje's mission," Father Kawalski said. "So I was happy to come along and lend a hand."

West and I exchanged a look. A free ticket for their inventor friend definitely indicated that someone was up to no good.

"And?" Sarah asked.

"Ellis and I decided to check it out for ourselves. We managed to convince Patrick not to go. I used his ticket, we got another ticket for the good Father, and Ellis went undercover," Daniels replied. "Father K and I checked out the show, Ellis spooked around the backstage areas, and we agreed to meet up and ransack the office. Which is when you showed up."

"We doubled back to get the office files," Sarah volunteered, surprising me. "We'll share what we find out if there's anything useful."

Ellis's eyes narrowed, and I figured that he thought his team should have dibs on the files, but we were all apparently making nice, so he didn't push the matter. Or maybe he didn't want to tangle with Sarah.

"The medium we busted was a wraith," West said, with an edge to his voice that told me he was still vying for dominance. "We think he was doing more than scamming the bereaved—he was compromising 'soft assets' who might have influence over key people or second-hand knowledge that might be valuable. And the prizefighting ring fits with experimenting with ways to make super soldiers."

"Our theory is that the circus deaths might have been attempts to control the minds of the targets and coerce them—efforts that went wrong," I added.

"Oh, for God's sake!" Sarah burst out. "Enough with marking your territory and dancing around each other. Could you get on with the collaborating part? I don't want to be here all night."

That drew a grin from Daniels and the priest and chagrined smiles from West and Lawrence. I just chuckled, knowing that Sarah was an unstoppable force.

"If we're right about the medium, the prizefighting racket, and the circus chasing the same goal with different means, then someone upstream is pulling the strings," West leveled with them. "And if it's not DSI and it's not the SSS, then either we're dealing with the Sinistram, the Occulatum, or a new group. Does Operation: Ferryman ring a bell?"

Father Kawalski and the others shook their heads. "I don't know anything about that. And whoever is involved isn't the Logonje or the Occulatum," the priest said. "I have friends among the priesthood who left the Sinistram and greatly repented of their association with that group. They still retain some ties to gather information—as a way to atone for the harm they helped to cause. I will make inquiries and see if they think the Sinistram is responsible."

Lawrence and Daniels exchanged a look. "There've been whispers that some government folks who are worried about what's going on in Germany want to build their own hush-hush organization to weaponize anything supernatural, build magical defenses, and maybe create 'enhanced' soldiers," Lawrence confided. "They might be linked to this Ferryman group you mentioned."

"Damn," Sarah muttered. "Just like the creeps we stopped in Reading."

Lawrence raised an eyebrow. "That was you? Nice work."

"Those dangerous idiots tried to raise an eldritch power from the depths," I remarked. "There was one secret society that recruited foot soldiers and another group for the rich people who stood to benefit. We closed down the Reading operation, but it wouldn't be a surprise to find them in other cities."

"A new government agency preparing for another Great War, with magic and monsters instead of machine guns. Wonderful," West said, heavy on the sarcasm. He ran a hand through his hair, and I figured he felt a headache coming on.

"And we believe that some—if not all—of the weapons our friend invented were shunted in that direction after they got confiscated," Daniels added, contempt clear in his voice. "That was another reason we didn't want Patrick to attend the circus. He rarely leaves the house—too much chance that someone will try to grab him for what he knows."

"We think we've found another, related situation—if you'd like to join us in shutting them down," Lawrence said, and I looked up sharply. I hadn't expected to "make the team" quite so quickly.

Then again, if "Double Trouble" were coming out of retirement for the effort, this was likely to be unofficial, bootleg, and maybe illegal as all hell. I could get behind that.

"What did you have in mind?" West asked.

Lawrence yawned and pushed away his empty pie plate. "How about we tackle that tomorrow? Supper, same place? I don't know about you, but we've got paperwork to fill out."

West gave a rueful chuckle. "Yeah, so do I. Meet you here for dinner at eight tomorrow."

We paid our bill and headed out to the parking lot. That was when I noticed some subtle protection sigils worked into the diner's decorations and a row of protective plants behind an iron fence in the small garden that ringed the building.

"It's a safe meeting place for our sort of folks," Lawrence replied to my unspoken question. "The sort of thing that comes in handy."

Father Kawalski drove away in his Oldsmobile, and we watched the two DSI agents roar away on their motorbike.

"God, I hope I'm still that crazy when I'm their age," West said, shaking his head.

"I'm older than they are, and I'm not that crazy," I replied.

No one said much on the drive back to the William Penn. We veered off to our rooms, intending to meet in the parlor. West and I were just pouring drinks when Sarah joined us, holding a cream-colored parchment envelope.

"This was on my nightstand," she said. "Handwritten. We are invited to lunch with Glenn Philips at his home tomorrow." Then Sarah held up the note for us to see, with its prominent protection sigil drawn at the bottom. Someone who didn't know our world might take it for an intricate seal or decoration, but for us, it clearly marked the invitation as professional, not personal.

"Philips—as in Willard-Philips ? The antique auction house?" West asked, raising an eyebrow in surprise.

I struggled to remember a connection and felt a flash of satisfaction as I grasped the memory. "As I recall, the company is rumored to have two very particular specialties. One is reuniting long-lived beings with favorite possessions that were 'misplaced' over the years. The other is getting dangerous supernatural items out of the wrong hands."

"Hmm," West murmured. "I've heard the same stories—never anything to back them up. Do you know Philips?" he asked Sarah.

"Not personally, although our families attended the same boarding schools over the years, which counts," she replied.

"Any idea what prompted the invitation?" I asked, unsure whether this was good or bad.

Sarah slid the invitation back into the envelope. "If I had to guess, I'd say that either we've run into common colleagues, or they have an interest in the cases we've worked. Maybe both." She set the envelope aside, poured herself a measure of gin, and settled onto the couch to enjoy a nightcap with us.

We'd succeeded in closing down the Macabre Menagerie, and while West and I would have some sore muscles tomorrow, none of our party were seriously hurt, for once. The Ringmaster and monsters were dead, the audience had been protected, and any infernal spirits present had been banished.

We still had to slog through the files—and compare notes with Ellis and Lawrence—to see if our hunch about the circus's role in recruiting "talent" held true. And while we had shut down this version of the menagerie, there were surely others doing the same shadowy scouting for whoever was at the top. Not to mention the two other creepy events that were still part of West's assignment.

Our work wasn't done, but we'd had a good day. We deserved to celebrate our wins when they came our way.

"Here's to us." Sarah raised a toast. "And to a good night's work. Knock your drink back, boys. We've earned it."

4

We took Sarah's Duesenberg into Shadyside for our lunch invitation at the Philips house.

"Nice digs," West joked as we pulled up in front of the gray and white mansion that took up most of a city block.

Sarah shrugged. "I suspect it's been in the family for a while. The company was founded by the current owners' fathers. I guess it's a lucrative business."

A servant came to park the car, registering surprise when he realized that Sarah had been behind the wheel and not a hired driver. She was clearly enjoying the novelty of Steven having a few days off.

"Mrs. Harrison, Mr. West, Mr. Mack. You're expected and precisely on time," a butler said, welcoming us into the home's grand foyer. "Right this way, please."

We followed him into a large dining room, set for five. The door opened at the far end, and two well-dressed older gentlemen entered.

I guessed their age to be mid-sixties, but both wore the years well. One man's hair still had dark flecks among the silver, while the other had gone completely white.

"Welcome," the darker-haired man greeted us. "Thank you for coming. I'm Glenn Philips—"

"And I'm Curtis Willard," his companion added.

"Please—sit down," Philips said. "I promise that my reason for inviting you here is worth your time, but before we get down to business, let's enjoy some lighter conversation over good food."

We chose our seats, and servants brought beverages and the first course of deviled eggs and oysters Rockefeller. Philips and Willard kept the conversation going, inquiring about our lines of business and recent travel, swapping stories with Sarah about familiar places and common acquaintances, and giving us a quick "tour" of the notable artwork and antiques in the room.

An olive platter, mixed nuts, and leek soup came next, along with a champagne cocktail.

West traded stories of his exploits with our hosts, who had quite a few adventures of their own to share. And while I felt sure that all of them gave carefully edited versions, the tales still made for a lively discussion.

I hung back, listening to the others talk—analyzing—as the main course of sugar-glazed ham, puff potatoes, and peas was served. Conversation came to a halt as we ate, and I couldn't imagine how our host remained so slim if he dined like this every day.

"I've arranged to have dessert served in the parlor," Philips said when the dishes were cleared. "We can be more comfortable and talk at our leisure."

We followed the two men through a doorway into a well-appointed sitting room with couches and armchairs arranged around a large fireplace with an ornately carved wooden mantel. The temperatures hadn't dropped enough for a fire to be lit, but they would soon.

Once we were seated, the butler came with a tray of cakes, coffee, and glasses of port. After such a feast, I hoped I wouldn't struggle to stay awake, but I fully intended to enjoy the moment.

"Archie Dunning speaks well of you," Philips said with a moue like he had revealed a great secret. "So do Ellis and Isaac," he added, clearly on a first-name basis with the two DSI agents. "I take their recommendations very seriously."

I disliked being the last one in on the story. But since Sarah had been issued the invitation, I let her take the lead.

"We were wondering about that," she said after she'd had a bite of cake. Sarah is an intrepid investigator, but she also never passes up good desserts or top-shelf alcohol. "I had the distinct feeling this wasn't entirely a social call."

Philips and Willard both chuckled. "And you would be correct,"

Willard replied. "This is where I admit that I've thoroughly researched all of you and found that the truth exceeds your reputations."

"If you're acquainted with Lawrence and Daniels, what do you need us for?" West asked, in his usual socially-incorrect way.

"You're both younger, and Mr. Mack is immortal," Philips replied with a nod in my direction. "Much as I value Ellis and Isaac's instincts, I'm not going to send them into danger without backup."

"And that danger would be?" Sarah inquired, with an edge to her voice which said she hadn't quite been convinced to throw in her support.

"We're the ones who requested assistance from the Supernatural Secret Service about the Macabre Menagerie and the other suspicious events," Willard said, smiling at our surprise. "Ellis has already filed his report, and the unedited version that we received contained the theories you spun over supper about a new government agency with devious plans."

"We agree," Philips chimed in. "And after having seen how even the more benign agencies have treated our friend Patrick—the inventor—as well as Ellis and Isaac—"

"And our own run-ins with them, back in the day," Willard added.

"That too," Philips picked up. "We don't want to see another group come to power—particularly not one invested in using the supernatural as a weapon of war."

"I think we can all agree on that," Sarah replied, making them work for our support.

"So the first cases with the wraith-medium and the paranormal prize-fighting were tests?" I wasn't sure how I felt about that.

"Yes and no," Philips said, raising his hands in a placating gesture. "We wanted to believe the stories we'd heard about you; but given what was at stake with the Menagerie and the rest of the situations, we had to be sure."

I didn't like it, but I could grudgingly see their side.

Willard leaned forward. "We think that someone in the government is going about the process of identifying potentially useful people in a very organized way, moving from region to region. We've protected Pittsburgh for a long time—and from things a lot scarier than bureaucrats. We aren't about to stop now."

"We suspect that the folks behind this effort send an advance team into a location to size up the potential and scout for opportunities. They're looking for several key types of people simultaneously, we believe, and so they set up multiple entry points for their marks to come to their notice and be evaluated," Philips continued.

I didn't like the sound of that at all, and from the look West shot me, I knew we were on the same page. Sarah was at her most dangerous, playing the social doyenne, so her expression remained unreadable, but I figured she backed us on principle.

"So the medium identifies vulnerable people who have sensitive information, opens a trusted channel of communication, and introduces a way to emotionally manipulate them," Sarah summarized.

"The prizefighting racket recruits former soldiers and experiments on them to make them enhanced killing machines," West added.

Philips nodded. "Then the circus comes to town, and it attracts a different—but equally valuable—group of potential 'assets.'" The curl of his lip on that last word suggested he disliked it as much as I did.

"What was the circus's end game?" I asked. None of us seemed sure since there hadn't been time to go through the files we had "liberated," although we had plenty of theories.

"We think the people at the top are still experimenting," Willard replied. "Some of our witch friends believe that the entities tried to possess guests with valuable information and were a little too heavy-handed, hence the deaths."

"Possess them?" Sarah echoed.

"A spirit that could take possession of a body and mind would be privy to all its secrets. It could go in, riffle through the mental filing cabinet, as it were, and leave with the information. In theory, it could be done in a way the victim—asset—never even notices," Willard continued.

"Except they died." Everyone looked my way when I spoke.

"Guessing the spirit overdid things," Philips said. "No telling what would have happened to the VIPs who were invited to the Menagerie here, but we weren't going to risk finding out."

I remembered that their inventor friend was one of those who got an exclusive invitation and shuddered at the thought of the secrets to be mined in a brain like that.

"You said you thought the folks at the top were going after different groups. We've dealt with three. Who's next?"

"Wealthy donors and people who would make excellent warrior-generals," Willard replied.

"Sounds right," West agreed. "What's the con?"

"Identify the asset and lay claim to them—permanently," Philips said. "They might be working with vampires."

"Might be?" West countered sharply.

Philips shrugged. "That's what we need to find out. It's been more difficult than we expected to get good data. The events are invitation-only, small audience, only one night. The names of the troupes are always different, and cast listing is non-existent. We aren't sure it's the same group in each city—or whether it's a new fashion with a lot of copycats."

"And you want us to be bait?" I didn't like what I thought I was hearing.

Philips looked appalled. "God, no! *Curtis* and *I* are the bait. Believe it or not, we both have enough secrets rattling around in our heads to make what we know valuable to certain people."

I frowned, not following. "Then where do we come in?"

Willard glared at Philips. "As usual, Glenn skipped the whole first part of the story."

Philips cleared his throat. "Just letting you spin the tale with your usual dramatic flair," he teased back.

Damn, they argue like an old married couple.

Willard shifted his gaze to look from one of us to the next, assuring our attention. "We received a very posh invitation—by courier—a week ago inviting us to an exclusive one-night-only performance of the *Theatre de Fantomes*. Of course we were intrigued—and suspicious. Especially since it's going to be held at the Alvin, which isn't the showplace it used to be."

"The Alvin was one of the city's most magnificent theaters when it opened, but it's fallen on hard times since then. Practically a ghost of its old self—fading grandeur and all that," Philips supplied.

"We asked around and realized that the only people who received invitations were not just wealthy—they had served as senior officers in the Great War or been shadow operatives, as we were, in the Intelligence Corps," Willard went on.

"Ellis and Isaac unearthed more details. There have been vampire-themed shows in several cities, but we can't prove they're the same show or even related. People disappeared a few days to weeks after attending the show, but never with a direct enough connection for the police to get involved," Philips said.

"I hate to tell you this, but even with all of us, we can't take on a theater company of vampires." West didn't beat around the bush.

"We don't have to," Philips said with a predatory smile. "Our good friend Andre Bergeron has been Pittsburgh's master vampire for a very long time. He doesn't look kindly on any vampires entering 'his' city without permission—let alone a whole troupe. He's even less fond of any activity—like turning prominent people—that might draw unwanted attention."

"Of course, it would also be bad to wipe out a troupe of actors who were just playacting at being vampires," Willard said. "And Andre can't just show up himself because if they are real vamps, they'll cut and run to save their skins."

"Not every city is protected like Pittsburgh," Willard went on. "The other places where the show played didn't have a vampire guardian. That's another reason we think this might be part of a government project instead of vamp politics because even fledglings know you don't enter someone else's territory."

"If they're real vampires, Andre and his nest will handle it. If they're not, odds are good they're still some kind of supernatural creature," Philips added.

"And where are all the moral watchdogs? This sort of thing sounds... salacious." Sarah's tone made it clear that she didn't find that to be a bad thing.

Willard shrugged. "We suspect they've either been paid off directly or had a big donation made to silence their conscience for one night." His voice fairly dripped with disapproval.

"When is the show, and what's your plan?" Sarah asked, in the tough-as-nails voice she must have used successfully at board meetings staring down executives. "Not saying we'll agree. But we need to know the plan— all of it—or we're out."

Philips smiled. "I'd expect nothing less. Here's what we've got so far..."

THE ALVIN THEATER must have been a showplace when it was new. The tall, narrow stone facade presented an impressive entrance to the street. Its lobby was awash in faded luxury and tarnished glamor. The plush carpet might have been crimson when it was new, but foot traffic had worn paths in its pile. Faded flocked wallpaper marked the extent of the sun's reach from the large front windows.

An usher in a threadbare uniform led us to our box seats. Worn velvet upholstery and peeling paint showed the theater's age. The Alvin had good bones. Its ceiling soared overhead, painted to look like the night sky. Ornate plasterwork medallions surrounded the bases of crystal chandeliers, and the balcony railing's brass gleamed.

The real masterpiece was the Alvin's stage, framed by elaborate artwork, with a rich, red velvet curtain trimmed in gold fringe that hung in heavy folds which nearly hid patches and discoloration.

We still didn't know whether the "vampires" were real or not, but the faded glory fit the sense of decadence, decay, and old wealth the stories associated with the undead.

"Does anyone know what the play is even about?" West grumbled. "Lord Bannerworth's Downfall—sounds like some awful dime novel."

"Reminds me of a book about a vampire that I skimmed after someone had left it behind on a train," I replied. "Quite dramatic." I didn't add that I had enjoyed the overdone adventure, which broke up a long, and otherwise boring ride.

"There better be some action," West said. "Otherwise, I fall asleep at the theater. Same with the symphony, opera, and ballet." I wondered how many of those he'd attended with Sarah and which had been on assignment. I figured West was more of a motion picture kind of guy.

"Ever see *Nosferatu?*" I asked.

"Yeah. Not scary after you've fought the real thing."

West and I posed as bodyguards to Philips and Willard. Lawrence, Daniels, and Sarah were outside in an altered delivery truck, using some of Patrick's pilfered experimental technology to hear what was going on around us, thanks to wired contraptions that fit beneath our clothing. A tiny hidden camera enabled West to snap pictures.

Willard and Philips played their roles to the hilt. Their goal was to be visible, making a splashy entrance, greeting the other attendees, and making sure everyone saw them. We hung back, watching the reactions of the theater's small staff and the performers who mingled among the patrons during the pre-event reception.

So far, none of these are vampires. I had activated Krukis's magic when we came to the theater since fangs couldn't penetrate my metal skin. With my heightened senses, I felt certain that I would sense the undead, but whether or not I could tell if a human had fallen under their sway, I wasn't sure.

Could that be the missing connection? Vampire thralls doing the work, with a handful of real vamps as the main performers?

The house lights dimmed, music swelled dark and ominous, and patrons settled nervously in their seats as the curtain rose.

Later, I might ask what the story involved, but as a bodyguard, I couldn't afford to get distracted. I looked everywhere except the stage, constantly scanning for threats, and sizing up the other members of the audience.

Occasionally, I spared a glance toward the stage, making sure I didn't get wrapped up in the story. From what I heard and saw, the show had everything except a good plot. Sets, costumes, actors, all looked top-notch. But the script rambled, something even the best actor couldn't overcome.

"To save our lands and lineage, we must have a sacrifice!" A character —perhaps Lord Bannerworth himself—shouted with melodramatic fervor.

I glanced at Philips and Willard, only to find them leaning forward, seemingly engrossed in the performance. *To each his own, I guess.*

They recoiled as if remembering where they were when the actors jumped down from the stage or filed down the steps and fanned out through the audience. The performers moved with spooky grace, but I couldn't tell whether that was supernatural or just a trick of trained dancers.

The thespians angled themselves toward startled audience members, scenting them.

"Is it you?" they asked again and again in malevolent whispers, hissing that first word. They didn't touch, although their clawed hands hovered mere inches from the hapless patrons, whose momentary terror turned to self-conscious chuckles once the performers moved away.

Once the actors had worked their way through the entire theater— although not our box since we'd locked the door—they slunk back toward the stage.

Abruptly, one veered off and snatched a woman by the wrist, pulling her along with them as she screamed.

A fearful murmur rose, but most seemed to think the abduction was part of the show, despite the woman's protests. West nearly rose from his seat, but I pushed him down with a forceful hand on his shoulder and shook my head, earning a glare in response.

As the creatures on the stage wrestled the hapless woman onto a table, a narrator's voice boomed over the ominous, stirring music.

"Lo! 'tis a gala night, within the lonesome latter years! An angel throng, bewinged, bedight, in veils, and drowned in tears, sit in a theatre, to see…a play of hopes and fears."

I recognized those lines. Edgar Allen Poe—*The Conqueror Worm*, my memory supplied. While I hadn't had much opportunity for education before I died, books had been my constant companions ever since. I read to learn, to provide solace in the lonely hours, and to distract myself on the many nights sleep proved elusive. Poe was an old favorite I had enjoyed many times.

I had never envisioned the poem brought to life quite like this.

The narrator continued his dispassionate reading while gasps and screams rose from the audience as the "vampires" swarmed their prey. Blood that looked all too real ran across the stage.

At the crescendo of the music, the vampires fell back as if tossed aside, and the victim stood—unharmed but now dressed in scarlet. Her assailants crawled toward her to kneel at her feet, some sort of unholy resurrection.

What the hell are we watching?

With a bang like a gunshot, the door stage right slammed open, and a man clad in a mantled leather cloak strode in carrying a crossbow.

"I have come to send you back to the pit from whence you came!" the vampire hunter shouted as the music swelled once more.

I tensed, expecting a pitched battle. The vampires scuttled and slithered toward the outnumbered hunter, whose arrows didn't slow their advance. They overwhelmed him, covering him with their bodies and bearing him to the stage beneath them as the music swelled once more.

The narrator continued, dispassionate. "Out—out are the lights—out all! And, over each quivering form, the curtain, a funeral pall, comes down with the rush of a storm."

As the audience watched in stunned horror, the writhing, bloody mass of actors gradually disentangled. The poem continued to its ultimate deadly conclusion.

The performers stood, gore-covered but apparently alive, and took their bows to the thunderous applause of a standing ovation.

"That's it. We're getting out of here right now," West said, rising. I followed his lead.

I led the way out of our locked theater box and found a smarmy tuxedo-clad usher waiting for us.

"I hope you enjoyed the show. You're invited to a VIP back-stage reception with refreshments and *beverages*," he said with a tone that made it clear alcohol would be served.

"I'm afraid we aren't able to stay," Philips replied as West and I stood between him and the usher.

"But we insist."

The usher met my gaze, and I felt the tug of supernatural energy trying to fuck with my mind. Since I belonged to an ancient god, I'd already been claimed.

"Yes, that sounds good," Philips echoed in a far-away voice. Willard murmured in agreement.

I moved with nearly vampire speed and had the usher up against the wall by the throat. "Try to glamour us again, and I'll rip your eyeballs out of your undead skull and make you eat them," I growled.

I took his squeak as agreement and let go, adding a little flick of my wrist to toss him out of the way.

"What happened?" Philips asked, shaking his head to clear it. Willard looked equally unnerved.

"Vampire glamour. Which means we really *don't* want to go to the reception," West said tightly.

"Stay close, don't get distracted, and don't make eye contact," I warned. I went first, with Willard and Philips behind me and West bringing up the rear. We wove through the crowd, shouldering dawdlers out of the way, down the stairs, and through the lobby. I figured our hosts could blame any social errors on me, and I'd willingly take the heat if it kept them safe.

Fortunately for our escape, most of the audience was drawn by the allure of meeting the cast, snacking on delicacies, and enjoying illegal hooch. That meant we weren't fighting to get to the exit, but it left a theater full of potential victims to deal with later.

We didn't stop until we reached Philips's town car. I'd been the chauffeur tonight and remained wary until everyone was inside and the doors were locked.

"What the hell was that?" Philips exploded as we pulled out of the lot.

"Trouble," West replied tightly.

"We've seen this kind of thing before—in the old days," Willard reminded his friend. "Whether it's a witch or a vampire doing the manipulating, it's all the same in the end."

"Now we know how the vamps are controlling their targets," I said. "They don't have to turn their victims—not right away at least. They glamour them into submission, make them open to their will."

"That makes sense," Willard agreed. "While the audience was hand-picked, it's still too large a group to all get turned and have it not be noticed."

"But once they're glamoured, they could go on for a long time, letting the vamps turn people selectively, as needed," Philips picked up where he left off.

"This is not good. Not good at all," West muttered.

I pulled the car up in front of the Philips' residence. A tall man with thick, dark hair and deep-set brown eyes appeared between one blink and the next, standing at the foot of the stairs.

I reached for my gun, but Philips put a hand on my shoulder. "It's all right. That's Andre Bergeron. He's expected."

Bergeron—the vampire.

"You trust him?" West's tone was skeptical.

"With our lives, more than once," Willard replied.

I knew without having to look that West wasn't completely convinced, but this was Philips's party, and we were backup. At least we had a working theory of what was going on, which was more than before.

The truck with the two DSI agents and Sarah pulled into the service driveway. We got out of the town car, and a servant rushed to drive it to the nearby garage.

"Andre, welcome," Philips greeted his new visitor. "Let's go inside."

We were quiet as we filed into the house, following Philips back to the parlor where a cart of cheese, dried fruits, port, brandy, and scotch awaited. Bergeron stood by the unlit fireplace while the rest of us took seats.

"Glad to see that you've all returned alive and well," the vampire replied. He looked me over with a sharp, appraising stare. "You're not mortal."

"Good for your friends, I'm not," I replied. "The vampire who tried to glamour me didn't get far."

"Tell me everything."

Philips and Willard took turns relaying the events of the night. West and I broke in occasionally with additional observations. Sarah and the DSI agents added to the tale where their recording equipment had over-heard something the rest of us might have overlooked.

Bergeron listened silently, and his expression changed from serious to grim.

"I believe you are correct in your assumptions," Bergeron said when we concluded. "Glamouring is strongly frowned upon among ethical nests, but clearly that hasn't stopped these vampires. Manipulation or turning without consent is reason for grave punishment, including destruction. That they came into *my* city and ignored all warnings is even greater provocation."

"That's why we think these are government vamps, following orders," West replied. He laid out the recruitment theory, which deepened Bergeron's scowl.

"Even worse, if you're correct," he said. "You've provided an invaluable warning—for my nest and the larger community. My people will take it from here—discreetly," he added with a faint smile that barely exposed the tips of his elongated eye teeth.

"If they're government-sent, destroying one troupe will just mean a replacement gets sent to the next city," I warned. "Someone's readying for war. Losing one team won't stop them."

Bergeron looked pensive. "I know more than I care to about war, as do you," he replied with a look that silently shared the losses of immortality. "One defeat won't dissuade their plan of attack, but the proverbial 'shot across the bow' can serve notice that such things won't be accepted without a fight."

Shortly afterward, Bergeron excused himself while the rest of us compared notes and talked about the evening. When we returned to the William Penn late that night, we saw a plume of smoke rising into the sky. Fire engines passed us, alarms blaring, lights flashing—responding to an all-out, five-alarm blaze.

After we parked Sarah's car, we paused in the lobby to speak to the doorman.

"What's all the excitement?" Sarah asked.

"The Alvin Theater is on fire," he replied. "Looks like it might be a total loss."

"That's a shame," Sarah responded, with an expression of concerned surprise that gave nothing away. We hurried back to our suite and met back in the parlor.

"What about the people who were glamoured?" Sarah asked once we reached the privacy of our rooms.

"To my understanding, if the vampire who did the glamouring dies, the bond dies with them," I said, and West nodded.

"So it's over?" Sarah went to her stash and poured herself a drink.

"It is for Pittsburgh," West replied, taking the bottle when she offered it and doing the same. I begged off since it didn't have any effect on me, and I wasn't in the mood.

"The government doesn't give up that easily," I added. "They'll put new teams together and try again—but not here. And now they know that someone's watching."

"Speaking of not giving up," West segued, "we've still got one more situation to handle before we can call it a day. I called headquarters to sic them on the prizefighting ring, so that'll be taken care of promptly."

"Let me guess—the phantom of the opera turned out to be a real phantom? They want us to bust the three ghosts in *A Christmas Carol?*" I felt like after what we'd been through, the snark was well-deserved. After all, everything so far had been a form of entertainment turned deadly.

"Nope—just a vicious vaudeville show," West replied with a grin.

He had mentioned the fifth item on our list before, but there was a lot of water under the bridge since then. I tend to focus on things in the order in which they're trying to kill me, and the last suspicious event had to wait its turn until we had handled the four before it.

"Want to explain?" Sarah asked, with a fond look that made it clear she thought West was an adorable idiot.

West sat back in his chair and savored a sip of his drink. "Apparently, there's a vaudeville company touring in the tri-state with a mesmerist—Spellbinder—headlining the show." He held up a hand to forestall interruptions.

"Yeah, lots of shows have magicians and mesmerists," West said, anticipating our comments. "But apparently there've been reports of people acting strangely after attending the show. As if whatever stage magic happened during the performance didn't end when the theater's lights came back on."

"Like what?" I didn't care for the possibilities that sprang to mind.

"One guy can't stop scratching his ear like a dog. Another meows like a cat whenever he hears the word 'mouse.' Standard stage hypnosis tricks—but they aren't supposed to be permanent," West said.

"Were they up on stage with this Spellbinder guy?" I asked.

West shook his head. "Not according to the complaints. They were in the audience, minding their own business. It's pretty much impossible to track down all the people who had tickets. Those folks aren't likely to respond to a newspaper ad, even less if they're embarrassed."

"If we're right about this secret government organization wanting to get ready for the next Great War, being able to control groups of people with some kind of hocus pocus would come in real handy," I suggested.

Sarah nodded. "That's what I was thinking."

"Then we're all on the same page," West declared. "I'm going to see if Ellis, Isaac, and Father K are up for taking in the show. Could be an interesting way to spend a Friday night."

FRONT PAGE HEADLINES in the morning confirmed that the Alvin was gutted by a "fire of unknown origin." The newspaper said that a traveling theatre group was missing and presumed dead. Pittsburgh's fire chief stated that no evidence suggested foul play and mentioned the many perils of old theaters—bad wiring, too-hot footlights, flammable sets.

Everyone agreed it was a tragedy, but once the embers cooled and the wreckage had been cleared away, I knew the troupe would be forgotten by the public—just as Bergeron intended. The government agency that sent them would decode the warning, and other vampires got a stern reminder of who protected Pittsburgh.

"Well, that certainly sends a message," Sarah said with a snap of the paper as she folded it and tossed it to the end of the couch. "Don't imagine whoever's behind the project will miss that."

"More like sending up a goddamn signal flare," West growled, pouring himself another cup of coffee. "I thought vampires were supposed to be subtle."

"Not when it comes to their territory." I grabbed some coffee for myself even though, like alcohol, it had a limited effect on me. Some habits, even death can't erase.

"Four down, one to go." Sarah stretched her arms overhead and arched her back like a cat. "I've got to admit, this is the most *entertaining* set of cases we've ever worked. We could all end up *bon vivants* if you're not careful."

Compared to some of the places we've gone during a case, Sarah had a point. We'd trekked through abandoned mines, old warehouses, haunted tunnels, and scandal-scarred hotels, among other "scenic" spots. With that in mind, tackling evil at the theater and the amusement park sounded like a lark, although it had been just as deadly.

"I'm still shaking my head over Willard and Philips being behind the request to the Supernatural Secret Service," West grumbled. "They must still have friends in high places to get a team assigned on their say-so."

"Turned out to be a good thing," Sarah noted. "If anyone was going to handle these, I'm glad it was us. I wouldn't trust many other people to do it right."

"Since none of them are available, the world is stuck with us," I joked. "So we'll do the best we can."

5

"Now this is more like it," West said as we drove past the Sheridan Square Theater on Penn Avenue. The vaudeville venue had a line for tickets, and its marquee promised *Spellbinder: The Amazing Mysterious Mesmerist.*

According to Archie Dunning, "Spellbinder" was born Jacob Hinner-shitz. I could see why he changed his name.

"A bit more your speed?" I joked. After the opulence of the vampire theater, the vaudeville show looked far less fancy. I'd been to many such shows, both on cases and seeking a night's reprieve from solitude. The dozen different acts usually ranged from amusing to pitiful, a mix of comedy, singing, dancing, skits, juggling, and magic, but it remained the best entertainment forty cents could buy.

Unlike the audience for the vampire theater, which drew the upper crust, vaudeville's cheap seats were usually filled by an audience of working people for whom even the modest ticket price meant forgoing other purchases.

West shrugged. "It's homey. Familiar. You can see a show in Kansas City and one in Boston, and they'll have pretty much the same line-up. It's nice to know what you're getting when you pay for your ticket."

I sometimes forgot that West's life as a secret agent was likely as solitary—and sometimes lonely—as my own. In all our time together, he never spoke of family, and while I occasionally shook my head at the flirting between him and Sarah, I didn't really think it meant anything. The three of us had formed our own little damaged family, and I wouldn't trade it for anything. Knowing I would outlive my friends made me cherish their friendship all the more.

We parked at a lot a block away, making sure we could make a quick exit.

"Father Kawalski said he'd meet us here." I looked for the priest as we walked back to the theater.

"And here I am." The priest fell into step with us, dressed once more in black without his clerical collar. I wore a brown cloth jacket over a plaid shirt and tan pants, a millworker's best outfit.

"Ellis and Isaac should be in position by now," I murmured. We had stayed up late the night before working out the strategy with Lawrence and Daniels, and I had to admit that I liked and admired them. They kept Willard and Philips updated while their friend Archie fed us any leads he uncovered.

West, Sarah, and I made an awesome team by ourselves, but I had to admit that it was nice to have reliable, competent backup and expanded research resources. People who might, over time, become friends. Our business didn't lend itself much to those connections, so I valued the opportunities when luck favored us.

"Let's hope tonight goes better than the last time," West muttered. "They might get suspicious if another theater catches fire."

"We didn't do that." I felt certain that Andre Bergeron had been behind the fire that killed the troupe of rogue vampires, and since no innocent bystanders had been harmed, I couldn't find it in my heart to fault him.

"Just saying," West grumbled.

He and Sarah walked arm and arm, just a regular couple out for a night's entertainment. They dressed the part, leaving aside the snappy tuxes and New York gowns for less remarkable outfits. West wore a canvas jacket over a white shirt and dark trousers. Sarah's dress flattered her, but probably came off the rack at a department store.

We were running a different con this time. Ellis and Isaac were supposed to ransack the theater office for records and be ready to cut the lights or interfere with the show if things got dire. Father Kawalski and I were muscle, but since regular people didn't have bodyguards, we had to keep our distance.

I wasn't sure exactly what we were up against with this Spellbinder guy, but I knew it wasn't anything good.

If we're right that there's a government agency looking for magical weapons or ways to make super soldiers, then I wonder what might be of value to them with the show. Is Spellbinder's ability real? And do they want to conscript him or learn his tricks?

Compared to the Alvin Theater, the Sheridan Square was a modest affair. It mimicked the plusher venues with cheaper substitutes—plain red wallpaper instead of flocking, sturdy brocade upholstery instead of velvet. Glass chandeliers pretended to be crystal. The murals on the walls lacked the skill of the artists who adorned palaces like the Alvin, and none of the ceilings had the ornate plasterwork that graced upscale theaters.

Sarah and West had seats up front, where they could get a good look at the mesmerist's tricks. Father Kawalski and I were in the back row, where we could watch the audience as well as the performers. I could cross that distance in seconds, although I couldn't attest to how spry my companion might be.

We settled into our seats, and I glanced at the priest. "Ever been to a show like this before, Padre?"

He smiled and shook his head. "No. It's not forbidden—I just don't get much time off. When I do, the library calls to me more than the theater."

I remembered that the Logonje priests shared a cloister. Maybe Kawalski had plenty of company and needed the solitude. Libraries were also like a second home to me, so I couldn't fault his choices.

Since Spellbinder was the main attraction, he was the last to perform. We came early enough to get seats but sufficiently late to miss the warm-up acts, which were usually not as good as those that came later on in the program.

The crowd looked exactly like the kind of people I expected—factory workers, shop girls, store owners, mill folks. Vaudeville provided a much-needed diversion. Radios were expensive, and libraries only served those who could read—or read in English. Although it had been several lifetimes ago, I remembered the struggle to learn a new language from my native Hungarian. Much of the performances here could be enjoyed even without understanding the words.

The theater filled as time passed, with the smell of cheap perfume mingling with the scent of cigarette smoke and macassar oil. The singers were passable, and the comedy team used enough pratfalls and physical jokes that language wasn't a barrier. A juggler only dropped something once, and a pair of dancers knew how to cut a rug.

After the danger and tension of the last few days, I found myself enjoying the show. Father Kawalski also seemed to be having a good time. I didn't let down my guard, but it was nice to have a few moments when we weren't in a life or death situation.

The good feelings slipped away the closer we got to Spellbinder's act. Nothing about any of the other performances made me suspect magic or ill intent. As shows went, it was one of the better lineups I'd seen.

I resisted the urge to look around for Ellis and Isaac, who were somewhere in the darkened theater. Government restrictions meant their inventor friend wasn't supposed to create any new contraptions or recreate any old ones, but apparently, a few items had managed to slip through the cracks. The ghost-summoning/repelling box was one, and the altered cattle prod hidden beneath my coat was another.

Hearing Ellis and Isaac's stories about their friend's long-ago experimental weapons made me envious for that kind of technology—and worried about what the government intended to do with the items and blueprints they had confiscated. *Nothing good. They'll use them to kill people.*

Spellbinder was up next. I called on Krukis's magic and felt the subtle shift as my skin changed. I've always been grateful that while my skin becomes steel, I don't turn silver. No one notices—unless they try to attack me.

Father Kawalski must have sensed the magic because he turned to look at me and met my gaze. "Gotta say, that's impressive."

"It comes in handy." That much was true, but my enhanced abilities could never be worth what they cost me.

The musicians played a rousing number to welcome Spellbinder, who walked onto the stage to thundering applause and shouts. It had been difficult to get a good sense of the man from the posters outside. I guessed his age to be late thirties. He carried himself like someone accustomed to money and wore a good-quality tuxedo. Rings glinted on his fingers. His slicked, dark hair accentuated high cheekbones and dark eyes —"motion picture handsome," as Sarah would say.

He grinned and bowed, then raised his arms for silence. "Welcome, Ladies and Gentlemen," he boomed in a voice clearly trained for the theater. "I am Spellbinder, and tonight I will perform feats of mesmerism that will shock and amaze you!"

An appreciative murmur spread through the crowd. I rolled my eyes, and a glance told me that the priest was equally unimpressed.

"This is not magic!" Spellbinder announced. "Nor is it sleight of hand. No—what you are about to witness is based in the science of the mind."

His voice rose and fell in all the right places to gin up the crowd's enthusiasm.

"Invisible forces surround us. Gravity fixes our feet to the ground so that we don't drift away. Sunlight and wind have no form but are real nonetheless. I call upon the invisible force of magnetism and the energies of the world to plumb the depths of the human mind—and perhaps, the soul."

He might be a charlatan, but he was also one hell of a showman.

"Think of what can be accomplished if we harness the true power of the human mind! Imagine the paradise that could be created by aligning our thoughts with the harmony of the universe." Spellbinder's deep voice rumbled through the theater. I wondered whether his so-called abilities enhanced his effect on the audience, like the vampires' glamour affected their prey.

I didn't feel any odd effects, but my magic might have provided protection. Father Kawalski also didn't seem to be swayed by the mesmerist's introduction, but he also had magic that might buffer any repercussions.

Glancing around at the audience, people looked excited and swept up in Spellbinder's oratory, but then again, that thrill was what brought them here and what they paid to see.

"Are you ready to see something amazing? Something that will defy your expectations?"

The crowd clapped and cheered, and Spellbinder grinned. He went to the side of the stage and returned with a wooden chair, which he set in the center.

"Then let's get this show started! And to do that, I need a volunteer from the audience."

Hands went up all over the theater. This was one of the reasons West and Sarah situated themselves in the front. Depending on how the performance went, Sarah had offered to try to be selected so we could get a first-hand report. I didn't like it, but West and the others overruled me.

Thanks to Ellis and Isaac, I had a bit of "insurance" beneath my coat in case everything went to hell.

Spellbinder picked a young man from near the front. His clothing suggested that he had come off a shift at a factory.

"What's your name?" the performer asked.

"Johnny," the man replied, suddenly bashful in front of the audience.

"Well, Johnny, it's nice to meet you," Spellbinder said in a warm tone. He saw Johnny's gaze drift toward the audience.

"Don't look at them. They aren't here. They don't exist. It's just you and me. You look like you did a hard day's work today. Is that true?" The mesmerist went on.

"Yes, sir. Put in a long shift."

"I bet you could use a nap. Would you like that? To close your eyes and feel almost as good as getting a night's sleep?"

"I sure would."

"Have a seat, Johnny, because that's exactly what's going to happen." Spellbinder waved toward the chair, and Johnny sat down.

"Johnny, I want you to know that you are completely safe. Nothing is going to happen that you don't want. I'm going to help you relax, and you're going to feel really good. Are you ready to get started?"

"Yes, sir."

Spellbinder stretched out his hand, palm up. "Press down on my hand." Johnny complied, looking a bit lost.

"Close your eyes."

Johnny's eyes drifted shut.

"Sleep."

Johnny's head lolled to the side, and a gasp went up from the audience. Spellbinder turned to them and put a finger to his lips.

"Johnny, I'm going to count down from five, and with each number, you will find yourself growing more relaxed. Five—You are warm and comfortable. Four—your shoulders and neck feel relaxed and loose. Three—your mind is clear, and your heart is light without a care in the world. Two—as you breathe deeply, you feel good health spreading through your body. One—your body is sleeping deeply."

Johnny let out an impressive snore that sent the audience tittering.

Spellbinder waved his hand in front of Johnny's face, snapped his fingers, even nudged the man's head from side to side. He appeared to be fast asleep, snoring loudly.

The mesmerist turned toward the crowd. "Imagine if everyone could sleep peacefully at night so easily! This power can change the world."

He turned back to his volunteer. "It's almost time to wake up, Johnny. I'm going to count up to five. One—you are warm and comfortable, more relaxed than you have been in a long time. Two—your fingers and toes get a pleasant tingling. Three—take a deep breath and let it out. Four—

you are feeling more awake like you've had a full night's rest and good dreams. Five—Open your eyes. You are rested, happy, and at peace."

Johnny blinked several times and looked up at Spellbinder in amazement. "That was unbelievable. I really do feel like I slept all night."

"Give Johnny a round of applause," Spellbinder said to the audience as he gave his volunteer a hand to pull him out of his chair. The crowd clapped enthusiastically. Spellbinder let him enjoy the moment, then a stagehand came to escort him off the platform.

"Now that you've seen a practical application of mesmerism, let's have some fun," Spellbinder announced. "Do you want to have some fun?" He grinned like a cat with cream at the wild cheers.

"For my next demonstration, I need someone who doesn't mind being a little silly. Do I have a volunteer?" Hands again shot up, and Spellbinder chose another young man, long and lanky like a scarecrow.

"Are you a good dancer?" he asked the boy.

"Not really, sir."

"What's your name?"

"Bill, sir."

"Bill, today you are going to be a great dancer," Spellbinder assured him. Once again he took the man through his relaxation countdown, keeping him standing this time.

"Strike up a lively tune," Spellbinder told the band, which immediately began to play a song I'd heard from the doorways of many dancehalls.

Meanwhile, Bill stood with a blank expression, arms hanging loosely at his sides.

"Bill, you are completely safe here. In fact, you feel happy—very, very good. You are with friends, so you don't have to worry about anything. You feel so good that you want to dance. Go ahead, Bill. Dance!"

The shy boy began to hop around, shaking his arms and flopping to the music. The audience began to snicker, but Spellbinder put up a hand in warning, and they quieted.

After a minute or so, the mesmerist motioned for the band to stop, and Bill once more stood awaiting instruction.

"Before I wake him up—can you imagine the possibilities? No more missing out because of shyness. No more cowards. If only every soldier knew of this, they would never fear the Hun or any foe!"

That's it. That's the con. Soldiers without fear. Super soldiers without self-preservation. Cannon fodder.

From the expression on Father Kawalski's face, I figured he had reached the same conclusion.

Spellbinder brought Bill out of his trance and sent him back to his seat as my mind spun. After a few moments, I realized that I'd been so busy thinking about soldiers I missed Spellbinder's foray to find another volunteer.

Sarah.

Everyone clapped when he drew her up on stage. She flashed a bright smile, putting on the act I recognized as giving people what they wanted to see. I spotted the back of West's head and could see from the way he held his shoulders that he had tensed, ready to spring.

"What's your name?"

"Sarah."

"Are you enjoying the show?"

"Very much."

"I'm going to help you relax," Spellbinder promised. He reached out and laid a hand on Sarah's shoulder as he counted back from five.

That's different. He hadn't touched the other volunteers. *Is that because she's female?*

I could have sworn I saw a shiver pass through Sarah and felt my gut tighten. *Something's wrong.*

"Why did you come to the show tonight, Sarah?" Spellbinder asked in his soothing voice.

"To have a good time," she answered, although her expression looked like she was concentrating instead of feeling peaceful.

"But that's not the only reason, is it, Sarah? Why did you really come tonight?"

Sarah hesitated, brows furrowed, as if fighting compulsion. "We came to find out…what you are. What you're up to. Who you work for."

Fuck.

A fire klaxon shrilled through the theater, and given the Alvin's recent fate, the reaction was immediate as the audience rose to its feet.

"Don't panic. Move safely to the exits," a voice shouted from somewhere in the back. I felt certain it was Isaac. "Exit the theater now."

West had already vaulted to the stage, putting himself between Sarah and Spellbinder. Father Kawalski went right, and I veered left, moving against the crowd as we shoved our way toward the front.

"Stop!" Spellbinder roared, and all of the theatergoers who hadn't made it out yet froze.

"What did you do to her?" West demanded, gun drawn and pointed at the mesmerist's chest.

Father Kawalski closed in from one side as I came from the other. I caught a glimpse of Ellis behind the curtain, backstage.

"I'm in her head. If you want her back, let me go." Spellbinder didn't seem worried. The audience remained frozen where they stood.

"You're not in a position to make threats," West growled. "Let her go."

"On your knees. Drop the gun." Spellbinder focused his attention on West, who watched his body betray him as he knelt and put his gun on the floor. He looked like he fought the order every second—and lost.

Shit. He's whammied everyone in the audience—except for maybe Father K and me. Were Ellis and Isaac too far away to be affected?

"Who sent you? I was warned they'd send a team after me, maybe assassins," Spellbinder replied. "Which required taking a hostage. When I'm free, I'll let her go."

Sarah's face lacked the blissful look of the other mesmerized volunteers. She looked uncomfortable, perhaps even struggling. Sarah wasn't the kind to go quietly, and I bet that she was fighting Spellbinder's hold.

"We're going to go now," Spellbinder said with a smug, confident smile as he put his hand on Sarah's shoulder again. "And you're going to let us walk right out of here."

The mesmerist looked to the audience still unmoving where they stood.

"Attack."

The people turned around, expressionless, and started walking toward us. They didn't run—didn't have to. There were at least fifty of them—and only three of us.

Suddenly the temperature dropped until I could see my breath and I remembered something important.

Every theater—especially one as old as the Sheridan Square—is haunted.

Ghosts howled and moaned, taking form between the audience and the stage. They wore clothing from a variety of time periods, some clearly costumes, and others their everyday outfits. At least a dozen spirits materialized, looking nearly solid, and I guessed Ellis used his inventor friend's box to summon them and lend them power.

The mesmerized audience continued their relentless approach, failing to heed the silent warning.

That's when the ghosts let out an ear-splitting shriek and rushed the bewitched theater-goers, pushing and shoving, knocking them off their feet, gliding right through their bodies to disrupt the onslaught.

The audience members struggled forward, but the ghosts pushed back, keeping them at bay and perhaps straining the bonds of compulsion that put them under Spellbinder's control.

I raced forward with a burst of super speed, closing the distance between me and Spellbinder in the blink of an eye. I had a long prod in my hand, and I jabbed the glowing end of it into Spellbinder's abdomen, making him double over in pain as the electricity snapped and sparked.

Ellis had assured me that the supernaturally souped-up cattle prod was guaranteed to send a strong enough jolt of the right electrical frequency to disrupt the magic and energies Spellbinder used for his trances.

Father Kawalski intoned a binding spell as our target sank to his knees, gasping and clutching his stomach, then the priest rushed forward to slap magic-neutralizing, runed, silver handcuffs on the mesmerist.

Sarah and West broke free with a sharp inhale.

The audience members muttered and cried out, surprised and alarmed to find themselves missing their memories of the last several minutes and hedged in by shrieking, moaning, and all-too-real ghosts.

Just for good measure, I prodded Spellbinder again, a bit longer this time. Father Kawalski gave me a disapproving look.

I shrugged. "He twitched. I needed to be sure."

West turned to steady Sarah as she took several deep breaths and looked around, trying to get her bearings. She quickly focused on Spellbinder, who remained on his knees.

"You bastard." Sarah broke away from West and ran toward Spellbinder, giving him a swift kick in the knee followed by a solid right hook to the jaw.

"Leave him in shape for questioning," West told her, pulling her back by the shoulders. "Then you can work him over to your heart's content. I don't think anyone would get in your way."

Ellis turned the dial on his strange box, and the ghosts vanished. The terrified theatergoers ran for the exits.

"What's going on here!" A burly man in a badly fitting suit strode down the center aisle, clearly not in a good mood. I guessed he was the proprietor. "What's the meaning of this?"

West, Ellis, and Isaac flipped open their badges while barely sparing the outraged theater manager a glance. "Federal agents. Taking this man for questioning. Stay out of it unless you want us to look very closely at your tax returns," West snapped.

The owner paled. "Yeah, sure. I never laid eyes on him before this week."

We heard sirens in the distance and figured someone had alerted the fire department and the police.

"We'll bring him to our office," Ellis said. "It's close. You can follow us there."

Isaac joined us just in time to help drag Spellbinder to his feet, ignoring the man's protests. I handed the paranormal prod back to Ellis.

"That's a handy gadget. I'm guessing we can't order one?" I asked.

"Can't order what technically doesn't exist," Ellis replied with a sly grin.

Two hours later, Ellis and Isaac gave up questioning Jacob Hinnershitz, aka Spellbinder, and put him in a cell.

"Well, that was frustrating," Ellis said, returning to where the rest of us waited in the main Department of Supernatural Investigation office.

"But worthwhile," Isaac countered, taking his partner's pique in stride. "We got answers—even if they weren't ones we liked. Hinnershitz has low-level natural telepathy—mind manipulation more than mind reading. He was 'recruited' by scary government people, and he did what they wanted to keep from getting stuck in a secret site somewhere. He's a dangerous pawn, not a mastermind."

"And his whole act really was about finding highly suggestible people and figuring out how to make everyone suggestible to help create super soldiers," West said, looking chagrined that Spellbinder had gotten inside his head.

"We proved it didn't work as well as they thought it would," Sarah replied. She seemed shaken by the experience but didn't appear to be taking it as a personal failure.

"That's a good thing," I said. "And we know three ways around it— ghosts, banishment ritual, and a powerful paranormal-energy cattle prod —in case we run into it again."

"Yeah, but we don't know anything more about the higher-ups than we did when we started," West grumbled.

By now, it had to be close to dawn. I didn't need much sleep, but the adrenaline had long faded for the others, and no amount of coffee would fill that gap.

"What now?" I asked, with a jerk of my head to indicate the direction where they'd locked up Hinnershitz.

"The Department of Supernatural Investigation has a warded transport coming for him in the morning—fuck, later today," Ellis said, scrubbing a hand down over his face and blinking with exhaustion. "They'll take him somewhere and put him on ice—and see what other agency tries to spring him loose. As long as he doesn't get out, he's no longer our problem at that point."

"We've shut down four operations here in Pittsburgh and made it clear that between Andre Bergeron and our agencies, the city is protected," Isaac said. "Thanks for that—couldn't have done it without you."

"And while we were busy with Hinnershitz, the Supernatural Secret Service busted the prizefighting ring," West reported. So that's actually *five* groups we shut down. Damn, no wonder I'm tired."

"What about your inventor friend?" Sarah asked. "Is he going to get dragged back into this?"

"Not if we can help it," Isaac replied. "That's why we've got to be so careful not to let on about the few pieces of equipment that didn't get confiscated. We think the new Operation: Ferryman grabbed many of his inventions, and I don't like to think about the kind of uses they might be put to."

"About that," West said. "I got a telegram before the show tonight about the whole 'Ferryman' thing. Our intelligence folks say it's a code name for a new top-secret government organization like we were afraid it might be. Sounds like Washington's counterpart to the Vatican's Sinistram. Reports to a Cabinet-level boss, big budget, operates pretty much outside the law to deal with supernatural threats."

West's tone made it clear how much he loathed the idea. "My guess is that their mission is all about weaponizing the paranormal—cryptids, magic, the whole shebang. I don't think they're archivists or academics. My gut says that they're preparing for something big—like the next Great War."

"If 'Ferryman' is the code name, do we have a real title for this group?" I asked.

West nodded. "Yeah. It's an acronym—don't know what the letters stand for yet, but it explains the alias. They're calling it C.H.A.R.O.N., and I think it's going to be a dangerous pain in our asses."

Isaac leaned back in his chair. "Maybe so. But we've already put a serious crimp in its plans. Shutting down five recruitment efforts? That's a big deal. They probably put a lot of money and manpower into making those happen, and we closed them. Maybe they'll pop up elsewhere, but that's going to cost them time and more effort."

"We also lifted the rock and let the other organizations see what scurried out," I added. "DSI and SSS might have had suspicions, but now they've got proof. Whoever is championing C.H.A.R.O.N. is going to get pushback, maybe get asked for justifications. If they were operating off-the-books before, they aren't now."

"Their patrons might not like being in the spotlight," Sarah added, and her voice had the dangerous purr of a cat about to catch its prey. "This wouldn't look good in the papers. I imagine their political rivals will make hay out of it. We all want to beat the bad guys—but it doesn't look good to *become* them trying to do it."

"We've also created a blueprint for shutting them down when they pop up elsewhere," West noted. "DSI, SSS, the Logonje, and Occulatum—they'll know what to watch out for and what worked. I wouldn't be surprised if the C.H.A.R.O.N. people will need to drop out of sight for a while, which nixes big public events. We put a spoke in their wheel—and we can do it again."

I sat back, enjoying listening to the others talk, taking consolation from the company. This was the upside of immortality—these people born long after I died who had become friends, allies, and family.

There was no telling what would happen with the tension in Germany or whether there would be another Great War. I hoped not, with every fiber in my being. We might not be able to prevent war, but what we'd accomplished these last few days might keep our side from using monstrous means to achieve their ends. I'd learned that even small changes could make a big difference.

Whatever happened, we'd see it through together. That certainty gave me something I never thought I would feel again—hope.

The End

ABOUT THE AUTHORS

Gail Z. Martin writes epic fantasy, urban fantasy, and steampunk for Solaris Books, Orbit Books, Falstaff Books, SOL Publishing, and Darkwind Press. Recent books include *Vengeance, Assassin's Honor, Tangled Web, Sons of Darkness, Convicts and Exiles,* and *The Dark Road.* As Morgan Brice, she writes urban fantasy MM paranormal romance. New books include *Witchbane, Burn, Dark Rivers, Badlands, Lucky Town, The Rising,* and *Treasure Trail.*

Larry N. Martin is the author of the new sci-fi adventure novel *Salvage Rat,* and the new portal fantasy series, *The Splintered Crown, A Tankards and Heroes novel.* He is the co-author (with Gail Z. Martin) of the *Spells, Salt, and Steel: New Templar Knights* series; the Steampunk series *Iron & Blood;* and a collection of short stories and novellas: *The Storm & Fury Adventures* set in the Iron & Blood universe. He is also the co-author (with Gail) of the *Wasteland Marshals* series and the *Joe Mack - Shadow Council* series from Falstaff Books.

Find them online at www.GailZMartin.com, on Twitter @GailZ-Martin and @LNMartinAuthor, on Facebook.com/WinterKingdoms, at www.DisquietingVisions.com blog, on www.Pinterest.com/Gzmartin on Goodreads https://www.goodreads.com/GailZMartin and BookBub https://www.bookbub.com/profile/gail-z-martin. Gail is also the organizer of the #HoldOnToTheLight campaign www.HoldOnToThe

Light.com Never miss out on the news and new releases—sign up for our newsletter: http://eepurl.com/dd5XLj

Join our Shadow Alliance street team so you never miss a new release! Get all the scoop first + giveaways + fun stuff! Also where we get our beta readers and Launch Team! https://www.facebook.com/groups/435812789942761

FALSTAFF BOOKS

Want to know what's new
And coming soon from
Falstaff Books?

Try This Free Ebook Sampler

https://www.instafreebie.com/free/bsZnl

Follow the link.
Download the file.
Transfer to your e-reader, phone, tablet, watch, computer, whatever.
Enjoy.